This book is dedicated to the memory of Brian Connell.

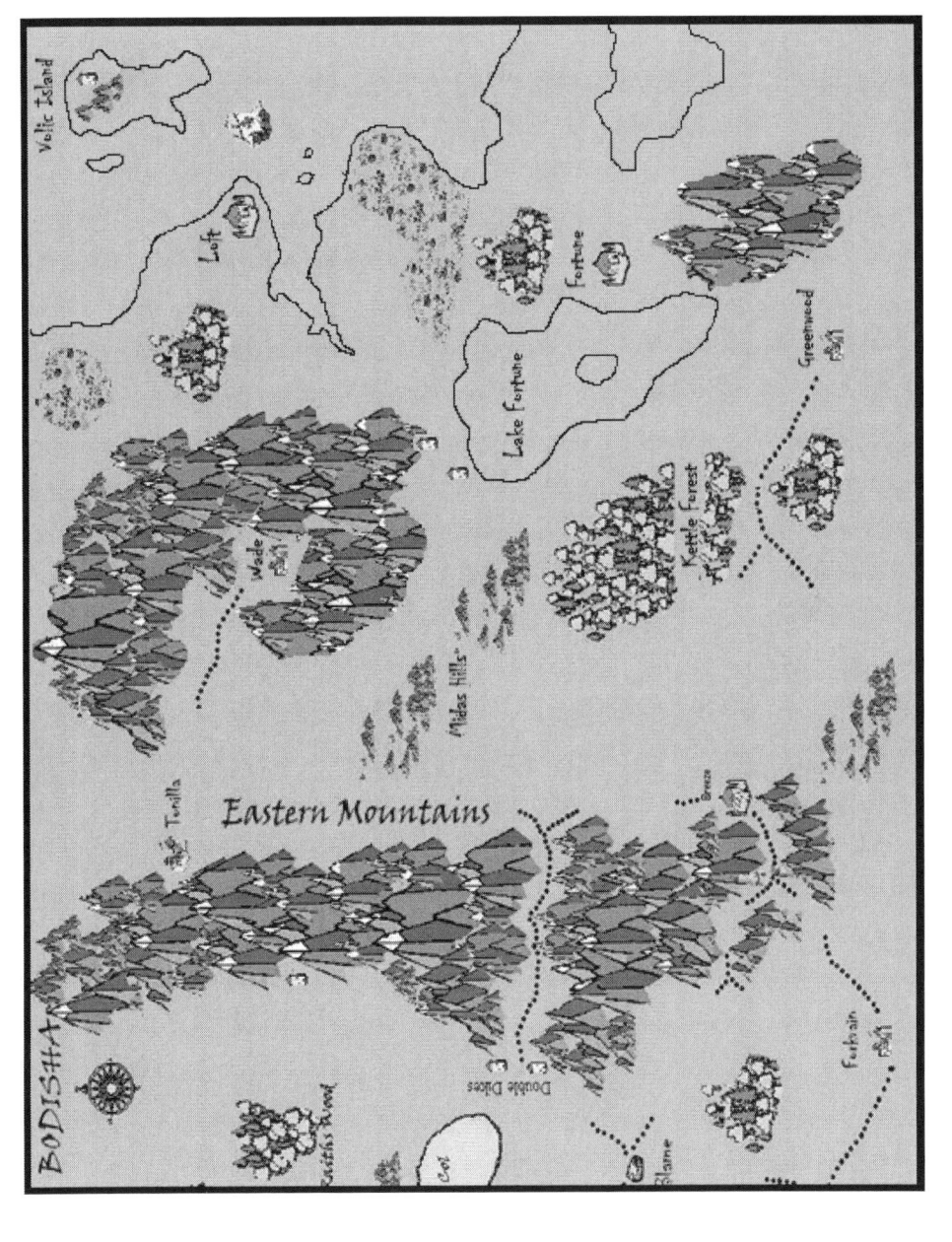

Front cover: Kern Ocarn Looking down upon the King's Soldiers

Chapter One
The King's Promise

The king sat on his lavish throne, its high back rising two feet above his head. The wooden throne had been carved by the finest woodworker in Bodisha, and rumour had it that King Moriak's father—the late King Milnok—had ordered the execution of the carpenter so he could never make anything more magnificent. The throne was covered in gold leaf and ivory edging with vines and leaves carved into the wood, twisting and twining as if they were growing up the sides and over the top.

He wasn't an elegant king by any means. His grey beard hung down to his belt and covered half his face, which was pitted and scarred. His sunken eyes were darkened by the rings surrounding them, and each line on his face told a story of war and battle.

He wore a gem-encrusted golden crown and a red robe hung on his shoulders, lined with snow leopard fur; it was held in place around his neck by a clasp in the shape of two golden hands. A bright silver sword hung by his side; it was more of a showpiece than a weapon—but once drawn, the blade could not be sheathed until it tasted blood. There were many legends about the sword, and a song often sung in the taverns of Bodisha claimed *those who see it being drawn, will meet the dead before the dawn.* Above King Moriak's head was his shield crest, a sword spearing a lion.

Next to King Moriak sat his son and heir, Prince Hordas. He was a small child for fifteen; his legs dangled from his miniature throne—a copy of his father's—and barely touched the floor. He was dressed in black armour and a crown sat upon his head, he had a silver short sword hanging by his side; the cloak he wore was black with white trim. He wore all black, thinking it would make people fear him and give him a menacing look. But his facial features were sleek and, with his long blonde hair tucked behind his ears, he looked almost feminine.

On Moriak's other side was another smaller throne, in between the king's and the prince's in size. This was Queen Cherian's throne, but on this day it was empty, as the queen was on a royal visit to the Elven lands north of Bodisha.

The thrones sat at one end of the enormous room with steps leading up to them. On either side of the thrones were a set of steps curving upward to a door-lined balcony directly above the king. A red carpet ran from the entrance of the throne room—a set of enormous oaken double doors directly opposite the dais—to the steps leading up to the thrones, embroidered in patterns of paisley in golden thread all down its length. Stone pillars lined each side of the room, and a guard was positioned at each one, complete with full armour, shield, and spear. Behind the stone pillars were tapestries, at least twenty feet in height, hung from massive ropes. The tapestries were embroidered with great battle scenes, kings on horseback fighting against orcs.

Other doors were situated in between the tapestries. The ceiling was thirty feet high, and hanging from its centre was an elaborate wooden chandelier. The bottom circle had at least a hundred candles, and smaller wooden rings above were also covered in candles. A rope above this ran through a sheave, then along the ceiling through another, sending it down the east wall to the floor, for ease of lowering and lighting the hundreds of candles that lined the circular rings of wood.

The king took a long look down at Conn. "Where are my dragon eggs?"

"We… lost them, my lord."

"You lost them? How exactly did you lose them?"

"The convoy was ambushed by orcs and the chests were taken."

"Well, go kill those damn orcs and retrieve my chests!" King Moriak shouted. He slammed his fist down onto the arm of his throne, then coughed.

"We did, Sire."

"So you *do* have my chests, then?"

"Not quite, my lord. We retrieved them at the orc tower of Sanorgk, but as my guide was returning them to me, he was killed and the chests were taken once more."

"Your guide, eh?" The king paused and stroked his long grey beard. "You sent one *guide* to collect my dragon eggs from an orc tower. Conn, please stop with these lies; they grow tiresome. Now tell me what happened to my damn eggs before—"

"Kill him, Father. He lies to his king," Prince Hordas interrupted.

"Oh, my dear son. I have known Conn longer than I have known your mother. He will tell me the truth. The king—your father—promises you that. But if he doesn't," he said, turning and looking at Conn, "you can give the order again."

"Yes!" Hordas clapped with delight. "Speak up, Conn. Let us hear your lies," the young prince said with an evil smile.

Anger grew inside Conn's chest at the young prince's outburst.

"We hired three.... *thieves* to retrieve the chests, because we didn't have enough men to spare to go to war with the orcs at Queen Valla's tower. We sent Solomon with them as a guide. He was my own flesh and blood, Sire."

"Spare me the heartache," the king said coldly. "People die. Carry on."

"Well, the plan worked—to an extent. They stole the chest and Sol… my guide managed to get away from them. He was killed on his way back to Raith."

"Yes, yes, I get all that. But where are the chests now?"

"As far as I am aware, the chests ended up back in the hands of our thieves by some divine intervention. So we sent the wyverns and twenty of our finest men to collect the chests and kill the thieves."

"And?" the king said impatiently.

Conn bowed his head in embarrassment. "The thieves killed a wyvern along with the score of guards, then delivered the eggs back to the mother dragon."

"What!" The king rose up from his throne in a rage. "Delivered them back to the mother dragon? Killed twenty of my men and one of my wyverns?"

"Yes, my king."

"Who are these *thieves*? I will hire them to protect my castle!" the king raged, and Hordas clapped his hands in excitement.

"My lord, I have someone who can help us find these men—someone who knows them personally. Someone who was there when your men died."

"Who is this man?"

Conn spun round and nodded at Belton, who was stationed near the main doors of the throne room. Belton opened one of the doors and waved an arm. Two of the king's guards dragged a man into the room, his head bowed and his body limp. The guards came as far as Conn, then threw the man to the floor. His clothes were ripped and torn, and blood and lash marks lined his back.

"Who is this man?" the king asked again. "He looks like a tramp."

Conn poked the end of his staff under the man's limp body and rolled him over onto his back. His face was bloodied and bruised. His lip was cut and a vicious slice down one cheek had swollen up, doubling the size of his face.

"This, my lord, is Bok."

"Bok? And who might this… *Bok* be?"

"He knows what happened to your eggs and, as I said, he was there when your men died."

"Bring me water! Two buckets of water!" the king shouted.

Two guards hurried off, returning a few tense minutes later with wooden buckets. The king pointed at Bok, and they emptied the contents of the buckets over his face.

Bok sat up, spluttering and spitting as the freezing water soaked him. The guards dropped their buckets and, one at each arm, hoisted Bok to his feet and dragged him toward the king. King Moriak rose from his throne, coming close enough to touch Bok's chin and lift his head.

"Where are my dragons?"

Bok's eyes rolled in their sockets as he tried to focus on the king. "H…h…hatched."

"Have they gone back to their mother?" the king said with a cough.

"Y…yes, in the mountain… west of Tonilla."

"What about the thieves who stole my chests? Where did they go?"

"I killed one, but the other two lived. Don't know where they went."

"But you could find them again, right? You do know what they look like?" Bok nodded.

"What about the dragon's lair? Could you lead a garrison back to the lair?"

"Yes. It is secret and hidden from view. You wouldn't find it in a million years; only one or two people even know of it," Bok said, lying in an attempt to make himself more valuable to the king, "but I know exactly how to get there. You won't find anybody else who knows of its whereabouts."

Conn stepped forward. Moriak nodded and let Bok's head fall, then returned to his throne. A servant approached the king with a towel, and Moriak wiped the blood off his hands.

"You said you killed one; which one did you kill?" Conn asked, using the end of his staff to lift Bok's head.

"The Rat. I killed Ty 'The Rat' Quickpick."

"Are you sure?" Conn asked, forcing Bok's chin higher.

"Yes. I stuck an arrow into his heart and watched him die. He killed the boy with the chests. I avenged his death," he lied.

Conn leaned on his staff and let out a sigh of relief. *A sort of closure for Solomon's death,* he thought.

"What would you like me to do, my lord?" Conn asked the king, who stood with his hands behind his back, looking out the window.

"I would like you to go capture two young dragons, and kill the mother dragon and two petty thieves. Bring me their heads in a basket so I can place them on spikes overlooking the gates to Raith. No one makes a mockery out of me! Kill *my* men and *my* wyverns?" The king shook his head. "Take fifty men—no, one hundred men, one thousand! Take as many as it takes! And do it properly. Otherwise I'll send my son. He would do a better job!"

"Yes, my lord. It shall be done."

"One more thing, Conn—one more *small* thing."

"Yes, my king, anything," Conn said, bowing.

"If you fail me this time, it'll be *your* head on a spike."

"Yes, King Moriak. I understand." Conn bowed and backed away before spinning on his heel and walking towards the exit. Belton opened the door as he approached, then followed Conn out of the throne room.

*

"Father, you should have punished him for being incompetent."

"Oh, my boy, you have so much to learn. Conn has been a good advisor to me and has been at my side through many wars, but sometimes you just need to shock them. Complacency will swallow all men, so every now and again you need to adjust their focus," the king said, looking down at his son.

"Yes, Father."

"Soon you will rule Bodisha—but first you will need to learn how to rule your men. Without them, you are nothing. Without the right people around you—people you can trust—you will not last the first week. These vultures will kill you in a heartbeat, just to gain control of a tenth of what you have. Trust no one; believe nothing you hear and only ten percent of what you see."

"Yes, Father."

"You have so much learning to do, and I fear I don't have the time to pass on what I know."

"Rubbish. You'll be here for years," Queen Cherian said from the balcony above.

"Mother, you're home!" the prince said, leaving his throne and rushing up the stairs to greet the queen.

"Hello, my queen. You are back early," King Moriak said.

"I couldn't stand it any longer. Those elves bore me so much."

"How did you manage to get away?"

"I told them a lie about needing to be in Fortune for the summer solstice festival."

"What did they say about the war brewing in Tonilla?" the king asked.

"They agreed that help would be available. They will be sending some of their army. I think Guldir is going to arrange a meeting with you soon. He wouldn't say too much to me. I don't think he values my input about wars. I told him you were unwell and unable to attend, so he said he would come here," she said, gracefully making her way down the stairs with Prince Hordas in tow.

Queen Cherian wore a tight-fitting dress of red silk that trailed behind her, highlighting her elegant figure. She lifted the hem as she moved to keep from falling over it. The dress was cinched with a golden belt, exaggerating the slimness of her waist. She was beautiful for her age, and her golden hair hung down her back in a simple braid. She never wore a crown except at royal events—she always thought it pointless around the castle, although the king felt differently. The sleeves on her dress flared at the wrist, and the edges were trimmed with gold.

As she reached the bottom of the stairs Moriak grumbled, "I will send a messenger to invite Guldir and his entourage… and his fucking wife."

The queen laughed. "You don't like her, do you?"

"Like her? She's a whore! Always sticking her nose in; it's like talking to him through her. The man has no independence. He's frightened of her; I'm sure of it."

Cherian took her seat next to the king. "I'm sure *he* wears the crown, my dear."

"I bet she picks which one, though," the king said with a laugh, but the laughing soon erupted into coughing.

Cherian called to the guards, "Get Murtal! Now!"

The king was hunched over on his throne, coughing; a trickle of blood stained his beard. He held one hand to his chest and the other on his throat. Hordas watched without so much as a flicker of emotion as the guards raced from the throne room.

"Murtal!" Queen Cherian shouted.

Murtal rushed into the room, followed by two assistants carrying bags, towels, blankets, and buckets of water. They spread blankets in front of the king's throne and helped him lie down so Murtal could examine him. The physician produced a bottle from his bag and gave the king a sip, the coughing gradually eased as the king lay still, his breathing heavy.

"It's getting worse, my queen."

"Let's get him to his quarters. It's not dignified for the king to lie on a stone floor in front of his guards."

"Agreed. I will make the arrangements," Murtal said, then turned to his aides and began giving commands.

The queen sauntered down the line of royal guards. She knew they were loyal men, faithful to their king and fearsome in battle, but after a few ales in the local inn, tongues will wag. The whores had the uncanny knack of asking just the right questions at just the right moments, and most men couldn't resist sharing whatever information they had with an attractive, attentive woman. The next day, hardly any of them would even be able to remember having a conversation, let alone recall the details of what they had said.

"What you saw today stays in here. If word of King Moriak's illness gets out, I will personally execute every one of you. Do you understand?"

The guards replied simultaneously, "Yes, Queen Cherian."

"DO YOU UNDERSTAND?" she demanded again.

They answered again, even more loudly.

"Good. Now go about your duties. You!" She pointed at a guard. "Tell Conn he is needed in King Moriak's chamber."

"Yes, my queen."

*

Conn entered King Moriak's chamber and joined Queen Cherian and Murtal next to the king's bed. Two maids, one on either side of the bed, dampened the king's brow with cool wet towels. The massive four-poster bed sat dead centre against the wall opposite the door; to its left was a great stained-glass window, which opened outward. A set of drawers and a few lavish chests lined the walls.

"How is he, my queen?"

"Not good, Conn. He has a fever from hell and we cannot control it. It's burning him up from the inside. I can slow it, but not stop it."

"There must be a way," Conn said, looking down at the king. "Is this this a flare up of that damn assassination attempt two months back?"

"Yes, indeed it is. The buckthorn poison from *that* arrow?"

"Why after two months?"

"We were able to stop the fever initially by combining three herbs—the fighort leaf, sorrwell wood bark, and willow rose petals. Unfortunately we don't have any of the petals or leaf left."

"Well, we will go gather some my Queen, easy."

"It's not that easy, Conn. The fighort leaf is only found in the Dungeon of Dreams on the Voltic Isle, and willow rose only grows in the west—though we don't know exactly where. The last time any was found, it was down near Lake Fortune."

Conn paced next to the bed, thinking to himself.

"Couldn't we just send some soldiers to go collect it all?" Queen Cherian asked.

"My queen, you don't send soldiers to a dungeon any more than you would send thieves to war." Conn caught Cherian's eye. "But I have a plan."

"It better involve petals and leaves," Cherian replied.

"The king wants me to go capture two new-born dragons and kill two thieves."

"Yes, but how is that going to help?"

"The thieves returned the dragons to the mother. They obviously have the dragons' best intentions at heart. So if we capture the dragons, we can offer them a swap."

"You've lost me," she said, placing her hands on her hips.

"Me too," Murtal added.

"Look, it's simple: They will go gather the fighort leaf from the dungeon and then go find the other ingredients. In return, we promise to release the dragons."

"What makes you think they will agree?"

"I will think of something. We can use the prisoner—Bok—to help set a trap."

"Whatever you are planning, plan it quick," Murtal said, looking at the king. "He will only last another month, and without these herbs he will die."

"I will put the wheels in motion. Trust me, it'll work. We get to kill the thieves and the dragons too."

"I hope you are right, Conn."

"There's only one thing, my queen."

"Yes, Conn, what is it?"

"You know that with the king here like this, the prince will have to step up and—"

"I know. Let me worry about my son; you just worry about getting the king back on his feet. Now go."

"Yes, my queen." Conn bowed and turned toward the door.

Chapter Two
Scarred for Life

Bok sat on his wooden bed in the small cell. Another human lay opposite him, an old skinny man with long grey hair and beard whose clothes looked as old as him. Bok stared at him. *I wonder how long he has been here.*

The room had windows and one door, and was lit by a single torch on the wall—*too high to grab*, he thought. A bowl in the corner completed the damp cell. Every now and then a rat would scurry from under Bok's bed and disappear behind the bowl. *Even here he haunts me*, Bok daydreamed, *but he is dead and Bok got his man.* He got up and stretched his legs and arms. They ached, but not as much as his face did. The cut down his cheek still throbbed. He prodded it as tenderly as he could, feeling the scabbed blood on his face. The worst ache of all, though, was in his back. Every movement he made could be felt in the lash marks.

How stupid was he to travel back into west Bodisha and drunkenly shoot his mouth off about the dragon? The fact that the off-duty guards had chanced to be there to hear him was unbelievable, but not as unbelievable as his crowning bit of bad luck: One of the guards had lost a brother to the dragon.

He heard a key turning in the lock on his door and flinched, stepping back in preparation for another savage beating. In doing so he stepped on the bowl, and two days' worth of urine soaked his feet and the bottoms of his ragged trousers.

The door opened and two guards entered. "Come with us," one of them ordered.

"You can wake up too, old man," the second guard said, kicking the sleeping man in the back and laughing. The man groaned and rolled over onto his stomach, placing his hand on his back.

"All right, I'm coming. No need for violence," Bok said.

He was led out of the cell and down a few corridors until they reached Conn, who was outside an open door speaking to Belton.

"—sort those instructions out, and I will sort this little situation. And Belton, remember, it's a matter of urgency." Conn turned to face Bok, standing between the two guards. "Bring him in."

Conn strode through the open doorway and into a small study. Bok was pushed in behind him by one of the guards.

"That will be all," Conn said, waving a hand. "Wait outside."

The two guards left the room silently, closing the door behind them.

Bok quickly eyed the room. It was a square study with a cluttered desk, with two plain wooden chairs in front of the desk and a bigger leather one behind. The window to his left was closed, and the bookshelf that took up the wall behind the desk was crammed with books, papers, and parchments. A large wooden chest, encrusted with sparkling gems, sat in a corner of the room.

"Sit down, Bok," Conn said, taking his own seat in the leather chair behind the cluttered desk. Bok did as he was told and waited sullenly for Conn to speak.

"We need you to do your king a favour."

"Why should I do anything for him? Look at me! Look at what his guards did to my face!"

"Yes, I must apologise about that… unfortunate incident. I understand one of the guards had a brother who died in the fight with that dragon." Conn fixed Bok with a stare. "Wrong place, wrong time."

"That's not going to heal my face."

"Very well. If you aren't interested in what I have to say, I'll call the guards to return you to your cell." Conn began to rise from his chair.

"Hold on—at least tell me what you want," Bok said hurriedly.

Conn smiled and settled back into his chair.

"We need those two thieves to go retrieve some herbs for us from a dungeon."

"With all respect, *your holiness*—"

"Cut the shit, Bok. Treat me like a fool and your face will be the least of your worries."

"They are not thieves. I killed the only thief; what you have left are a ranger and a fighter."

"It doesn't matter. They can survive without the halfling."

"Oh yes, I'm sure they can. But in a dungeon you have traps, hidden doors, and locks to pick. They wouldn't get through the first two rooms."

Conn leaned back in his chair and rubbed his chin, deep in thought, before finally speaking.

"You will join them. Replace the thief you killed."

"*Join* them?" Bok sat back and laughed. "Yeah, right, I'll just walk into the inn and say, 'Hello, I'm the man who killed your friend!' They would cut me down where I stood," he sneered.

Conn shot up, knocking his chair back into the bookcase and sending books falling to the floor. Bok's laughter froze in his throat. He cringed as Conn grabbed his staff; the eyes in the top glowed red as he pointed it at Bok.

"We will change your appearance, then!" Conn bellowed.

The torchlights in the room flickered and Bok held his hands out to ward off the advancing wizard. "NO! Please, no!"

With an upward flick of Conn's staff, Bok flew from his chair. His body slammed up against the door behind him, his piss-soaked shoes two feet off the floor. He was pinned and couldn't move. "No! I will join them! Please, no!" he screamed.

Conn flicked the staff again, to the side, and Bok's right arm flew against the wall as if magnetised. Another small flick did the same to the left arm.

"Please, I'm begging you, stop!" Bok blubbered. "I'll go, I'll do as you—"

Conn held the end of his staff a few inches from Bok's face; the heat it generated made Bok's eyes water. "NO…!"

Conn pushed the head of his staff into Bok's cheek, and he screamed as the pain raced through his body. Every vein felt like it was flowing with molten lava. The stench of burning flesh filled the room. Still Conn pushed and Bok screamed, until finally Bok's head slumped downward, unconscious with pain, and the screaming stopped.

Conn pulled the staff away and studied Bok's charred face.

From his eye to his jawline the flesh was black and smoking; even his nose and ear had been burnt. Conn raised a hand, then gently lowered it, and Bok's body slid down the door, ending in a heap on the floor.

Conn reached down to grip Bok's head in one hand, and closed his eyes. In his mind's eye he saw the entrance to the dragon's lair and watched the arrow hitting Ty. The vision lasted only a few seconds, but it was long enough for Conn to know where the lair was and how to get there. He opened his eyes and released Bok's head.

"Guards!" he shouted, returning to his seat behind the desk. The door opened, pushing Bok's body along the floor, and the two guards stepped over it and stood at attention in front of Conn's desk.

"Take him to Murtal. Tell him to stop the wounds getting infected and heal him, but not to fix his face. I want him disfigured and unrecognizable. Give him a haircut too. And hurry. Time is of the essence."

"Yes, my lord," the two guards said in unison. They turned and grabbed Bok under the arms, dragging him away.

*

Conn sat at his desk studying a map of Bodisha. "Where the hell do we find willow rose?" he muttered. There was a knock at the study door. "Enter."

The door opened and Belton stepped in.

"Sit down, Belton."

"Thank you." Belton took one of the chairs in front of Conn's desk. "How did you get on with convincing Bok to help capture the thieves?"

"Not well, to be honest. He made a very good point: He killed the only real thief out of the three of them. They would be unlikely to get through a dungeon without him."

"Can't they just hire another?"

"Yes. I have told Bok to join them."

"Bok? Won't they just kill him in retaliation for killing their friend?"

"That's exactly what he said. So I changed his features a little."

"You did *what?* How?"

"I burnt his face on one side. The other already has a scar from eye to jawline. He will look like he has been fighting with a Balrog once it's all healed."

"Sounds delightful."

"It wasn't nice, and the smell of burning flesh has only just cleared," Conn said, waving a hand at the open window.

"I thought I smelled something - *nasty* - when I entered. I didn't like to say," Belton said with a cruel smile.

"Yes, that'll be the smell of pain. I shouldn't have done it, but we are running out of time and—well, in that moment I lost it. I know the king is old and most of his decisions are being forced upon him by others. We don't agree on most, but he has been good to me. If he dies, Hordas' rule of Bodisha will be a reign of terror. I know for a fact he would pull the armies back from Tonilla; it would be overrun with orcs within days of Moriak's death. We mustn't let that happen."

"I agree completely. So what is your plan, exactly?"

"Moriak still wants us to capture the dragons; furthermore, he has declared war against Kern and Galandrik. He wants them dead—to prove a point, if nothing else."

"I can see that. They did steal his dragons, kill twenty—"

"Yes, yes—whatever. Murtal needs some particular herbs to stop the fever, so we send the thieves to collect the herbs and bring them to us."

"How do you intend to get them to gather the herbs?"

"This is the tricky part. My first thought was to capture the dragons, then have Bok tell them that we have them and will only release them in exchange for the herbs. Then once they bring us what we want, we kill them *and* the dragons, and heal the king."

"Excuse me for my ignorance, but why would they go to all that trouble for two baby dragons?"

"That's what I am worried about, so I have a contingency plan." Conn rose and approached the open window.

"This should be good," Belton murmured, folding his arms.

"We capture Kern's father. Kern will either do as we ask, or we feed his father to the dragons."

"That would work—but I thought he and his father fell out?"

"Yes, but blood is thicker than water. He won't stand by and let his father die."

"This may be a stupid question, but why don't we just hire three adventurers for the same quest?"

"I did think about that, but we still have to kill Kern and Galandrik anyway. And they have proven their skill—they did kill a wyvern, and escaped two bounty hunters *and* twenty of the king's guard. We may as well kill two birds with one stone." Conn shrugged.

"Good point. How will you find Kern's father?"

"No idea. I have sent scouts out already. If we have no luck, I will simply use Jakob and his illusions."

"You have it all worked out, I see."

"Yes. To set it all in motion, we just need Bok to find them and drag them to us. Where, though, I haven't quite figured out yet."

"You said you are capturing the dragons?"

"Yes."

"I take it you will be capturing them in their lair?"

"…Yes, I guess so."

"Do it there, then. They will see the dragons captured and Kern's father, illusion or flesh. It's also halfway between here and the Voltic Isle. Perfect," Belton said with a smile.

Conn folded his arms and stared at Belton, his mind racing with ideas. "That might just be the way. Belton, you're a star." He patted his friend's shoulder and eased down into his chair again. "Yes, that's perfect. I will have Bok drag them—somehow—to the mountain, and there we will make them the offer they simply cannot refuse."

*

The following morning Conn was back behind his desk studying maps of Bodisha, old treatises on herbs and their habitats, books on the history of healing—anything that might help him place where willow rose could possibly be found. After studying the facts about temperatures, moisture, and daylight hours needed for the plant to thrive, he agreed with Murtal's comment from the previous day: Lake Fortune was their most likely bet.

A knock sounded at the door and Conn answered without looking up. "Enter."

The door opened and a guard entered. "We have the prisoner for you, sir."

"Well, show him in." Conn sat back in his chair and stretched his neck as the guard shouted, "Bring the prisoner," into the hallway.

Bok was hauled into the room by two guards. His hands were bound and he wore a loose hood which, with his head so deeply bowed, concealed his face.

"Leave us. Wait outside," Conn told the guards with a wave of his hand. "Sit down, Bok," he added.

"I'd rather stand."

"Your choice. How's the face?" Conn said with a smirk, leaning back in his chair.

Bok raised his head, flicked the hood back, and glared at Conn. The left side of his face was grotesque; his cheek looked like it was covered in black dragonscale. His eyelid drooped where the scarring had hardened, tugging it down. His right cheek bore a scar from eye to chin, which Murtal had healed well; the wound was dry and closed, but otherwise it looked like it had been cut this very morning. His head had been roughly shaved, and nicks and scrapes covered his scalp. He wasn't even recognizable from the previous day.

"Well, aren't you a pretty boy?" Conn sniggered.

"Fuck you," Bok answered, staring directly at Conn.

"Now, now. There is no need for that sort of attitude," Conn said, rising from his seat and taking hold of his staff.

Bok flinched, taking a step backward.

"If you agree to help me, I will fix your face."

Bok stepped to the side and fell into the chair to hide the sudden weakness in his knees. "And if I don't want you to fix it?" he said, trying to sound confident.

Conn snapped his fingers. Instantly, the burning pain returned, consuming Bok's face. He arched back in his chair, then lurched forward onto the floor, rolling back and forth with his hands clenched to his face.

Amongst the screams Conn could hear him sob, "Make it stop!"

"Sorry, what was that? You agree to help your king?" Conn said, bending down and holding a cupped hand to his ear.

"YES! The pain! Make it stop!" Bok's face was contorted even further with agony.

Conn stood up straight. "Now there's a good boy. Question me or swear in my presence again and that pain will never stop."

"Make it go away!" Bok said, still rolling, his tied-up hands covering his face.

Conn snapped his fingers and the pain vanished.

Bok lay still on the floor, gasping for breath. He would've rather been dead at this precise moment, he thought, as tears welled in his eyes.

Conn rested his staff against his desk and sat back down. Clasping his fingers together, he rested his elbows on the table.

"Now get up off the floor and sit down," Conn ordered. Bok got to his knees, then stood defiantly next to the chair. Conn shook his head and reached for his staff.

"No," Bok said, sitting down.

Conn smiled. "You're learning. Slowly, but you're learning. Right—this is what you are going to do," he said, clasping his fingers together again. "You are to go to Tonilla and pick up Kern's trail. Find him and his dwarf friend and bring them to the dragon's lair at midnight on the last moon of the month. This should give you plenty of time to find them and get them there. Do you understand?"

"Yes, I understand," Bok answered coldly.

"Tell them we have the dragons, and if they do as we say we will release them. Can you remember that?"

"I will try."

"Remember this, then: If you are not there with them on that day at that time, the pain will come back *and it will never stop.*"

Bok shuddered involuntarily. "I would kill myself rather than go through that. Nobody could live with it."

"Then make sure you're there with Kern and Galandrik. Simple."

"Yes. I will make sure of it."

"If the capture of the dragons isn't enough to convince them, tell them we have Kern's father captive."

"I will get them there."

"Oh, I know you will." Conn opened a leather pouch on his desk and pulled out a small ruby on a chain and two folded pieces of paper. He held them out to Bok. "Take these. They are paperfinches. Simply cup one in your hand, tell it your message, then whisper 'Fly' and release."

Bok took the two square pieces of paper and nodded. "What's the ruby for?"

"That's for the finches to find you. They will home in on whoever has the ruby."

"I see."

"Guards!" The door opened and two guards entered the room.

"Take our *friend* Bok, here, and get him kitted out with whatever he needs. Send Reyheld with him—just for the company, you understand," Conn said with a smile.

"I don't want the company, nor do I need the help," Bok said, standing up.

"Ah-ah-ah," Conn said chidingly. "What did I say about questioning me?"

Bok bit his lip. "Whatever you want."

"Send Reyheld and make sure their mounts are fed, watered, and shoed. And remember what I said, Bok."

Bok didn't reply.

The guards led him out of the study and down to the servant's quarters, where he was untied and given clothes and armour. He changed into a new set of dark brown light leather armour and boots with a matching cloak. He pulled the hood up, covering his face. A servant brought a backpack with the standard adventurer's equipment—bedroll, rope, flint and tinder, torches, rations, blanket, and a canteen of water. Another servant brought him a longsword, complete with belt sheath, a crossbow with a dozen bolts, and two daggers. There was nothing special about the weapons, but Bok felt more comfortable with them at his side.

He was led out to the castle's enormous stable. There were at least fifty mounts in separate compartments, along with twenty young boys grooming them, feeding them, and washing the floors.

"This is your horse," the servant said, pointing at a brown mount. "His name is Jade. Reyheld will be here in five minutes," the servant added.

"I can't wait," Bok said unenthusiastically. He grabbed an apple from the top of a barrel, then approached the mount and offered his new horse the snack. Jade looked like a fine horse from good stock.

As the servant had predicted, a man marched into the stable and up to Bok exactly five minutes later.

"Greetings. I am Reyheld." He was well over six feet tall and dressed in chainmail. A dark brown cloak hung over his shoulders and a longsword hung by his side. He carried his helmet in one hand and a backpack in the other.

"I'm Bok. You know what we are doing?" Bok replied, keeping his face covered by his hood.

"Yes. Lord Conn has explained that we are to find Kern Ocarn and Galandrik Sabrehargen. You must convince them to go to the mountain where the dragon lives."

"That's about the size of it," Bok said, leading his mount out of the stable. Reyheld moved a few stalls down and unbolted the gate, leading his own mount out to stand next to Bok.

"Let's go then," Bok said, stepping up into the saddle. Reyheld mounted his own beast, and they rode toward the main gates.

*

Conn sat behind his desk, Belton in front of him once more. "I need you to sort out the dragons."

"All right. What exactly do you need me to do?"

"Take twenty—no, thirty—no, take *one hundred* men to their lair and capture the blasted creatures. Keep them there until the last moon of the month and wait for our thieves to show up. Then tell them what we need them to do." He slid a piece of parchment across the table. "Here is a map of western Bodisha; the highlighted areas are places where the herbs are. Well, where I think they are. I have searched, studied, and researched."

Belton unfolded the map and studied it. "And if they say no?" he asked absently.

Conn's temper snapped. "Torture them! Feed them to the dragons! I don't care, just get it done!"

"I will make sure of it. You mentioned using illusionary methods?" Belton queried.

Conn sat back, remembering the idea.

"Yes. Take Jakob the Illusionist; get him to work on Kern. I think he will succumb easier. Try the dragons first, then Jakob if that fails."

"That sounds like a plan."

"It should take them the best part of the month to complete this. We can only hope the king will last that long. Murtal did say he was showing signs of improvement."

"I will make sure they know the urgency of their quest."

"Yes. Tell them when they find the herbs, they are to take them to the western entrance of the Double Dikes. That should be the quickest way back to Raith. And when this is done and you have the herbs in your hand, make sure your sword is in Kern's heart and bring me their heads for Moriak to place on spikes."

"But he has never met them, so he doesn't know what they look like. We could give him any old heads; he wouldn't know the difference."

"All right, then bring me two heads, one human and one dwarf—but if he finds out they are not who we say they are, it'll be *your* head on the spike!"

"Point taken," Belton said, leaning back into his chair.

"Or hopefully not, in this case."

Belton laughed at Conn's jest. "Who should I send to lead the troop?"

Bok pondered for a few seconds, then said coldly, "The Gorgon and the Black Guard."

"The Gorgon… Will he not find this a little beneath him?"

"Tell him his king orders it. No—tell him there's a fully grown dragon to defeat. He will probably want to go alone."

Belton chuckled again. "Consider it done."

"Send him to me after you have given him the mission. I need to tell him where the entrance to the dragon's lair is."

"You can tell me and I can—"

"Belton, if I wanted you to know, you'd know."

"Yes, Lord Conn. I shall send Gorgon to you."

"I know you will." Conn smiled, leaning back into his chair. "And I will send word to the towns in the east."

Chapter Three
Light at the End of the Tunnel

"Go to the hills, you said! Steal some goblin loot, you said! It'll be a doddle, *you* said!" Kern shouted, running as fast as he could down the tunnel while holding a bag of loot.

"Just run! They weren't that far behind!" Ty shouted back, carrying a sack of his own.

"Where does this tunnel lead to?"

"I don't know! I didn't think to ask them!"

They ran a few hundred yards more; then Ty spotted a light at the end of the tunnel. "Quick, we are nearly out," he said, struggling to keep up with Kern.

Kern reached the end of the tunnel and came to an abrupt stop. What he had hoped would be a pathway out was no more than a hole in the side of the mountain. He could see Tonilla in the distance and the Eastern Mountains behind, against a bright blue sky without a cloud in sight. Twenty feet below were the tops of the trees spread out around the skirt of the mountain. The drop wasn't sheer but he knew he couldn't walk down, and it would be a very painful slide.

He dropped the sack on the ground, shouting in dismay just as Ty reached him, skidding to the edge of the drop and sending stones rolling down the mountain.

"This doesn't look good," he said, panting.

"Doesn't look good?" Kern said, looking down at Ty. "That's a slight understatement."

"It could be worse."

"Really? How the hell could it be worse?"

"Oh, I don't know. There could be giant spiders," Ty said, leaning out and looking for some way down.

Kern grabbed Ty by his tunic and spun him round. "Easy, you said! We will pop in and grab the loot, you said."

"And? We have the loot," Ty said, glancing down at the bag he was holding.

"A few necklaces and some gems!" Kern shouted, kicking the melon-sized bag he had dropped.

"You didn't have to come! Nobody made you," Ty shouted back, dropping his own bag on the ground and grabbing Kern's wrists. "In fact, it'd be easier without you!"

"You wouldn't have got past the first room without me!"

"Rubbish! I'd probably be back in Tonilla by now, drinking with Galandrik!"

"Oh, of course you would! The great Ty the—"

There was a noise, and both men slowly turned their heads and looked back down the tunnel. Thirty goblins stood there, swords drawn, watching the squabbling pair. The tunnel wasn't massive but it was easily wide enough for eight goblins to stand side by side.

Kern turned back to Ty then glanced over the edge. Looking at Ty once more, he raised his eyebrows. Ty didn't need to answer; he just nodded his head slightly and forced a smile. Kern let go of Ty's tunic and straightened it out where he had crumpled it. As he did so, trying to be surreptitious, he kicked the bag of loot over the edge.

"I don't suppose we could—"

The goblins charged them, screaming.

Kern and Ty both spun on their heels and, with a dual shout, they stepped out and fell.

They landed only a few feet down from the entrance and began sliding on the loose stone and slate that peppered the sides of the mountain. Ty folded his arms over his loot bag, holding it tight to his chest as they gained momentum. He could see the tops of the trees getting closer.

"If we survive this I'm going to kill—argh!"

Kern and Ty slid over a ledge and flew through the air into the trees. Spinning and crashing, downward they fell, knocking off branches as they went, until at last they landed on the ground with a thud. Leaves and broken branches drifted down and landed all around them.

After a few moments, Kern sat up very gingerly, trying to regain his focus after his world had been spun around and upside down. He started feeling where the aches and pains were, hoping not to feel any blood—or even worse, bones.

"I think I've broken my arm," he heard from behind another tree.

"Oh, you survived then?" Kern said, still checking his limbs, making sure nothing was broken.

"Seriously… that was… bad," Ty groaned.

"I am *seriously* never trusting you ever again," Kern said, getting carefully to his feet. He rolled and stretched his neck.

"Come help me. I am stuck… I think my neck is broken, too."

"Pity your mouth wasn't. I haven't decided yet if I am leaving you here, anyway," Kern answered. He picked up his sword from the forest floor, noticing his leather belt had broken in the fall. "Damn."

He examined the ground. It was soft underfoot; not a lot of sun reached here, but it was humid and warm. The dead leaves, plants, and animals that had decayed over the centuries had made the floor almost cushioned. How ironic, he thought, that it was the decomposition of life that had saved his own, and not his leather armour. The armour had probably helped, though: there were rips on the legs and arms, showing the bloody scratches underneath. Shaking his head, he began searching for Ty, still rolling his neck round and round.

"Where are you?"

"Over here."

Kern followed the voice and peered around the trunk of a large tree, then burst out laughing at what he saw.

Ty was upside down with his legs sticking upward, his left foot caught between two branches, which made him dangle somewhat. His head was tilted against his shoulder and buried under the leaves of the forest floor; one arm was twisted behind him while the other was still holding the bag of loot.

Kern bent over with his hands on his knees, laughing uncontrollably.

"It's not funny, I think I have broken everything!"

Kern straightened, then stopped laughing as a sharp pain shot up his spine. "Oh, me too," he said, stretching out the pain. He grabbed Ty's leg and worked it out from the two branches and—by no means gently—lowered him to the ground.

With a groan, Ty rolled over, then sat up, expecting to feel something broken—but apart from slight nausea and dizziness, he felt all right. After stretching each limb in turn and feeling his head for lumps, he held out a hand to Kern, who accepted, pulling Ty to his feet. Ty was slightly unsteady on his feet, and he didn't let go.

"You okay?" Kern asked, trying to sound concerned.

"Yes, I think so," Ty answered, rolling his head. "How close was that?" He smiled, letting go of Kern's hand and looking at the rips and tears in his friend's armour.

"Too close. I wonder where my bag went?"

They searched the area where they landed, but gave up when it was apparent the bag wasn't to be found.

"Can our luck get any worse?" Kern said, shaking his head.

"The fall could have killed us. Anyway, we'd better move if we want to get to Tonilla before nightfall."

"Good point. I wonder how far they pushed the orcs north?"

"No idea. The last news I heard was they were a good mile or so."

"Rumour mill has it that King Moriak has made an alliance with Guldir, and he'll be sending the elves to help."

"I'll believe that when I see it." Ty put the loot bag in his backpack, making sure he had left nothing behind. His backpack was ripped from the slide but he made a quick repair—laying some large doc leaves inside in the bottom, covering the rip—and they headed west, toward Tonilla.

It wasn't long before they reached the edge of the trees. They could see the city in the distance, the massive Eastern Mountains behind.

"I wonder if the other dragon egg ever hatched," Ty mused as they made their way toward Tonilla.

"Where did that come from?" Kern asked.

"I don't know; it seems to be constantly on my mind."

"It must have by now. It's been a month since we handed it back."

"Do you think we could ever go back?"

"I don't think dragons invite humans around for dinner."

"You know what I mean; maybe just to have a look."

"I'm not listening to you. The last idea you had was 'let's rob the goblin cave because they've gone to help the orcs.' Look how that turned out."

"Yes, but Heldar said—"

"Heldar knows shit! He also told us that the orcs had marched on the town of Wade, and the next day they were on Tonilla's doorstep. He spends too much time in the Orc's Armpit listening to every piece of gossip that's going."

"He knew where the goblins' cave was."

"Fat Mary knows the whereabouts of the goblin cave."

"Fat Mary knows a lot of things," Ty said with a smile. "Okay, so Heldar gets the occasional thing wrong. But we did get *some* loot."

"Look at our armour. I doubt if that loot will even cover the cost of two new sets."

"I know someone in the market who will sort us out some quality armour, and cheap, too."

"See, that's you all over: *quality* and *cheap* in the same sentence. Doesn't that ring alarm bells?"

"Just trying to help."

"No, you are just trying to redeem yourself after a useless idea given to us by that idiot Heldar."

No further words were spoken until they had reached Tonilla's main street. Ty said, "I'll go sell the loot. Meet you in the Factory Inn?"

"Yes... and bring it *all* back."

"Trust me," Ty replied with a wink.

"I think therein lies my problem," Kern said, heading for the inn.

*

Kern walked into the Factory Inn and spotted Galandrik sitting with another dwarf in the corner. The inn was packed with traders, adventurers, and everyday townsfolk enjoying a drink after a hard day's work.

He made his way over to Galandrik's table, nodding at the innkeeper as he passed. The fat innkeeper begrudgingly nodded back, still remembering Kern's *'Fine establishment'* remark from their last meeting.

"May I join you?" Kern asked, approaching the table.

"Kern, you're back! Of course you can. This is my friend Gronli," Galandrik said, offering Kern the seat next to him.

"Hello, Gronli. I'm Kern," he said, sitting down.

"Hello, Kern. Galandrik has been telling me all about you and your friend Ty the Rat."

"All bad then?" Kern sniggered, lifting one finger and mouthing the words 'one more' when he caught the maid's eye.

"What the hell happened to you, anyway?" Galandrik asked, looking at the rips in Kern's armour and the scratches on his face.

"Ty's idea of 'popping in, grabbing the loot, and popping out' was… well, was Ty's idea."

Galandrik laughed. "Where is he, anyway?"

"He has gone to sell what little loot we found."

"At this time of night? What shop is open at this time?"

"I didn't even bother to ask him."

"So it wasn't a *complete* disaster, then?" Galandrik said, slapping the maid's behind as she placed three jugs of mead on the table.

"Well, apart from jumping out of a cave, sliding twenty feet down a rocky mountain face into a cluster of trees, falling down through them hitting every branch on the way, and landing on the forest floor, it was a complete success." Kern forced a smile and took a long drink.

"I see what you're saying," Galandrik said, gulping down another mouthful of ale and wiping his mouth with his hand. "Gronli was telling me that there are temples appearing up to the north of Wade Mountains. One of those mad cults that worships goats or something."

"They worship a spider god, not goats," Gronli interrupted. Galandrik smiled back. He had known it was spiders, but it never hurt to let someone else feel important.

"What has that got to do with us, then?" Kern asked.

Galandrik gestured at Gronli to continue.

"Well, they brainwash the members, who go out and recruit other members. It's growing like wildfire. All the cultists have jobs to do—some work the farms while others go collect for the cult or build the new temples."

"Go on…"

"They say the money collected is huge, and they store it in their temples. The main temple—that's where Therliyn lives, the cult leader—is supposed to have riches beyond belief, but all their temples contain a certain amount of treasure."

"You said just said, 'they say.' Who's they?"

"One of my contacts in Wade found a wagon tracks that had been ambushed by orcs on a path northwest of Loft, near the marshes. There was a detailed inventory list with information about where it was heading. There was lot of gold on that convoy. The orcs got lucky, I'd say," Gronli said, leaning back in his chair.

"Orcs, ambush, gold—sounds familiar," Kern said, looking at Galandrik.

"Doesn't it just."

"Also, my contact spoke about magical weapons. They drain the magic from them for some reason. Axes, swords, daggers, and lots more."

"Just don't mention it to Ty yet. He'll have us leaving in the morning." Kern smiled.

"You spoke the little shit up," Galandrik said, his cheeks reddening slightly. Kern glanced round and saw Ty making his way through the crowd to their table.

"Hello all," he said with a smile.

"Welcome back! This is my friend Gronli."

Ty forced a smile, then turned to Kern. "Not bad at all. We had a good result on the—" He glanced over at Gronli. "—you know. It sold well."

"Loot?" Gronli said, smiling at Galandrik.

Ty stared at Galandrik. "Loose lips sink ships."

"Nonsense. Gronli and I go back long before you picked your first pocket."

Ty pulled out the chair next to Galandrik and sat. He made eye contact with the maid and held up four fingers; she nodded back and smiled. Ty placed his backpack on the floor, wrapping the shoulder straps around his foot. Reaching into his tunic, he pulled out a pouch and dropped it on the table in front of Kern. "All yours. Now that all the inn apparently knows," he said, glancing at Gronli, "you may as well have it."

"Thanks." Kern opened the pouch and peered inside. "Mm, better than I expected."

"I told you it wasn't a complete disaster," Ty said as Kern threw a gold piece onto the table top.

"Right, I'm off. Have a think about what we spoke about, Galandrik, and get back to me. You know where to find me." Gronli pushed back his chair and left, nodding at the other two as he passed.

"Will do, Gron. See you soon," Galandrik replied.

"Where did he appear from?" Ty asked, finishing off his first jug.

"I have known him for ages; tight bastard never buys a drink."

"A bit like—" Ty began, and Kern fixed him with a stare, knowing what was coming. Ty grinned. "…someone I used to know," he finished, then shouted for the barmaid.

"So did you find out anything else while we were gone?" Kern asked.

"Else? Did I miss something?"

Galandrik ignored Ty's question. "Yes, there is work about, but nothing close by."

"Save it for the morning, then. I need a hot bath," Kern said, stretching.

"I've just ordered your ale," Ty protested.

"Keep it. I'm off. There's a gold piece; have it," he said, getting up from his chair. "See you in the morning sometime; we can talk about more profitable work then," Kern said, with a knowing glance at Ty. He picked up his sword and broken belt and strolled through the side door that led up to the rooms, nodding at the innkeeper as he passed.

"Glad he left it. I am nearly skint," Ty said.

"Skint! How can you be skint?"

"I gave him all the loot," he said sheepishly.

"*You*... you gave away all your profit? Well, you do surprise me."

"Yes, just to keep him happy. If I'd halved it, he would have moaned." Ty looked glum. "So it's easier this way. Easy come easy go, I guess."

"Now you're the one moaning. I thought you always say, 'It's not the loot, it's the looting'?"

"Yes, but I don't think Kern thinks that way! Anyway, I am going out tonight. I need a good hit and by what I see in here, there isn't a decent mark in sight."

"Mark? What are you talking about now?"

"It's how they trained us at Lake House. When you work in pairs, one of you would find somebody with potential, someone who looks worth robbing, and 'mark' him, usually with chalk on the back. He was then the mark. Your partner would distract him and you make the hit."

"I see. Where's the Lake House?"

Ty gave Galandrik a wry look and raised his eyebrows.

"Oh, I get the point. You could tell me but you'd have to kill me."

"Something like that. So tonight I'm off out and I'm not coming back unless I get a haul. I don't care if it takes all night. I need to go." Ty paused. "Well, I guess I can stay and finish my drink."

The pair continued to talk until the innkeeper rang the bell that hung behind the bar. It was an old ship's bell, and fairly large; on the side it had the words *Green Dragon* with an anchor engraved.

"That's your lot! Go home," the innkeeper bellowed. "It's well past the hour of midnight and some of us need to tidy up, so drink up!" His announcement was met by a chorus of moans and groans.

"Well, that's my cue to leave," Galandrik said, getting up and patting Ty on the shoulder as he passed. "Don't get caught tonight, lad."

"I will try my hardest," Ty chuckled in return.

The inn gradually emptied as Ty finished off his ale. *How many drinks was that exactly?* Ty wondered. He never drank more than three before going out to 'skim some loot,' as he called it, but even three was more than advisable. Standing up, he wrapped the cloak tight around his shoulders and flipped his hood up. He picked up his bag, set it on the chair next to him, and reached in, pulling out his black leather climbing gloves. He slid his hands inside, making fists to stretch the leather, then slipped his pack over his shoulder and stepped out of the inn.

He glanced up and down the street; it was quiet. He headed for the marketplace. He hadn't tried this end of the city.

He reached the end of town where the marketplace was situated. During the day it was full of traders, but at night it was a ghost town. A few carts with broken wheels lay abandoned around 'the rows,' as the area was called when the market was busy, because of the many rows of market stalls.

Ty saw a fat, well-dressed man plodding along in his direction on the far side of the marketplace. He was staggering from side to side, and sometimes even backward. How many drinks he'd had was anybody's guess, Ty thought. He must have been wealthy, though; even at this distance the buttons on his tunic shone resplendently in the moonlight. The man leaned against a wall and bowed his head. Ty walked slowly, keeping a close eye on the drunken stranger. The man pushed himself off the wall and pivoted on his heels, rocking back and forth, trying to stay upright. Once he was nearly stable, he walked forward, but after only a few steps he stumbled into an old cart, rolled over it, and lay on the dirty marketplace cobbles, looking up at the stars. Ty even heard the *chink* of coins rattling as he fell.

Never one to look a gift horse in the mouth, Ty quickly checked out his surrounds. Everywhere was quiet, not a soul in sight. *That will be the most expensive drink this man ever had,* Ty thought as he skipped over a puddle toward the fallen stranger.

He stood looking down at the fat man. He wore green trousers; over the top of his brown tunic was a blue coat with shiny gold buttons. He wore long socks with his trousers tucked in and brown leather shoes. A fat pouch hung from his belt on his left side.

"How the other half dress," Ty chuckled, looking around again. After making sure it was all good to go, he bent down, kneeling next to the drunk and releasing a dagger into his palm.

But before he had time to cut the leather straps, the man hit him around the left ear with something heavy, sending Ty rolling over and onto his back. He lay there for a moment, his world spinning and his head throbbing, looking up at the night sky and trying to work out what had just happened. Then he tried to roll onto his front to get up. As he did, he saw the drunken man towering above him.

"You are one greedy little bastard."

"Wa... wait... I was going to... help!"

Ty saw the man swing again and then—darkness.

Chapter Four
Gone Missing

Kern left the shop dressed in his new armour, the same style as he usually bought: light-leather armour, dyed forest green by a process that involved boiling the root of foxgloves, and a cloak that matched his armour perfectly. He approached Galandrik, who was looking in a shop window across the street.

"See anything you like?"

"Plenty. I just can't afford it. I'm glad I prepaid for the room! We need some work and we need it as soon as possible. We are nearly broke. What about these spider temples?"

"I'm up for it. Let's wait for Ty and we'll work out a plan. We sold the horses, remember; it's a fair walk."

"Sounds good, lad. Maybe you can buy three cheap mounts?"

"This armour has emptied my pockets. We'll need to get Ty to put his hand in his purse," Kern said, walking toward the Orc's Armpit.

Galandrik knew Ty was skint from the conversation they'd had the night before, but didn't mention it. "What time did you say you would meet him?" he said, jogging to catch Kern up.

"I didn't, but we usually meet around this time."

The pair entered the inn and headed for a table, ordering two jugs of ale on their way past the bar. It was mid-morning and the inn's only other customers were a couple of men at the bar chatting. Kern and Galandrik sat at the table and began discussing work.

"So, these temples—are we thinking of trying just a smash-and-grab sort of operation?" Kern asked.

"Sure. I wouldn't think they'd be particularly heavily guarded, would you?"

"If there are magical weapons and gold, it'll be guarded."

"You really think so? In a religious temple?"

"Definitely. If it was yours, would you not guard it?"

"Yes, of course, *I* would, but inviting outsiders into a temple? I can't see it. Maybe a few cultists trained in the way of the sword, but I just don't see hired guards," the dwarf pointed out.

"I see your point. Best not to take chances, eh?"

"Us, take chances? As if we would!" Galandrik smiled.

"I guess we will have to get there and see. Where the hell is Ty?"

"No idea," Galandrik muttered.

"Well, when he gets here, we'll have to pool our gold and see exactly what we have and what we need."

Galandrik just nodded and sipped his ale.

*

It was mid-afternoon and they were still in the inn, having just finished off a lunch of rabbit stew and herbed bread. The inn had filled up, and most of the tables were taken by people eating and chatting.

"Well, that was the finest *rakib stum* I have had in a long while," Galandrik said, finishing the sentence with a belch.

"Where's that Rat? He's never this late."

Galandrik stared silently into his empty bowl.

"Galandrik… is there something you are not telling me?"

"Hmm," Galandrik muttered, still looking at his bowl.

"Galan—"

"All right! Last night after you left he said he was going to 'skim some loot.' I told him to be careful! My last words were 'don't get caught.'"

"Did he say where?"

Galandrik shook his head.

"I bet the fool got caught and is now being beaten in some rich farmer's basement… or worse."

"Nah, knowing that lad he's had a good haul and is off sleeping with Fat Mary somewhere," Galandrik said, trying to lift the mood.

"Wait here," Kern said, shaking his head as he rose from his chair. "Innkeep!" he shouted across the bar. The innkeeper approached from the far end of the bar.

"How may I help you?"

"Has my other friend been in today?"

"The little guy? No, haven't seen him since last night when he was with you," he answered, ramming a dirty rag into a wooden mug and twisting vigorously.

"Thanks," Kern replied, flicking a couple of copper pieces onto the bar.

"You're *too* kind," the innkeeper said, raising his eyebrows.

"It's all I have!" Kern shouted back as he returned to his seat opposite Galandrik. "He hasn't been in since last night."

"Look, it's only mid-afternoon," Galandrik said.

"I know, but he is never this late, especially after 'skimming some loot.' He cannot wait to tell me how he did it, who from, and how much."

"Aye, it is strange. Usually he's bounding through the door with a story to tell. But as I said, it's only early."

"True. Shall we take a walk, see the cheapest price we can get on some nags, and come back later? We can leave a message with old Mr Clean behind the bar."

"Sounds good."

They left a message with the innkeeper for Ty to wait if he arrived, and headed off into the hustle and bustle of the town.

*

Ty came around in darkness. His head was covered with a sack and throbbed where he had been bludgeoned the night before, and his hands and feet were bound tight. He was in a seated position with his back against something hard; by the noises he could make out, he guessed he was on the back of a wagon. He could feel somebody on either side of him. He tried to speak but the gag tied around his mouth was tight, and a muffled moan was all he could achieve. He did get one back from the person next to him, though there was no way to really communicate.

The wagon travelled for what seemed like hours as Ty drifted in and out of consciousness. Judging by the changing light and shadows, he knew they had been traveling for at least six hours, and he wondered how long he had been unconscious.

Eventually the wagon stopped and he could hear a commotion from outside—muffled voices and footsteps. A few groans came from inside the wagon. He couldn't see who was making the noises, but whoever they were, he thought, they must have been in the same position as him, tied and gagged. After a good hour, the wagon moved on again.

Ty concentrated on freeing his hands from the restraints, but he knew it was a waste of time. *Whoever tied these really knew what he was doing.* He felt the warm trickle of blood run down his wrist and into his palm, then his head drooped and he slept again.

*

Daylight had faded to darkness. The inn was full, and Kern and Galandrik were back at their regular table. Music played in the corner—the same crude banjo, flute, and cowskin drum players as always, with three or four drunken townsfolk dancing around them.

"The innkeeper hasn't seen him. What else did he say last night? Anything that could lead us to him?"

"No, apart from… he wouldn't want you to know this, but I suppose it doesn't really matter now. You know that loot he gave you?"

"From the goblin haul, yes."

"He gave you his share, too."

"His share? He wouldn't give you the steam off his shit," Kern scoffed.

"I'm telling you, he did. He thought you were well annoyed; he did it to keep you happy."

"He's a bloody fool. Yes, I was annoyed, but *he* annoys me!" Kern snarled.

"That's what he does, it's what he always does. If he didn't, something would be wrong! And to be honest he's annoying me more now than ever."

"Should we check the guard house? Maybe he was caught and locked up."

"Good idea. We will, first thing in the morning."

"He could be anywhere—trapped, locked up, beat up… even dead."

"I don't think he would be trapped for long. It's hard to trap a rat." Kern smiled. "I personally think he has been caught, but he'll escape. He always escapes."

"What if he's… gone?"

"Gone? Gone where?"

"No, I mean gone. Done a runner, had it on his toes, done the midnight flit."

"Why? That doesn't make sense."

"I don't know. He is a loner at heart, and if he thought you were ready to quit anyway…"

"You could be right there. When I had him by his throat in the goblin tun—"

"You had him by his throat?" Galandrik interrupted.

"It's a long story. Anyway, he said he would have found it easier without me, that no one made me go."

"See? I think he may have been planning this for a while."

"You could be right—giving me the loot as one final gift."

"I remember now! He said he wasn't coming back until he 'got a good haul,' and he needed to get out of here."

"That little shit," Kern said, picking up his ale.

"I think he may have gone," Galandrik said morosely.

"Maybe. I think we should still check the guard house tomorrow."

"Yeah, it can't hurt. If he has gone it will be a shame, because I liked the little shit. He had a certain charisma you don't see often."

"He had something, all right."

*

The next morning, they met up and checked the guard house, but nobody fitting Ty's description had been picked up in the last few days. They visited a few other inns, but if any of the local gossip mongers actually did know anything, they were keeping it quiet. None of the traders at the marketplace nor even Fat Mary had anything to tell.

By early afternoon, they stood in the town centre, their mood sullen.

"Well, that's it then. The little shit has deserted us, gone to find the greener grass," Galandrik said, slightly deflated.

"It certainly looks that way. I still can't believe he buggered off without even a final goodbye."

"If he didn't walk out of here, he was carried. Either way I can't see us finding him."

"You know what he was like. Remember in that cave under the Eastern Mountains, when we jumped into the flowing river and got spat out into the pond?"

"How can I forget?"

"He couldn't even do that without the extravagant exit that nearly got him killed. So I just can't see him taking off without a final fanfare," Kern said, kicking a stone across the marketplace. "Saying that, disappearing is just as crazy, I guess."

"Sure is. Oh, I contacted my friend, Gronli. He should be here in two days. He is bringing some horses—for a larger cut of the loot, obviously."

"All right, we will go to the spider temple, but it'll be strange without him. And I don't want this to sound out of turn, but we will need another thief who can pick locks."

"True. We can cross that bridge when we come to it."

*

Gorgon sat his mount at the front of the troop, with Belton at his side. He was a huge man for a human, certainly the biggest man Belton had ever seen. He wore thick leather boots, the tops lined with fur. His legs were bare and showed his many battle scars. His massive thighs were wider than Belton's chest and rippled with muscle. Only a leather loincloth covered his modesty. His torso was protected by thick brown leather armour, crisscrossed twine pulling it together down the centre of his chest. His arms were huge and bare, apart from his metal wristbands. His shoulders and neck exploded with muscle, matching his monstrous thighs. Even his horse was massive; at least a foot taller than Belton's own, this was the sort of mount that pulled carts, not carried men.

Thick black matted hair hung slightly past the Gorgon's shoulders, tied back into a ponytail. It looked caked with mud or blood, and had probably not seen water for a year. His face was serious and intense, his stare like two black coals burning deep into your soul. A scar ran down his left cheek from above the eye to his chin, which was slightly covered in stubble. He was awesome, Belton thought, and he had never seen anything like the two swords that hung at Gorgon's hips. Both blades were curved and serrated on the front edge, with three barbed hooks on the back. Belton shuddered to think of the damage these had done. No one had lived to say they'd fought the Gorgon.

"How long till we reach the lair?" Belton asked in the most commanding voice he could muster.

Gorgon didn't answer; he just pointed forward at the mountains in front of them.

Belton stared up at the Eastern Mountains. They stretched as far south as he could see, and roared up out of the ground like a stone tsunami. The tips were white with snow, glistening like pearl necklaces on the throats of giants.

Belton breathed deeply and said, "I know *where* it is. I want to know how long until we *get* there."

Gorgon slowly turned and stared at Belton. "I estimate by midnight." His deep voice was harsh.

"And once we are in, how do we capture the dragons?" Belton asked, keeping his face forward, not wanting to catch that stare again.

"We have ways. Magical ways."

"Would you care to enlighten me?" he asked, trying to keep his voice steady as he imagined Gorgon reaching for a sword and slicing through him like a hot knife through butter.

"Magic ropes and nets. In those boxes on the cart behind, we have some large modified crossbows. We fire ropes up into the walls in a crisscross pattern, stopping the dragon from flying up or down. The nets and ropes are magical and she won't go near them."

"That is truly ingenious. What about the baby dragons?" Belton relaxed a fraction.

"Same thing, but we fire nets at them. The crisscrossing ropes are close enough together to stop a fully grown dragon, but once the nets hit and capture the babies, they will fall down through our magic web to the ground."

Feeling more confident now, and somewhat distracted by his own curiosity, Belton asked, "Excuse my ignorance here, but what's stopping the dragon from just breathing fire down at us through the ropes? In fact, what's stopping her burning the ropes up?"

"I told you, the ropes are magical. She will flee."

"I hope you are right. Ropes don't usually stop fire," Belton said, then realised that questioning Gorgon wasn't the brightest thing to do. He kept staring forward, as if his words had meant nothing.

"This isn't the first time I have done this. Trust me. She will flee," Gorgon rumbled.

"I do trust you, and I'm sure she will. In fact, I am positive she will," Belton said smoothly.

"Now, let me ask *you* a question," Gorgon said, turning his head.

Belton could feel the gaze burning into the side of his face; he felt like an ant being burnt by a magnifying glass. Trying to look unfazed by the uncomfortable stare, he replied, "Sure, you go ahead."

"Why do we need to capture baby dragons to lure two petty thieves out of hiding? Just sprinkle some gold about; they'll come for it like mice for cheese."

"It's not that simple." Belton explained the need for the herbs, and how one only grew in a dungeon. Using these thieves to retrieve the herbs was perfect, he said, because King Moriak wanted them dead, too, along with the capture of the dragons.

"It's sort of like killing three birds with one stone," he finished off.

"Three birds? What birds?"

"Not real birds." Belton bit back his next comment, then continued. "What I mean is, we are doing three jobs at the same time: killing the thieves, getting the herbs, and capturing the dragons. This is sometimes called 'killing two birds with one stone.'"

"You said three birds."

Belton bit his lip. "Yes, you are correct. Indeed I did. In *this* case we are doing *three* things—or 'birds,' as it were—but the saying usually only has *two* 'birds.'"

"So you could have four birds?"

Belton, now slightly agitated, replied, "What? Yes, of course."

"But always one stone?" Gorgon asked.

"Of course only one stone! That's the point, doing multiple tasks at the same time! The time is represented by the stone, and the birds represent the number of tasks." Belton swallowed hard, belatedly realizing his tone was probably harsher than any Gorgon had heard in a very long time. He still refused to look to his left, but he could feel Gorgon's gaze on him.

"I think I understand now. So if I ripped… *someone's* arms, legs, and head off, I would be killing five birds with one stone?"

"Well… if the task was ripping limbs off, then yes, but if the task was simply the kill, then no."

There was an uncomfortable silence before Gorgon spoke again. "I'm going to check on the men, Belton Five Birds." He manoeuvred his mount and rode back down, talking to his troop of men as he went.

Belton felt sick; his skin went cold and clammy. *He couldn't possibly be thinking he could kill me. Could he?*

*

As they got closer to the Eastern Mountains, the ground became rougher and the pace slowed. They picked up a pathway that led up and into the mountains, twisting and turning as it climbed upwards. The air got colder as the night drew in. It was a couple of hours before midnight when they came to a fork in the mountain pathway. One path led southward and through to western Bodisha; the other path led up higher, toward Shalamia's lair.

Gorgon stopped and looked back at the troop of men.

"The wagons and horses will stay here. The dragon will smell this many horses from a mile away. No fires and no noise. Shalamia could hear a pigeon shit at five hundred yards. Billou, you will stay here and guard them. Go pick ten men you want."

"Yes sir!" Billou said quietly, and scurried back along his troop, pointing and ordering.

Gorgon swung his mighty leg over and dismounted his horse. He glared at Belton. "We walk from here."

Belton got down from his own mount and watched as the men unloaded the crates from the carts, removing the wooden cotton reels, which were coiled with an unusual rope that shone metallic blue in the moonlight. The large crossbows and their stands were dismantled. Jakob the Illusionist removed bags from his mount. Other wooden boards and even makeshift wheels were being unloaded and readied to carry, while other men scurried about doing their duties. Belton wanted to know what all the wood and wheels were for, but thought it better not to ask.

Once all the equipment was ready, the troop began the long trek up the winding mountain path, Gorgon at the front keeping a quick pace, with Belton just behind. After two hours of nonstop marching they reached a small clearing. Belton wasn't used to this pace and the hike had exhausted him. *God knows how the men who carried the equipment must feel*, he thought, but then he realized—these weren't normal men; these were *Gorgon's* men. These were his elite soldiers, men who could march for two days then fight a two-day war. It was rumoured the fifty elite guards—and Gorgon—had defeated five hundred orcs, among other tales of valour and inconceivable, against-all-odds battles.

This wasn't the entrance to any cave or the summit, but Gorgon seemed to know exactly where he was. Below them and to the west, they could clearly see the lights of Tonilla. A path curled down toward the west side of the mountains.

"Right, Fucan," Gorgon said to another one of his guards, "this path leads to the entrance of the dragon's lair. Tell the men we need the two net crossbows, and make sure they are fully loaded. These need to go up front first. If the dragons are there, we net the two smaller dragons. I will enter alone and attack Shalamia. As soon as I go in, the second attack will be the two rope crossbows. Fire these directly above Shalamia's head. Aim them into the wall behind her, in a crisscross pattern. I will try and slow her whilst you're loading the crossbows. Hopefully I can, and once the rope crossbows have fired for the second time, she will be trapped. Then we can butcher her. Every man in and using ranged weapons. She won't leave her babies and that love will be her downfall. Her flame range is about thirty feet, but the heat travels a good ten or twelve feet past. It will burn like a bitch, so tell the men to have shields ready."

"Yes sir," Fucan said, taking all the instructions in.

"You want me to explain again?" Gorgon said.

"No sir."

"Well, move then!" Gorgon growled.

With this, Fucan ran down the line of men, relaying Gorgon's orders. The troops began scurrying around, readying their equipment.

The troops were well trained and within minutes the two net crossbows were readied, each one carried by four soldiers. Behind them were the rope crossbows; another four guards carried each of these, along with two more behind each carrying the bobbin spools with the glowing blue rope on. A wooden pole went through the centre of each spool, and a soldier lifted it on either side. Then came ten men, each carrying a kite shield and spear—*ready for the butchering,* Belton thought. Another ten archers followed, and backup soldiers carrying spears finished the troop.

At last Fucan gave a signal and the soldiers left their gear in position to gather around Gorgon. Belton stood off to one side, observing. Any other leader would have needed to stand on a box, he mused, but not Gorgon; he was a foot taller than all his men.

"Right, men," the Gorgon began, "down this path is a dragon. A big fucking dragon, and big fucking dragons don't like men. Especially men who want to capture her babies and rip out her heart, so be on your guard and remember your training: Use your shields. They will heat, but they'll stop your face from melting off. Use wet cloth wrapped around the handles so you can hold it longer without burning your hands. Together we will defeat her!"

The men gave a subdued cheer and raised their swords. "We will move quickly down the path and hit the bitch. We don't want to spook her and spoil our surprise, so move as quietly as you can. We work as one and remember…" There was a pause as Gorgon looked sternly at his men. "Be your brother's keeper!"

Gorgon raised his hand and the troops dispersed, resuming their positions and taking up their gear with impressive silence for their numbers.

Belton could see that these men were in absolute awe of Gorgon and would follow him into the pit of Hades itself, but what surprised him was his command of tactics. He knew Gorgon was famed for his victories in battle, but Belton had always pictured him to be a berserker barbarian full of rage, taking on ten foes at once, swinging his swords wildly as blood and gore filled the air—not as a general of men, complete with tactics. He wondered now if the soldier had known what 'killing two birds with one stone' meant all along. Perhaps the whole thing had been intended to make a grudge with Belton, to see how far he could push him.

Gorgon turned to Belton, "Ready, little bird?" he muttered.

"Ready for the slaughter, you mean?" Belton replied, distractedly.

"You disagree with your king's wishes?"

Belton looked up at the giant man. "Did I say that?"

"I heard it in your voice. You're against the killing of the dragon."

"Don't be ridiculous. It's just a dragon."

"Maybe just the last dragon, and one that you would rather keep alive."

"Kill it, and the young. Kill it for your king!"

"Watch your tone with me; you don't realise who you are speaking to."

"Oh, I realise all too well, *high general Gorgon*. But you should be careful to whom you speak, as well."

Gorgon held Belton's gaze for a few seconds. Then, with a hint of a smile, he whispered, "Oh, I know who I am talking to… *little bird*." Gorgon's eyes burned into his skull, but Belton refused to look away this time, keeping his eyes locked onto Gorgon's. Eventually Gorgon turned and headed down the slope, waving for the troop to follow.

Belton looked down at his hand and saw the tremble. He had never felt fear like this. A bead of sweat rolled down his temple.

"Careful what you say to the Gorgon," Fucan said quietly, appearing next to him.

"Why, I suppose he holds a grudge?"

"Holds a grudge? No… worse."

"Worse? How can *not* holding a grudge be worse than holding one?"

Fucan glanced over his shoulder to make sure no one was close enough to hear. "He doesn't *hold* a grudge. He cuddles it close to his chest, and he hand-feeds it the choicest tidbits and keeps it safe so it can grow up to be big and strong. Be careful, my friend." He clapped Belton on the shoulder, then marched past him and toward his leader, who was speaking to Jakob.

Belton balled up his fist in an attempt to stop it shaking.

Chapter Five
Better Dead Than Red

Kern swung his sword in a wild arc in front of him. "Come out and fight me, you little whore!" He spun around, his sword again circling and slicing through the air. "Show yourself, you bastard," he cried as he swung his sword wildly, turning round and round like a blind man. A small cloaked figure holding two daggers stepped out from behind a tree stump and crouched in front of him, ready to attack. Kern swung again and the small figure rolled under the arc of the sword then lunged forward, stabbing Kern in the thigh. Kern swung to the side where the attack had come from but sliced thin air as his attacker rolled under the sword and squatted, holding his daggers up, ready to attack again…

Ty was awakened by the wagon coming to an abrupt stop. His head banged against whatever was next to him. *The same dream again,* he thought. His body ached and he wanted to scream every time he moved his wrist. He could hear the commotion of the wagon being opened from the back. Even though he wore the sack, the sudden influx of light made his vision slightly brighter.

He was dragged to his feet without warning and pulled from the back of the wagon. He fell to the ground with a thud, winding himself in the process. He realized how hungry he was, too.

He heard a muffled voice say, "I'll take this little shit. I thought we weren't feeding it halflings or dwarfs because of the thick hair."

"Yeah, it was mentioned. We shave them first now," another voice said.

Ty had to concentrate to hear the speakers clearly through the hood over his head.

"I'll carry him. He can't weigh five stone soaking wet. It wouldn't even fill me up, let alone Old Seven-Legs."

"I'll take this one. She looks like she could be some fun."

"Leave it! You know Therliyn said no fucking the women before the sacrifice."

"He'll never find out, though, will he?"

"You better hope not."

There were moans and groans from the other captives as they were bundled off to wherever it was they were being taken. He longed for his two companions, but deep down he knew they would not be coming. He was on his own.

He was picked up and it felt like he was thrown over someone's shoulder. He could hear the sound of keys rattling; doors being opened, closed, unlocked; captives' groans and moans. He was carried through doorways and down long, echoing corridors.

"He soon got heavy for a little one," he heard as he was thrown to the floor, which felt damp and cold. He was grabbed again and pushed against a wall. Then he felt hands fumbling at his wrists, and the rope around them suddenly loosened. The pain of the blood rushing back into his deadened fingers was terrible, but no sooner was he untied than his arms were pulled up above his head and shackled again, this time in metal restraints. What little struggle he did make against his captors was soon dismissed with a punch to his stomach. Choking into his gag, he stopped struggling as his ankles were untied and then re-shackled as well.

The room he was in was noisy; he could hear other chains and struggles around him. This went on for what seemed like hours, until eventually all was quiet apart from the odd muffled moan. He heard the door open and footsteps entered the room, then the door slammed shut behind them.

"Right, listen up," a harsh voice announced. "We are now going to remove your blindfolds and gags. When we do, I don't want to hear no screaming and shouting. If I do, then it all goes back on and you will have no food." Ty felt the sack on his head lift off, followed by the blindfold. He squinted in the torchlight and tried to let his eyes adjust to the light.

From across the room he heard, "You have the wrong man! If you let—" The voice turned from shouting to coughing. Ty's eyes finally focused, and he could see a man hanging in shackles across the room, head bent, coughing and spitting.

Ty looked around the room. It was a square with one wooden door directly opposite where he hung. The sobbing man hung to his left, and a young woman was hanging on the wall to his right. Next to him hung an old man dressed in rags with a long grey beard. He was slumped over and appeared to be dead. Everyone had been stripped to their leggings and undershirts; even their footwear was missing.

"What did I tell you?"

The angry voice brought Ty's focus to the two men in the middle of the room. They were each six feet tall, wearing hooded robes—one in white, the other in red. The robes were plain and unornamented, save for the belt each man wore with a curved dagger tucked inside.

"But I have riches and if—"

The red-robed man slapped the captive across the face.

"We don't want your money. We want your soul," he said, smiling.

"Please... I have a family," the man said, sobbing. "I have kids... two kids. Why won't you let—"

The man received another slap. He hung his head and sobbed, "You can't do this... you just *can't*."

"Has anybody else got anything to say?" the red-robed man said, looking around the room.

"What's for dinner?" Ty said, bracing himself for a slap.

The man moved toward him and stood with his nose inches away from Ty's.

"Ah, we have a joker in the pack, do we?" he said.

"Not a joker, just a hungry halfling," Ty answered, just now realizing he had been completely stripped of his armour. For the first time since he was a child, he felt frightened. No daggers, armour, potions, or poisons to help him. Not even a friend. He was afraid, alone, and scared.

"So what would you like? How about some meat?"

With a forced smile Ty replied, "Yes, that'll do nicely."

"Then meat you shall have." The robed man pulled the dagger from his belt and held it up in front of Ty, twisting and turning it, the point facing directly at Ty's face. His smile disappeared, and the robed man laughed.

Spinning on his heel, he faced the man who was still sobbing and strode with intent over to him. He grabbed the man's hair in his left hand and yanked his head up.

"Felkk, remove his tunic." The white-robed man, Felkk, obliged, ripping the man's shirt open.

"No, no! What are you doing? Make him stop! No!" the man screamed.

"Enough! You've made your point," Ty shouted as he watched the sobbing man thrash about.

"Hold him still, Felkk!"

Felkk gripped the captive's forehead and pushed it back against the wall. The man in the red robes drew his dagger and cut a line across the man's chest as if checking the sharpness of the blade, then began hacking at the sobbing man's ear. When he turned around, he was covered in blood, dagger in one hand and half an ear in the other.

"You are sick," Ty said, staring at the blood-stained man.

"Oh, I haven't finished yet," he said, moving towards the thief with an evil smile.

"Don't even think about it!" Ty said, rattling his chain restraints.

"*You're* the hungry joker. *You're* the one who wanted meat."

"Not human meat, you sick bastard."

"Felkk, hold Mr Joker. He's hungry."

"No! I'm going to cut out your heart and—"

Felkk grabbed Ty's head and held it back. Ty struggled and refused to open his mouth, clenching his teeth together as hard as he could. The red-robed man stepped back and spun round, looking at each of the captives. "This is what happens when people are *jokers,* this is what will happen if you try to escape, and this is what will happen if you disobey us." Ty's head was bent backward but his mouth was still firmly shut. The red-robed man punched Ty in the stomach three times. Ty screamed in pain and Felkk seized his jaw, holding Ty's mouth wide open, as the other man rammed the human flesh into his mouth.

Felkk forced Ty's jaw up, closing his mouth. The man in red robes held Ty's nose and said, "Eat, my child, eat."

Ty coughed and spasmed as if choking, but still they held his mouth shut. Ty's eyes widened and his face turned red. He couldn't breathe.

"He's going to choke to death!" the girl shouted across the room. The red-robed man glared at her as if she had woken him from a dream, but he let go of Ty's nose.

"Let him go, Felkk, it's upsetting his bitch."

Felkk relaxed his grip, and Ty immediately threw up onto the floor. Coughing and spluttering, he spat the chunk out, along with what little he had left in his stomach. He hung limp, head bowed, only his hand restraints keeping him from collapsing in a heap.

"Let this be a warning to you all. Next time it won't just be a little cut ear." The two men left the room and silence fell.

"Thanks," Ty said, between coughing and spitting out pieces of sick and ear.

"You bloody idiot! Why say anything?" the young woman said. Ty lifted his head to study the girl. She was dressed in rags, but still her beauty shone through. Her hair was nearly white and tied back in two braids, and her pale complexion was dotted with freckles. *Not a skinny girl; just about right,* Ty thought.

"I'm sorry. I thought I would get a slap. Not… *him* over there."

"The name is Ronnick. I'm just a farmer. I don't deserve to be here," the wounded man said, looking up. The blood and tears were still trickling down his face and neck.

"None of us do. My name is Ty."

"I'm Lan'esra. If he doesn't get treatment for that ear and chest he'll get an infection." Just then, a rat scurried across the floor and grabbed the piece of ear, then scurried back into the darkness. Even Ty's shouts and the flicking of his feet weren't enough to put the rat off.

Ty noticed something glistening in amongst the sick. He reached out with his toe and prodded about. It was what he thought—the little diamond he had swallowed a couple of days ago. He thought he had lost it. *Lots of gems get lost when swallowed; well, forgotten about—*

"What is it?" Lan'esra asked, interrupting his thoughts.

"It's a diamond." On any other given day Ty would have lied, but the truth had come out before he knew it.

"A diamond? Why on earth is there a diamond in your pile of sick?" Ronnick asked, staring at the thief.

"I don't know. He must have dropped it."

"Yeah, of course he did. The pockets on those robes are just bursting with gems!"

"Maybe it was here before we got here?"

"Why did you swallow a diamond?" Lan'esra asked. "Actually, let me guess: You got caught somewhere you shouldn't have been and swallowed the evidence so the search wouldn't reveal it."

Ty grinned. "Something like that," he chuckled, then winced at the reminder of the stomach blows he had received.

"Can you sick up a set of keys and a couple of swords?"

"I wish. This will come in handy though."

"How? He wants our souls, not money. Remember?" Ronnick added.

"No, not to pay them with. Faceted diamonds have a sharp point. If I use this correctly, I may as well have sicked up a key."

"It's on the floor under your foot. How do you intend to get it into your hand?"

"I'll fall down when they unlock me and grab it."

"Full of ideas, aren't we?" the girl said, trying to force a smile.

"I'm Ty the Rat. No prison can—" He stopped mid-sentence. *Bragging 'no prison can hold me' would seem pretty pathetic at the present moment*, he thought.

"You're Ty the what?" Lan'esra asked.

"Never mind. Let's try and rest."

"Rest? Have you seen where we are? We are shackled with our arms tied up above us! How on earth are we going to rest?"

"Just slump and sleep," the old man hanging next to Ty chimed in.

"I thought you were dead!" Ty said, looking at the man next to him, shocked.

"Play dead and they leave you alone."

"I'm Lan'esra. How long have you been here?"

"I did hear. My name is Rye. I'm not exactly sure, but it's been months."

"Just tied up here?" Ty added.

"Oh no, above us is a Spider Guild temple. The two that were in here were Felkk and Luthian. Luthian, in the red robes, runs this temple—he is one evil man. The main man is Therliyn. He lives in a massive temple a couple of hours' ride from here."

"So what do they want from us?" Lan'esra asked.

"Someone has to clean the carcasses out of the cave. You three are now 'feeders.'"

"What carcasses? What cave?" Ty said.

"They worship a spider god, see. There are catacombs below us where they feed and look after a giant spider. It's like a pet. They send us in to grab the leftovers and clear the cave floor, but there is always that chance that Old Seven-Legs is still hungry and grabs one of us for an extra snack. I've been lucky. Twice he has grabbed the person with me."

"Feeders? You must be kidding me," Lan'esra spat.

"Oh no, not at all."

"And where are the spider god disciples during all this?"

"They stand above and watch. It's like a circular pit, and they clap and cheer. I think it's to make the spider wild and attack."

"I take it the spider lost a leg—any idea how?" Ty asked.

"Rumour has it that a feeder fashioned a weapon out of a previous victim's leg bone that had been left on the floor. While the spider attacked one of the feeders, the other one cut through one of its legs. His mate got eaten by the spider, and he was skinned alive. His skin is hung in the temple as a warning to others."

"So what do they actually feed it? Carcasses of what exactly?" Lan'esra asked.

"Men. Women and children, too. Sometimes they get an animal but it's usually human."

"Sick bastards! We need to get out of here as quickly as possible," Ty said, pulling at his hand restraints.

"Save your energy," Rye said. "Even if you somehow broke free, what are you going to do? You have no key and I expect that even if you could pick a lock, you have no tools." Ty glared down at his bare feet and sighed. "But even if you did, you'll never walk out of here. Don't take this the wrong way, but I don't think you're a warrior, so you're not fighting your way through. So just save your energy. The gods will decide your fate now."

"Fuck the gods. They've never helped me. You make your own fate and if there's a way out of this shit pit, I'll find it. This isn't the first time I've been locked up and it won't be the last. You'll see," Ty said, looking around the room as if to spot some sort of miraculous answer. Inside he was worried, though. Indeed he had escaped from a few jail houses—and once even broke *into* one—but he'd had tools and accomplices. He had held all the cards on those other occasions, but this time his hand wasn't looking very good.

"Well, I admire your enthusiasm. I hope you do get out—even more so if you take me with you. But I fear your enthusiasm may be quenched very soon," Rye said.

"I believe in you, Ty," Lan'esra said earnestly. "If we all stick together, we will be just fine."

*

They rested as best they could under the circumstances. Three hours went by before they heard the keys to the door being rattled. It opened, and Felkk and another two cultists entered, dressed in white robes and carrying drawn swords. The two men stood on either side of the door as Felkk moved to the middle of the room.

"I'm sure Rye has explained to you that trying to escape is pointless. Any problems from you lot and you'll be Dago's next meal."

Ty spoke up first. "You'll get no problems from us."

"Good," Felkk answered, turning around. "Come!" he shouted and two more cultists entered, one carrying a little table, the other with a tray of food. As soon as the food was set down, the pair began unshackling Ronnick.

"What you doing?" Ronnick asked, a panic-stricken look on his face.

"We are going to get your wounds cleaned, that's all," Felkk explained.

"I shouldn't be here," he said as he was shoved and dragged to the door by the cultists. "I have a family."

"Don't worry," Felkk replied. "You'll see them soon."

After Ronnick had been led away, Felkk unshackled Rye. The old man fell to the floor in a heap, rubbing his ankles where the iron restraints had been. Lan'esra was released next, and did the same. Then Felkk stood in front of Ty.

"I am watching you. There are many men outside these walls and you will be cut down within seconds."

"Many a sparrow killed a hawk," Ty answered. Felkk stared at him for a few seconds then, with a slight hint of a smile, unshackled him. Ty didn't fall to the ground; even though he ached to rub his wrists and ankles, he stood strong. Felkk turned and walked to the door, waving an arm for the other two cultists, who followed him out. As soon as the door closed behind them Ty dropped, rubbing his wrists and ankles.

"Why do you put up such a fight?" Lan'esra asked.

"Why do you give in?" Ty countered.

"We are not giving up or in. We are shackled in a dungeon cell somewhere, surrounded by armed guards. What's the point in fighting?" she said, examining the food.

"She is right," Rye added, "and the sooner you learn that, the better for you."

"Look, you two do what you want and I'll do what I want," Ty said, making his way around the room, feeling the walls and examining the lock. "Hmm. Double-barrel tube-core lock; I reckon I could open this with a couple of toothpicks."

"Which we don't have," Rye said around a mouthful of stale bread.

"Always the pessimist," Ty said, as he picked up his diamond. *Not a massive gem*, he thought, *but should fetch a couple of gold*. He went to slip it in his pocket, then realised he had none. With a small shrug, he put his hand down the back of his leggings.

"That's gross," Lan'esra said, frowning as she watched him.

"All right, here you are. You hide it in you," Ty answered.

"No way! That's even grosser."

"Exactly. I'll do it then," Ty said, inserting the gem with a wiggle. He walked over to the table and looked down at the food—mouldy bread, blue cheese, and water. Grabbing a chunk of bread, he continued to survey the floor for anything he could use as a lock pick, but found nothing.

"Found your toothpicks?" Rye asked.

"Leave him," Lan'esra butted in. "Let him do what he wants."

"I haven't," Ty said, sifting through a pile of dirt on the floor, "but when I do, I'll be sure not to unlock yours."

At that moment they heard the door being unlocked again. Felkk re-entered the room, four armed cultists behind him.

"You two come with us," Felkk said, pointing at Ty and Lan'esra with an evil smile. "Dago's house needs cleaning."

They were pushed out of the door and into a corridor at sword point. To their left were stairs leading downward; to the right, the corridor had three sets of doors on either side. Felkk led the way down and the others followed until they reached another corridor. Felkk turned right. The corridor got wider until it ended at a set of large double doors.

Felkk looked at Ty and Lan'esra. "Behind these doors is her lair. You'll see a couple of carcasses and other bits; drag them into the hole to the left. When you have cleared the bodies we will open the door again. Until then, it stays shut, so try not to wake him up."

"We are just lambs to the slaughter, you—"

Felkk backhanded Ty across the face, spinning him around. A trickle of blood seeped from his lip.

"Anything else you want to add?" Felkk asked.

Ty didn't answer; he just stared, trying his hardest to ignore the pain in his cheek.

"Good. Open the doors," Felkk ordered two of the guards. The two guards stepped forward and pulled out the wooden block holding the doors shut, then pulled the doors open, toward them. Ty and Lan'esra could hear cheering from above, but neither one moved. Then the tips of the swords forced them in and the door shut behind them.

The room was circular with an arched opening directly in front of them, some ten feet away. Spider webs spanned in different directions, and torches attached to the wall all the way around lit the room. On the floor in front of them was a man's torso, face-down, with no legs and one arm. Another half-eaten corpse lay to their right. The smell was terrible. Above them, circling the edge of the pit, was a baying crowd all dressed in white robes. The noise was deafening as they clapped and cheered. Directly above the lair entrance stood Luthian in his red robes, looking down with folded arms.

"Quickly," Ty shouted, "you grab that one. I'll do this one." They dashed to the corpses as the crowd cheered wildly. Ty grabbed the arm of the corpse and began pulling it toward the hole. As he got it to the edge, the body flipped over and he could see the half-eaten face of Ronnick. He rolled what was left of him over, and the body fell in. Ty saw that Lan'esra was struggling to pull her body toward the hole; he jumped forward and grabbed the other arm, and together they pulled.

"Look!" Lan'esra shouted over the noise of the crowd above, nodding to the spider's lair.

Ty could see two legs coming out of the darkness. Both were black and hairy, and two black claws rested onto the ground. "Hurry, get it in the hole," Ty said. They dragged the body and rolled it into the pit. Looking around for something to defend them with, Ty snatched up an old leg bone.

"Pick up a weapon, anything you can swing," he told Lan'esra, holding the bone out in front of him.

Another two legs protruded from the entrance, bending like the legs of a stringed puppet. These two were a lot longer than the first two, and Ty could see the size of what was coming out. Lan'esra stood next to Ty; he pulled her away from the hole and toward the door they had entered through.

"As soon as it opens, get out. No matter what is going on, run," Ty said.

"All right," Lan'esra agreed, nodding frantically.

"Get to my left, and make yourself look tall. Wave your arms and scream," Ty said, doing so himself.

Lan'esra did the same. Only the width of the door separated them as they shouted and waved their arms. This seemed to have worked, but only for a few seconds. The spider's head gradually emerged from the darkness—two black bulbous eyes with four smaller ones in a line below them, thick dark brown fangs hanging down below the eyes like stalactites.

Lan'esra froze. Her eyes widened and the bone she was carrying dropped to the floor. The noise from above stopped and all the cultists held their hands together as if praying.

"Keep shouting, Lan'esra! Wave your arms!" Ty checked the door with the heel of his foot, pushing against it. "Lan'esra! Keep waving your arms! The door is still locked!"

Dago—now nearly all the way out—was only a few arms'-lengths away from Lan'esra. Ty screamed and shouted, waving the bone. Dago was completely out of the cave now, and Ty could see the stump of the spider's missing leg. The spider lowered its body to the floor and Ty knew it was getting ready to attack. The legs and abdomen twitched, but the beast was completely ignoring Ty. Its back three legs bent, and Ty took a single step, then jumped toward Lan'esra, pushing her out of the way, just as the spider sprang forward. Ty and Lan'esra tumbled to the ground and rolled as Dago's fangs struck the ground inches away from their feet. They scrambled forward on their stomachs for a few feet, then spun up and around, sprawling on the stone floor and facing Dago. Ty held his arm across Lan'esra's chest, pushing her slightly back. Dago edged towards them, then stopped, her claws rattling as he moved.

"Pass me the bone," Ty said quietly. Lan'esra did, still without speaking.

Dago lowered herself again and his legs started twitching.

"She is going to strike again. Stay behind me." Ty shifted up into a squat, holding the bone out straight as if aiming it to throw. He could feel Lan'esra shift her body behind his.

"Please don't let me die," he heard from behind him.

"No one is dying today," Ty answered without looking back.

Dago pounced, her giant head and fangs coming down directly toward Ty. He held the bone up and rammed it in between her huge fangs. The force of the attack slammed Ty and Lan'esra back. Ty lay under the spider, gripping both ends of the jammed bone and using all his strength to stop the spider's fangs from penetrating his body. A drip of yellow poison fell from a fang onto Ty's chest where it sizzled, burning through his cloth shirt and into his flesh.

"Lan'esra, hit him! Do something!" Ty shouted.

Lan'esra sat motionless, staring at the huge arachnid. The spider's strength was far greater than Ty's, and the poison fangs were now inches away from his chest.

"LAN'ESRA!" Ty screamed.

Her head twitched and she blinked as if awakening from a dream. Her eyes focused on Ty.

"Hit the spider! NOW!" Ty shouted.

Lan'esra jumped to her feet and picked up a fist-sized stone.

"Hurry!" Ty pleaded, the fang tips now touching his flesh as he strained under the weight of the spider.

Lan'esra ducked under Dago's frontmost leg and smashed the stone into one of her smaller eyes. Dago sprang backward, shrieking, then scurried into the blackness of her cave. From above they heard a chorus of shouting and booing.

"Kill them!" the cultists jeered.

"Quick, the door," Ty said. "Follow my lead."

"What?"

"Just do as I do! Follow me. It'll be all right," Ty reassured her.

The door opened and they ran through it into the corridor. Ty bent down gasping, trying to regain his breath. The two guards stepped past them and picked up the wooden block to bar the door. Felkk stood in front of them, glaring, two guards on either side.

"That was very stupid, what you did," Felkk said.

"We were supposed to just die?" Lan'esra answered.

Ty leapt up from his crouching position and struck Felkk in the face with the bone, breaking it in two. Felkk staggered, falling into the guard next to him, who stopped him falling completely over. Ty ducked under the other guard's lunge and sprinted down the corridor, shouting, "Quick, Lan'esra, run!"

As Ty reached the end he glanced over his shoulder. "Lan'esra, this w—"

The guard was holding her by her hair, and his sword rested against her throat.

"Please don't let me die!" she screamed.

His instincts screamed for him to carry on running. His muscles tensed, but then he looked back to Lan'esra. His heart sank and he knew his fate was sealed. He fell to his knees, bowing his head.

"Take him to the torture chamber," he heard Felkk order.

Chapter Six
Dragon Bait

Bok and Reyheld trotted their mounts through the gates of Tonilla. It was evening and the streets were emptying: Farmers rode their carts home after doing their daily trading; market traders pulled barrows of fruit and veg, silks, and other unsold items; and other folk just wandered home after a hard day's work.

"How do you know where to find them?" Reyheld asked.

"They will be in one of these inns; they are creatures of habit and live in these places. Even leaving aside the pull of the wine and women, they find all their work in the inns."

"Work? They *work?*"

"Yes. Well, they don't go ploughing fields or running a market stall. They adventure. Go find the riches that lay around Bodisha."

Reyheld snorted. "It's hardly what I call working."

"Oh, trust me. You go into a dungeon and risk life and limb for a bag of gold, you've earned it."

"And then what do they do? Drink it all away, I guess?"

"Yes, I guess they would drink, but they also spend it on improving their armour and weapons and so forth. The more powerful they become, the more advanced the dungeon they can enter; therefore, the better the rewards."

"How do they know which dungeons are hard and which are easy?"

"Exactly! That's my point. The inn is the best place to hear the stories. If you hear that there's a cave with a dozen goblins, that'll be easier than the cave with four fire elementals."

"But where does it end?"

"End? I don't know, when they die? When they get fed up? Too old? Too rich? Meet a woman? Who knows. I once heard of somebody becoming a demigod through dungeoneering."

"A demigod? Don't be absurd."

"It's true! He completed masses of dungeons and got so many rich rewards and spells cast upon him giving him ever more strength, intelligence, and dexterity that, over the years, he became a demigod. He could wrestle a ten-foot bear and carry huge boulders."

"Well, I will take your word for that one."

"Take what you like. It's true."

They rode through the town until they came to the Factory Inn. "Let's eat. We can look for them in the morning," Reyheld suggested.

"You don't have to ask me twice," Bok replied.

They tied the horses up outside and Reyheld gave the stable boy a couple of silver pieces, saying, "Look after them, lad."

"Aye, sir, I shall. I'll take them round the back and feed them," the young boy replied.

As they entered the inn, Bok covered his face, hiding the grotesque scarring. The bar was packed with all races and trades; farmers, adventurers, traders, and townsfolk mingled together, enjoying a drink after a day's work. Pipe tobacco from all over Bodisha mixed in the air, making a smog that smelt of lavender, rose, vanilla, and various other tobacco types. They sat at one of the few empty tables that were left, and ordered some chicken stew and two pints of mead.

"When we do finally meet them, I need to get them back to the dragon's lair, so let me do the talking," Bok said.

"What are you going to say?"

"Well, I will use the dragons, which we will have captured by then, as the first reason for them to help. If they don't want to help for the creatures' sakes, then I will tell Kern they have his father."

"But we *don't* have him."

"Yes, but Gorgon has Jakob the Illusionist."

"Oh, I see."

Bok tilted his head and studied Reyheld, sitting there in his shiny armour. "In fact, I think this is where we must part."

"Part? But—"

"Look at you. You stand out like a new pin. If I am to convince them that I'm a thief and want to join them, the first thing they'll ask is 'Why are you with him?'"

"You think?"

"No, I know. You can shadow us, make sure I don't run, but they'll never believe I hang around with you. Maid! Where's my fucking drink?"

"Okay, I get the point." Reyheld said.

"There they are," Bok said, nodding toward Kern and Galandrik as they entered the inn. The maid placed the food and drink down on the table, but Bok ignored her. Instead he watched as his quarry claimed a table on the other side of the bar and began to chat.

"I'll go over and get the ball rolling; they want us at the lair tomorrow at midnight, so there's no time to lose."

"Why not let them have ale first? It might soften them up."

"Good point. I'll eat the stew, then I'll go over. They won't venture over to this side of the bar."

*

Bok enjoyed a very welcome bowl of chicken stew and washed it down with a couple of ales. He and Reyheld sat and watched as Kern and Galandrik did the same, until an hour had gone by.

"Right. Let's get this thing started," Bok announced. "Remember, don't let them see you following."

Reyheld stared at him, agog. "I am not stupid, Bok."

"I'm just saying, if they spot you and think I'm setting them up, they might want to attack you. I'd have to help them to prove I'm not with you."

"I'll take my chances against three thieves," Reyheld growled.

"Never underestimate them, Reyheld. Friendship is a powerful weapon."

"Just go," Reyheld grunted. "And good luck."

*

"So when is your friend Gronli coming?" Kern asked.

"He arrives the day after tomorrow. I'm really hoping this temple has some good loot. We need some work."

"Indeed we do. It's a shame Ty cleared off. He would have been a big help."

"Yeah, I hate to agree but his skills would have come in handy, to be honest,"

"Well, it was his choice, so we can't dwell on it," Kern said, and raised his jug. Galandrik tapped his against it, spilling ale onto the table. Together they said, "To the future!"

"May I join your celebrations?" Bok said as he reached their table.

"That depends on who's asking," Kern answered, trying to see into Bok's hood.

"Let me introduce myself. I am Kob, and I have been sent here with a message for Kern Ocarn."

"I am he. I suggest taking a seat."

"Thank you." Bok sat down next to Kern. "What I have to say is from Conn—and please, I am just the messenger, earning some coin."

"Conn? I wondered when he would come looking," Kern said, looking at Galandrik.

"Aye, lad, surprised it has taken this long," the dwarf answered.

"He wants you two to gather some herbs for the king."

"Herbs? Why does the king need us to gather herbs?" Kern asked. He waved to catch the barmaid's eye, and shouted for three ales.

"Because they are in some dungeon. He needs adventurers to find them, not soldiers."

"Why should we? Conn lied to us before, so why trust him again?"

"Because he has recaptured the dragons you took back to their mother. If you don't do his bidding, he will slaughter both of them."

Kern stared at Galandrik, his mind racing.

Galandrik spoke up. "It's a trap."

"No. I can assure you it's no trap," Bok said. "I found you. If he wanted you, he would have sent twenty guards and just grabbed you."

"He has a point, Galandrik."

"I still don't like it. Smells like bullshit to me."

Bok lowered his voice. "The king is ill. His physician needs the herbs for the king's medicine. I promise you this is true: He needs your help."

Kern rubbed his chin for a few seconds, staring at Galandrik, then said, "No. Go tell Conn and the king that we won't fall for his bullshit again."

"And if wants to send twenty, then let him," Galandrik added.

"There is one more thing," Bok said quietly, not knowing how Kern would react.

"Go on," Kern answered.

"They have your father with the dragons."

"My father?" Kern's hand shot out and he grabbed Bok by the front of his cloak. "You better speak the truth or I swear to the gods I will cut you down right now," he said, his voice rising in anger.

Bok's head jolted back and his hood slid off, revealing his burnt face.

"Sorry! I knew you would react like this. I am just a messenger!"

Kern stared for a few seconds then pushed Bok away, letting him go.

"Speak. Tell me what's happened."

Bok pulled the hood up over his head again. "They went looking for you in your homeland, but obviously never found you, so they grabbed your father instead. Look, I am sorry. If it were up to me—"

"Yeah, spare me the 'just the messenger' crap."

"He is being held with the dragons in Shalamia's lair. They ran her out and are holed up in there, waiting for you."

Kern rested an elbow on the table and rubbed his forehead.

"What are you thinking, Kern?" Galandrik asked.

"What choice have I got? I can't believe it's a trap. Like Kob said, why not just send an army here to take us out? Why go to all this bother to get us to the lair? Damn it! He's fucked with my family, Galandrik!"

"If you want to go, I'm with you all the way, trap or not."

"Thanks, Galandrik. I know you are."

"Like I said, the king needs these herbs," Bok interrupted. "I can even offer my services for the journey."

"And what exactly do you do, Kob?"

"I can pick locks and find traps, if that's any help."

Kern thought for a few seconds. "Well, we do need a thief…"

"Aye, lad, that we do."

"Yes, I didn't want to bring up the death of your companion, but I'm sure I—"

"Death?" Kern said, surprised. "How do you know about this?"

Bok thought as quickly as he could, cursing his slip of the tongue. "I—that is, Conn told me. They have spies all over the place. They know everything!"

"How did he die?" Galandrik asked.

"I was told a bounty hunter took him out, an arrow to the chest."

"Can this day get any worse?" Kern mumbled, finishing his ale and nodding to the maid for a refill.

"I'm sorry about your friend," Bok said, trying to sound sincere.

"No, it's all right. We needed to know," Galandrik answered.

"Needed to know what?" Bok asked.

"About his death. We didn't know anyone knew. Anyway, what happened to your face?" Kern said.

"Yes, Conn knew. He's the one who did this to me," Bok said, pulling his hood aside and pointing to the horror of his scarred face.

"Why did he do that?"

"Because he can. He is an evil man and if you stand up to him, he punishes you—*badly,*" Bok explained, covering his face once more.

"Yet you still work for him?" Galandrik questioned.

"I can't run. He'll bring the burning pain back if I do. That's why I would like to come with you—to get away from him and his cruelty. It's not running, but I'll be away from him."

"When have we got to go to the lair?" Kern asked.

"Tomorrow at midnight. His associate Belton is waiting there to explain exactly what you will need to retrieve in order to free your father and the dragons."

"All right. Meet us outside here, tomorrow morning at dawn. And unless you want to walk, we need two horses."

"I will arrange that. Thank you, Kern, and thank you, Galandrik. I will be here at dawn." Bok finished his ale, then got up from his chair and left the table. He walked out of the inn without so much as a glance at Reyheld.

"What did you think of that rubbish?" Kern asked.

"Very strange. Why go to all the trouble to capture your father?"

"Because they knew we wouldn't do it otherwise. Bastards!" Kern raged.

"They won't let the dragons go, even if we do find these blasted herbs."

"I think you're right, Galandrik. Even if they have my father, can you see them letting him *and* both of us walk free, after what we have done?"

"No, not a chance. We killed his men and gave back the dragons. He wants us dead."

"But I do believe he wants us to get the herbs, for some reason. Like you said, it doesn't seem right to send a messenger and not an army if he just wanted to kill us."

"Best we go and see what's to be seen then, lad."

"Yes, you're right. My father will be seething."

"I bet. And I don't think it will cheer him up any when he finds out it's because of you, either."

"He wouldn't have been pleased to see me even if he hadn't been captured, so that's no big deal, but the northern armies will be raging. Trust me, King Moriak will not have heard the last of this, if I know my father."

"It should be an interesting conversation." Galandrik smiled.

They both drank into the early hours, telling stories of their childhoods, adventures, and of the times they'd spent with Ty, good and bad.

*

Reyheld watched as Bok left the inn and followed him out a few minutes later. There was a half-moon sitting in the sky and Bok was nowhere to be seen.

Where has he disappeared to? he wondered as he entered the stable.

Bok sat on a bundle of hay, talking to the stablehand.

"How did it go?" Reyheld asked.

"Superb. I think they bought the lot."

"Well done. When are you meeting them?"

"Dawn, outside here. I gave them a sob story about hating Conn. I said if I could go with them, that would get me away from him," Bok said, smiling.

"Did they fall for that too?"

"I think so. He was so upset about his poor daddy being captured he couldn't see the wood for the trees."

"Let's hope you're right. I spoke to a man in there; he said if you go down this main road there is another inn called the Eagle's Claw. Head there in about ten minutes. We don't want to walk in together," Reyheld said, flipping Bok a couple of gold coins.

"Oh, on the subject of gold, they will need two horses."

"They don't have horses?" Reyheld said, shaking his head. "Fine. I will sort them out."

"Thanks. See you in the Claw."

"See you there."

*

The next morning at dawn Galandrik and Kern waited outside the Factory Inn.

"What the hell did you do to me last night?" Kern asked.

"Me do to you? My head is thumping."

"Can you remember arm wrestling for ten silver?" Kern laughed.

"Did I? Did I win?"

"Yes… I think you did. Some dwarf you knew."

"I do remember! Jongo! I hadn't seen him in ages."

"That's it, Jongo. He fell asleep and slid onto the floor… I think."

"He never could handle it. His sister was gorgeous. Aye, I had many a dream over his sister." Galandrik laughed.

"Did she have a ginger beard?"

"Yes, but not—"

"Good morning," Bok interrupted as he rode around the corner, trailing two mounts behind him. Kern and Galandrik returned the greeting.

"You two look rough. Late night, was it?"

"You could say that. I can't remember much," Kern replied, rubbing his head.

"Looks like you had a good one. Here are your mounts, Blossom and Venture."

"Thanks. They look good quality," Kern said, stroking the nose of Venture.

"Don't thank me, thank the king," Bok said, smiling.

Kern and Galandrik mounted their horses. "Let's get a move on then. We wouldn't want to keep our guests waiting," Galandrik said, kicking his horse into a trot. They rode toward the gates of the town as Reyheld watched from a distance.

Chapter Seven
Illusionary Tactics

Gorgon stood with his back against the mountain. In his right hand was a kite shield that curved around like an almond shell. In his left hand he held two spears with barbed points. The entrance to the cave was only a few feet in front of him. Arrayed behind him were twelve guards: two holding the bobbin with the blue sparking net, two supporting the crossbow itself, and two with the javelin-type arrow—six feet in length and as thick as a man's arm—to load into it. Then came the same again, but with the bobbin rope instead of nets. Gorgon nodded to Fucan, who held up his hands and counted down silently to one, dropping one finger at a time.

When the last finger fell, Gorgon stepped into the entrance. Shalamia spun her giant frame around and immediately opened her giant wings to either side of her. Hovering just off the floor, she stayed in front of her children, Sleeper and his sister Erella, who both flapped and flew just behind her. Gorgon sidestepped to his left, forcing Shalamia to turn slightly as she examined him.

"Gorgon. What are you doing in my cave?" Shalamia asked.

"I have come to kill you and take your children away," Gorgon said smugly, facing the dragon.

"You are no match for me!" Shalamia cursed as she arched her neck forward, launching a spiral of fire.

Gorgon spun round and crouched as the flames engulfed his shield. As he did, his guards stepped from around the corner. Two pairs of guards squatted on either side of their crossbows while two more held the bobbin behind, waiting for the rope to be uncoiled. One guard on each bow placed the arrow on top and pulled back on the draw rope.

"Fire!" Fucan said. One of the standing guards on either crossbow pulled a pin and the two javelin-sized arrows flew from the bows, slamming into the walls behind Sleeper and Erella. On striking the wall, the javelins shattered into bright blue sparkles of light, and the rope that trailed behind them splayed open like a fan.

Like a sparkling electric blue spider web it fell, capturing both young dragons and dragging them to the floor. Shalamia spun round and looked at her children, caught under the bright blue web of rope.

"No, it is you who is no match for me!" Gorgon shouted, dropping one spear and launching the other at Shalamia. It lodged in her shoulder and she reared back and dropped to the floor, landing next to her babies. Sleeper and Erella looked up at their mother, their frightened, tearful eyes asking for her help, but Shalamia could feel the magic on the rope forcing her back.

Gorgon grabbed his kite shield and stood firm.

"Fire the ropes!" Fucan shouted as the first wave of men moved their equipment out of the way, then grabbed shields and spears, readying themselves for battle. The next two crossbows were brought forward.

Belton watched in amazement as the soldiers went about the business of capturing the dragons, moving as smoothly and efficiently as a well-oiled machine. Within seconds the next two crossbows were readied. Shalamia, now in a blind fury, sprang from the floor at Gorgon. She was halted by a massive crossbow bolt trailing a blue rope flying past inches from her head, and thundering into the wall above and behind her. She manoeuvred around and lunged for Gorgon again. Arching her neck forward, she unleashed another wave of fire at Gorgon. Again the fire engulfed his shield. Another rope was fired above her, and she could see that the trap was being set. She needed to move swiftly or she would die in front of her young. Turning and twisting, she moved to an opening next to the ropes.

"Fire second ropes!" Fucan shouted.

Another bolt, followed by the electric blue rope, flew directly above Shalamia's head. Ducking, she twisted and flew down. She spotted the last gap on the other side and flew for it as fast as she could. Her wing brushed against a rope as she flew, and she could feel the burning as the stream of magic raced through her body. She knew this was her last chance for freedom, the last gap big enough for her to escape through. With a desperate burst of speed, she flew toward it as the last crossbow was being loaded and aimed at the final spot needed to trap her.

Belton watched Gorgon as he dropped his shield and picked up the last spear. Shalamia was closing in on the gap, and Gorgon took aim.

"Fire! God *damn* it!" Fucan shouted.

At that moment, one of the archers ran past and Belton impulsively stuck out a leg, tripping him. The archer lurched forward into the soldier firing the crossbow, and they both tumbled against the side of the huge bow, knocking it out of alignment just as it launched.

"Gorgon! Look out!" Fucan shouted as the arrow raced straight toward him.

Gorgon arched backward, desperately trying to avoid the crossbow bolt. Dropping his spear, he fell backward over his shield. The bolt sliced through his armour, catching his shoulder and slamming into the wall below the dragon as she soared through the opening in the ropes, up and up toward the exit from the mountain.

Archers ran into the lair, firing a volley of arrows at the dragon as she made her escape—but most just bounced off her hardened scales. She flew up and up, only stopping once she was high enough to be out of any arrow range. She hovered, her giant wings flapping as she stared down at her captured babies, and a tear welled in her eye. She grabbed Gorgon's spear from her shoulder with her talons and pulled it free. Blood trickled from the wound. She dropped the spear and pressed her claw over the wound. Wisps of smoke emanated from her fingers. After a few seconds, she turned and flew upward into the night. A roar was heard around the lair, echoing anger throughout: "*I will return, my children, I will return!*"

*

"You fucking idiot!" Fucan shouted at the archer.

"He tripped me, sir!" the archer said, standing to attention.

"Who tripped you?"

"He did, sir," the archer said, pointing at Belton.

"I never did! How dare you accuse me of this? Complete lies! I want this soldier arrested!" Belton shouted.

"No one is arresting any of my soldiers," Gorgon said, stalking over to them as he patted out a flame on his arm.

"But he has accused me of—" Belton began.

"I said, no one is being arrested. We have the dragons. It's very unfortunate that we missed Shalamia, but shit happens," Gorgon said, staring at Belton. "Now bring all the equipment inside. Retrieve that last bolt from the wall and re-fire it, into its intended position, just in case she returns. Get four guards on the front entrance rotating every two hours, and start cooking some food," he said over his shoulder as he strode over to the other men. "I am fucking starving."

Fucan turned to Belton once Gorgon was out of earshot. "I don't know what game you are playing, but tread *very* carefully, my friend," he murmured.

Belton did not answer, pushing his way past and heading down the slope into the cave toward the captured dragons. They were each about the size of an adult sheep, but were otherwise the very image of their mother. Both dragons hissed at his arrival, showing their razor-sharp teeth.

"My men don't lie," he heard Gorgon say from behind.

"The man tripped and fell, nothing more and nothing less," Belton answered without turning around.

"If I were a betting man, I'd say you tripped him so she could escape."

"Then you would lose your wager."

"I'm not too sure about that. In fact, I wouldn't mind getting a truth potion back in Raith. You know—just to make sure my men aren't lying to me. We cannot have liars in the troop, now, can we?"

Belton swallowed hard. "Do what you want. I have nothing to hide."

"Oh, I will, little bird. I will," Gorgon said. He left the cave, shouting orders to his men as he went.

Belton looked down and watched as his hand shook, he knew Gorgon was a dangerous man and cursed the day he left to find this damned dragon.

*

Gorgon approached Jakob the Illusionist. "Get ready for their arrival."

"I'm ready."

Gorgon scowled at Jakob, who was resting on the rocky ground, his back up against a boulder. "Then where's the illusion? Don't just loll about. Call it up now so it's ready when he gets here."

Jakob laughed. "I *can't* do it now. The illusion all depends on the victim's imagination."

"I thought you just created an image of whatever we want him to see."

"Oh no. I cast the spell on the person, and *they* create the illusion."

"I see. I didn't think it worked that way."

"How can I possibly cast an image of his father? I have never seen him, heard him—nothing. It's impossible."

"I see. Let's just hope Bok has lathered the story up then."

"Oh, and keep the dwarf away. He will not see the illusion. Can't have him giving the game away."

"All right." Gorgon sounded sceptical.

"Think of it as an intelligence test, just for Kern. If he passes, he will not see anything, but if he fails he will see whatever we want," Jakob explained.

Gorgon smiled grimly, tapping Jakob on the shoulder as he returned to his men. "Do well, Jakob, do well. Right, lads, what food is left?"

*

Kern pointed up the mountain path toward Shalamia's lair. "It's just around that bend and up a few hundred feet."

Galandrik wrapped his cloak tighter around his shoulders. The wind had risen and now a cold rain began to fall. "I think the weather is turning."

"Yes, most definitely is," Kern agreed.

"When we get up there, let me go first," Bok said. "They don't know you, so I'll get the all clear."

"They soon will know me," Kern growled, thinking about his father as a prisoner.

They pushed on up the rocky foothills and followed the bend that led up to the entrance. The pace was slow as the horses manoeuvred carefully along the stony path.

"There is the entrance. Wait here. Let me go up and clear the path," Bok said, dismounting.

"Very well," Kern said. As Bok walked away, Kern turned to Galandrik. "If this goes all wrong, I will fight to the end."

"I know. We will give them hell."

Bok walked his horse up the path to the entrance, where two guards approached him.

"Name yourself," one of them called, holding a hand up to shield his eyes from the rain.

Bok glanced back to make sure he was well out of earshot of Kern and Galandrik. "It's Bok. I have brought Kern and Galandrik to see Gorgon."

"Halt. Do not come any further," the guard replied. He snapped an order to the second guard, who ran up and into the entrance. After a couple of minutes, he returned with Gorgon.

"How did it go?" Gorgon asked.

"Well. I don't think they care too much about the dragons, but he wants his father released."

"Anything else I should know?"

"Not that I can think of—oh, other than that I told them my name is Kob."

"All right, bring them up. Karlog, take his horse up the path to shelter from the rain with the others, then return for the other horses," Gorgon said to one of the guards.

Bok went back down the path to Kern and Galandrik.

"They are ready. Follow me," Bok said.

Kern and Galandrik dismounted and led their horses up to the entrance. Karlog returned just as they arrived, and took their mounts up the path to join the other animals.

The three men stood at the lair's entrance. Guards lined either side of the cave, some with cocked bows, others with their hands on their sword hilts, ready to draw. Gorgon stood in the centre; Kern and Galandrik could see the shining blue net behind him which held the two captured dragons.

"Come down," Gorgon said, his voice deep and gravelly.

Kern and Galandrik exchanged glances.

"Shall we?" Galandrik asked with a half-smile. Kern simply nodded back.

As they approached Gorgon, Kern studied the enormous man. His arms and neck looked almost unreal, he thought.

"Well, well—the Gorgon. The king got *you* to speak to me? The war must be quiet," Kern said.

"The war is ongoing, but your reputation precedes you. Twenty of the king's guards and one of his pet wyverns died at your hand. This time he wanted no fuck-ups."

"The only *fuck-up* here is the king's decision to capture my father. Where is he?"

"Over there, in that alcove," Gorgon said, nodding towards the back of the cave.

"I want to see him," Kern said sternly.

"You seem very sure of yourself, Kern Ocarn, for one who is so well outnumbered."

"There is nothing impossible for those who will try," Kern answered.

"There is a fine line between bravery and stupidity, my friend."

"Let me see my father."

Gorgon headed towards the alcove. "Follow me."

Kern and Galandrik followed.

"Just you," Gorgon said without turning.

Two guards stepped forward, one on either side of Galandrik. Kern hesitated, then gave Galandrik a nod. "Stay here and don't start anything," he said with a wink. Galandrik nodded back.

Kern followed Gorgon to the alcove in the corner of the lair. He rounded the pillar behind which Jakob was hiding. As he passed, Jakob blew a green powder into Kern's face, and instantly his eyes rolled in his head.

"Speak to your father, Kern. We have him," Jakob said softly as Kern fought the spell.

"My… father," Kern muttered.

"See him, speak to him. He is in the cage. To free him you must do as we wish, Kern."

"Father…?"

Gorgon gestured at Jakob as if to hurry him along.

"Kern, your father is waiting to speak to you," Jakob said as Kern struggled to see. Then his vision cleared, and his father appeared in front of him, on his knees in a cage, gripping the bars.

"Thrane!" Kern said, bowing his head to the illusion.

"Son, you must help me. Get me out of here."

"I am sorry I got you into this."

"Don't worry, Kern. Just do as they say and everything will be fine."

"But… but… it was never fine. I let you down."

"That's all in the past, son. Gather the king's herbs and free me."

"Yes father, I will. I will make you proud."

"That's all I ask."

Kern turned to Gorgon. "What must I do?"

"Come with me, Kern," Gorgon said, nodding to Jakob.

Kern looked to his father. "I will not let you down again."

He followed Gorgon up toward the dragons where Belton was standing. Galandrik was ushered down and stood with Kern. Sleeper recognised them immediately, and began to whimper.

"Belton, explain what's asked of them," Gorgon said.

"There are two herbs you must find. The first is fighort leaf, which is only found in the Voltic Isle Dungeon of Dreams. The second is willow rose. Nobody knows exactly where this grows, though we think it may be found down near Lake Fortune."

"We'll find these and bring them to you," Kern said.

"Wait a minute," Galandrik interrupted. "If you don't know where to find this willow rose, how will we?"

"We will find it, Galandrik. We must," Kern said, eyes wide.

"But we don't—"

"I'll go alone if you don't want to come," Kern said, staring right through the dwarf.

"What's got into you?" Galandrik asked.

"We can make inquiries about the herb when we get to Lake Fortune. We must save my father!"

"I understand that, but we can't just walk blindly into this."

Kern ignored Galandrik's protests. "We will leave now and return with what you seek."

"You must be quick, Kern. The king's health is deteriorating. We *need* those herbs," Belton added.

"Fuck the king. I do this for my father."

Gorgon stepped forward. "Be careful what you say about the king," he said angrily. "There are other thieves."

Kern turned and looked up at Gorgon. "I don't see any. All I see are the king's sheep."

"Let's not end this before it has started," Belton interrupted, moving between the feuding pair. "Come, let's get you moving." He put an arm around Kern and ushered him and Galandrik up the slope to the entrance. "Get their horses," he called to one of the guards. "Now, Kern, I want you to take Kob with you. He's a dab hand at picking locks; he will come in handy."

Kern didn't answer. He just stared silently out over western Bodisha. The rain was coming down heavily.

Galandrik pulled his cloak around his shoulders and looked at Kern. *Something isn't right.*

Two guards came down the path leading the horses. All three mounted and Kern rode down the path without a word. Galandrik shook his head and followed.

Hanging back, Bok raised a hand to Belton and said, "Four weeks."

"Be quicker. The king does not have long."

Bok didn't answer. He just kicked his horse and rode down the path after Kern and Galandrik.

*

Belton approached Gorgon, who was overseeing his men's efforts to get the dragons into the wooden crates they had assembled.

"I wondered what all the wood was for," Belton said to Fucan.

"Gorgon doesn't miss much," he replied.

"No, I see that. His troops are well-trained. They operate like clockwork."

"The best. He vets every last one and would die for all of them."

Gorgon shouted for Belton. "I better go see what he wants," Belton said. As he passed Fucan and headed up to the entrance to the lair he called, "What is it?"

"Walk with me," Gorgon asked.

Belton pulled his hood up, shielding his face from the blowing wind and rain, and fell into step with Gorgon.

"Listen, Belton, we never got off to the best start."

"You do your job and I'll do mine. I see that what you do is well-run and I will report as much to Conn."

"I think this operation went well, apart from Shalamia escaping."

"Yes, that was very unfortunate. People slip," Belton lied.

"They do. And of course, killing her wasn't our main objective."

"True. We have Kern and the baby dragons. That should suffice."

The pair walked in silence around the bend of the path, then stood in the lee of the wind, looking out over Tonilla and western Bodisha. The mountain below sloped down hundreds of feet and the trees in the distance below were tiny.

"The trouble is, Belton, I hate failing my king."

Belton's ears pricked at the change in Gorgon's tone. He realised he was alone with the beast, and suddenly he felt apprehensive. No—frightened. Side by side, the two men gazed out over Bodisha.

"You never failed, Gorgon. You did splendidly. I will make sure the king knows of your good work."

"But I only killed *two* birds with my *one* stone," Gorgon said, placing his hand on Belton's shoulder.

"Like… like I said, the king will be pleased… trust me. I—I think we… should get back to the men," Belton said, visibly scared.

"Nonsense, *little bird*. I think we should see if you can fly," Gorgon said, gripping the collar of Belton's leather armour.

"No! You can't," he screamed, trying futilely to twist out of Gorgon's grip. Gorgon slowly lifted Belton up like a rag doll, clearly savouring the moment, then stepped forward until his feet were on the edge of the cliff.

"Stop this! Now! Put me down, the king will have your head!" Belton pleaded, trying not to look down at the drop below. Stones kicked loose by Gorgon's feet tumbled into space.

Gorgon raised his other giant hand to grip Belton's throat, then released his grip on the man's collar. Slowly he squeezed.

"Plea… you… can't… put…" Belton choked and gasped, grabbing Gorgon's arm. He kicked out wildly, but the few blows that made contact elicited no response from the giant man. Gorgon didn't even flinch. Blood trickled from Belton's bulging eyes and nose, his face turning blue as the last ebbs of life drained from his body. He tried to speak, but made no sound.

"Maybe now I have killed my three birds, eh, Belton?"

Belton just stared back, bloody tears streaming down his cheeks.

Then Belton stopped struggling. His arms dropped to his sides and hung there, motionless. Blood ran down his face and over Gorgon's gloved hand.

"Fly, little bird," Gorgon said, as he released his grip on Belton's throat, dropping the lifeless body down the side of the mountain. Belton's corpse bounced off rock and stone as it fell. "*Fly.*"

Chapter Eight
No Pain, No Gain

Ty woke up with a stabbing pain in his chest, right where his heart was. It felt like somebody was pushing a dagger into his chest, twisting it as they went. His vision swam in and out as lights flickered through every colour imaginable, flashing and changing in front of his eyes. The sea of colours swirled left to right and back again, and a black circle appeared dead centre of his vision, growing wider and wider as the colours around it swirled and twisted like rainbow snakes. Slowly a vision began to form within the black circle. He saw Kern and Galandrik talking to a giant human with long black hair. Next to the giant was a smaller man, who was speaking to Kern. Behind them he could see Sleeper and another dragon, caught like two fish in a magical blue keep-net. Sleeper was staring at Ty, unmoving. Ty heard, "Help us, Ty, help us…"

The pain—and the vision—vanished. He opened his eyes.

"Right, wake up, you little shit," said a grimy fat man next to him. A few straggling remnants of hair were whisked over his bald head. He wore a black leather apron that hung down to the floor, and long black leather gauntlets. His face was filthy and his teeth—or what was left of them—were black.

Ty was laid out on a wooden block, his arms and legs tied by rope at the ankles and wrists. His eyes crossed as he tried to get a glimpse at his bare chest, half-expecting to see a dagger protruding from it, but there was none. He then looked around the room. With his first glance, he knew exactly where he was—and it was grim.

Table upon table was stacked with every torture device imaginable. A circular coal-fire pit burned in the corner, smouldering red hot. Shackles lined the walls to his left, and the floor under them had a crude groove cut into it, to let the blood flow out of the room. To Ty's left stood an Iron Maiden, and next to that was the dreaded Chair of Torture—a high-backed seat that looked a little like a throne. The arms and headrest had straps to hold the person immobile, and there was a hole in the seat like that of a privy. The torturer placed coals underneath the seat to cause severe burns while the victim was still conscious. It was a device that brought fear to even the most hardened men—just watching someone else's sufferings was enough to make most prisoners talk… though they would still probably end in the same fate, themselves.

Ty turning his head to the man. "Look, can we cut a deal here?" he said in desperation.

"Trying to bribe Bull the Torturer, eh?" the fat man said, with a smile that revealed two badly rotten teeth.

"No, not at all, but I'm sure I could make it worth your while to somehow… erm… let me go?"

The man waddled over to where Ty's feet were tied, and Ty craned his neck to see what he was doing. The man began turning something that looked like a ship's wheel—eight cylindrical wooden spokes all joined by a central hub. The ropes went through snatch blocks, then up across the ceiling and down through a second set of blocks, their ends tied around Ty's wrists. He felt himself being stretched and lifted from the bed as the man turned the wheel towards him, drawing up the ropes.

Ty screamed as the mechanism tugged against his arms and legs, the ropes growing tighter and tighter until Ty's limbs seemed in danger of being pulled from their sockets. But the torturer knew exactly how far to go without ripping the victim limb from limb. With each movement of the wheel, his limbs were stretched further, and his screams grew louder as the pain intensified. He had never felt pain like this. Bull was slowly stretching Ty to the breaking point.

"Please make it stop," he screamed. To his amazement, the torturer eventually did, releasing the taut ropes and allowing Ty to drop back onto the wooden bed. "I swear…" Ty said, panting for breath, "if you let me go… I will give you riches… beyond your wildest dreams."

"If I had a gold coin for every time somebody said that to me, I'd be richer than my wildest dreams already," Bull said as he lumbered over to the fire pit. He plucked a metal branding rod from the coals, holding it by its wooden handle.

"Please, for the love of Hades. Don't. I have wealth. I can go get it right now," Ty begged, tears rolling down his cheek.

"Oh, I don't do this for money, Mr Halfling," he said, walking back over to Ty with a grin. "I do it for pleasure."

"No, honestly—I'm talking real wealth!" Ty lied.

"Now where do you want this put?" the torturer said, grinning. Ty could feel the heat from the red-hot end of the branding iron as it hovered above his chest, then moved down toward his groin.

"I'm going to cut your heart out and eat it, you fat bastard," Ty shouted.

"Oh, now that's the real you. It always comes out in the end," Bull said sadistically, moving the hot iron back across Ty's chest. "I know. What about HERE!" Bull shouted and pressed the hot iron into Ty's ribs. Ty screamed as it melted his flesh, thrashing about in response to the unbearable pain.

For thirty seconds Bull held the brand into Ty's side, before finally pulling it away. Bending down, he examined his work.

"Do you know, I think that's the best I have ever done," he said, looking pleased with himself.

"I'm going to enjoy killing you," Ty sobbed, smelling his own burnt flesh.

"Of course you are. But let me tell you what you are *really* going to do, shall I? You are going to be stuck here with me until they call for you to be thrown into the pit with Dago. Then he is going suck out what blood is left inside of you after I have taken my share. Basically your last *very few* days left will be… let's just say 'unpleasant,'" the torturer said cheerfully.

"Let *me* tell *you* what I am going to do. I am going to stick a dagger in your stomach and make you apple-bob for hot coals in that fire pit until your face has melted off. Now do your fucking worst," Ty replied, staring up at the ceiling.

"Oh, I haven't even started. I think I'll see what toenails can be removed first, before I remove your dirty pickpocketing little fingers," the fat man said, laughing as he stepped over to the instrument table.

Ty pulled on the ropes, trying to somehow squeeze his hands through, but it was futile. He glanced over to the torturer, who was holding some rusty pliers up to the torchlight. He winced with the agony of his burnt ribs and sobbed at the knowledge of what was to come.

*

Galandrik, Kern, and Bok rode in silence for three hours from the rocky foothills of the Eastern Mountains onto the flat grasslands. Galandrik spoke once or twice, but got no reply from Kern. The rain still came down heavily and all three were soaked to the skin. The moon was full and lowering in the night sky.

"I think we should head back to Tonilla," Galandrik said, having had enough of riding in the rain.

Kern blinked the rain out of his eyes. He shook his head, trying to get some water from his hair before pulling up his hood. "Yes, of course, Galandrik. We need shelter," he said.

"What is up with you? You haven't spoken for three hours," Galandrik asked.

"Nothing. Has it been three hours?"

"Yes. What did they say to you in the cave?"

"I spoke to Thrane. He is in a cage and it's my fault. We need to get him out."

"I gathered that. But what did they say to you? You've been acting pretty strange since you saw your father."

"It's probably the shock of seeing his father locked in a cage. I know I would be devastated," Bok interrupted. Galandrik stared at Bok, trying to work out if he knew more than he was letting on.

"Kob is right. It really hit me hard."

Galandrik thought there was more to it than that, but he reluctantly changed the subject. "We need to speak to Gronli in Tonilla."

"Yes, the spider temple. I forgot all about that."

"Spider temple?" Bok said. "But we are going to the Voltic Isle."

"Yes, but first we need to do a job en route," Kern said, nodding to Galandrik.

"Very well," Bok said, not wanting to press the matter.

"When are we meeting Gronli?" Kern asked Galandrik.

"Tomorrow morning, outside the Factory Inn."

"How are we paying for the rooms tonight?" Kern asked of no one in particular.

"Don't look at me," Galandrik answered, looking at Bok.

"I can't afford it. The horses cost me a fortune," Bok lied.

"Then we sell the horses. Simple," Kern said.

"What, and walk to the Dungeon of Dreams?" Bok sounded appalled.

Kern smiled at Bok. "No, my friend, we will ride to the Dungeon of Dreams, but tonight we need shelter, and these horses will pay for that. Tomorrow, Galandrik's friend Gronli is bringing us some other horses. We will rob the Spider Cult's lair to pay Gronli for the mounts and be on our way, horses paid for and coin in our pocket."

Back to normal, Galandrik thought to himself.

"Of course, Kern, whatever you say," Bok said, nodding.

"Best way, lad, best way," Galandrik said.

*

Gorgon and Fucan led the troops down the path. When the path split, they took the southwest branch, which led through the mountain and into East Bodisha. The troops followed along behind, carrying the crated dragons. Four guards were assigned to each dragon crate, which they carried by means of poles slid through pre-made holes, while the crossbows and rope-bobbin spools were distributed amongst the rest of the soldiers.

"Where is Belton?" Fucan asked.

"Who?" Gorgon said nonchalantly.

"How long have I served you? I know perfectly well he didn't just disappear." Gorgon was silent. Finally Fucan sighed and gave up waiting for an answer. "Will Conn say anything about this?"

"Let him. It isn't my fault he lost his footing and fell. The man wasn't made for this line of work; he was careless and didn't stay on the track. He simply got too close to the edge and the loose stone gave way."

"Yes," Fucan smiled. "He was very careless indeed."

"Gorgon. Nice to see you again," they heard a voice say.

Gorgon looked to the side of the path, where he saw Reyheld sitting on his mount. "Hello, Reyheld. Finished babysitting that weasel Bok?"

"Yes." Reyheld smiled. "I can't believe the jobs Conn dishes out lately. What ever happened to the good old days?"

"Not enough good men to do the tasks. They've got me capturing baby dragons, for fuck's sake. I did this for fun when I was a lad."

All three men laughed.

"Oh—Reyheld, this is Fucan. He's my number one."

"Nice to meet you, Fucan."

Fucan nodded. "You too."

"So what's the plan now?" Reyheld asked.

"Get the horses and my other men, head back to Raith," Gorgon said. "Give the king his damn dragons."

"Surprised to see you marching. I thought you would rest first. I was heading up to the lair for some food. Your men must have been out here for hours."

"Exactly. They are *men, my* men, and they can march for a week," Gorgon said proudly.

"I meant no offence, Gorgon," Reyheld said, inclining his head.

"I didn't think you did, but I'm sick of these soldiers who need a break every two hours because they are hungry or tired."

"You don't change," Reyheld laughed.

*

The soldiers continued west down the rocky path. The rain had eased off now and the dark was being slowly swallowed up by the dawn sun. Just before they reached the bend that would lead to their troop, they saw a figure lying in the middle of the path.

"Quick, that's one of ours!" Fucan said, kicking his horse into a trot. They reached the figure and saw it wore the black armour of Gorgon's men. Fucan jumped down and knelt beside the man, then rolled him carefully over onto his back. His front was burnt completely, head to toe, his face black and blistered and nearly unrecognizable. Fucan lowered his head to the man's chest and listened for breath. "He's alive," he said, glancing up at Gorgon. "Sorin! Sorin, speak to me. What happened?"

Sorin's eyes flickered, "Dragon," he whispered.

"*Shalamia.*" Fucan swore under his breath.

"Water," Sorin whispered.

Reyheld tossed down a canteen of water and Fucan trickled some onto the injured man's lips, gently lifting his head up. He coughed and spluttered as the water went down his throat.

"Sorin, was it Shalamia? Can you tell us what happened?"

The soldier's voice was halting and he struggled for breath between words. "Dragon... fire. We were trapped. Please... help me."

"It's going to be all right," Fucan lied, looking up to Gorgon, who nodded back. Fucan pulled a dagger from his belt and held it to Sorin's chest. The front of his black leather armour had burnt and melted away, leaving only the charred remains stuck to his chest. "Sleep well, Sorin. I will drink with you soon."

"Yes... sir."

Fucan plunged the dagger into the soldier's chest. Sorin flinched and his mouth opened wide, then his head slumped to the side.

"Get the men to take his body. We can't leave him here for the vultures," Gorgon ordered.

"I will see to it," Fucan replied, staring at Sorin. "Such a waste, and for what?" he muttered under his breath.

Gorgon and Reyheld rode further on as Fucan remounted; then they stopped, looking over the site that had once held their troop. Fucan caught them up and saw what they were surveying. The remains of all the men, horses, and carts lay blackened and burnt. Some of the carts still smouldered.

"I think Shalamia was angry we took her babies," Fucan said.

"Damn these thieves! How many more lives will be lost because of them?" Gorgon said as they trotted through the burnt-out carnage of the wagons and dead bodies. The rest of the troop followed behind, tight-lipped with rage and grief for their dead companions.

"Damn Kern and this damned mountain!" Gorgon said angrily.

"Blame this on the dragon, not Kern," Fucan said.

"Kern is the dragon. These good men died because of those thieves and Belton's stupidity. He deserved to die, and Kern does too."

*

Kern, Galandrik, and Bok entered Tonilla early that morning. Wagons and carts filled with fruits and vegetables rolled towards the marketplace, and shopkeepers opened their doors, some offering greetings to the trio as they passed.

"Kob, are you going to sell these horses?" Kern asked.

"Yes. I will go sell two and meet you at the inn."

"Thanks. We will order you some food."

Once inside the inn, Galandrik and Kern found seats and draped their soaked cloaks over the chair next to them. The maid took their order for three cooked chickens and ale.

"I could sleep for two days," Galandrik said, yawning.

"It has been a while. We'll get this food in us, speak to Gronli, and sleep. We can leave first thing in the morning."

"Good idea. Earlier you were hell bent on going straight there. You never even answered me."

"Sorry, Galandrik. It's all a blur. I think seeing my father in the cage really twisted my mind. Kob was right; it was quite a shock."

"I don't trust him. Just a messenger, and now just a thief? He's trouble."

The maid brought their food and drink and placed it on the table.

"Thanks," Kern said. He took a long swallow of ale, then said, "I'm not so sure, Galandrik. By the look of Kob's face, he's been through the wars with Conn. No wonder he wants out."

"You are too trusting, lad. I can smell trouble."

"Well, keep a close eye on him, then. But is he really any less trustworthy than the next cutpurse we hire to pick locks?"

"Good point," Galandrik answered, ripping off a chicken leg.

At that moment, Bok entered the inn, spotted Galandrik, and headed over to their table. "Chicken, my favourite," he said, taking his seat.

"Tuck in, Kob. You're paying, after all," Galandrik said with a smile.

"Well, strictly speaking the king is. He paid for the horses I just sold," Bok said absentmindedly, thinking of Reyheld.

"I thought *you* bought the horses," Galandrik said lightly.

"I did," Bok answered, taking a bite of the chicken.

"Then how did the king buy them? Is there something you are not telling us, Kob?" Galandrik asked, leaning back in his chair.

Bok thought quickly, damning himself for letting something slip that could jeopardise his cover.

"Well, I work for the king, so in a roundabout way he did pay," Bok said, washing down the chicken with a swallow of ale.

"But your pay is your pay, no longer the king's," Galandrik said, continuing his line of questioning.

"Listen, I have more hatred for the king than most! If you don't want me here, I'll go. I'm not bothered," Bok said, revealing the burnt side of his face.

"You must forgive our dwarf friend here. He is very inquisitive," Kern interrupted, placing a hand on Bok's shoulder and frowning at Galandrik.

Galandrik shrugged. "I didn't mean anything. You just have to be careful who you are dealing with."

An uncomfortable silence hung over the table for several minutes, but was broken by Gronli's arrival.

"Galandrik, how's it going?"

"Gronli, you're early," Galandrik replied.

"Yes, I got the horses around the back, and also three other dwarfs. I think we may need them on this smash-and-grab. No messing about. In, grab the loot, and out. If they try to stop us, they will pay the price." Gronli smiled. "Oh, sorry. Hello, Kern, and…?"

"Kob. This is Kob. After the spider temple we are heading to the Dungeon of Dreams, so we need someone who's good with locks and can spot a trap."

"That's a bad place," Gronli said. "Let me give you a little tip: Take an old weapon with you. One you won't mind losing."

"Old weapon? You'll have to do better than that," Kern said.

"Rust monsters! They spit acid and damage your armour. They are red in colour and about the size of a dog, covered in red scales. They are tough buggers."

Galandrik shrugged. "I'll just cover my axe up."

"No, you miss my point. When you strike one, they infect your weapon with rust. After about ten strikes your sword will fall to the floor in a pile of red dust."

"What a load of rubbish," Galandrik muttered, shaking his head in disbelief.

"Oh well, don't blame me when your axe head falls off. Right, I'm going to get the others. Do you mind if we join you?"

"No, please do. You can introduce us to them," Kern answered.

When Gronli came back in he was accompanied by three other dwarfs. They all joined the table.

"Kern, Galandrik, and Kob, let me introduce Gizzir, Gamrot, and Forkhil." Greetings and welcomes were exchanged, and soon all seven companions were eating and drinking.

"So what's the plan for tomorrow?" Kern asked the table.

"Get there, get in, grab the loot, and get out," Gronli said with a smile.

"Oh, if only it were that simple," Galandrik chuckled.

"It will be simple—trust me," Gronli reassured them. Kern thought of Ty and all the times he had said 'trust me,' and sighed at the memory of long-lost friends.

"How many guards do you anticipate?" Kern asked, shaking away the thought of his old friend.

"I'd guess six to eight. The tower we are heading to isn't that big, so it shouldn't be guarded heavily. The hardest part will be getting them to open the door."

"I guess we will see when we get there," Kern mused. "One more thing—

once we have finished this, Galandrik and I will be moving on, and would like keep the horses. Obviously you can keep a larger share of the loot to compensate."

"Oh, that's right. You're heading to the Dungeon of Dreams."

"It's full of rust monsters, that place," Gizzir interrupted.

"Don't you start. That's what *he* said," Galandrik said, with a nod at Gronli.

"Well, it is. My friend Toshol went once and came out with no armour or weapons! And he said it was full of traps," Gamrot added.

"We shall see when we get there. What time are we leaving?" Kern said, changing the subject.

"I suggest we leave at dawn," Gronli said, waving to the maid.

"Good suggestion. We haven't slept in ages."

"We will get the supplies, then we'll all meet in the stable at dawn. Your mounts are the two on the left side of the barn. The stable boy will saddle them before your arrival."

They ate happily and exchanged stories until Kern, Galandrik, and Bok slipped off to their respective rooms. The others went into town and restocked their supplies for the journey ahead.

Chapter Nine
The Raid

Ty hung on the torture chamber wall, his feet inches off the floor. Both wrists were shackled by iron bands which hung from short chains, affixed to the wall by an iron spike and ring. His shoulder sockets burnt like fire; he felt certain they would be pulled from his body at any second. His upper body was covered in whip marks, red lines peppering his torso. On his ribs was the branding burn that had been inflicted two days prior. It was red-raw and oozed bloody pus. His head drooped and his eyes were shut, trying to block out the pain from all his horrendous injuries. The door opened and Bull the Torturer entered the room.

"Right, let's get you down from there, shall we?" He grinned, pulling a set of keys from his belt. Ty gingerly lifted his head, revealing his bloodied and bruised face. One eye was closed and his lip was swollen to double its normal size.

"Fuck you," Ty said, and spat in the torturer's face.

Bull flinched and wiped Ty's spit from his cheek. "That wasn't very nice, now was it? Why have you got to be so nasty?" Bull said, then, without warning, punched Ty in the stomach. Ty groaned from the blow and began coughing, blood dripping from his mouth. Bull held the keys up and unlocked one of Ty's wrist restraints. With one arm freed, Ty spun round, dangling from the other arm. Bull unlocked the second one, Ty crumpled to the floor in a heap, agony flooding his arms as the blood rushed through them to his fingertips.

"Now then, over here," Bull said, grabbing Ty by one arm and dragging him into the centre of the room. He walked to the table and Ty could hear as he rummaged for his instrument of choice.

"Here it is," he said. Ty, lying on his side on the floor, looked up to see Bull standing above him, brandishing a cleaver and sharpening stone. With a sadistic grin, the torturer rubbed the stone slowly along the side of the cleaver's blade. "I love this noise, don't you?"

Ty didn't answer.

Bull plodded back over to the table, set the sharpening stone down, and picked up a foot-long length of wood. He knelt down next to Ty's head, placing the piece of wood and cleaver down on the floor out of Ty's reach.

"Now this may sting a little," Bull said, turning Ty onto his stomach, as he grabbed one of his arms and pulled it outstretched in front of him. Ty struggled, gripping Bull with his free arm and trying desperately to free his arm, but it was pointless. He didn't have any strength left; even the punches he did manage to land on the torturer's ribs were a fruitless effort. Bull barely seemed to notice them. He knelt on Ty's upper arm and slid the piece of wood under his wrist.

Bull picked up the cleaver and kissed the blade. "Say goodbye to your hand," he laughed as he raised the blade.

"No!" Ty shouted, shutting his eyes involuntarily.

The door burst open and Felkk entered the room, staring at the scene: Bull kneeling on Ty's arm, holding the cleaver aloft; the halfling limp on the floor. "What the fuck are you doing?" he shouted.

Bull scowled at Felkk. "My job."

"You want him to bleed out, you fool? Luthian wants him upstairs now to feed Dago."

His fun spoiled, Bull tossed the cleaver aside and heaved himself up. "Take him, then, and send me the girl."

"Be careful, Bull. Don't get above yourself or you might find that cleaver stuck in your head."

Bull didn't answer. He retrieved his cleaver and set it on the table next to the sharpening stone.

"Take him," Felkk said as two white-robed men entered the room. They picked Ty up and dragged him towards the door.

"See you soon, you fat fuck!" Ty shouted as the men dragged him away.

"Of course you will my love!" Bull answered waving at the theif with a smile.

"I'll send you the girl, but don't kill her. She is next for the feeding. Just… soften her up." Felkk said slamming the door behind him.

Ty was carried down a couple of flights of stairs, then down a corridor into a square room, empty apart from a table and two chairs. On the table lay a set of white robes and a belt.

"Get him dressed. I'll bring Theol," Felkk said before disappearing back down the corridor.

The two men pulled the robe over Ty's head. He winced with pain as they lifted his arms through the robe's sleeves. Then they pulled the belt tight around his waist and pulled the hood up over his head.

One of the men produced a short length of rope and tied Ty's hands together in front of him. "Doesn't he look the part?" he said, standing in front of Ty.

"Pity the robes will be red soon," the other man replied, laughing.

Felkk returned, entering the room with a grey-bearded man. Opening a bag hanging from the belt of his grey robe, the man—*This must be Theol,* Ty thought dazedly—pulled out a vial, handing it to Felkk. "This is for you."

"What is it?" Felkk said holding it up and examining the liquid inside.

"It'll make him forget the pain. Make him drink it; new orders from Luthian. He will fight harder against Dago and the battle will last longer. You know the pain of Dago's fangs usually renders them unconscious within seconds," Theol said.

"He must want a real spectacle for this one. Hold his head," Felkk ordered. The two men spun Ty around and forced his head back. Felkk tipped the liquid into his mouth and held it shut. Ty spluttered and coughed, but finally swallowed the liquid.

Theol watched, then nodded at Felkk. "I will see you in the feeding chamber," he said, and left the room.

"Follow me," Felkk ordered, and the two men each grabbed one of Ty's arms, virtually dragging him along.

Ty didn't mind, though. In fact, he felt better than he had in a long time. His injuries had all stopped hurting, even his ribs. His eye was still swollen shut, but whatever the liquid was, it had numbed the pain.

They led him down the corridor until it reached a set of double doors. Felkk banged on the door with his fist. The doors creaked opened inward and Ty was led through by the two robed men. The circular room was filled with men in white robes. To Ty's left, Luthian sat on a throne overlooking a massive hole in the ground. On the right was a table filled with candles, bowls, and various other items. Behind the table was a chest brimming with gold coins, goblets, necklaces, and gems. All the cultists stood like statues, their hands together as if in prayer, forming two lines for Ty to walk through. Ty was led to the edge of the pit. He could see, on the opposite side of the pit, the door he and Lan'esra had entered through earlier. Remembering the girl, he thought of Bull and what horrible things he might be doing to her at this very moment.

The men spun him round so his back was to the pit as all the cultists slowly walked toward the pit, making a humming noise. Within moments all the cultists were surrounding the pit, still humming, apart from the two standing on either side of Ty. Both had their daggers drawn and held to Ty's neck.

Luthian clapped and the humming stopped instantly. He rose, coming around the pit until he was in front of the thief. Ty nervously looked back over his own shoulder, peering at the drop below.

"How dare you attack Dago? The Spider God has spoken and you shall be punished for your actions."

"He was trying to eat—" Ty started to say.

"Silence!" Luthian shouted and the two men on either side of Ty pushed their daggers deeper into his neck. Ty didn't move.

Luthian spun on his heel and glided to the table. Picking up some petals, he threw them into a bowl, then picked up a vial and dripped a liquid from it onto the petals. He mixed them together and crushed them in a mortar. He held the bowl aloft and began chanting, his voice echoing around the chamber.

O Mother of the Web, Lady of Death,
ARANEAE, REGINA, MORTEM, TELAM!
Queen of the Dark, Venomous Mistress,
ARANEAE, REGINA, MORTEM, TELAM!
Spawn of Nightmares, Blood Bound with Web,
ARANEAE, REGINA, MORTEM, TELAM!
We call to you…

Luthian walked back towards Ty, holding the bowl in front of him. The silence was broken as the cultists resumed their eerie humming. Luthian dipped a finger into the red liquid and wiped a line down Ty's forehead, then one line down each cheek. The humming was getting louder and the cultists began stepping from side to side, stamping their feet. It sounded like men marching. Ty figured it was to wake Dago, and he began looking in earnest for a means of escape. Luthian placed the bowl back on the table, then raised his arms above his head. His hands began to shake as the stamping and the humming got louder and louder.

Ty's mind raced. Feeling utterly abandoned, he watched Luthian—who was now spinning, looking up to the gods, chanting in an ancient tongue. He had seen no potential means of escape, but he looked around the room again, hoping he had missed something. He bent his head forward and glanced at the door. It was hopeless.

Then Luthian fell still and all the noise stopped. He raised his head and glared at Ty, then approached the thief and placed his hand on Ty's fore

*

Kern, Bok, and the dwarfs were astride their mounts outside the stable by the time Gronli appeared from around the corner of the barn.

"Morning," Gronli said, heading for his horse.

"Sleep in?" Kern said with a smile.

"I couldn't sleep all last night. Must be the excitement of the raid," he answered, climbing onto his mount. "Shall we?"

Kern looked over to Galandrik. "We shall," the ranger said.

The group left the barn and headed out of Tonilla, toward the northwest edge of the mountains surrounding the town of Wade. It was only a four-hour ride and before they knew it they could see the spider temple in the distance.

"This is a raid," Kern said to the group, "not a slaughter. We only kill if we have to."

"What do you take us for?" Gronli answered.

"Look! There's a wagon heading to the temple," Galandrik pointed out.

"The gods must be smiling on us. That's our way in," Forkhil added.

"Remember—no killing. We will never get in with blood-stained robes," Kern said.

The group made for the flat-backed wagon. Two cultists sat in front, and the back was loaded with something that was covered by a hemp sheet. The party came alongside the wagon, then overtook it and turned their mounts to face it, blocking its progress. The four horses pulling the wagon stamped and snorted, and the cultists' eyes were wide.

"Morning," Kern said to the two men.

"What is it you want?" one of them asked.

Gronli interrupted. "You wagon, your horses, and your clothes."

"You dare steal from Therliyn? He will hunt you down and feed you to the crows," the other cultist said, rising from his seat.

"Get off the wagon peaceably," Kern said, "and we won't hurt either of you. Put up a fight and your robes will be stained red."

The two men exchanged glances, then did as they were asked and stepped down from the wagon.

"Here, Galandrik," Kern said, passing him the reins as he jumped over to the wagon seat. "Follow me to the tree line."

Kern rode the wagon to the edge of a small circular crop of trees, then jumped down. He lifted the sheet covering the back of the wagon and peered underneath. It appeared the cultists had been making a supply run: They carried crates of fruit, sacks of flour, barrels of wine, and other basic food supplies.

Gizzir, Gamrot, and Forkhil shepherded the two men into the trees, and

Kern followed on foot. Several yards into the woods, the dwarfs dismounted.

"Take off the robes," Gizzir ordered.

"But these are our—"

Gamrot slapped the cultist in the face.

"I'll ask you again. Take off the robes."

This time, the two humans complied.

"Tie them up over there behind the trees," Gronli ordered once the two had disrobed. Then he threw one robe to Kern and one to Bok. "Put these on."

"Wait a minute," Bok argued.

"I think they'll notice a ginger-bearded dwarf sitting there. You two fit the bill. You'll have to do it."

Kern said, "Dump a barrel from the back of the wagon, and you five should fit under there. Hopefully we can sneak you all in."

"Four. I'm leaving Forkhil here to guard the horses and our two friends," Gronli said.

"Why do I have to stay behind?" Forkhil argued. "I always miss out."

Gronli rolled his eyes. "Because I said so! Now stop arguing and think of a game to play with our friends."

"Always me," Forkhil mumbled as he marched off, kicking at the dirt in disgust. "Don't know why I bother…"

While Bok and Kern put on the cultists' robes, Galandrik, Gronli, Gizzir, and Gamrot climbed up on the wagon and got under the sheet. Kern placed his sword out of sight in the footwell of the wagon, and Bok did the same.

"Hey, Forkhil, ask your friends if there is a password or sign to enter the temple," Kern called.

Forkhil approached the pair who were tied up back to back on the ground. "You heard him."

Neither man spoke.

"All right, then, let's do it the hard way," Forkhil said, pulling out his dagger and squatting down next to them. He held one man's chin and pointed his dagger at his eye.

"Hey, Gronli," he called. "Is it the left eye or the right that hangs lower after you gouge it out?"

"Left. Now hurry up; it's bloody uncomfortable back here."

"All right! All right!" The cultist squirmed. "It's 'bluebird.' Just get to the gate and say 'bluebird.'"

Forkhil slapped his cheek. "See, wasn't that hard, was it? But if it isn't 'bluebird,' you won't speak another lie ever again."

"No… it is, I promise. It's 'bluebird.' Just say 'bluebird.'"

"Thanks." Kern smiled when Forkhil delivered the code word. "We're ready, then. How do I look?" he asked Bok, flicking his hood up and tightening his belt.

"Like an idiot! As do I. I can't believe I'm doing this," Bok moaned.

"It'll be fine. Mount up, cultist!" Kern said, trying to lift Bok's enthusiasm. Bok shook his head and climbed up, pulling his hood over his head.

They steered the wagon back onto the path and slowly made their way toward the wall surrounding the temple. Two massive oak gates barred their way. The tower wasn't as tall as Kern had expected, but it was a considerable size all the same. A few windows were dotted around the tower's higher levels, and the top had a spire.

"Make sure you cover your face. They may realise we're not who we should be," Kern cautioned Bok as they approached. They could see two guards up on the wall on either side of the gate. As they neared the wall, Kern reined the horses in.

"What supplies have you?" one of the guards called from above.

"Food supplies," Kern shouted back, without looking up.

"What bird flies south this coming winter?"

"Bluebird."

They heard the gate being unbolted from the inside, then it opened inward. Kern flicked the reins and the horses moved forward, pulling the wagon into the courtyard. The main doors of the tower were shut, and two more white-robed men stood guard before them.

"Which way, left or right?" Kern whispered.

"I don't know… Left," Bok whispered back. Kern flicked the reins and steered the horses to the right.

"I said left."

"I know. That's why I'm going right."

They rounded the tower and came to a barn with two horses tethered in it and stable boys going about their chores. As soon as the boys saw the wagon, they walked over to the wall of the tower, lifted two wooden hatches, and secured them.

"This must be where they unload the food," Bok suggested.

"Yes, I think you are right," Kern agreed, pulling the wagon up next to the hatch. Kern and Bok jumped down from the wagon and approached the two stable boys. Kern nodded at Bok, then grabbed one boy around the head, holding his mouth shut.

Bok swung a punch at the other boy. The blow smashed into the boy's chin, spinning him around and dropping him unconscious to the floor.

"What the fuck are you doing?" Kern hissed angrily.

"What? It was only a slap."

"Galandrik, get out here," Kern said as quietly as possible. All four dwarfs climbed out of the wagon and gathered around the hatch.

"Tie him up," Kern said, pushing his captive to the dwarf. Galandrik swiftly bound and gagged the boy, and laid him out in the barn on a bale of hay.

Kern was kneeling next to the other stable boy. "He's alive," he announced with obvious relief.

"See? It was only a slap," Bok reiterated.

Kern faced Bok. "You ever punch a child in the face in my presence again and I swear, that burn on your face will be fuck-all compared to the pain I will inflict on you," Kern said, nose to nose with Bok, staring him straight in the eye. Bok said nothing, but Kern's gaze intensified. He was silent for several moments, staring into Bok's eyes, then he asked suspiciously, "Do I know you from somewhere? Have we met before?"

Bok quickly turned away. "No, we haven't. I'm sure if you had seen this scar you'd have remembered it," Bok said, keeping his hood up.

"Come on, we need to move," Gronli interrupted.

Kern shook his head. "Yes, sorry, you're right."

"What about the guards on the front gate?" Galandrik asked.

"Don't worry about them. We will get in first," Gronli said, looking down at the hatchway in front of them.

"Let me go first," Kern said, grabbing his sword and taking the lead. There was a set of steps leading downward. "Kob, follow me."

They headed down into the cellar. The only exit was a single wooden door, and the room was filled with barrels and foods: fruits, breads, meats, and dry goods. After ensuring the coast was clear, Kern and Bok beckoned the others down. Kern cautiously opened the door and peered down the corridor, which was lit by wooden lanterns along its length. They moved carefully down it until it turned right. Another twenty paces in front of them was a set of double doors. Kern approached the massive wooden plank that secured the door, then lifted it with care and leaned it against the wall. As gently as possible he opened the door a crack and peered in. Directly in front of him was a cave entrance, strands of spider webs stretching from wall to wall in every direction. He could tell he was in some sort of pit with a room above. Above the cave, on the floor level, stood two men in white robes, each gripping an arm of a smaller man who stood between them. Another man in red robes stood facing them, holding some sort of bowl.

"Go that way," Kern whispered, closing the door and replacing the plank.

They quietly made their way along the corridor and up a flight of stairs. When their heads came level with the top step, they could see two soldiers guarding a door.

"Kob and I will go up; the robes may give us the element of surprise."

"Am I allowed to punch this time?" Bok asked.

"Do whatever you want. Just do it quietly," Kern answered.

Kern and Bok pulled their hoods forward and held their daggers behind their backs, leaving their swords with the dwarfs.

"Walk slowly and calmly," Kern said, nodding at Bok to follow.

They finished climbing the stairs, keeping their heads down, and headed toward the guards. The guards stood silent and nearly motionless, only nodding as the robed pair approached. Kern nodded back, then swiftly smashed an elbow into the closest guard's stomach, doubling him up instantly. He bought the elbow down again onto the back of guard's neck, rendering him unconscious.

Bok had flicked his dagger out when Kern began his assault and held it to the other guard's neck. The guard held his hands up and offered no resistance. Bok gestured for the guard to walk down the corridor toward the dwarfs. As soon as he did, Bok smashed the butt of the dagger down onto the man's neck, knocking him out cold. The dwarfs joined them and Galandrik handed Kern his sword.

"What's behind that door?" Bok whispered.

"Just some ritual. We need to continue this way," Kern explained.

"Let me have a peek," Bok said, sliding open the wooden peep-hatch.

Bok peered through and saw a man in red robes carrying a bowl toward some men in white robes, who seemed to be holding a shorter man captive. The red-robed man dipped his hand in the bowl and wiped something on the short man's head. Bok could hear the cultists stamping their feet and humming with a sound like a swarm of giant bees.

"I think there's going to be a sacrifice," he said, watching. The red-robed man stepped back to the table and placed the bowl down. Lifting his hands in the air, he started to chant some more strange words. The captive man bent forward, his battered face staring straight at the door.

Bok stepped backward, mouth wide open.

Kern frowned at him. "What's the matter with you? You look like you have seen a ghost."

Bok didn't answer, just slid the hatch closed.

"What was it?" Kern asked.

Bok stared at the floor for a second or two and then answered, "Nothing. Let's move on." His face was as white as his robe.

"Let me have a look," Kern said, placing his hand on the hatch.

"No! It's just a sacrifice," Bok said, placing his hand on Kern's.

Kern pulled his hand away. "Move," he said, staring Bok in the eye.

Bok stepped reluctantly away. Kern opened the hatch a little and peered through the slit. The man in red robes now stood with the palm of his hand on the captive man's forehead.

"Bok's right. It definitely looks like a sacrifice," Kern noted.

"Male or female?" Galandrik asked.

"What does that matter? Hang on, that looks like—he's in the way. If he would just move his hand… It almost looks like a—*TY!*" Kern said, his whisper strained.

"A Ty? You mean a halfling?" Galandrik asked, confused.

"No, not *a* Ty, *Ty!* Ty the bloody rat! That Ty!"

"Ty? You said he was dead!" Galandrik said, looking at Bok.

"Who? What the hell is going on?" Gronli said, confused.

Kern didn't answer. He stepped back and, without a second thought, kicked the door in. It flew open and he strode into the room. Galandrik stepped in right behind him, hefting his axe.

*

Luthian jerked his hand back from Ty's head at the sudden explosion of noise. As if in slow motion, Ty saw the door swing open, and watched as Kern and Galandrik charged into the room. The two guards on either side of him immediately lunged toward them, but they were cut down instantly. Kern and Galandrik tried to fight their way forward to come to Ty's aid, but the stampede of cultists running to the door held them back.

Ty leapt forward and hit Luthian in the stomach, sending him falling backward to the floor. The room turned to chaos as the cultists ran for the door, screaming and shouting. Luthian jumped to his feet and grabbed a sacrificial sword from the table, spinning to face Ty. Then he ran, waving the sword above his head. Ty braced himself and, as the blade came down toward him, he held his hands up and caught the blade between his wrists, its edge against the rope restraints. He leaned into the sword and ran his wrists upward along the blade. The rope cut free just as he reached the end of the sword, and the blade sliced his robe.

Luthian stood in front of Ty, sword in hand. "Time to die," he hissed through gritted teeth. He swung the sword but Ty arched his body, stepping back and just managing to miss the swinging blade. As he bent forward, he could see between his legs to the drop below. His feet teetered on the edge of the pit, and he waved both arms in a circular motion in an attempt to regain his balance. He managed to straighten up, both arms still waving.

"What's up? Nowhere to run, eh?" Luthian said, and lunged forward.

Ty sidestepped the attack and grabbed Luthian's arm. "Dago is hungry!" Ty said, swinging Luthian round and watching as he fell down into the pit.

Luthian landed face-down with a groan. He shook his head, pushed himself up, and rolled over onto his back, looking straight into Dago's lair. Ty watched as two hairy legs appeared from the cave entrance below.

"No!" Luthian shrieked as the giant spider jumped onto its victim, sinking its fangs through his gown and into his chest.

Kern finally broke free of the last of the fleeing men, shouting "Ty!" as he ran into the room, followed by the dwarfs.

"Good to see you, Kern, even if it's with only one eye," Ty answered, forcing his battered and swollen face into a smile.

Galandrik stood next to Kern. "It's good to see you, friend," the dwarf said.

"You too, Galandrik."

"Lovely. Now where is the loot?" Gamrot asked.

"Behind that table," Ty answered.

"It *is* good to see you, but we need to go and we need to go *now*," Kern said.

"One thing before we do. Let me have your dagger, please," Ty asked.

Kern slipped the dagger from his belt and handed it over. "Why do you need it?" he asked.

Ty smiled. "You'll see. Follow me."

"Will we need the others?" Kern asked.

"No, you and I will be enough," Ty said.

"Right, you four clear the way. We will be out in ten," Kern said to the dwarfs.

Kern followed Ty down the corridor and up a few flights of stairs, until they got to a closed door.

"Back me up," Ty whispered. Kern nodded back. Ty placed his hand on the handle and pushed the door open.

Bull was standing in the middle of the room. He spun round at the noise of the door being opened and stared blankly for a second at Ty and Kern.

Lan'esra was tied to the torturer's table against the wall. "Felkk!" he shouted, holding his hands up and backing away.

Ty launched his dagger; it stuck Bull straight in the stomach. Screaming, the big man bent over, clutching at the dagger handle. Ty moved calmly forward and grabbed Bull by the neck. Turning him around, he pushed him a couple of steps to the fire pit.

"No!" the torturer shouted. Blood dripped from his mouth onto the hot coals, his face inches away.

Ty reached to the table and grabbed the piece of wood. "I love the way this sounds!" he shouted, and whacked the back of Bull's head, forcing it down into the coals. "This may sting a little!" Ty shouted again and struck him again, this time pressing the wood against the back of Bull's neck, crushing his face in the red-hot coals. Flames engulfed his head, whipping up and around.

Ty let go and stepped back as Bull lurched away from the fire pit, holding his blackened and burnt face. He fell to the floor, rolling and shouting in agony. Ty reached down and plucked the branding iron from the middle of the fire pit. He held it up, noticing that the brand end was fashioned into a spider. He stared down at Bull, who lay on his side, his body shaking, holding his face. Ty placed the branding iron against Bull's ear and pushed down with all his weight. Smoke bellowed up as the torturer screamed, and as the smell of burning flesh filled the room Bull stopped moving, either unconscious from the pain or dead.

Ty tossed the iron aside. He pulled Kern's dagger out of Bull's stomach and spat, then stepped across to the table where Kern stood, having already untied Lan'esra.

"Am I glad to see you, Ty," she said, wrapping her arms around his neck. Ty winced as the pain of his injuries came back.

"Sorry," Lan'esra said, hearing the groan.

"That's all right. Just go easy," Ty said with a half-grin. "This is my friend, Kern Ocarn."

She wrapped her arms around Kern's shoulders, too. "Thank you, Kern."

"Come on. You can thank us both later," Kern said, turning towards the door.

They left the torture chamber and headed to the main entrance, checking the cells for people as they left. Kern was adamant that they mustn't leave any of the cultists' captives behind. Ty was too weary to argue the point, but was secretly relieved when they found no one else who needed to be rescued.

When they reached the front entrance, the doors were already open. Four guards and Theol lay dead on the floor, their robes all stained with blood. Ty bent down and grabbed the small vials from Theol's belt pouch. "I think I'll need these."

Gizzir, Gronli, and Gamrot sat on the back of the wagon, with Galandrik up front on the driver's bench holding the reins. "Get on," he said.

"Come on, let's go," Ty said, taking Lan'esra's arm.

With some help from the dwarfs, Kern, Lan'esra, and Ty stepped up onto the back of the wagon.

"Wait, where's Kob?" Kern said, looking around.

"He disappeared. No one has seen him since the fight began. I told you he was a bad apple, lad," Galandrik said, snapping the reins.

"He saw something that spooked him in that room, I could tell by his face. He went ashen white, like he had seen a ghost," Kern said.

"I think the ghost he saw was Ty," Galandrik replied.

"What do you mean?" Kern asked, puzzled.

"Well, he told us Ty was dead, didn't he?"

"You're right, he did," Kern agreed thoughtfully.

"Me, dead? And who the hell is Kob?" Ty asked.

"Just a thief we had with us," Kern explained.

"A thief?" Ty frowned. "Hang on a minute—you thought I was dead so you got *another* thief? Before my blood was even cold?"

"Your blood never went cold," Kern answered.

"*You* didn't know that!"

"What did you want us to do? Sit and mope around for months?"

"Well, at least a few *days* would have been nice! Not just, 'Oh, poor Ty is dead, let's hire another thief!'"

"What about 'thanks for rescuing me,' instead of moaning about someone else who picked a lock better than you?"

"I had it under control! I was about to—"

"You had it under *control*? You couldn't control a—"

"Enough!" Galandrik finally interrupted.

"He's unbelievable," Kern said, moving up to the front to sit next to Galandrik.

"Kob. What sort of name is that?" Ty said, folding his arms.

The dwarfs all smiled as the wagon rolled on to meet Forkhil.

*

Felkk stepped out from behind the iron maiden and looked down at Bull. *You pathetic fool,* he thought. "Ty and Kern Ocarn," he mused aloud. "Therliyn will rain the fires of hell down upon you."

Chapter Ten

Back as One

Queen Cherian glided into Conn's room without knocking. He glanced up irritably from behind his desk, but when he realized it was her he stood up. "My queen," he said, bowing his head. Two of the queen's elite guards closed the door behind her; he knew they would be there standing guard until she left.

"What news do you have for me?"

"Nothing yet. Gorgon should be back today, my queen."

Queen Cherian walked to the window with her hands behind her back. "You know we must prepare for the worst," she said, staring down at the gardeners working on the grounds beneath the window.

"My queen, we will get the necessary ingredients and heal the king," Conn said, stepping round his desk to stand next to Cherian. "We must have faith."

"Even if we succeed, Hordas will be king sooner rather than later. Moriak plans to step down."

"I'm sure your son will make a fine king, Queen Cherian."

"Rubbish, and you know it! The boy hasn't got a clue. I love him dearly, but he could destroy what we have built."

"With your advice, he will be a good king."

"Speak to Moriak and convince him to stay on the throne. Make him stay at least until the boy is ready."

"My dear queen—"

"Oh, cut the 'my queen' nonsense! I'm asking as a friend."

Conn stared at Cherian as she reached out and took his hand in hers. "Please. Talk to my husband."

"I will do what I can," Conn replied, extricating his hand from hers and returning to his desk. There was a knock at the door, and Conn shouted, "Enter," in response. It opened, and Gorgon entered.

"Welcome back, Gorgon. I hope you have some good news for me," Conn said, taking his seat.

Gorgon bowed to Queen Cherian. "My queen," he said, and she graced him with a nod. Gorgon turned to Conn and stared down at him. "I have some good news and some bad news."

"What's the good?"

"Kern, Galandrik, and Bok search for the ingredients, and we have the two baby dragons under lock and key."

"That's brilliant. Now what's the bad?"

Gorgon paused for a few seconds, taking a deep breath. "Shalamia escaped."

"That's nothing. I thought you said bad news."

"That's not all."

"Go on, spit it out, man," Conn said with anticipation.

"She killed eleven of my men in her escape."

"Train others, then. Soldiers die," Conn said coldly.

"And Belton fell to his death," Gorgon said abruptly.

Conn glared up at Gorgon at the news of Belton. He lowered his head into his hands, then smashed his balled-up fists down onto the table.

"How did you let this happen?" he said angrily.

"It was dark, wet, and very windy. He walked up and around the side of the mountain to fetch his mount, and must have got too close to the edge," Gorgon said without a flicker of emotion.

Conn doubted the truth of Gorgon's story, but knew he needed to keep his temper. "We have lost a good man in Belton," he said, rising from his seat.

"And I lost good soldiers," Gorgon said, looking down at Conn.

Conn stood looking up at the giant human, but couldn't read his face. He knew that trying to magic the truth out of Gorgon would send the massive soldier into a rage, and a whirlwind of violence rushing through the palace was the last thing he needed.

Conn turned away and sat back down behind his desk, forcing his anger down. "Fair enough. People make mistakes; people die. Maybe I should have gone. First Solomon and now Belton," he muttered. There was a moment of silence, then Conn said, "My thanks for what you have done, especially returning those dragons."

"It's my honour to serve my king," Gorgon said, stealing a glance at Cherian as he spoke.

"We will need you to dispatch Kern and Galandrik as soon as they have the herbs we require. Stay local; train some new men. I will call for you when you are needed."

"As you wish, Lord Conn." He bowed to Conn, then to the queen. At her nod, Gorgon left the study, ducking under the frame of the door as he squeezed himself through the opening. The door shut behind him.

"Do you think he's lying?" Cherian asked. She had seen the pain flash across Conn's face when Gorgon broke the news of Belton's death.

"Fell off a mountain? Belton didn't just fall off a mountain; I don't care how windy or wet it was. I knew him from an early age. I trained with him. Apart from being in very good shape, he was surefooted. He may not have looked it, but trust me, he was too sharp to simply fall off a mountain."

"But why would Gorgon want to harm Belton? I can't see any reason for it."

"Nor can I, but it's the only explanation. If he'd said the dragon killed him, perhaps I could believe that, but to fall from a ledge? Pushed, more like."

"Don't jump to conclusions, Conn. Do your research first."

"Yes, you are right. I will. I'll send a paperfinch to Bok; maybe he can shed some light," he said.

"Speaking of messages," Cherian said, "I have sent a message to Guldir and put off the meeting. I can't let Hordas make critical decisions about the Orc Wars."

"What about the king's war council? Couldn't they hold the meeting along with you and Guldir?"

"I suppose we could, but Guldir doesn't want to discuss war with me. He will only speak to Moriak. The only woman Guldir listens to is his wife."

Conn smiled at Cherian. "I did hear he was henpecked."

"I left Murtal with Moriak, so I'd better get back," Queen Cherian said, turning and gliding effortlessly to the door. "And remember what I said, Conn. The king must remain in power—until my son is at least twenty."

"I remember, my queen," he answered. The door slammed behind her. "If we get the herbs, that is," he muttered under his breath.

He lifted a pouch from a nearby table, then pulled a piece of paper out. Holding it to his mouth, he whispered something, then opened his hand. A bird flew from his palm, straight through the open window.

"Fly, my baby, fly," he said softly.

He sat back down at his table. He leaned back in his chair and began to think.

How many people have died? Thirty guards, Belton, Solomon—and Ty, his bastard murderer. How many more before this ends—and for what? To bring two dragons to the king for a sacrifice, a ludicrous idea that fools believe will please the gods. When this is over I am gone. I'll be just an old name in the book of life, and I will walk the land far away from this chaos and insanity.

*

Bok squatted down behind a little bunch of trees and watched as the wagon rolled past. He could see Galandrik up front next to Kern, and the dwarfs in the back along with Ty and a young woman. He watched as it headed toward the small cluster of trees where Forkhil was waiting. He turned and sat down with his back to the tree. *How is he alive?* He pulled a small leather pouch from his tunic and opened it, then pulled out a small square of paper and held it in his hand. *What do I say to Conn? I told him Ty was dead; I told him I watched him die.*

He felt his face and the hardened skin. *I can't go through that pain again. Think, Bok, think.* He felt sick to his stomach thinking about the agony he would go through when Conn found out he had lied. A lump filled his throat and he coughed, spitting onto the ground. *I won't say anything. Just let him think all is well; he will never know! I will just follow them and keep a close eye.*

Bok scrambled to his feet and peered around the edge of the tree. *Damn, I need a horse. I know where they are going; I could just catch them up. Maybe they will head to Wade on the way; I could grab a horse there and follow.* He slipped the paper back into his pouch and watched as they entered the trees in the distance. He remembered seeing Ty again in the Orc's Armpit; he remembered getting arrested after taking Ty's gold in the toilet; he pictured Joli and the chests. *Oh, you will die next time, Ty. Even if I have to rip your heart out and hold it still beating in front of your stinking face, you will die.*

*

Ty lay on a bedroll as Lan'esra gently lifted the robe that covered his injuries, while Gronli and the dwarfs sat counting out the loot they had taken from the spider cult's tower.

"They look bad, Ty," Lan'esra said, looking at the hundreds of fine cuts on his back.

"Will I die?" Ty answered as calmly as he could.

"Not right away, but any infection and you could."

"Right, then. I must head back to Tonilla," Ty said, sitting up and letting Lan'esra inspect his closed eye.

"I'm afraid we can't go back, Ty," Kern said, looking down at the injured thief.

"What? Why not?"

"It's Conn. He's given us a task. And he's captured Sleeper and his sister dragon. If we don't do what he says, he will destroy them."

Ty knelt and Lan'esra examined the burn on his ribs. Thinking about Kern's news, Ty remembered his dream. "Were they caught in a magical blue net?" he asked, wincing as Lan'esra poked his ribs. "Ow!"

"Oh, be quiet, you big baby," she replied with a smile.

"Yes, in Shalamia's lair. How did you know?" Kern said, squatting down.

"I dreamt it… I think. Was there a tall human there, the size of a troll?"

"Yes, the Gorgon! He was there."

"And another man, a smaller man who was talking to you."

"Yes. That was Belton."

"Strange. I dreamt this. Who is the Gorgon?"

"He is a great warrior from over the seas to the east. When he first appeared and fought for King Moriak they called him 'the Beast from the East.' He controls the king's finest troop of fighting men, the Black Guard. There are many stories about them—defeating countless armies despite being greatly outnumbered, that sort of thing."

"I take it we really pissed the king off, then?"

"Just a bit. But there is more," Kern said.

"Go on. I am all ears," Ty said, pulling his robe down.

"He has my father, too."

"Your father? Why the hell has he got him?"

"Double security. They didn't honestly think we would go just to save two dragons. Who would risk life and limb for a couple of dragons that would probably eat them in a heartbeat?"

Ty stared up at Kern for a second. "They asked me to help."

"Who did?"

"Sleeper did."

"It was a dream. You imagined it, Ty," Kern said, shaking his head.

"Tall man with matted black hair, arms and thighs like tree trunks. The smaller man had shoulder-length brown hair. Well-spoken, wearing black leather armour with gold trim. Two dragons about the size of sheep, caught together under a shining blue net... still think it was just a dream?"

Kern paced over to the dwarfs and watched silently as they divided the gold into piles under Galandrik's watchful eye. He thought of what Ty had said, and slowly walked back.

"Admittedly it's close, but could still be coincidence. And none of it changes the fact that my father is being held prisoner. We need to do what they ask."

"Which is?"

"There are two herbs we must find. The first is fighort leaf. It's found in the Dungeon of Dreams on the Voltic Isle. The other probably grows near Lake Fortune—willow rose."

"The Dungeon of Dreams—that's a bit out of our league, isn't it?"

"Nobody is making you go, Ty," Kern said, staring at the thief.

Ty remembered their exchange in the goblin tunnel. With a smile he replied, "No, I know this, but we are a party and we stick together. Plus, you wouldn't last five minutes without me."

Kern rolled his eyes, then turned to Lan'esra, who had been dressing and bandaging Ty's wounds as best she could while the two men talked. "How bad are they? Will he live?" he asked her.

"He will live, but they need to be seen to. They are weeping and need some healing balm. The potions he has will not last forever, and right now he thinks he's fine, but when the potion wears off, he will feel differently about that. And the spider's poison in the chest is spreading. It needs to be isolated," she answered.

"Right, that's settled. We will go to Wade and get him sorted, then through Wade Mountains to Loft. Maybe we can grab a boat there to the Voltic Isle."

"Sounds like a plan," Ty said. "You may have to loan me some gold for some armour and weapons."

"I'm sure we can afford that. Gronli should be finished dividing the loot."

"Am I in this split?"

"I can't see Gronli letting you have a share."

"Why not?"

"Have a think about it. We found you in there," Kern said, shaking his head and walking over to the four dwarfs.

"How is the split going?" Kern asked.

"Not a great haul, to be honest. It may have been brimming, but under it all was a load of rubbish. We have kept the bracelets and goblets, since you won't want to be carrying them to the Dungeon of Dreams. Your share is all in coin."

"We are going to Wade first now; we could have sold our share of the jewellery and things there."

"No worries. It's easier this way. I have taken the cost for the horses out, so that leaves you and Galandrik thirty gold each," Gronli said, tossing one bag to Kern and another to Galandrik. "Also there were two teleportation potions. I gave your group one and we're keeping the other."

"Not bad at all, lad," Galandrik said tucking the pouch into his tunic.

"Where's my share?" Ty said from behind Kern.

All four dwarfs stared at Ty, then looked back and forth at each other and broke into laughter. Then Gronli stepped forward. "And why would we give you a penny of this-hard earned loot?"

"Well, the way I see it, Kob disappeared, so we should get his share of the loot."

Gronli looked at Kern. "Is this fucking idiot for real?" he said, folding his arms.

"Be careful who you insult, dwarf," Kern replied, placing his hand on the hilt of his sword.

"Those goblets you have so *kindly* taken were worth far more than the gold you shared out," Ty added.

Gronli's face changed. "What do you know about goblets?"

"The same as you, enough to know they are valuable."

"The cut was fair; Galandrik watched."

"You said they were just gold-plated. Are you trying to cheat us?" Galandrik said with a snarl.

"The cut was fair!"

"I wouldn't advise robbing us," Kern growled.

Gronli looked to Galandrik. "Sort these clowns out, Gal, for the love of Hades!"

Galandrik stepped next to Kern, placing his hand on the hilt of his axe. "These *clowns* are my brothers. You rob them, you rob me."

"Gal, you choose these two over your own kin? We fought side by side!"

Galandrik face didn't change.

Gronli stared at the trio for a few seconds, weighing up his options. "This is the thanks I get," he muttered, opening up his money-pouch. Reaching in, he pulled out a handful of coins and threw them down into the dirt. "Here's your damn gold. Don't come to me the next time you need work."

The dwarfs mounted up hastily and left, heading off toward Tonilla.

"Never did like him. Tight bastard never buys a drink," Galandrik said when they were gone, smiling at Ty.

"Let's get going to Wade," Kern said.

Ty bent over, wincing in pain.

"You okay?" Lan'esra asked.

"It'll be fine," Ty replied, holding his hand to his chest. As he did, he felt the strange new hardness of his skin through his tunic. He reached under it gingerly and felt his chest. It was a small patch, just where his heart would be, and firm—almost hard—to the touch.

"What's the matter?"

"I said I'll be fine!" Ty fired back, then stood up straight, grimacing.

"Sorry for asking. Here, drink another one of these," Lan'esra said, passing Ty another healing potion.

He took the potion from Lan'esra and drank it, watching silently as Kern pulled her up behind him onto his mount.

"Hold on tight," Kern said with a smile, and Lan'esra did, wrapping her arms around the ranger.

"Pass me your hand, Ty," Galandrik said, trotting up next to the thief.

"Thank you," he mumbled, still watching Lan'esra smile like a smitten schoolgirl. He rubbed at his chest again. It was like a plate beneath his skin.

*

Bok watched, whispering under his breath, as the four trotted off toward Wade.

Find the rat,
Snatch the rat,
Smack the rat,
Until he's flat!
Squash the rat, dead!
Dead! Dead! Dead!

Chapter Eleven
The Baby Snatcher

The party travelled southeast along the path toward the town of Wade. The giant rock face to the north naturally curved around, leading into the heart of the mountains. The only entrance to the town was still a day's ride away, and the only way into Wade was this path, which led into the horseshoe-shaped mountains and was known as the Gateway of Stone. The entrance was heavily guarded, with mountains on either side; it was the only way in and the only way out.

The town was run by Lord Heilo, one of King Moriak's cousins, who ruled with an iron fist. His punishments were legendary, and the most famous of all was the Sleeping Balrog. This torture consisted of a cast iron statue of a balrog laying on its side with a hinged door on the back. The victim would be forced into the iron balrog, and the door would be locked behind him. Wood and coals would then be lit under the balrog, heating the cast iron to an unimaginable heat. The only two holes were placed in the balrog's nostrils, and when the victim screamed as he melted to his death it echoed out, giving the impression that the balrog was roaring.

This pleased Heilo and he prided himself on having the idea. It hadn't been used for many a moon, but sat in the town centre as a reminder to all who lived there of what could happen to the opportunistic criminal. As a result, Wade was known for its safety and lack of crime.

Having Nowhere to run to made Wade virtually impossible to raid, and thieves who did commit crimes there were usually caught and subjected to hideous punishment. Those who escaped went on the run, living as bandits in the mountains surrounding the town, hiding in the caves and scavenging for anything they could kill and eat. These outcasts were known by the locals as Baws—historians said it stood for 'Banished Away from Wade,' but no one really knew. The Baws often entered the town to steal sheep and other livestock in the dark of night—activities which, if they were caught, always ended in death by hanging or worse.

The leader of the Baws was an infamous criminal called Retch, known as 'the baby snatcher,' and his stories were just as well-known as those of Heilo's torture. The most famous tale was of the time Retch had been caught stealing livestock; he had been captured but had escaped that very same night from the town's cells, eluding six guards and, as he left, stealing Lord Heilo's prize pig Peggy. Peggy's head was delivered back the next day, complete with a fancy bow. Retch was the only bandit in Wade's history to have been caught and escaped.

His nickname—'the baby snatcher'—had been given after the disappearance of six babies, taken from their cots in the middle of the night, over the last ten years. Locals said he stole them for his own to turn them into bandits, for the first five of the six stolen babies had been boys. But other tales told of infant sacrifices to please the Baws' gods, and of babies' skulls left on top of poles for crows to eat their eyeballs.

*

After an uneventful ride, they stopped to eat and rest the horses in a small sheltered cluster of trees. Ty and Kern gathered some kindling as Lan'esra and Galandrik sat talking.

"So what are you going to do when we hit Wade, Lan'esra?" Galandrik asked.

"I don't really know. I need to get to the Midas Hills. My people are there."

"Is that where you were snatched from?"

"Yes. I was gathering herbs to the north of the Midas Hills. I was in a field, harvesting, when a wagon rolled up and asked me some directions. The next thing I knew, I was bound and gagged in the back."

"Bloody freaks. These cults are popping up everywhere."

"Yes, there have been many people vanishing from the villages around us."

"So you will need a mount and supplies then?"

"Well… I didn't want to ask, but if Kern would cover my expenses, I could offer my healing skills as partial payment."

"I'm sure he would be more than willing to help. What would you suggest?"

"Well, with the right herbs and materials, I am a very good cleric. And I can fight. My father was a soldier, and he taught me and my brother Kulo well."

"We can always use a cleric fighter. We shall see."

"I would be very grateful. I'm sure I would come in handy."

Kern and Ty returned to the clearing, carrying the wood for the fire. Ty looked pale and drawn.

"I told you not to carry anything; your wounds won't heal," Kern said.

"Since when have you been *Doctor* Kern?"

"You don't have to be a doctor to know that you need rest and treatment, not carrying bundles of wood about."

"I'm fine. And since when did you start to care? You'll just get another thief after—"

"Still on about that? I need you fit and healthy. It's going to be a long, hard journey in the next couple of days, and a half-fit thief is no good to me."

"Oh, I work for you now? So much for us being a team," Ty replied, dropping the kindling down next to Galandrik.

"We *are* a team," Kern said, dropping his bundle onto Ty's.

"Enough! Let's just eat," Galandrik interrupted.

Ty sat down next to Galandrik and grabbed some food out of his backpack. Kern sat next to Lan'esra. "Do you lot always argue like that?" she asked the ranger.

"It's not an argument, just a… discussion."

Lan'esra chuckled at the reply. "I have a question."

"Fire away," Kern answered with a forced smile.

"Well, I have no money, but I was wondering how I can repay you."

"You don't owe us anything, my dear."

"I think I do, and…"

"Go on, spit it out." Kern said.

"Well, I was wondering if I could travel with you and your party for a few weeks, just long enough for me to earn a mount so I can get back home."

"Travelling with us, doing what?"

"I'm a cleric and know how to fight. I can wield a mace."

"You're a cleric fighter, eh? We could use a healer in the party, and the extra weapon is always welcome. What do you two think?" he said, looking over as Galandrik lit the fire.

"Good idea, lad. A good cleric is priceless."

"What about you, Ty? What do you think?"

"I'm sure a cleric would fit nicely into *your* party," he answered, not looking away from the pot he was placing vegetables into.

With a slight shake of his head Kern looked at Lan'esra. "That's settled, then. You're in."

"Thank you, Kern. I will not let you down," Lan'esra said, unable to contain her smile.

*

Bok stared down at the dead farmer, his mouth and eyes still open wide and staring sightlessly at the sky above.

"Don't look at me like that! The rat killed you, not me!" He bent down and pulled the dagger from the old man's chest, then stabbed him again. "The rat made me do it!" He thrust the dagger into his chest once more. "Stop looking at me!" He stabbed again and again, blood splattering his face. "Ty the Rat did it! Not me!"

Eventually he stopped and pulled the dagger free, wiping the blood on his victim's tunic. He tucked it into his belt and looked down at the blood-drenched body of the farmer. Bok wiped the blood from his cheek and gazed at his bloodied palms; clenching his fists, he shut his eyes, picturing Ty. "Why won't you die?"

Shaking his head, he grabbed an arm and dragged the corpse to the side of the road, where he covered it with leaves. After cutting the farmer's leather pouch away, he walked the wagon off the road and cut the horses free. He slapped one horse on the rump and watched as it galloped off across the fields and into the morning sun. Then he grabbed the other one by its mane and swung himself up.

Bok pulled his cloak up over his head just as Conn's paperfinch landed on his shoulder. He heard a whisper in his mind: *How did Belton fall from the cliff?*

Bok panicked. Instantly he felt sick, but there were no more questions. He waited for several tense seconds, but nothing else came. Carefully he reached up and cupped the paperfinch, removing it from his shoulder. When he opened his hand, tiny pieces of paper blew away. He stared as they danced and spun in the wind before disappearing, and he began to think.

Belton's dead? Can things get any worse?

Bok pulled the tiny square piece of paper from his pocket and cupped it in his hands.

I know, I will tell Conn that Ty did it… No, he will ask why I hadn't already told him and then make the pain return for lying about Ty's death. Damn. I will just say Belton was alive when I left. That is the truth, after all. I need to rejoin the party, tell Kern that I was spooked by something… No, what if Ty recognises me? He cannot—I am grotesque, a freak; and all because of him! But he will see through it, I know he will. Damn. I need to kill him, then rejoin the party, that's it! Once he is out of the picture again, I will simply rejoin them. I told them Ty was dead; I thought he was! Why didn't they question me?

After several more moments of frantic thought, Bok finally whispered something into his hand and said, "Fly little bird, fly."

*

Retch sat playing cards with Alexe in the bandit's cave. The caves were a natural formation, the result of flowing streams thousands of years ago, when water covered Bodisha. The cave they were in wasn't too far back in the mountain, but deep enough that their fire inside didn't make it light up like a beacon at night. Fissures and cracks in the rocks above made ideal vents for letting the smoke escape. There was one main entrance, which led out to the south of the mountains that surrounded Wade. At the back of the cave were gaps and crevices large enough for the bandits to squeeze through and weave their way deeper into the heart of the mountain, twisting and turning in a maze of rock. The few times they had been attacked, these escape passages, and the hiding places they concealed, had saved the bandits' lives.

Retch wasn't a typical-looking bandit; his clothes and skin were clean, for one thing. His brown leather leggings and white tunic would have been welcome in any establishment in Wade. Two katanas lay at his feet, shining resplendently in the torch light. His long brown hair was tied back into a ponytail and despite his years of rough living, his handsome features could still turn a head. The only regrettable blotch on his features was a scar that crossed down over his right eye, forehead to cheek; it had been inflicted by a Wade guard a few years prior. Retch always took pride in his appearance and loathed being called a bandit. He especially hated the nickname 'the baby snatcher.' In his own mind, he was simply the leader of the Baws.

"So are we going for it tomorrow night?" Alexe asked, flipping a card down onto the crudely-made table. Alexe was a thick-set human with a bald head and moustache. In contrast to his leader's, his own brown leather armour was dirty and tatty.

"Well, if the others don't come back with a mountain goat, I don't see any other option," Retch answered, picking the card up. "Ah, just what I needed."

"You're so lucky at this it's sickening. Have you thought anything more of trying to contact that fat fuck Heilo and ask about leaving the mountains?"

"Yes, but I can't see him entertaining it for one minute."

"You never know your luck. Out," Alexe said, slamming his cards down on the table.

Retch shook his head and collected the cards up to deal again. "I've had hands like feet all day. I know my luck, all right, and if I never had bad luck I wouldn't have any."

"What's that now? Three-one, to me?" Alexe said, smiling under his bushy moustache.

"Rubbish! Two-one," Retch said, shaking his head as he dealt another hand of cards.

"So what's the plan for tomorrow? If there's no food here in the next couple of hours, I mean."

Retch leaned back in the chair and placed his hands on top of his head, interlocking his fingers.

After a lengthy pause, Alexe looked up from his cards. "You playing or what?"

"We snatch a baby," Retch replied.

Alexe's cards dropped to the table and he stared at Retch, eyes wide. "Have you lost your tiny mind? Just because they *call* you the baby snatcher doesn't mean you have to *do* it! Baby snatching? Count me out."

"Hear me out, Alexe," Retch said, standing up. "In two days, it will be the Carnival of Light or whatever they call it."

Alexe folded his arms. "Go on, I'm listening."

"Well, that fat fuck Heilo always has his fat relatives attend just so he can gloat over the fireworks display—which the townsfolk pay for with their taxes, of course. Anyway, the display will be the ultimate distraction. As soon as the bangs start, we snatch one of his relatives, the smaller the better."

"Okay, bangs and lights, we nip in, snatch a kid, nip out. But we will still be hungry. Unless you plan to eat the—"

"Don't! Don't even say it. We use the little brat as a bartering tool to escape. We can't just walk out, because our faces are on every post in Wade. We can't bribe the guards, because he changes them so often. We can't go through the mountains because they are impenetrable."

"So you think he will trade the life of a third cousin to let us just walk out of the gates?"

"It's definitely worth a go. I have been here for ten years, Alexe. I cannot go on anymore. I want out."

"Out? But you're Retch the baby snatcher—the most infamous bandit in western Bodisha," Alexe said with a smile.

"That's exactly it! What a load of shit."

"You are what you are."

"We have never killed *anybody* we didn't have to. We loot people and take what's theirs because we have no choice. We raid the town every now and again when the mountain goats climb high, because without food, if we didn't steal we would starve to death here. We live like… well, we live like bandits."

"That's because we *are* bandits."

"He's made us *into* bandits! He needs us out here, don't you understand? It's like a game to him; it keeps people on their toes. If we weren't here, they wouldn't need him and his iron fist. They think he protects them from us. Hanging the odd bandit keeps the town in fear. Without us, he would be seen as soft, weak—and he doesn't want that. He needs to justify his existence."

"You think?"

"Yes! He created me. He wants me out here; he *needs* me out here! Take my nickname, 'baby snatcher.' You know I've never touched a fucking baby."

"True, but they do go missing. Before I was caught robbing that shop, my friend Aguis's baby was taken. At the time, even I thought it was you."

"Exactly. But it *isn't* me. And it isn't wolves, or orcs, or giant birds. It's him."

"Lord Heilo steals the babies?"

"What's so unbelievable about that?"

"Who would sacrifice babies just to make someone into their nemesis?"

"The same man who would lock someone in a metal balrog and heat it until they cook, that's who."

"Okay, agreed, he is an evil bastard but—killing babies? That seems over the top."

"Well, it isn't me, so it's someone else."

"Or some*thing*."

"Thing, it, him, her, whatever—it's taking them, and it's making me look like a right arse," Retch said with a smile.

"Your deal, arse," Alexe answered, watching Retch take his seat and pick up his cards.

"When the others come back, I will explain what I'm going to do. None of you have to go with me, but I need to do this."

"I'm in. I want out as much as you. But you know this is risky."

"Yes, I know. But it's time the baby snatcher dies."

Chapter Twelve
Cotton Candy

Kern, Ty, Galandrik, and Lan'esra trotted toward the entrance to Wade. In front of them stood a wall that spanned from the northern stretch of the Wade Mountains to the curved end of their southern point. The mountains were sheer and went up into the clouds; there was no going over, under, or through these rock formations. The wall stood thirty feet high and over three hundred feet in length. Dead centre stood two massive wooden doors, each one ten feet wide. Little guard towers lined the top of the wall every thirty feet, and two guards stood watch in each one. Six guards stood outside the massive gates, speaking to the travellers and traders waiting in the long queue to enter. In front of the party were six carts filled with vegetables, barrels, livestock, and six horse-drawn carriages. Kern trotted to the carriage in front of him, with Lan'esra sitting behind.

An elegantly dressed man sat on the rider's bench holding the reins. The curtains of the carriage twitched as Kern approached.

"Excuse me, sir, what is the holdup?" Kern asked the driver of the carriage.

"You don't know? Where have you been, boy, in a dragon's cave?"

Kern smiled back at the driver, raising an eyebrow. "Well…"

"It's the Carnival of Light, the biggest festival in all of Bodisha. It celebrates King Moriak's coming to power. This happens every year."

"Oh, I see; the Carnival of Light. Yes, I had heard of it, but just never had the chance to go."

"Well, you do now! A little tip for you—round the back of the arena where Lord Heilo sits is the best hog roast seller in all of Bodisha. Get the garlic bread, too. Bidol's hog roast is to die for, boy."

"Thank you, I will keep that in mind," Kern replied as he went back to the others. "We are in luck," he said when he reached them. "It's the Carnival of Light. We'll go in and grab a room for the night, tomorrow get the injuries seen to, and leave the day after."

"We'll need to go all the way back nearly to Tonilla and then north around the mountains," Galandrik said with a sigh. "It will take a week just to get to the other side."

"I heard there is a way straight through the mountains to Loft," Kern replied.

Ty pointed to the mountain to the north. "Have you seen them? Those are solid; there hasn't been even a crack."

"Our only other option is to head south past the Midas Hills, to Lake Fortune, then up to the Voltic Isle," Kern said.

Ty saw Lan'esra's face change and knew that she wanted stay with them. "Yes," he said. "That's a better idea, definitely."

Galandrik glanced over his shoulder at Ty. "You seem keen to journey south, lad. Any particular reason?"

"No, it just makes sense. Why waste all that time journeying around these bloody mountains when we can just go south? It makes perfect sense to me."

"Yes, I agree with you, Ty," Kern nodded.

"That's if there is no way through the mountains," Lan'esra quickly added.

"We will see once we get inside, if this queue ever goes down," Kern said, smiling.

"No, I say still travel south. There is no point going north now just to come back south!"

"But there are loads of bandits near the Midas Hills. And it would be difficult enough to pass through with just the bandits, but you *also* have the Spider Guild probably looking for you," Lan'esra said, reinforcing her side of the argument.

"Hmm. She has a good point," Kern answered.

"Rubbish! Bandits won't attack us and the Spider Guild was north," Ty said, slipping to the ground and stretching.

"Let's just wait until we get inside. No point arguing if there is no way through," Galandrik yawned.

"Ah, the voice of reason! Not another word said until we find out, then," Kern replied.

Lan'esra slid down from Kern's mount. "Want me to inspect those wounds?"

"No, not really. I will get them seen to tomorrow," Ty said.

"All right. Here is the last potion," she said, handing Ty the small vial. "That should ease the pain until it's seen to."

"Thanks."

*

After two hours, they stood at the main gate into Wade. The mighty wooden gates were impressive this close up. The iron hinges were as big as Ty and the bolts that ran through them were as thick as a giant's fist. A smaller passage was built into the right-hand door, easily big enough for a cart to fit through. Two scribes dressed in green robes sat at a table laden with writing paper, quills, and two huge leather-bound books. Two guards stood on either side of the smaller gate, and two more stood to confront the party.

The older-looking guard asked brusquely, "What's your business in Wade?"

"We come to join in the Carnival of Light festivities," Ty replied. The scribe at the table dipped his quill and scribbled as they spoke.

"Been in Wade before?"

"No sir. This is the first time for all of us."

"Names?" the guard asked as the second guard walked around the party examining their equipment and mounts. Before Ty could answer, he heard, "Galandrik Sabrehargen, Ty Quickpick, Lan'esra, and I'm Kern Ocarn."

The scribe at the table was still writing, and the second one hurriedly flicked through the pages of the leather-bound book.

"How long will you be staying?"

"Just a couple of days, then we will be on our way," Kern answered.

The scribe called the guard over and whispered something in his ear. He turned and stared at Kern as he listened to what the scribe had to say, then returned to the party with a slight smile.

"Well, well. It looks like a celebrity has come to Wade," the guard said, looking at Ty.

"A celebrity, eh," Ty said with an ear-to-ear smile.

"Apparently so. It says a giant slayer."

"Well, it's nothing to—"

"Welcome to Wade, Kern the Giant Slayer and his party!" He nodded at the guard by the gate, who banged twice on it. With a creak, the small wooden door began to open inward.

"News travels fast," Galandrik said.

"Yes, it does. Too fast," Kern answered, then kicked his horse on to trot through the small door, followed by Galandrik. "Thank you, good sir."

"It's all my pleasure. At least we will be safe from attacking giants now you're here," the guard replied with a laugh.

"Slayer of giants, eh? Well, Kern is full of surprises," Lan'esra said.

"Unbelievable," Ty muttered under his breath.

*

They were completely surrounded by mountains, a near-perfect circle of rock reaching up out of the ground and traveling up and up into the clouds. Behind them was the Gateway of Stone and in front of them, dead centre of the rock circle, was Wade. The town was also surrounded by another wall with guard huts dotted around the top. It felt more like a huge garrison than a town. The party could see why it was known as impenetrable—first the mighty outer wall, then another around the town. Straight ahead they could see another massive gate with the same people queueing to get in. The space between the town and the mountains was easily half a mile in every direction, and luscious grass surrounded the town. Even though Raith claimed to be the biggest town in Bodisha, that honour definitely went to Wade. There were more residents here than traders; most traders tended to avoid the town because of the high security and the way Lord Heilo ran things.

To their left were rows of tents, all perfectly aligned. The town's guards went about their daily business, cleaning armour and swords, washing uniforms, and resting before the start of the night shift.

They travelled forward along the path that led straight to the gate of Wade. The terrain all around the perimeter of the city, in the grassy area between the wall and the mountain that encircled the town, was dotted with rows of small tents, some in lines and some forming circles; it was like a town outside a town. People moved here for the safety, sick of the constant warring with the orcs. They also knew the Baws wouldn't attack because they had nothing to take.

Vegetable patches lined the pathways outside some tents and women, men, and children were busy working their plots. Other children played together. The happy shouts and screams of the kids was something none of the group had heard for many moons. Some children chased dogs, skipped, or played ball.

"Well, this seems a happy place," Lan'esra observed as the children played.

"I couldn't agree more. I haven't seen people this relaxed since… well, I haven't ever," Galandrik said.

"It certainly looks safe enough," Kern added.

"Easy pickings, then," Ty said, knowing what was coming.

"Don't even—" Kern started to say.

"I know—don't steal, don't fight, don't—"

"Just *don't*," Kern laughed.

After an uneventful hour of trotting through the tent city, they reached the main gate of Wade. "Hello. You must be Kern and party," the guard at the gate said.

"We are just four travellers, wanting a rest in your good town," Kern explained.

"Well, whoever you are, that'll be one gold piece," the guard replied, revelling in his position.

"You're charging us one gold? What for?" Ty barked.

"You have weapons and we have to keep peace in the town. The gold collected here pays our wages."

"We won't start any trouble, lad!" Galandrik said.

"They all say that. Then they go straight in the Horse's Head Inn, and two hours later they want to take on the world."

"Very well, we will pay," Kern said, reaching into his tunic. He flipped a gold coin at the guard, who caught it in his gloved hand.

"Each," the guard said, smiling at Ty.

"Each? I don't have any weapons!" Ty said, spinning around to emphasise the fact.

"Listen," the guard said, bending down to Ty's eye level, "the queue is building up behind you. Either you pay the gold you owe or fuck off."

Ty stared at the guard, knowing damn well he was being robbed blind. "Kern," he said, not taking his eyes from the guard.

"Here's your gold," Kern said, flicking more coins onto the ground. The guard stared at the three gold coins lying in the dirt and looked back at Ty.

"Pick them up, there's a good boy," the guard said, standing up straight. Another guard stepped forward to pick the coins up, and the first guard shouted, "Stop! Mr Halfling here was about to do that."

"You must be kidding me. I am not touching those coins; ram this shithole of a town," Ty answered, folding his arms.

"Well, you might as well just turn—"

"I'll pick them up," Lan'esra said, stepping past Ty and grabbing the gold coins from the ground. She handed them to the second guard.

"Let them through," the guard shouted, "and have a nice stay," he added with a smirk, gesturing for the party to enter.

"Thank you. I'm sure we will," Kern answered, trotting past and into the town.

"Don't bother, Ty, he isn't worth it," Lan'esra said quietly.

"I won't," Ty replied.

*

Kern and Galandrik dismounted and stood next to Ty and Lan'esra. All four stared in awe at what was in front of them. All the houses were ablaze with colour—fiery reds, bold blues, vibrant greens—and stood in lines, each building cleaner than the next. Each shop had hanging baskets of flowers affixed to shiny black iron brackets. Planters made of half-size wooden barrels were dotted around, sprouting colourful flowers. The floral smell was overpowering as it wafted through the air. A marketplace was set off to the right, awash with colour as well—the cloth roofs of its stalls in all different shades, the brightly coloured clothes of people scurrying about doing their daily business amidst all the hustle and bustle.

"What the hell is this?" Ty asked.

"A colourful, happy place," Lan'esra remarked.

"Colourful is putting it mildly," Galandrik added.

"You are right there. This is like nothing I have ever seen," Kern said.

"Let's go find an inn. I am famished," Galandrik said, rubbing his aching belly.

"Me too. My last meal was an ear, and I spat that out," Ty laughed.

Kern and Galandrik looked at Ty and said simultaneously, "An ear?"

"Come on. I'll tell you all about it in the inn."

*

They made their way through the main street of Wade, still marvelling at the colours of the houses and the flowers blooming all around, until they came across the Horse's Head Inn and entered. It was a large inn, twice the size of the Orc's Armpit but with the same basic layout: a bar at the far right, tables and chairs scattered about in no particular order. A thick drift of pipe smoke hung from the ceiling like mountaintop clouds.

"Over there, next to the window," Ty said, heading for a large round table. He pulled a chair out for Lan'esra, but she didn't notice and sat next to Kern.

"Why, thanks, Ty. You must have picked up some manners on your travels," Galandrik said, plopping down in the chair and grinning.

"What can I get you four, then?" a busty maid asked as she approached the table.

"Four ales, please," Lan'esra answered.

"You like an ale, then?" Kern asked.

"Oh yes, I can drink with the best of them!"

"I bet you can," he replied with a smile.

Ty watched as Lan'esra batted her eyelashes and sent flirty looks in Kern's direction. He kept his face neutral, but inside he was seething. *He* had met Lan'esra first. She was *his* find, not Kern's.

"There was this one time—"

Ty leaned forward and groaned, breaking up the conversation.

"What's up?" Galandrik asked, placing his hand on Ty's shoulder.

"The pain is returning. I think I'd better go get these looked at," he replied with a wince.

"I'll come with you," Kern said.

"Thanks," Ty answered, getting to his feet and holding his ribs.

"Oh well. Two each for us, then, girl."

"Yes! See you soon," Lan'esra said, as Kern and Ty left the inn.

They stood in the street and stopped the first person who walked past, an old lady carrying a basket of fruit.

"Excuse me, my love, would you know the way to a healer?" Kern asked.

"Of course I do; I have lived here for sixty years. Mr Klay's is the closest. Before it was a healer's shop, old Mother Bagfoth sold her fruit there, but that was before all these walls went up," she answered, putting the basket down.

"I'm sure old Mother Bagfoth wouldn't mind. Can you tell us where it is?"

"Yes, I was getting to that. Go along here and take the first right. Or is it left? My memory isn't what it used to be, you know."

"So, is it right or left? I'm dying here!" Ty moaned.

"Left? Or right," the old woman mused. Then she brightened. "Yes, that's it—you go up here and turn right. It's just up on the right-hand side, opposite the old well," the old lady answered, picking up her basket.

"Thank you. Have a good day," Kern replied as the old lady shuffled off, muttering something about old Mother Bagfoth.

"Let's go before you die," Kern grinned.

"Yes, let's," Ty answered, taking a bite out of a luscious green apple.

"You stole off that old woman?"

"I was hungry. It's only an apple."

"You will never change."

The pair took the route the old lady had given them and found the well she had mentioned in the middle of a large square, with shops lined all around and two fruit-and-vegetable stalls standing next to the well. The healer's shop was on the far side, a sign with the traditional red cross hanging outside.

Kern and Ty entered and the bell rang out. It was an unremarkable little shop, and remedies and potions filled the shelves. Parchments and books lined the tables, and the cupboards were filled with ingredients.

A middle-aged man came into the front of the shop. "Good day, what can I do you for?"

"We're looking for a Mr. Klay. We were told he's a healer."

"At your service." He sketched a slight bow. "Which of you is ill?"

"I have some wounds I'd like you to take a look at and, if possible, heal."

"That's what I do. Come through to the back, please."

Ty and Kern followed him into the back of the shop, where a bed was readied and all manner of instruments lined a side table.

"What are we talking about here?" Mr. Klay asked, hands on his hips.

Ty lifted up his shirt, revealing the bruises on his stomach. He turned to let Mr. Klay see the branding on his side and the whip marks on his back.

"My word, you have been through the wars."

"You could say that. Can you help?"

"Of course. It'll take a couple of hours but it should be fine. Let me go get what I need."

"I'll get back to Lan'esra and Galandrik," Kern said, dropping ten gold pieces on the table next to Ty.

"Thanks. You like her, don't you?" Ty asked.

"She's all right. Makes a change from Fat Mary! See you in a couple of hours—and don't disappear this time," Kern said, chuckling as he left the shop.

"I'll try not to," Ty replied. He waited until the door closed behind Kern before taking his shirt off.

"Right, I think I have everything," Klay said, placing a load of small bottles and cloth bandages on the table next to Ty.

"Can you tell me what this is?" Ty said, touching his chest. Klay examined it and pressed into the hard skin above Ty's heart, prodding and examining from several angles. He went back into the front of the shop and returned with a large leather-bound book. He lay it on the bed and flicked through the pages.

"A-ha! Here it is. It looks like the start of dragon shielding to me."

"What in Hades is dragon shielding?"

"It is a gift from a dragon. When humans bond with such a creature, it can give the human certain 'gifts'—in your case, it's dragon shielding. But this is usually after the dragon has touched the inner soul of the human. It's very rare, to be honest. Dragons don't usually give such a gift unless they…" Klay flicked the page and a plume of dust filled the air. "Resurrect the human, it says here."

Ty felt the hardness of the shielding under his skin. "What happens then?"

"Well it says here, 'Once the dragon gives the gift of life to the human, the human will begin to suffer random side effects such as "claw fingers," "dragon shielding," "wingback," or "cat eye."' And it looks like you, my friend, have dragon shielding."

"I thought you said it's a gift."

"Resurrection *is* a gift! And in the eyes of a dragon, shielding is also."

"Read on. When does it stop?" Ty said anxiously.

Klay flicked through a few more pages and, after a blow and a wave to clear the dust, began reading aloud. "Well, it says, 'Dragon scales form under the skin and vary in size and shape. Eventually the skin on top of the scales will dry and split, allowing the scales to protrude out.'"

"But when do the scales stop… growing?"

"It doesn't say. There have only been two cases documented here. In both cases the dragon shielding started on their backs, covering the whole top half. And because of the scales' hardness and how the human—or halfling—body is made up, so much soft tissue and muscle, it restricted movement, causing agony for the bearer."

"What happed to those two?"

"It doesn't say, sorry. That was the last input. Oh, and mood swings; another side effect is a dramatic change in mood."

"That's all I need. Can it be treated?"

"It doesn't say."

"Brilliant."

"Right, let me get to work. Oh my, what are these burns on your chest?"

"That is spider poison. Straight from a fang, dripped on me."

"Dragons and spiders, eh? You must love to live dangerously, that's all I can say."

"Sometimes too dangerously."

Klay went to work, treating all the wounds with different balms and treatments, bandaging each as he went. Ty stared up at the ceiling, thinking about Lan'esra. It took Klay nearly two hours before he finally finished his treatments.

"Right, all done. The wounds will heal fine, as long as you don't take the bandages off. If they get dirty or start to weep, re-dress them and use this ointment," he said, holding up a jar of grey paste. "The burn on your ribs needs dressing every three or four days, and use this," Klay said, holding up a little jar with a brown paste, "and your spider poison should be okay. If it flares up, use the brown paste and re-dress. Other than that, you are good to go. I will put five potions in the bag; if you do open any wound up and the pain is strong, one of them should numb it for twenty-four hours. It won't heal you; it'll just numb the pain."

"Brown for burns and grey for others. Got it."

"Right. Finish dressing, then come through the front and I'll sort out the payment."

Ty gingerly put his shirt back on, then pocketed the ten gold pieces and went through to the front of the shop.

"All right then: bandages, balms, fig ointment, time, stitching, and five potions... that'll be four gold pieces."

"I'm not even going to argue, since I feel a hundred times better already—and as my friend paid, too."

"Thank you, sir," Klay said, taking the gold from Ty.

"No, thank *you*," Ty replied, exiting the shop.

Time to find some armour and weapons, he thought, then stepped into an alcove between two shops and reached down the back of his leggings to retrieve the diamond. *Better just sell this little baby first.*

*

Kern, Galandrik, and Lan'esra sat eating in the Horse's Head Inn. "So what is the plan then?" Lan'esra asked, finishing her bowl of stew.

"Get Ty fixed up, grab you some equipment, and head back out. We'll go through the Gateway of Stone and head east round the mountain's edge, then south towards Lake Fortune," Kern answered.

"We will go past my home."

"Aye, you will be able to go home again." Galandrik smiled.

Lan'esra paused for a few seconds. "I don't want to."

"I thought you wanted a mount to get back," Kern said, leaning back in his chair.

"Well, I do—but I want to have some adventure, see some other places, meet other people. It's so boring where I live, and there's nothing to do but study."

"Knowledge is good, Lan'esra. I'm sure if Kern and I had studied more, we wouldn't have to go into half the hellholes we visit."

"But that's the whole point! You have an eventful existence, even if you do risk life and limb."

"It's not all fun and games, Lan'esra. People die all the time. We do some horrible things to get where we need to go," the ranger added.

"I don't care! I *want* to do horrible things! I want to do what you do; I want to take those kinds of risks."

"Really, it isn't all that good—and the rewards are usually not worth the danger," Kern explained.

"When Ty and I fought Dago, the giant spider, I was scared out of my wits but I felt alive. For the first time I was *alive*."

"Yes, I know the feeling," Kern agreed.

"Well, can I come?" she asked in anticipation.

"I guess so, Lan'esra, as long as you are sure. You okay with that, Galandrik?"

"Yes. The more the merrier, lad."

With that Lan'esra wrapped her arms around Kern's neck and kissed him on the cheek. "Thank you both so much!" She got up from the table. "I need the toilet."

*

Ty peeked through the window just in time to see Lan'esra kiss Kern's cheek. He sighed and stared down at his new armour and clenched his leather-clad fist. He had hoped it was going to impress Lan'esra, but now he knew that what he had suspected was true: She had eyes for Kern. He watched as she got up and left the table.

She has to go, he thought.

He joined them in the inn, dressed in his new black light-leather leggings and tunic. A cloak hung down to the floor and a hood covered his head, again all black. Black leather boots and gloves finished off the new look.

"Well, what do we have here, then?" Galandrik said, looking at Ty as he approached the table.

"Black? You turned chaotic evil?" Kern joked.

"I thought I already was," Ty said, sitting down next to Kern and pushing Lan'esra's mug across the table. "Any stew left?"

"It might be cold," Galandrik said, passing Ty a bowl.

"So how did the healing go?" Kern asked.

"Very well, thanks. I have some healing balms, potions, and bandages to change the dressings, but I should be good to go. He's wrapped me like a mummy under all this."

Lan'esra walked back to the table and stood next to Ty for a moment. She was slightly disgruntled that he had taken her chair, but finally she went round and sat next to Galandrik. "How do you feel?"

"Better than I did. Mr. Klay did well. The healing balms he added should heal everything quickly."

"That's good then," Lan'esra said, picking up her mug.

"What's the plan?"

"Head south, past the Midas Hills and to Lake Fortune," Kern explained.

Ty glanced up from his bowl at Lan'esra. "Dropping you off on the way then?"

"Nope, I'm staying. Kern has let me ride with you."

Ty dropped his spoon into his soup. "I thought you wanted to go home."

"I did, but fame and fortune have tempted me."

"Fame and fortune? You are deluded! We are heading to the Dungeon of Dreams, not some cotton-candy-covered joyride!"

"She knows the dangers, Ty. We have explained this to her."

"Well, explain again! She shit herself against a spider not too long ago," Ty said, leaping up.

"That was a giant spider! It was huge!"

"What do you think will be in that dungeon, baby rabbits? I am not having this conversation any more. I'm off."

"Where are you going, lad?" Galandrik asked.

"To get my weapons and supplies."

"We have paid for four rooms here tonight. Maybe see you later?" Kern asked.

"Maybe," Ty answered as he walked out the inn's main door.

"What's up with him?" Lan'esra questioned.

"He doesn't like change, but he'll calm down. He will be different in the morning," Galandrik explained.

"He was so nice in the temple—he gave himself up to protect me."

"Maybe he doesn't want to do it again," Kern said, calling the maid over.

"It won't happen again," Lan'esra answered.

Kern paid the maid, then got up from the table and stretched. "Give Lan'esra a couple of gold for some supplies and a mace. I'm going to have a look about for a couple of decent mounts."

"All right. I am heading upstairs for a lie-down. I could sleep for a week. When are we leaving Wade?"

"I think we should go the day after tomorrow. We can enjoy the carnival tomorrow night and let everybody relax, and that gives Ty another day's rest. It's going to be a long journey."

"That sounds good to me, lad."

"Me too," Lan'esra said. "Thanks for the gold, and I *will* pay it back. I will see you all in here later, then." She picked up the gold from the table and left the inn.

"Should I watch her? She could just do a runner," Kern said, watching Lan'esra cross the road.

"Do a runner? You must be blind, lad. She is like a smitten schoolgirl around you."

"Don't be stupid."

"I am telling you, Kern, she likes you. She likes you a lot."

"I'm not having that. Anyway, I am going to get two horses," he replied.

"Get one, she can share yours," Galandrik laughed.

Kern waved a dismissive hand as he left.

"Yes, please, one for the road," the dwarf shouted to the maid.

Chapter Thirteen
The Beginning

Conn walked with Queen Cherian in the garden of the castle. The morning sun shone brightly through the clouds and he could feel the heat on his back. "How is Moriak?" Conn asked politely.

"No change, but he isn't getting any better. Murtal has contained the fever but says he will become progressively worse."

"It shouldn't be long now before our thieves return with what we need."

"Yes, the sooner the better. What is your plan once they have returned with the herbs?"

"Keep them locked up until the king is healed and let him deal with them… and the dragons."

"Have you had word from that vile creature, Bok?"

"Yes, I had a message this morning. They are heading to Wade and when he left Shalamia's lair, Belton was alive."

"You still doubt that Belton fell to his death?"

"Oh, I know he fell to his death—but was he *pushed*? That is the question."

"What about Fucan? He was there and seems like a very loyal man. Couldn't he tell you how it happened?"

"He would never contradict Gorgon; he is like a brother. Gorgon has saved his life more times than you or I have had a glass of fine Bodishian wine."

"I guess we may never know then. One thing is strange—I thought Kern would head to the Voltic Isle first, then down to Fortune and across to Double Dikes."

"So did I, but who knows what is happening? Maybe they had a lead, or need to speak to someone there for the whereabouts of the herbs."

"But going to Wade will add a week to their journey."

"I know. They must know something we don't."

"I don't know if it was a good idea, sending those thieves to do this."

"They will get the herbs. Kern thinks his father is our captive, so he will do all in his power—and trust me when I say they are versatile."

"I hope you are right. They are our only chance of keeping Moriak alive, and we need him back. Guldir has been sending messages asking about the meeting, and if we don't hold a council soon he will turn his back on us. We have armies returning from the south soon; they need to be led north of Tonilla. It's all a mess."

"You are doing a fine job, my queen."

"I have no interest in or understanding of war. I rely on Brithuim to keep control, and I just voice his plans. He knows what the king was planning better than anybody."

"Brithuim is the king's chief in command. He will keep you right. Why not announce that he will be taking over while the king is… away?"

"Yes, I have thought of that, but if they get a sniff that the king is ill… You know how traitorous people can be."

"Hordas would be easy pickings for sure. They would fill his head full of perfidious nonsense for their own gains, and spin a web of lies poisoning him with their deceitfulness."

"Well said. So for now I will keep control. They won't threaten me. I have had a thought: The king's cousin Heilo runs Wade. Why not send him a message to see what our thieves are up to?"

"Good idea. I think it's the Carnival of Light this week; I had my yearly invitation to go. The man does this every year. It's a sickening show of self-gratification."

"Yes, I went once. Heilo loves the power. He has made Wade into some sort of fortress. No one goes there anymore. He has spoilt what was once a beautiful town."

"I will send a message and let Heilo know why they are going there, and what they are doing for us."

"That would be wise. If they fail us…"

"I know, my queen, but as I have said—if anybody can retrieve what we need, it is Kern."

"I just hope you are right."

So do I, Conn thought.

*

Galandrik and Lan'esra sat eating breakfast in the Horse's Head Inn; the plate in the middle of the table was full of bacon, sausages, eggs, mushrooms, and slices of homemade sweet bread.

"I needed this badly," Galandrik announced.

"Where did you go last night?"

"I went to my room and fell asleep. Never woke up until early hours of the morning, and couldn't get back to sleep again."

"Kern said Ty didn't come in either."

"Not surprising. He is a strange character, to say the least. He doesn't mean any harm with his words. He is just… spirited."

"Well, you know him better than I do."

"You spoke him up, look."

Ty approached their table with a spring in his step and a smile on his face. "Good morning. That looks delicious! I could eat a horse," he said, sitting down next to Lan'esra.

"Morning, Ty. Where did you get to last night?" Galandrik asked with a sly wink at Lan'esra.

"I think the potions and healing balm made me drowsy. One minute I was sitting on the bed and the next I was sound asleep. Only been awake an hour," he explained, plating up a full breakfast.

"Did you sort your weapons out?" Lan'esra asked.

"Yes, I will pick them up later. They are making them to the weight and size I requested, as well as new dagger holsters to fit my wrists. I think I may have lost a few pounds in the spider temple. Where is Kern?"

"He's been and gone. I have no idea where."

"Something to do with the horses, I think," Lan'esra added.

Ty spotted a poster on the wall and got up from the table to examine it. He ripped it off and sat back down. "That's a nasty looking scar. Wonder who he is," he said, looking at the face on the paper.

"It's Retch the baby snatcher," Lan'esra answered.

"How do you know?"

"It says his name on the top of the poster," Lan'esra giggled.

"Oh—I know that; I just didn't notice it," Ty replied with embarrassment.

"One hundred gold for the capture, or fifty dead," she added.

"Now that's easy money," Ty said, passing it to Galandrik and picking up his fork again.

The inn door opened and Kern entered. "You are all still here then?" he said, sitting next to Galandrik.

"Yeah, I slept like a baby right through to this morning," Ty explained.

"I thought you might. Same for you I take it?" he said, looking at the dwarf.

"Yes, couldn't get my head off the pillow," Galandrik admitted.

Ty called the maid over to order some ale. While he waited for her to arrive, he pointed at the face on the poster and asked Kern, "Have you heard of this guy?"

"Retch the baby snatcher. He sounds delightful."

"He's the ghost bandit who lives in the mountains that surround us," the maid said, slipping up behind Ty. "He runs a group of outlaws called the Baws—ruthless assassins and mercenaries who will kill you in a heartbeat. Retch sneaks into Wade in the middle of the night through cracks in the wall, steals livestock for sacrifices, and takes our babies for food. He goes in through the window as a snake and snatches them, never to been seen again. He is evil," she explained, looking over her shoulder and making sure the innkeeper wasn't watching.

"A snake, you say?" Galandrik questioned, raising an eyebrow at Ty.

"Yes. My friend Molly said her friend said he can turn into a snake, and he eats the babies whole."

"I would tell your friend Molly to tell her friend that it's probably old wives' tales," Kern said with a reassuring smile.

"Well, how do you explain the missing babies, Molly said—"

"I'll give you 'Molly said'! Get over here and serve these people," the innkeeper shouted. As the maid scurried away, he turned to the table and said, "I am sorry about her. She's not all there."

"No worries; just make sure she doesn't forget our four ales," Galandrik replied.

"Coming up. I will bring them over."

"Missing babies, eh?" Ty said, pushing his plate to one side.

"Probably birds or lizards. It definitely isn't a shapeshifter called Retch who lives in the mountains," Kern laughed.

"Can people change into other things?" Lan'esra asked.

Ty stared at Lan'esra. "You really haven't ever been out of the Midas Hills, have you?"

"Yes I have! I just haven't heard of that," she answered defensively.

"Ever heard of a magic potion that can change your appearance, a potion of disguise?"

"No, I haven't. Have *you*?"

Ty glanced at the others and grinned. "Just the once."

"I remember it well, Tyla!" Galandrik laughed, as the innkeeper set their ales on the table.

After the innkeeper left, Kern asked, "Did you sort out your weapons?"

"No, I have to pick them up today. They didn't have wrist holsters in my size, and they are changing the weights of the daggers."

"Ten gold pieces went a long way then. Healing, armour, supplies, and weapons," Kern said suspiciously.

"It's surprising what you can buy with a bit of a haggle."

"Surprising what you can buy with a diamond…" Lan'esra said, smiling at Ty. He knew the remark was a riposte to his earlier disguise potion comment.

"Loose lips sink ships, Lan'esra. You would do *very* well to remember that," Ty lectured.

"A diamond, eh?" Kern said, smiling and leaning back in his chair with his hands upon his head, fingers interlocked.

"Yes. Remember the diamond I swallowed in the orc temple?"

"Erm, no. I was digging for ore, remember?" Kern replied.

"Oh yes, and I was with Solomon. Well, I did, and it must have got stuck. When I threw up in the spider temple, it popped out."

"And you have held it all this way?" Galandrik asked.

"Yes, up his arse," Lan'esra said with a smile.

"Sink ships," Ty answered, shaking his head. "Yes, in my arse. It fetched thirty gold pieces, which I have spent on weapons and armour. Here, if you don't believe me!" Ty pulled out a pouch from his tunic and emptied it on the table. Two gold, five silver, and six copper pieces tumbled out, and Kern caught one as it rolled off the table.

"I wasn't questioning you, friend," Kern smiled.

"Didn't sound like it," Ty said, scooping his coins into the pouch. "I need the toilet," he said, and left the table.

After Ty was out of earshot, Kern leaned on the table and looked at Lan'esra. "I agree with Ty. We don't tell tales on each other."

"I was just—"

"Just think before you speak, next time. The worst thing you can do is tell tales on a thief, especially Ty. Remember you'll be sleeping with him guarding you very, very soon, and if he thinks you will rat out the Rat, it'll be a very long sleep."

Lan'esra swallowed hard as Kern kicked Galandrik's foot under the table. "Er, yes," the dwarf chimed in. "He is not to be underestimated. He would take a blade for you, but people who talk too much and tell tales on others generally don't live that long. It's their code."

"I'll watch what I say in the future," Lan'esra said, looking down at her empty plate like a schoolgirl who had just been scolded by her mother.

"Now go apologise to him," Kern advised.

"That was a bit harsh. She'll think Ty might murder her in her sleep," Galandrik said once Lan'esra had gone.

"I don't think he will be telling her much from now on, do you?"

"No lad, you know how secretive he is. He hates anybody knowing what he has or how he does things."

"Strange halfling indeed," Kern said shaking his head.

"Innkeeper! Same again, please."

*

Ty stood facing the wall in the toilet, remembering the meeting with Bok and Joli in the Orc's Armpit many moons ago. He glanced nervously over his shoulder, but the toilet was empty. He finished and headed for the door, then stopped, reached into his pocket, and pulled out six gold pieces. He admired them briefly, then smiled and put them back. When he got outside, Lan'esra was waiting patiently, with hands behind her back.

"Ty, I'm sorry I mentioned the diamond. I was just trying to wind you up."

"You certainly know how. Listen, all we have is each other—we rely on trust, friendship, and the knowledge that we have each other's backs."

"If all we have is trust, then why is it a problem that your friends know about your money?"

"That's not the point. The point is, you told people. What else will you tell, and to whom?"

"Yes, I see. It won't happen again."

"All right. I'll see you back in the bar," Ty said, walking off.

"Wait, Ty. Just one more thing."

Ty stopped and turned. "Yes?"

"If you want me to teach you to read, I'd be more than happy to."

There was a tense silence. "Thanks. I will keep that in mind," Ty said with a false smile.

*

Retch and Alexe stood in front of the Baws. Retch's group had dwindled to less than half its earlier numbers. The last group of men had left a few weeks prior, planning to head through the mountains even though Retch had told them it was a suicide mission. Still, they were sick of the bandit lifestyle so they set off, searching for a path through the mountains to freedom. Now there were only eight bandits left.

"Right, Alexe and I have decided we need to get out of this shit hole, move away, and live a normal life—not live as bandits—being hunted daily, scavenging for scraps of food. Tonight we make a stand!"

The Baws all cheered at Retch's speech, and Keefa stepped forward. He had been with the Baws longer than any of the others, and he hated Retch for his fame. He felt he should have been the group's leader; he should have had that fame—not Retch. "How do you intend to do this?"

"We are going to kidnap one of Lord Heilo's relatives and hold it for ransom. A child for our freedom!"

The Baws cheered again.

"Lord Heilo is a bastard. He would rather see the child die than give us a pardon."

"Well, you are more than welcome to stay, Keefa, and live like a dog."

Keefa scoffed. "How are we going to snatch a kid?"

"It's the Carnival of Light and everybody will be distracted by Heilo's pathetic light and firework displays. We will bide our time and wait. As soon as a little brat wanders from the pack, we will pounce like lions on a young calf." Again the cheers rose and echoed around the cave.

"And then what?"

"We come back here and send a message to Heilo: Leave the gates open, clear the guards, and let us have a free ride out. As soon as we are clear of the gates, we will let the kid go."

"Sounds good—but if we fail, you know we are heading to the Balrog."

"Fuck the Balrog. We've all got to die!" Retch said, raising another cheer.

"Maybe, but being melted by unfathomable heat in a metal balrog isn't the way I want to go."

"Like I said, Keefa, you don't have to go. Right—everybody who *isn't scared,* get geared up and ready. All black and limited weapons; we don't want to be encumbered. This isn't a raid, it's a snatch and grab. Hopefully the only weapon drawn will be the dagger to scare the kid silent."

*

Bok entered Wade and trotted through the rows of tents, watching as children played and ran around laughing—mostly young boys fighting with sticks, pretending to be great warriors. *How simple life could be. I could settle here, grow my own food and disappear from the eyes of everyone. Get a wife and have children... I could watch them fight with sticks, and show them the right ways of combat... No, Conn would find me. I must kill the Rat. While he lives, I am dead.*

*

Kern, Ty, Galandrik, and Lan'esra walked through the streets of Wade, watching the townsfolk scurry around preparing for the Carnival of Light. At the far end of the town was a wooden arena with hundreds of large wooden seats circled around it, open at one end to let the entertainers enter the arena floor. Facing the opening were the royal boxes where Lord Heilo and his companions sat, and traders were busy setting up their stalls around the perimeter of the arena. Kern spotted Bidol's hog roast stall, which the old man outside the gates had told him about.

"I'm definitely getting a hog roast tonight. I cannot even hazard a guess at the last time I had a good greasy hog roast roll," Kern said, pointing at Bidol's stall.

"Sounds good to me, lad!"

"It should be a good night. It looks like everything is almost prepared," Lan'esra added.

"Watch your pockets tonight. I can tell you from experience, this will be a pickpocket's paradise," Ty said.

"Good point. He is right; keep your wits about you," Kern said, placing his hand on Ty's shoulder.

"Anyway, my daggers should be ready so I'm going to collect them. Are we meeting at the inn later?"

"The carnival should start when the sun goes down. Shall we all meet then?"

"I'll come with you, Ty. I may get my axe sharpened for the journey," Galandrik said.

"You mean you're going to use it?" Ty quipped.

"I'll use it sooner than you think, thief!"

"Yeah, I know, you've pushed bigger people out of the way to get to a fight!" Ty laughed, remembering his first encounter with Galandrik in Conn's cells.

"Come on, let's go," Galandrik said, stomping off.

"See you two soon," Ty said, running to catch up the dwarf.

"What shall we do, then?" Lan'esra asked Kern with a smile.

"I'm sure we can think of something," Kern answered, smiling back.

*

The sun had long gone behind the western side of Wade Mountains. A full moon was out and the moonlight lit up the grassland around the town. Retch, Alexe, Keefa, and Sali ran across the open swath toward the north wall of Wade, darting from tent to tent, keeping low and out of sight of the watchful eye of the tower guards. When they reached the wall, Retch felt about on the ground for the trap door handle. He quickly found it and lifted, and without saying a word, the other three dropped in. Retch followed behind them. The tunnel sloped down and under the footings of the outer wall, then, after a twenty-foot crawl, ended at a wall with a wooden ladder leading upward. The tunnel was consumed in blackness but, after years of entering the town this way, the journey was second nature to the Baws.

Alexe climbed the ladder and pushed up the trapdoor, just enough to see out. They were behind the blacksmith's, inside the north end of Wade, and the area was deserted at this hour. "All clear," he whispered down. He pushed the door open stealthily, then climbed up and out. Reaching down one by one, he helped the other three up. When they were all out, he closed the trapdoor behind them, its covering of sod blending seamlessly into the expanse of lawn. They squatted behind the building, backs against the wall. No tower could see here, and even if it could have, the shadows hid them well.

"Right, blend in and mingle. We all know where to be. Keep an eye out for guards. When we get the nod from the others watching from inside, we will strike. Now go—and Keefa, keep out of the inns."

Keefa just shook his head, then flicked his hood up and disappeared around the corner of the blacksmith's. Sali gave a nod and darted off in the other direction.

"Well, this is it, old friend," Alexe said, extending his hand.

"It certainly is, Alexe. Be careful."

"You too."

Chapter Fourteen
The Carnival of Light

Heilo was an evil man, and increasingly mercurial. He imprisoned or executed—sometimes both—anyone who stood against him, or even people who just disagreed with his tyrannical ways. He sat on his throne like a king, surrounded by loyal servants scurrying around to prepare him for the Carnival of Light. His purple robe with its golden belt was stretched tight around his bulging midriff, and draped over his shoulders was a red cloak identical to his cousin Moriak's, its hems lined with the white fur of the snow leopard. His shoulder-length hair was dyed jet black to match his goatee. His trusted advisor Vaelyn stood by his side with ink and parchment, taking orders down for the upcoming event.

"Make sure the performers come out first. They bore me but the crowd seems to love them, so get them on first and out of the way."

"Yes, lord. Was there anything else?" Vaelyn looked down at the long list he had written.

"No, that is all for now. Just make sure the wine keeps flowing."

"Yes… wine," he said, and scribbled it down.

"Oh, one other thing. I have had word from Conn, that wretched wizard who sucks up to my cousin Moriak."

"Really? Don't tell me he is skipping the festival again this year! That's two years running he hasn't shown up."

"No, he isn't, but that's not why he sent the message. Apparently we have a party here led by a ranger named Kern. He has a dwarf with him named

Galandrik and a thief who's one of the king's men named Bok, but the party thinks his name is Kob."

"What is their significance here?"

"They have been sent to gather some herbs for Moriak. I have spoken to my physician and he informs me that the ingredients they seek are for a severe illness. I think my cousin is ill."

"That's sad news, my lord; my cond—"

"Sad? It's brilliant! If the king dies, then only that horrible little shit Hordas stands between me and the throne," Heilo said, smiling.

"You are most forward-thinking, lord. I would never have—"

"Stop the arse-licking. Here is what I want you to do: Make sure they leave here tonight in one piece, but they must never return with those herbs."

"What do you suggest, my lord?"

"Hm… let me think… KILL THEM!" Heilo shouted.

"Yes, lord. How stupid of me. It shall be done," Vaelyn grovelled.

"Make sure it is. Let me know when they're dead. Meanwhile I will think of a way to get rid of that imbecile Hordas."

"Yes, my lord. It shall be done," Vaelyn repeated, bowing.

"Oh, and when the carnival is in full swing, make a baby disappear. It's been a few months," Heilo said, lowering his voice.

"Another baby? What—"

"Don't just stand there. GO!" Heilo shouted at Vaelyn, then turned to a servant, "You there! Bring me more bloody wine."

Vaelyn ran down the steps to the main door of the throne room.

*

Kern, Ty, Galandrik, and Lan'esra sat in the Horse's Head Inn. It was full to the brim with people—townsfolk and travellers from around the land who had come to experience the Carnival of Light. Every imaginable race joined in the merriment and joy of the night's upcoming events.

"Busy tonight!" Galandrik shouted over the noise of the inn.

"Yes, it's the Carnival. People have come by the hundreds to join in the fun," Lan'esra said, smiling and watching as the townsfolk danced.

"I don't like it. Too many people bug me," Ty moaned.

"Where's your sense of fun? We leave tomorrow and it isn't going to be fun and games then," Kern said. "You'll soon wish you were here in a crowded inn!"

"Rubbish. This is bad news—too many people and too much drink. It'll end in tears, trust me," Ty warned.

"Finish these and we will head to the arena and see what all the fuss is about," Kern suggested.

"Sounds good to me, lad," the dwarf agreed.

They finished their ales, then headed toward the arena. Jugglers, fire breathers, and acrobats performed along the busy streets, entertaining the crowds for copper pieces. The smells from food stalls selling cooked meats and roasted nuts lingered in the air, and the moonlight shone bright on this glorious occasion. Music came from all around as bands played on makeshift stages, surrounded by townsfolk clapping and dancing. The atmosphere was electric as magic users cast firework spells for the groups of cheering children watching the displays of magic in awe.

Eventually they reached the arena. There were four empty seats near the entrance, and Ty sat down in one of them, saying, "This will do."

"Let's see if we can get in the thick of it," Kern said, looking at the rows and rows of packed seats that curved around the arena.

"No, this is good. Easy exit if anything happens," Ty said, folding his arms.

"You and your escape routes. Let's just join in and live a little. It's a long road ahead," Kern argued.

"You go. I'm quite happy here."

"No, let's sit here," Galandrik interrupted. "It's looking full anyway and we will only fight our way out at the end."

All four sat at the entrance to the horseshoe arena and watched as people continued to stream in. The place looked like it was already full to bursting, but still they came. The royal boxes had also begun to fill up; Kern saw men, women, and children standing on a balcony overlooking the arena floor, all dressed in fine robes with gold trim. Two guards stood at either end of the balcony, opening the doors for the nobles and the high-born. All around the top of the structure were patrolling bowmen, looking down into the arena.

"Here you go, lad! This'll warm your cockles," Galandrik said, pulling a silver hip flask from his tunic and passing it to Kern.

"What is it?" Kern asked, unscrewing the cap, which dangled on a chain.

"Try it, lad."

Kern did, and nearly spat it over Ty. "By the gods above, what is that shit?" he said, only just managing to speak.

"'Shit'? That, lad is Pugunary, the finest potato and lemon liquor money can buy, made by the dwarfs in Grimnoss."

"It should stay in Grimnoss," Kern said, licking his lips and pulling a face.

"Take it away," Ty said, holding up a hand as the dwarf offered it to him.

"I'll have some," Lan'esra said, taking the flask from Galandrik.

"Go easy, girl, it's… volatile."

"Nonsense. In the Midas Hills we make the best apple cider in Bodisha. I was virtually born up an apple tree." Lan'esra took a swig and immediately coughed and spluttered, spraying the liquor from her mouth and onto the floor.

"Volatile? More like violent!" she said in between coughs.

"You lot have never lived," Galandrik said, taking a swig.

"Obviously not," Kern replied, smiling.

*

After an hour, the entrance to the grounds was closed, as every seat in the arena had been taken. One guard in full battle dress stepped to the centre of the balcony, put his horn to his lips, and blew a fanfare. With that, the entire arena fell silent. Even the music from the surrounding streets stopped. The horn blower finished with a flourish, spun on his heel, and marched to the end of the balcony next to the other door guards. Lord Heilo pushed himself up from his chair and looked down into the still-hushed arena.

"Welcome, people of Bodisha!" A roar rose from around the arena as Heilo stood with arms outstretched, like a father beckoning his children to his bosom. The crowd cheered and clapped for him, and he clearly loved the applause. He stood soaking it up like sun's rays, then slowly lowered his arms, and the cheering stopped.

"Tonight we celebrate! Tonight is the Carnival of Light and we rejoice in its splendour. We marvel in its phosphorescent brilliance and its resplendent beauty!"

"What's he on about?" Ty whispered to Kern.

"He's just the same as all these people, making something more than what it is. It's only a few fireworks and some illusions," Kern replied.

"Tonight we drink! We eat and we enjoy the night, knowing that our walls are protected by men—not pathetic bandits, but *men*, men of honour, men of strength! Look around you—this very arena is protected by those men."

The crowd cheered wildly.

"And tonight we also have a special guest. He is a ranger from the north, but not any normal ranger—he is a tamer of dragons!" Confused murmurs could be heard around the arena. Kern glanced at Ty and Galandrik, and shook his head.

"When he has finished taming these mighty beasts, he amuses himself, saving entire towns by slaying hill giants!" The murmurs turned to cheers.

"Oh no, my good friends from all over this wonderful land. Not only does he slay hill giants, he also single-handedly kills wyverns!" The crowd roared and cheered wildly.

Heilo raised his arms again, and the crowd fell silent. "Please show your appreciation for this dragon-taming, giant-killing hero! Show yourself, Kern Ocarn!"

"What the hell is going on?" Kern shouted over the noise of the crowd.

"You're famous!" Lan'esra shouted back.

"Best you stand up, lad," Galandrik insisted.

Ty stared down at the floor. *Killer of giants and wyverns, tamer of dragons? I killed the giant, I killed the wyvern, and I tamed the bloody dragon,* he thought. "I'm going to grab a bite to eat," he shouted to Galandrik as Kern began to rise.

"All right, lad, no getting into trouble!"

And with that, Ty was gone.

"I'll go with him," Lan'esra said.

Galandrik nodded back and Lan'esra jumped down.

Kern was standing now, and Heilo pointed down at the ranger. "KERN OCARN!"

The crowd roared its approval. The people around Kern all patted his shoulders and shook his hand. Kern looked around the arena and smiled as the audience chanted, "KERN OCARN, KERN OCARN, KERN OCARN!"

*

Around the back of the arena, Bok was at a food stall. He had finally reached the front of the queue and was reaching for his lizard on a stick, when the sudden chanting of Kern's name made him jerk his head around.

"Son of a bitch!" He ran toward the front of the arena.

"Hey, your lizard!" the stall keeper shouted. Bok didn't look back.

*

"Ty, wait for me," Lan'esra shouted.

Ty glanced round and saw Lan'esra running up behind him. Out of the corner of his eye, he saw a man coming around the corner in front of him, but he was too late to react. They collided and Ty fell back onto his backside.

"Watch where you're going, you fool!" Ty said, holding his still-sore stomach and looking up at the hooded stranger.

Bok stared down at the angry person sprawled on the ground in front of him, and what he saw made him freeze. Sitting there large as life, holding up a hand, was Ty.

He was paralyzed, a million different ideas racing around in his mind. He couldn't stop it spinning. *Kill him, kick him, help him, squash him...*

"Help me up then," Ty groaned as a young woman raced up to the fallen thief.

Bok shook his head clear and held out a hand. "Sorry, I was in a hurry," he said, keeping his head lowered and roughening his voice.

"I should think so, too. Now be gone," Ty said, stepping past Bok and flicking the dirt from his shoulder.

"Sorry I distracted you. Awfully bad luck," Lan'esra said as Ty brushed the dust off his new cloak

"Not necessarily, Lan'esra. You see, luck is where preparation and opportunity meet."

"What are you on about?"

"Nothing; ignore me. Hog roast roll?" Ty offered with a smile. His hand tightened around the pouch in his pocket—which he had just stolen from the stranger who had bumped into him.

"The queue is twenty deep."

"It must be good, then. By the time we get served, Kern will probably have been made a lord."

"So are all those stories true? Did he really slay those creatures and tame a dragon?"

"No, *we* slayed those creatures and *I* tamed a dragon," Ty said angrily.

"So why does he get the credit?"

"Oh, I don't know, and I don't really care. I'm hungry. How long does it take to cook a pig?" Ty said, standing on tiptoe to see the stall.

*

Bok watched from across the street as Ty and Lan'esra chatted in the food stall queue.

Damn, you fool. You had the chance! That hapless girl couldn't have stopped you. You could have killed him there and then, pulled him up onto your dagger, straight through his heart. You missed it, you fool!. No, too many people standing around. Damn, I missed the perfect chance. Not next time; next time I will be ready.

Bok loaded his small hand crossbow and held it beneath his cloak. *Next time I'll be ready to shoot.*

*

Retch and Alexe stood at the back of the arena. Long black sheets of fabric were draped over the wooden structure, concealing the raw lumber. Twenty feet to their left was a food stall where people queued for a hog roast roll. Keefa was stationed near the entrance of the arena, mingling with the crowds and watching Heilo making his speech. Around the other side of the arena, a set of wooden stairs curved upward to the royal boxes. Two guards were stationed at the foot of the stairs, and they nodded to the guests as they made their way up; Sali leaned against a wall near the entrance, watching and waiting. A few people wandered around, but it was a quiet location.

"This is the perfect spot. If someone comes down the stairs and heads this way, no one will see us when we snatch a brat."

"What about that stall?" Alexe remarked.

"They are too busy buying food. They won't take any notice, and the noise from the arena will drown out any screams."

"I guess we just wait then."

"One will come soon enough,"

*

Lord Heilo raised his hands and the cheering stopped. "Welcome, Kern. You are our honoured guest." Kern simply nodded back and sat down. "Let the entertainment begin!"

With that, a dozen men ran into the arena, some dressed in black leather armour and hoods, and all carrying wooden short swords. One of the men was well over six feet tall and stood in front of the others. Another dozen men, dressed as town guards, ran in and stood facing the men in black. The trumpeter sounded his horn again, then shouted, "Please welcome Retch the baby snatcher!" The crowd began to boo, and threw rotten fruit into the arena as the tall man growled and waved his sword at the baying crowd.

"Let's hear it for your master, Lord Heilo," the trumpeter shouted. One of the men dressed as a guard threw down his cloak, revealing the purple robes favoured by Heilo. The crowd cheered as the fighting began.

As the entertainment unfolded in the arena, Kern turned to Galandrik. "I can't believe this. How did he know so much?"

"News travels fast in Bodisha, lad."

"Even so, not many people knew about Sleeper."

"True. I guess they do now."

"Where did Ty and Lan'esra go?"

"They went to grab some food."

"I take it Ty didn't want to stick around. We *all* killed the giant, and Ty did set light to the wyvern. I can see why he's upset."

"And he raised Sleeper while we languished in that cell."

"We will watch this act, then wander round to find them."

"What I can never understand with Ty is, he loves the sneaky side, the shadows and being so secretive—but as soon as there is the slightest hint of fame, he's all over it."

"That's Ty. I can't work the little shit out."

*

Alexe nudged Retch as a woman in a long green dress, holding a little boy by the hand, turned the corner towards them. The red cloak draped over her shoulders was tied with a golden cord, revealing the elegant cut of her dress and her brown leather boots. The little boy wore a blue shirt and trousers; a white sash completed his look. His black shoes had a shiny silver buckle on each and his trousers were tucked into his white socks. Keefa gave the nod and followed.

"This is it. As soon as they walk past, grab the boy—and don't let him scream. I will get the woman. We'll drag them behind that black curtain," Retch instructed.

"No problem. But if he bites, I'm going to quiet him down," Alexe said, rubbing his knuckles.

"Do what you like; just don't kill him."

Soon enough, the woman and child rounded the corner in front of Retch and headed toward the stairs leading up to the royal boxes. The pair of Baws stepped out and fell into step close behind them. The woman turned her head, saw them, and quickened her pace.

"Go," Retch murmured.

The woman saw the impending attack and managed to let out a yell just before Retch grabbed her and pushed her through the black curtain. Alexe cupped his hand over the boy's mouth and followed.

Ty heard the woman's cry. He spotted one man darting under the black curtain, another standing guard outside. The expression on second man's face was guilty as sin, and Ty's impression was confirmed when the man ducked under and into the blackness.

"I think someone is getting robbed. Quickly, follow me and be ready."

"Be ready for what?" Lan'esra asked, following Ty toward the black curtain.

"A fight," Ty answered.

Retch held his dagger to the woman's throat. "One scream and Little Boy Blue will have his guts spilled in the dirt, do you understand?"

The woman nodded, eyes wide.

"I am Retch the baby snatcher. Don't underestimate me, bitch."

The woman's head nodded frantically at his words.

Keefa quickly tied the woman's hands behind her back, and then pushed her to her knees. Retch took the dagger away, and Keefa forced a piece of rag into her mouth before placing a hemp sack over her head. Retch nodded and Keefa gave the woman's neck a forceful whack. She slumped to the ground, and the little boy instantly started crying and thrashing about.

"Listen, you little shit, stop all that crying or I will cut your eyeballs out!" Alexe said, bending down to meet the boy's eyes. The child froze in fear at Alexe's words.

"Can't you pick on anybody your own size?" Ty announced, stepping inside the curtain. It was dark under the arena, but the lantern lights penetrating through the wooden seats above made it easy enough to see.

Alexe spun around in shock. "Where the hell did he come from?" he said, lifting the boy quickly.

"Another baby to snatch, is it?" Ty said calmly.

"Listen, friend, this is none of your business. Now walk away or the kid dies," Retch answered.

Ty smiled. "You honestly think I give a fuck about that little kid?"

"What do you want then? Spit it out before I spill your guts!" Keefa said, drawing his sword.

"What *I* care about is the one hundred gold bounty on Retch's head."

"One hundred? Is that all? Ten years of terrorizing and he puts a miserly one hundred gold on my head?"

"That's if you're taken alive. Only fifty if you're dead."

"Just go before you get hurt," Alexe said, pushing the kid to Retch and drawing his sword.

"I don't think so. Drop your weapons and I will ask Heilo to go easy on you."

"Easy? We'll end up in the Balrog."

Alexe lunged forward with a straight thrust; Ty just managed to sidestep and flick his daggers into his hands. Keefa stepped forward and swung his sword wildly, sweeping down and arcing left to right.

Ty stepped back, keeping on tiptoes and easily avoiding the manic attack. Keefa stepped back and Ty could see his heavy breathing.

"Is this honestly the best the Baws have?" he said, looking at Retch. He skirted them in a wide circle, trying not to show fear as he flicked his daggers into the air and caught them.

Alexe lunged forward again, sweeping and arcing his sword at the thief's midriff. Once more Ty stepped and dodged the attacks, but he spotted his chance and brought his dagger slicing across the top of Alexe's hand. Alexe immediately dropped the sword and stepped back, blood spilling from the open wound.

Retch dashed away with the boy in tow as Keefa lunged forward again. Ty didn't dance; he simply sidestepped the crude attack and leapt up, plunging his dagger into his attacker's neck as his momentum took him past.

Keefa slumped to the floor, dead.

Alexe drew his dagger from his belt and pointed it at Ty. "Come on, then. One hand or two, I'll still have you."

Ty bent down and wiped the blood from his dagger on Keefa's back.

Alexe and Ty circled each other, each poised and waiting for an opening; Ty let Alexe come forward a few times and watched his opponent's movements, learning his style. At last he attacked, lunging forward and slicing left to right. Alexe blocked and countered until he had his back to the curtain. Ty saw Lan'esra step in behind him from the fold of the curtain where she had been watching. Ty slipped away and back, keeping Alexe focused on him while Lan'esra moved into position. She raised her mace and brought it down on the back of Alexe's neck, rendering him unconscious.

"I didn't think you were going to do it," Ty said.

"I was being quiet, unlike you. Luckily enough, a troop of children went by. Otherwise the entire hog roast queue would have heard you fighting."

"Where did Retch go?" Ty said, peering out from the curtain.

"Sorry, I didn't see."

"Let's try straight down the alley ahead. He wouldn't drag a kid past all those stalls, and the other way are guards."

"What about the other bandits?" Lan'esra said, running behind Ty.

"They won't earn me one hundred gold. *He* will."

*

Bok watched as Ty and Lan'esra ran up the alley searching for Retch and the boy. He followed them at a safe distance, dodging in and out of the shadows, keeping himself hidden as best he could. His heart raced as he lifted his light crossbow and doublechecked that the bolt was loaded. Now was the time to take his revenge. Now was the time for Ty to die—and this time the rat wouldn't escape.

*

Ty watched from about a hundred yards back as Retch stopped and set the boy down. The boy's weight was clearly a hindrance. After a brief pause, they disappeared around the corner at the end of the alley. Ty and Lan'esra followed the alley to its end and turned the corner into a large square. Ty remembered it well; the healer's shop was on his left-hand side. The market stalls were all shut, their owners probably all at the arena enjoying the night's activities.

Retch made for the well at the centre of the open square and stepped up onto the plinth that surrounded it. The few people in the square scurried away to hide behind a stall, peering out to watch the events as they unfolded.

"Keep away or the kid takes a swim," Retch said, holding the boy next to the edge of the well. The boy sobbed and tears streamed down his reddened face.

"I told you before, I don't care. Chuck him," Ty said calmly. Lan'esra stood silent next to him.

"I'm serious! Come any closer and he's going!" Retch lifted the boy and stood him on the edge of the well.

Ty and Lan'esra were within a few feet of him now, and Lan'esra tensed, ready to grab the child.

"I'm serious, too. This is the last baby you snatch."

"I have never touched a baby. This was just an insurance policy to get me out of town."

"You expect me to believe that?"

"I don't give a damn what you believe! Heilo created a monster to frighten the townsfolk. One hundred miserly gold for a monster like the baby snatcher? Think about it. He has them where he wants them."

"Neither here nor there. You're still worth gold and I am skint." Ty smiled.

"All right, then. Come and claim your reward." Retch abruptly released his grip on the boy's arm.

The boy lurched and then teetered on the edge of the well, his arms waving as he tried to shift his body weight away from the fall, but it was useless. He began to topple inward.

Lan'esra ran and jumped toward the boy, grabbing hold of his arm. He wasn't a large child, but big enough that his weight and momentum pulled her forward, and now she too was balanced on the edge of the well.

Ty released his daggers as he stepped forward; Retch dropped his sword and pulled two daggers from his belt.

Rolling his neck, Retch said, "I'm going to enjoy this."

He stepped forward, thrusting and slicing as Ty parried the blows. Their daggers clashed with frantic speed, sparks flying as the blades came together. The men drew back and circled, each taking the measure of his opponent. Then Ty lunged again, in a flurry of attacks. The blades almost sang as they sparkled in the moonlight.

*

Bok squatted, bracing his crossbow on a wooden spoke of the wagon's wheel. He aimed at Ty's back, but the halfling was spinning and turning too quickly for him to get a clear shot.

*

Using every ounce of strength she had, Lan'esra pulled the child up, using her body weight to arch back and lever him up. "Grab the edge!" she shouted. The boy reached up for the top of the well, his hand slipping on the moist brickwork. "*Grab it!*" she screamed. She felt her strength beginning to fade.

His next attempt was successful; the boy gripped the top lip of the well and heaved himself up, getting an elbow onto the top for leverage. She knew she had to let go for him to climb to safety, so she reached down and grabbed his leg to lift him. But she leant too far. Her weight shifted and she began to topple in.

Instinctively she reached for the rope in the centre, grabbing hold of it as she went over. She swung round and wrapped her legs around the rope, and held on desperately. She watched the boy clamber over the edge, and she could hear the blades clashing together as the two men fought above.

Need to go help, she thought, and reached for the edge of the well. It was several inches away and she tried to swing herself back and forth to gain the extra reach. Her fingers finally gripped the top and she gripped with all her strength, the rest of her body swinging around and slamming into the wall.

She rocked slightly, hanging there by one hand, then twisted her body to reach up and grab the lip of the well with her other hand. She strained to pull herself up, but all her strength had gone.

"Ty!" she screamed.

*

Ty twisted his head round at Lan'esra's shout, giving Retch just enough of an opening to cut Ty on the chin with a sweeping riposte. Jumping back, Ty wiped his face and saw the blood on his sleeve.

"Oh dear, what's it going to be? The gold or your bitch?" Retch said with a smile.

"She's not my bitch; I hardly know her," Ty said, taking a backward step closer to the well as Sali came running around the corner with her sword drawn.

"And now outnumbered," Retch said, nodding to his companion.

"TY! I'm going to fall," Lan'esra shouted as one hand began to slip.

"Choices, choices," Retch said, taking a step forward.

"There are no choices. I don't even know her."

Lan'esra's left hand slipped free. "Ty!"

"But she knows you!"

Ty saw Lan'esra's other hand start to slip. Lunging sideways, he reached out and grabbed her wrist. His burnt ribs and side scraped against the wall with searing pain. "Hold on, Lan'esra!" he shouted in agony. He raised his left hand and readied it to parry the oncoming attack.

"Kill him!" Retch shouted, just as Bok fired his crossbow. Sali jumped forward, her sword raised above the stricken thief, but it was the last thing she did. The bolt struck her right in the back of the neck, and she fell forward and toppled into the well, falling past Lan'esra.

"Damn that Rat!" Bok muttered.

Still holding Lan'esra's arm with his right hand, Ty parried, using his left leg and left hand the best he could. Retch's blade sliced his leg, his new leather leggings taking most of the damage. But Ty knew he couldn't hold Retch off much longer, and with one thrashing attack he was proven right, as his dagger went spinning through the air and into the dirt.

Retch didn't waste any time. He swung his dagger into Ty's chest.

Ty braced himself as the dagger clashed against the hard dragon shielding on his chest.

Retch looked at Ty with complete disbelief as he pushed on his dagger. Ty swung his fist and hooked the Baw right on the jaw, spinning him round. Letting the momentum carry him around, he grabbed Lan'esra's other wrist. Leaning against the wall, he looked down at the frightened eyes of the girl in the well and waited for the stab in the back.

*

Lan'esra stared into Ty's expressionless eyes; his face looked different, distant—as if he were staring straight though her. He wasn't trying to pull her up, either. She felt her hands slowly slipping through Ty's grip. She glanced down into the well. "Ty, pull me up," she pleaded. But he didn't—

he just stared down at her, as she began to slide from his hands and into a watery grave.

"Ty!" she screamed again.

Ty blinked and his face changed, as though he had woken from a dream. Lan'esra sobbed with relief as he pulled her up to the lip of the well.

Ty finished pulling Lan'esra to safety before turning to see what had become of the bandit. Retch knelt on the ground, Kern standing behind him with his longsword balanced on his shoulder. Galandrik came forward to help Lan'esra down from the well. "By the gods, lad, you just can't keep out of trouble," the dwarf commented.

"Never could resist easy money," Ty said. "Damn, girl, you are heavier than four bags of coal," he added, looking at Lan'esra.

"Thanks for that," Lan'esra said, still chilled from the intense look on Ty's face moments earlier.

"Looks like you caught the baby snatcher," Kern said to Ty.

Bok cursed and slipped into the shadows of the night.

Chapter Fifteen
The Reward

Kern, Galandrik, Ty, and Lan'esra entered the arena with Retch in front of them, his hands bound.

"You don't have to do this, you know. You could just let me go," Retch begged.

"One hundred gold pieces says differently. Plus, five minutes ago you tried to plunge a dagger into my heart," Ty answered from behind.

"If you were going to be melted in an iron balrog, you'd fight for your life, too."

"What about the missing babies, did they fight?" Kern snarled.

"You're as stupid as the townsfolk. Why would I take babies? He kills them to make me look like a monster! To keep the people scared. Now that I am as good as dead, he will simply find another way to keep the townspeople paying their taxes to ensure their 'protection' against the mighty baby snatchers."

"What about the boy at the well? Explain that!" Galandrik said, shoving Retch in the back.

"Insurance. I told you. We were not going to hurt him, just use him as our ticket out of this fucking shithole. We live like rats in the mountains. We were Heilo's invented enemies. Once he built the massive wall he had to get a threat inside! That's where I come in. We were just prisoners."

In the centre of the arena, six jesters entertained the crowd between acts. As the party entered, the crowd quietened and the jesters stopped, moving to the edges to let them through. There was a deathly silence; the only noise in the arena was from the people and music in the town outside. Heilo shot up from his seat and leaned on the wooden handrail, waving to the guard at the entrance.

"Kern, how dare you walk into *my* arena and stop the proceedings? Your reputation precedes you, but this is intolerable!" Heilo shouted, spit flying from his mouth as rage engulfed his reddened cheeks. Twelve guards ran into the arena and stood in an arc behind Kern and Ty.

"Lord Heilo, we give you Retch, the baby snatcher," Kern shouted, pushing the captive forward and pulling down his hood. The gasps from the crowd changed to boos and hisses, and eventually grew to a chorus of "Balrog! Balrog!"

Heilo turned to Vaelyn, his face contorted with anger. "How can this be?"

"I don't know, my lord," Vaelyn said, eyes wide in disbelief.

"Stop those guards! No babies can go missing now that he has been caught!"

"Yes, lord!" Vaelyn took off running through the door and down the stairs.

Heilo faced the arena, raising his arms until the chanting stopped.

"Well, tonight is a joyous occasion indeed. It looks like our hero Kern has captured the mighty Retch!"

The crowd went crazy and the chanting echoed around the arena: "Kern Ocarn!"

Kern couldn't explain that he had merely turned up, that it was in fact Ty who had done the work; the noise was too loud. He glanced at Ty and shrugged a shoulder. Ty replied with a slight shake of his head.

"Citizens," Heilo said, calming the crowd, "tonight we have even more reason to celebrate! Our babies will be safe from now on. Guards, take him to the cage!" Four guards ran forward and grabbed Retch by the arms, dragging him out of the arena.

"Enjoy your gold," Retch said as he passed Ty.

"Escort Kern and his friends to my house, and let the entertainment continue!" Heilo shouted. The remaining guards led the party out of the arena and through the streets of Wade. In the background, they could hear a chorus of

Kern killed the Retch!
Our babies all sleep well!
Kern killed the Retch!
Let the bastard burn in hell!

*

They followed the guards to Heilo's house. It wasn't as big as they would have thought, but big enough. A six-foot high wall surrounded the house and four guards stood guard at the gate. With a nod from one guard to another, the gate opened and the group was led up the path toward the house. At least thirty feet of grass surrounded the house, and the potted flowers on the lawn made it a joy to see. Lined up in rows, each pot was precisely positioned so that the effect was that of a snake winding through the grass.

"Looks like Heilo likes his garden," Galandrik quipped.

"When he's not roasting people alive," Ty answered.

The guard opened the front door of the house and led them inside. A giant staircase in front of them led up to a balcony. Guards were dotted about. Three closed doors on either side of the staircase were the only visible exits. Tapestries hung on the walls and antiquities stood on marble plinths in the spaces between each door. The guards led them to the right of the stairs and down to the last door, then opened it and gestured for them to enter.

"Make yourselves comfortable," he said as they entered Heilo's study.

"Thank you," Kern replied with a nod.

They entered the study and sat on a bench next to the window. A desk sat opposite the door and a bookshelf stood on the other side of the window. Everything was spotless. The desk was perfectly laid out, everything in order, and the mat on the floor looked like it had never been stepped on. The guard stood at the door, silent, as immobile as a statue.

After some time, the door opened again. Heilo and Vaelyn entered, without acknowledging the group in the slightest.

"Stand for lord Heilo!" the guard bellowed. They all stood up, even though Kern had to give Ty a stare. "Come stand here," the guard added, pointing in front of the desk. Ty rolled his eyes at Lan'esra, but joined the others as they lined up and faced the desk.

Vaelyn stood behind Heilo, who gazed down at his desk, then picked up a small leather book and opened it. He flicked through the pages and, after an agonizing wait, closed it again and set it down. Nodding to the guard, he leaned back in his chair.

"Bow for Lord Heilo," the guard announced and they did, all dropping their heads—apart from Ty, who stared directly at the fat lord.

"Bow for Lord Heilo," the guard said again.

"Not *my* lord," Ty said calmly.

The guard placed his hand on the hilt of his sword. "In the name of Lord—"

Heilo waved his hand before the sword was drawn. "Take him outside. He can wait there."

The guard grabbed Ty's arm and escorted him outside. A bench was hidden under the stairs at the back of the entrance hall, and the guard ushered him to sit on it.

"I have killed men for less," the guard hissed.

"I'm sure you have, sweetheart."

"I'll remember that," the guard said as he went back into the office.

*

"I have spoken to Phiella—the lady whose child you kindly saved—and she has explained what happened with her son and the Baws. For this act of bravery and kindness, I am truly grateful."

"It was Ty who rescued the boy," Lan'esra announced.

"Ty? Who's Ty?"

"The halfling you just kicked out," Kern said.

"The public doesn't want a two-bit halfling. They want a figurehead, a warrior, a great ranger from the north. Fuck Ty."

"Please don't take this as an insult, but you seem very ungrateful towards the person who just prevented another of Wade's children being snatched," Kern added.

Heilo stared for a second, then smiled. "You are so right. I do thank Ty, and this is how." He slid a desk drawer open and pulled out a bag of coins, dropping it on the table. "One hundred gold, as promised. Now—I have had word that you are heading to the east?"

"News does travel fast. Yes, we are heading east, though we may go south first."

"I can get you to Loft within a day."

"Loft in a day? But it will take three days just navigating around these mountains," Galandrik stated.

"Not around them. Over them," Heilo said, leaning forward.

"Over them? How in Hades will we do that?" Kern asked, shrugging his shoulders.

"You will go in one of our cargo air balloons. We send them to Loft every second day to deliver fresh fish and supplies."

"Air balloon? No thanks, I'd rather go by horse!" Galandrik sputtered at the thought.

"Hang on, Galandrik. Think about it. It'll cut a few days off our journey."

"Yes, but in the air!"

"It'll be fun," Lan'esra added.

"What about the mounts?" Kern asked Heilo.

"We will buy them for a good price and you can buy some more in Loft."

"We will speak with Ty, but it sounds good, thank you," Kern answered.

"I will meet you there then," Galandrik said, folding his arms.

*

Ty sat on the bench, watching the blood seep through the bandages on his side, where leaning against the well wall had ripped the scabs from his wound. With a shake of his head, he stood up and tucked his tunic in his leggings. He had a quick look down the line of doors; all was clear. He drew a dagger and with a faint whistle he started to inscribe 'The Rat' into the wood on the underside of the stairs. Just as he was finishing he heard two guards coming up the corridor. He sheathed his dagger and listened as they chatted, hiding in the comfort of the shadows.

"I can't believe Retch has been captured."

"Nor me. I bet Heilo is royally pissed off."

"Yeah, but he would have been even more pissed off if we had snatched that baby."

"That would have made things interesting, to say the least. Retch the baby snatcher behind bars and a baby goes missing!"

"I hated that job."

"I did, too. I dread to think what he did with them after we took them."

"Best not to ask him either."

"Do you think he will let Retch escape again?"

"I doubt if Heilo will let him go like last time. He flogged that guard, you know, even though he himself gave the order to let Retch escape. The man is sick."

"And if it happened twice, he would seem incompetent."

"Plus, Retch might kill another pig on the way out," the guard laughed.

"That's about the only crime he *has* committed. Okay, so they have robbed a few people, but they would starve if they didn't. I'm sure we would do the same."

"Retch the monster, created by Heilo, the even bigger monster."

"I think he will be in the Balrog. Heilo had Dulkin clean it out the other day."

"He did, really? What a shit job."

"Dulkin said it was the worst smell ever. He was gagging the whole time."

"I bet he was."

"He gets all the shit jobs. Did you hear about the latest one?"

"No. Cleaning the sewers?"

"Ha! Not exactly, but there is a rat involved."

"Capturing rats?"

"Nope. You know that ranger who is in town, the one that killed a dragon and a wyvern and tamed a giant?"

"I thought he killed the giant."

"Oh, I don't know. Well, Vaelyn has ordered Dulkin and Jurf to kill them."

"What? But why? And how do you know?"

"You know Vaelyn can't keep his big gob shut. Anyway, apparently King Moriak is sick, and Kern and his friends are on a mission to retrieve some medicines."

"So why kill them?"

"Are you stupid? If the king dies, Heilo can claim the throne!"

"I thought Moriak had a son."

"I don't know. Maybe he can bypass the son. It's just what I heard."

"So what's all this got to do with a rat?"

"Apparently one of the group goes by the name Ty the Rat."

Ty smiled to himself.

"Ah. So how is Dulkin going to kill them?"

"They are to be allowed to use the cargo balloons to journey to Loft as a 'reward' for capturing Retch. But when they get over the mountains, Ty will be a more of a bat than a rat!"

"Ah, the trapdoor flight. That's a shitty way to go. Apparently that advisor who argued with Heilo that taking the babies was insane—in addition to being morally wrong—ended up going through the trapdoor."

"Still, that's a better way to go than fighting Kern hand-to-hand. He *did* kill a dragon," the guard said as they turned on their heels to walk back down the corridor.

"No, he tamed the dragon."

"I heard he killed the giant, then killed the dragon with the giant's club later that afternoon."

"You just made that up."

"I did not!"

"Yes, you did! You'll be saying he flew in on the back of the wyvern next!" The guards disappeared around the corner to the stairs still arguing.

"The trapdoor flight, eh?" Ty said to himself.

"So that's settled then. Where are you staying?"

"We are in the Horse's Head," Kern answered.

"Well, enjoy the rest of your stay. I will have my guards escort you to the balloons just after dawn. Point out your horses to my men and we will sort out the payment for them. And make sure you take whatever you need off of them by morning. Be ready," Heilo said, throwing Kern the bag of gold, which he caught.

"Thanks," Kern said, feeling the weight of the bag.

"No, thank *you*," Heilo said, standing up. "You have saved our town from the vile Retch."

"What will his punishment be?" Galandrik asked.

"Never mind about his punishment. You go on and enjoy the hospitality of our town," Heilo said with a nod to the guard, who opened the door.

Lan'esra and Galandrik thanked Heilo and followed Kern from the room.

Kern walked over to Ty and threw the bag of gold into his lap. "Here, this is yours."

Ty opened the drawstrings. "Thanks. I think this is the most gold I have ever had."

"You earned it. Come on, let's go," Galandrik said, following the guard to the front door of the house.

On their way back to the Horse's Head, they passed the arena and looked in. Two men were fighting; one leg of each was chained to a wooden post.

"I can't be doing with this shit," Kern said.

"Me neither. Come on, the drinks are on me," Ty said. After a short walk through the busy streets of Wade, they reached the inn. It wasn't as crowded as previously, and there were a few spare tables.

"Over there," Galandrik pointed to a corner table. At the bar, a large human male stared at Kern and flicked his head up in an acknowledgment. Kern ignored the man and sat with his friends.

Ty stepped to the bar. "Barkeep! Please bring a meal fit for a king and four jugs of your finest ale. And keep them flowing until I say otherwise." He placed three gold pieces down on the counter. "If this runs out let me know."

The tall human gazed down at Ty. "You're not going to buy us one?" the man said, gesturing with a hand to his four friends next to him. All five men were armoured and loaded down with weapons, wearing dirty leather amour in shades of dark brown and black, with swords and daggers tucked into every possible strap, belt, and boot. They showed every hallmark of bounty hunters.

"Buy our five friends here a drink, too, barkeep," Ty said, staring at the large human. His bearded face was battle-scarred and his stare was intense.

Ty went back to the table. "I don't fancy taking them on. They look proper handy," Ty said, nodding toward the five humans.

"No, don't." Kern smiled, placing his backpack onto the floor. The human raised his jug and smiled at the thief.

"So, tomorrow we take a balloon!" Lan'esra said excitedly.

"I am not getting on a balloon," Galandrik said, thanking the maid as she placed an ale on the table.

"When you were inside with Heilo, I overheard an interesting conversation," Ty said, edging forward to lean over the table. "That balloon is a trap and we are the mice. Heilo is going to double-cross Conn and Moriak and hope the king dies, along with us. He will then try and get the crown for himself."

"Double-crossing pig!" Lan'esra said angrily.

"So that's how he knew so much about us," Kern remarked.

"So will we still take the balloon ride?" Galandrik asked.

"Well, I think so. We will have the drop—excuse the pun—on them, so we can easily take over the balloon before they pull the trapdoor lever," Ty explained.

"Yes, agreed," Kern replied.

"And Retch doesn't steal the babies. It *is* Heilo. He takes them and blames Retch. As long as the town is in fear, he can charge whatever he wants in taxes to pay for their protection. Now Retch has been caught, no more missing babies. The town will not be in fear of that monster."

"That crafty old sod," Galandrik said, as he drained his first jug.

"Retch was telling the truth. He nabbed the kid to try and escape. Heilo has invented this murdering bandit."

"Poor Retch. But he is still a dirty bandit," Lan'esra added.

"You made one hundred gold, too," Kern added.

"Yeah, fuck the gold. He is getting away with murder, literally."

"Don't even think about going up against him, Ty," Kern said, beckoning the maid.

"I'm not, but it pisses me off," Ty said, slamming his jug down on the edge of the table. It bounced off and fell to the floor next to Kern's backpack. As he reached down to pick it up, Ty quickly slipped his hand into the backpack, taking an item and slipping it into his tunic.

"We really don't have the time to mess around with these problems. If you remember, my father is in a cage. We are on a quest."

"No, you are right. And with the balloon ride, we'll gain back the two days we lost coming here to heal me, so all is well," Ty said, pushing back his chair.

"Where are you going?" Kern asked.

"I will be ten minutes. When I was outside waiting for you, that lady—erm, Katrina, I think she said her name was—you remember, with the boy that Retch had? She said to come and see the boy. He wanted to say thanks."

"Oh, all right. See you soon, then."

"Yes, I will just go look at his cut head. I'll be back before you have finished the next drink," Ty said as he left.

"That's a nice gesture," Galandrik noted once Ty was gone.

"Yes, apart from the fact that he isn't going to see any kid," Kern said with a smirk.

"What? But—"

"Remember? Heilo told us her name was Phiella, not Katrina."

"So he did! What's he up to then?"

"*And* he just pickpocketed the teleportation potion from my backpack. Well, actually, he failed miserably at that."

"You're not making any sense," Galandrik said, scratching his beard.

"He's going to free Retch."

"Free…? But—"

"Retch isn't a monster or a baby snatcher. Ty wouldn't let him burn in the Balrog."

"He does have feelings, then," the dwarf laughed.

"I'm not too sure. When he had me by the wrist in the well, I am a hundred percent positive that if you hadn't turned up, he would have let me fall," Lan'esra said, waiting for the response.

"Don't talk stupid. He can be vicious, as you saw with the torturer, but you haven't done him any harm," Kern said.

"What about when I mentioned the diamond?"

"Ty wouldn't kill you for that," Kern said angrily.

"I agree, lass."

"Well, maybe it was me, then. Maybe I was just so scared of falling I imagined it."

"Yes, and don't ever mention this again," Kern said, as three maids walked over with a roasted pig and all the trimmings.

*

Retch knelt in his cage, hanging a few feet from the ground in the town's central square. The Balrog stood several feet away, and Retch couldn't bear to look at it. Hordes of people had come to see him, spitting and poking, throwing mud and stones, and dried blood stuck to the side of his face where the missiles had cut him. The crowds had eased now and only four guards remained surrounding the cage, standing about ten feet away.

"Well, look who we have here, Ty the Prat," Retch laughed bitterly. Ty spat in the cage in full view of the guards and jumped up, grasping the bars while his feet rested on the bottom of the cage in between them. The whole contraption rocked from side to side.

"Shut it, you filthy scum!" Ty shouted. One of the guards started forward until another shouted, "Leave him. He is one of the ones who captured him." The guard stepped back.

"So, you got your one hundred gold coins and captured the big bad monster. Very well done. I bet you're so pleased."

"Listen, just shut up for a moment," Ty said quietly. "I was wrong and I apologise."

"Oh, well, that's okay then. I will remember that when I am roasting to death in that fucking iron coffin."

"Do you ever shut up? Just be quiet for one second."

Retch stared at Ty emotionlessly.

"Good, now listen. Next to my foot is a teleportation potion and gold coins." Retch immediately went to move. "Don't take it now, or *I'll* be in the Balrog!" Retch resumed his position.

"By all means get the items once I have gone, but don't drink it for at least an hour or until you've had at least one more visitor. They will guess it's me if you go now."

"All right, but there must be a catch. Why are you doing this?"

"Let's just say a little bird told me you don't kill babies."

Retch stared at Ty. "I will never forget you for this."

"How could you forget a prat like me? I will jump down and throw a stone at you. Make sure you roll over when it hits. That will give you cover to pick the items up."

"Thanks. Don't throw it too hard," Retch said with a smile.

"It has to be convincing," Ty said, jumping down.

Ty jumped down and picked up a stone. "What a piece of scum!" he said to the guard, launching it at Retch. It struck him on his arm and he rolled over with a groan.

"Make sure you burn him good," he said to the guard.

"Oh, we will. Don't you worry, Master Ty."

Ty smiled back, loving the fact that the guard knew his name, even if it *was* just because they wanted to kill him.

*

Ty entered the inn and joined the others as they were finishing off the food. "Hello. Told you I wouldn't be long," Ty announced, sitting down next to Galandrik.

"How's the kid?" the dwarf asked.

"What kid? Oh, I couldn't find them. They must have forgotten. The hog looks good," Ty said, slicing a piece of pork off.

"It tastes good too," Kern answered.

"I think I can manage a few more rounds," Ty said, remembering the pouch he had stolen from Bok. He emptied the contents on the table and counted out coins adding up to just under three gold, a ruby on a chain, and a folded-up piece of paper with a 'C' and an outline of a bird on it. "What's that?" Ty asked, examining the piece of paper.

"That is a paperfinch," Lan'esra said.

"A paper what?" Ty said, confused.

"It's a messenger bird made of paper. Whatever mage makes them gives them to people and they will fly back to the mage with whatever message you say."

"Oh yes, I have seen them before."

"Some more powerful mages can give them sight, and some speed. It all depends on the level of the spell. I think the ruby is what they call the finch's nest. If the mage sends a message back it will go to whoever has that ruby. It's worthless unless you have the other ruby that pairs it."

"Really? Listen to this, then," Ty said, holding the piece of paper to his mouth in his cupped hands. "Everybody is dead and I killed them. Ty the Rat killed them all," Ty said. Smiling, he held his hand open. "Fly," he said, and the finch flew up and out the open window.

"You're a bad man," Galandrik said, smiling.

"So are you looking forward to our windy, bumpy balloon ride tomorrow?" Ty asked.

"No. I'm not happy, lad."

"It'll be fine," Lan'esra said, shaking her head at Ty.

*

The fireworks had begun, and the night sky was lit up with lights of all colours as they exploded. The townsfolk all stood watching the annual spectacle.

Retch jumped at the sudden bang of the fireworks erupting in the sky. The town square lit up and all the guards looked up to watch. He held the pouch of gold and potion in his bound hands and flicked the cork stopper out. "Fuck you, Heilo," he muttered under his breath, then lifted the potion to his lips and gulped it down.

All around his body, little green lights like fireflies circled and twisted faster and faster, twirling and turning round and round until each one exploded into a tiny puff of green sparkles. The cage was empty and the baby snatcher was gone.

Bok sat at a table with his back to Galandrik and listened. "Balloon ride…" he whispered to himself.

Chapter Sixteen
The Balloon Ride

It was just after dawn and Kern, Galandrik, and Ty stood outside the Horse's Head Inn. Some townsfolk wandered home, still drunk and singing from the previous night's events.

"The walk of shame. It's been a while since we did that, eh Kern?" Ty laughed.

"Yes. Remember in Raith, when we got that drunk we couldn't remember where the horses were?"

"Yes, I remember. Ended up we never forgot where they were; we'd lost them at dice."

"*Who* lost them at dice?"

"Oh, so you can't remember where the horses were, but you can remember me losing at dice."

"I remember you trying to go bareback on the cow."

"Who went bareback on a cow?" Lan'esra said, walking around the corner with two of Heilo's guards.

"Never mind. You had to be there," Ty said, picking up his backpack.

Kern showed the guards which horses were theirs and the guard gave him some gold. All four grabbed their belongings and followed the guards through the town. The aftermath of the evening's events was plain to see; bunting and other rubbish blew all over the streets. As they passed the town centre, they saw that the cage in the middle was empty. Next to the cage were four men with their heads in stocks.

"Who are those men and what happened to Retch?" Lan'esra asked, trying to sound surprised.

"Didn't you hear?" one of the guards answered.

"Hear what?"

"He escaped last night."

"Escaped? How the hell did he escape?" Lan'esra questioned.

"He turned into a snake and slithered away while the guards watched the fireworks. They will be publicly flogged today."

"Turned into a snake? I thought he was a bandit, not a mage?" Kern interrupted.

"Retch is evil. He sacrifices babies to please his gods. The reward he gets is snake form."

They reached the north end of the town and entered a small courtyard. It was surrounded by a wooden fence, and a barrier blocked their entry until another guard lifted it as they approached. Crates, barrels, and boxes were spread all around, and men scurried about busily loading the cargo crates.

In the centre of the yard sat four massive cargo balloons. Their baskets were ten feet in the air and ladders leaned up against them. The balloons were huge, easily seventy feet from the basket to the very top. They were tethered down with ropes, and between the ropes on the ground under each basket were crates and barrels, all squashed together in huge cargo nets. Men rushed about, loading the nets with all manner of boxes and bags.

Fixed to the underneath of each basket was a long tubular pipe with a propeller at one end. Gnomes had the side covers of the pipe open and their heads buried inside, working furiously on each one.

"What are they doing?" Ty asked.

"Just last minute checks. They invented balloon travel. These gnomes are the engineers who will make your journey safe."

"Brilliant. We rely on these... gnomes?" Galandrik said, shaking his head.

At that moment, a male gnome walked up, wearing brown leather leggings and jacket, and a skull cap with a thick pair of glasses on top of his leather pilot's cap. He took off a leather glove and extended a hand to Kern.

"Hello, you must be Kern and company. I am Panoil Fizzlehouse, your pilot to Loft."

"Pleased to meet you. This is Ty, Galandrik, and Lan'esra," Kern said, introducing the party.

Panoil shook all their hands in turn. "I will be in the front balloon and you will be in the last. It's the personnel basket. You can't ride in the others because of weight issues with the cargo underneath."

"Weight? We don't weigh that much," Galandrik questioned.

"Well, if we consider a horizontal acceleration to negate the drag of the net external force and the weight of the gravitational constant, that is equal to thirty-two feet per second, then solving for the mass and substituting in the force equation is…" Panoil said, scratching his head.

"I believe you," Galandrik said, walking past Panoil over to the basket, examining the nuts and bolts.

"So, these baskets are all hitched together?" Ty asked.

"Yes, they can all self-navigate because they all have directional rudders, but these three only use them if they are separated from the pilot basket. The pilot basket does all the work here."

"So you steer the front and we basically get towed?" Kern questioned.

"That is exactly it. The thrust-to-weight ratio is directly proportional to the acceleration of the balloon. A balloon with a high thrust-to-weight ratio has high acceleration. For most flight conditions, an aircraft with—"

"Okay, okay. We understand! Just get us there in one piece," Kern interrupted.

"Of course, Mr Kern," Panoil said, nodding at Ty and Lan'esra as he walked past them over to the engineers working on the propellers. "No, no! Don't grease the oil rod injectors. And clean those gland expanders!" he shouted.

"Are you sure about this?" Ty said to Kern.

"Go buy some potions of featherfall just in case," Kern laughed.

"That is not a bad suggestion," Ty replied, remembering the jump from the orc tower's top window.

"Potions of featherfall?" Lan'esra asked.

"Yes. It does exactly what it says on the bottle. You fall like a feather."

"That is brilliant. I have never heard of them."

"There's a shock," Ty muttered.

Two men entered the courtyard dressed in brown leather armour, cloaks, and boots. Each man held a backpack and had a bastard sword sheathed at his side. They were identical, except for their faces.

Dulkin and Jurf, I take it? Ty thought.

"They could have brought some different clothes," Kern murmured.

"Hello!" Ty said as the two men approached them.

"Hello. My name is Dulkin, and this is Jurf."

"Well, hello, Dulkin and Jurf. I am Fotranus the goat trader, and these are my friends Petloriven and Kelsa," Ty said, indicating Kern and Lan'esra.

Dulkin frowned at Jurf. "Nice to meet… you."

"What's the matter? You seem a tad confused," Ty said to the pair of guards.

"Not confused, but… is this balloon the only one flying today?"

"I think there is another one leaving in about five minutes," Kern interrupted.

"Five minutes? From where?" Jurf stuttered.

"Heilo put a special one on for some famous group of adventurers. It's at the other end of town, near the main gate—"

Before Kern could finish, Dulkin and Jurf turned and sprinted from the courtyard.

"You two are bad men," Lan'esra laughed.

"No, *they* were bad men, ordered to kill us," Ty pointed out. "Remember?"

"Fotranus the goat trader?" Kern said to Ty.

"I was under pressure."

"I wanted to burst out laughing," Kern said.

"Mr Kern!" Panoil shouted, standing with one foot on the bottom rung of the ladder.

"Well, looks like this is us," Kern said, picking up his backpack, long bow, and quiver. All four climbed the ladder leading up to the basket and stood inside. The area inside the basket was a lot more spacious than they had expected.

"What was wrong with that ladder?" Kern asked in a whisper as they got settled. "It had like a thousand rungs!"

"Must be a gnome ladder," Lan'esra answered. "Short legs and all that."

"I'm not happy about this," Galandrik moaned under his breath.

There was one row of seats on either side of the basket and two seats at either end that folded up, allowing people to get in and out. The bottom of the balloon was about six feet in diameter and just below this was a large bowl suspended from the balloon by steel rods. Flames rose from the bowl into the balloon.

They each grabbed a seat and sat down. The atmosphere was sullen.

"Hello," a gnome said, getting into the basket. "I am Gelbus Finespanner." They greeted the gnome and watched as three other gnomes climbed up into their respective baskets. They could see Panoil waving, and each gnome waved back one by one. Panoil's balloon slowly started to lift. They could see the flame shooting up into each of the balloons, and jumped when the flame burst out of their own lantern into the open space of the balloon. Their basket slowly lifted as the gnomes on the ground released the guy lines. Once the balloons started to take the weight of the cargo, the flame burst got more ferocious and they could feel the heat as the cargo lifted from the ground.

"Here we go! Hang onto your hats," Gelbus said, firing another flame burst into the balloon.

All four balloons rose from the ground of the courtyard, Panoil's the highest, with the other three balloons in a line behind attached by thick hemp ropes. The cargo hung in nets below and the courtyard gradually got further away.

"Look," Lan'esra said, pointing down to the ground. Everybody peered over and saw Dulkin and Jurf run back into the yard, waving their fists up at the balloons. Ty waved back and smiled.

"Another two stocks required when Heilo finds out they missed the balloon," Lan'esra said.

"Yes, they will be punished, for sure," Kern answered.

Galandrik suddenly leapt up from his seat and leaned over the side. The contents of his stomach fell from the sky before he sat back down. "I don't like this," he said, wiping his mouth. The others all laughed.

*

Soon the balloons were high above Wade, and still rising. Even so, the mountains loomed far above them, and they wrapped their cloaks tighter around their shoulders against the cooler air. The grey-fanged mountains were awe-inspiring as the balloons rose into the morning sky. As they neared the top of the snow-hooded peaks, the party could clearly see the necklace of white encasing the summits. Clouds lingered around the tops of the mountains like pipe tobacco clinging to the ceiling in the Orc's Armpit. Soon the balloons were high above cloud and mountain, and Wade was a fast-fading speck in the distance below. They travelled east above the snowy peaks, and the sun over the Voltic Sea in the distance was lovely.

"That is some view," Lan'esra said. To the south they could see the great Fortune Lake and, even further to the south, the Greenwood Mountains. The Voltic Isle with its small collection of mountains looked like a small sailing vessel and its sails far, far in the distance under the rising morning sun. They could feel the warmth on their faces and the view from here left them speechless. Even Ty, for once, was at a loss for words.

Holding his hand up to shield the morning sun from his eyes, Kern looked for the town Loft. "I think it's directly in front, just to the left of that tree line."

"Yes, correct. We should be there by midday," Gelbus said.

*

An hour passed and the balloons had cleared the Wade Mountains. Below the balloons were the green open plains of east Bodisha, and Loft was visible now on the coastline. The Eastern Mountains appeared never-ending in the distance, spanning as far as the eye could see from north to south.

They heard a sudden screech, and the moment of surveying Bodisha's beauty was gone. Fear replaced tranquillity as Kern grabbed his long bow.

"Did you hear that?" Ty said, looking all around.

"Yes. Get to arms," Kern replied, notching an arrow.

The screech was heard again, louder.

"What is it?" Gelbus asked, rotating his head to pinpoint the noise.

"A wyvern," Kern said coldly.

"A wyvern?" Gelbus replied. "What's a blasted wyvern?"

"That!" Galandrik replied as Draygore appeared from the clouds above, soaring down toward their basket. Kern unleashed two arrows. One flew past Draygore, and one stuck the creature in the thigh. The wyvern's giant talons gripped the front of the basket, slashing as it took to the air again; the basket tore like paper, leaving one side ripped to shreds. One of the ropes that held the cargo was slashed, making it swing wildly underneath, tipping the basket forward. All five clung on as gravity tried to drag them out.

"Ty, cut the other cargo lines!" Kern shouted, regaining his balance.

Ty pulled up the split rope and quickly tied it around his waist. Gelbus sent a burst of flame into the balloon, trying to regain some control.

"Where is it?" Galandrik said, holding his axe.

"I don't know! It's disappeared!"

Draygore swooped down again, this time from the back; the beast's advantage in air combat was plain to see. Its twisting and turning was almost like a fish turning in water.

"Gelbus, watch out!" Lan'esra shouted, but it was too late. Flying past at devastating speeds, Draygore snatched the gnome in its giant jaws.

"Galandrik, help me. Ty, we need to get to the other balloon."

Galandrik and Kern started to heave on the rope and slowly closed the gap between the balloons. Draygore swooped down again, this time targeting the lead balloon, ripping at its basket. With the wyvern's second attack, Panoil fell, and they all watched in horror as he disappeared down toward the ground.

"That's it!" Ty shouted.

"What's it?" Kern replied, still pulling on the rope.

"The balloons are touching above, they won't get any closer." Ty pointed upward, and they looked up at the touching balloons; the gap between baskets was about five feet.

"Quick, get across and throw us some rope," Kern ordered as he tied off the rope to stop the baskets drifting apart again.

Ty didn't hesitate. With a quick leap, he skipped across the rope and jumped into the third basket.

Ty threw across two ropes. "This is it. Tie them around your waist and run."

"You must be kidding," Galandrik said, shaking his head.

"Look!" Kern pointed as the lead balloon, its basket in tatters, began to sink, dragging the others down.

"I'll go release the balloon. You three get across here," Ty shouted as he ran to the front end of the basket.

Kern had started to tie his rope when the wyvern struck the back of the basket, gripping with his claws. Lan'esra brought her mace down on its razor-sharp talons. With a screech, it disappeared up into the clouds.

Ty reached the second balloon, skipping across the ropes like a trapeze artist. "Can you steer this if I release the front balloon?" Ty asked the gnome. He got no answer; the gnome stared blankly into the bottom of the basket. Ty slapped the gnome across his face, waking him from his trance. "Panoil and Gelbus are gone! Can you fly this balloon if I release the front one?"

The gnome shook his head, as if to shake away the sight of his friend falling. "Yes, of course. Turn that wheel," he replied, pointing at a small wheel across the basket. "It's a safety device. It'll cut the rope that connects the front balloon underneath ours."

Ty stepped over and pushed with all his strength, but it didn't budge. "It's stuck!"

"The other way! Turn it the other way!" the gnome shouted, jerking his head in the direction he wanted Ty to turn. Ty pulled upward and the wheel started turning. After two turns Ty heard a crunch from under the basket, and the front balloon started to drift downwards.

"Thanks," Ty said.

*

"I am no tightrope walker," Galandrik moaned.

"Jump then," Lan'esra said, tying the rope around her waist.

"It's too far," Galandrik said, looking at the gap between the baskets.

"Rubbish!" She threw her mace across into the next basket and backed up, then sprinted and jumped. She landed, hitting the basket's handrail with her waist. She rolled over and in, then untied her rope and threw it back. "Your turn!"

Galandrik began fastening his rope around his waist, and looked at Kern. "You go first. At least if I fall, you can pull me up," he said.

Kern took the longest run-up he could, ran, and jumped, landing the same way Lan'esra had and rolling into the basket.

"Jump!" Lan'esra shouted to the dwarf.

Galandrik threw his axe, which Kern caught. He was standing at the back of the basket readying himself for the leap when Draygore flew down and ripped into the basket again. Galandrik fell over with the sudden impact as it rocked from side to side, and slowly the balloon started to descend.

"JUMP!" Kern shouted as the dwarf got to his feet. Galandrik leapt from the edge with no run up and only just managed to grab the bottom of the basket.

"Kern!" he shouted. The ranger leaned over and grabbed the dwarf by his collar and, using every ounce of strength he had, pulled him into the basket. The basket they had started in dropped with the weight of its cargo, and the rope joining the two baskets drew taut. Kern drew his sword, leaned over, and swung it. With two swipes, he cut the rope and the basket plummeted to the ground.

"We need to do something. Two baskets left and not for much longer," Ty said, climbing into their basket.

"What do you think?" Kern said notching another arrow.

"You're the leader," Ty replied, looking around in the basket as if for some sort of divine intervention.

"Oh, it's *my* group now!"

"Weight it down," Lan'esra said.

"Well, you always get the glory for *our* actions!"

"Weigh the wyvern done," she said, slightly louder.

"So that's what this is all about? Because they knew my name and not the mighty Ty—"

"WEIGH IT DOWN!" she screamed.

Ty and Kern stopped arguing and turned to Lan'esra. "Weigh what down?" they said together.

"The wyvern! If we can attach the balloon to it somehow, it'll fall from the sky," she explained.

Ty stared at Kern and raised an eyebrow.

"Why couldn't one of you two have thought of that?" Galandrik said, looking up at the oncoming wyvern. "And whatever you decide to do, do it quick."

Kern fired a trio of arrows. One missed, but two struck the wyvern in the shoulder blade, slowing Draygore for a second or two. Then it swooped again, straight toward the basket.

"Brace yourselves!" Kern shouted as the wyvern hit the basket. This time it stretched its head into the basket, its razor-sharp teeth dripping with saliva. Biting and snarling, it backed the foursome up against the basket wall, virtually squashing the gnome behind them.

Ty leapt forward, bringing his dagger up under Draygore's huge head. Twice he stabbed as green-black blood poured onto his hands. The wyvern thrashed its head, knocking Ty over the handrail. Then, with the dagger still sticking out of its neck, it took to flight, circling above the balloon.

"Ty!" Kern shouted as he looked over the basket handrail. He saw him below, underneath on the cargo net.

"I'm fine. If we can keep him close for a few seconds, I can jump up and tie one of these ropes onto his leg," Ty shouted up.

"Then where will you go?" Galandrik asked.

"I will jump across to that other cargo net."

"It's too far for a standing jump; you need a rope," Kern added.

"Throw me one then," Ty shouted upward, "and hurry! It's coming back."

Kern had just bent down to pick up the rope from the basket floor when Draygore hit the side of the basket, its claws ripping through.

Ty cut through one of the cargo ropes and started to climb up another, toward the basket. The wyvern's great clawed feet bit into the edge of the basket above him, and he threw the rope around one of the beast's legs and tied it as tightly as he could.

Draygore roared and lurched forward, snapping and snarling within inches of Lan'esra's face. She backed away, the vileness of the creature's breath filling her nostrils.

Galandrik steadied himself and swung his axe, smashing into the wyvern's shoulder just above the wing. Black blood sprayed out over them as Draygore screamed and pushed off into the air.

Ty let go of the rope he was holding and dropped, landing on the cargo net. Draygore flew ten feet before the rope around its leg tightened, pulling the basket. Kern, Galandrik, and Lan'esra held on as the basket tipped back and forth from the wyvern's thrashing.

Ty furiously hacked away at the next rope connecting the cargo to the basket.

Kern looked down at Ty. "Cut the ropes!"

Ty worked on the rope with his dagger. "What do you think I'm doing?" he shouted back up at the ranger.

The wyvern dived downward, trying to break its restraints. The rope again tightened, and the cargo swung and dipped with the force of the wyvern's struggles. Ty slipped and fell, just managing to grab the net. His dagger fell from his grip, falling to the ground below.

"I'm going down," Kern said, pulling up the second rope that Ty had cut and tying it around his waist. He climbed over the edge of the basket. Galandrik handed him his sword and he dropped down onto the cargo. Reaching down, he grabbed Ty's wrist and pulled him up onto the net.

Only two ropes of the original four were still connecting the cargo to the basket, Kern had a cut one around his waist and another was attached to the wyvern's leg.

"I'm going to slice this one; hold on!" Kern shouted as he swung his sword. It cut through the penultimate rope and the cargo net swung. Some crates fell from the net, plummeting to the ground.

"Tie that one around your waist," Kern said to Ty, raising his sword, ready to hit the last rope. Ty tied off the rope and nodded. Just then Draygore flew up, dragging the net, forcing Kern and Ty to lose their balance, then twisted in the air before heading straight toward them.

"Cut it!" Galandrik shouted from above. Kern swung just as Draygore reached Ty, grabbing Ty by his leg and lifting back into the air. Ty hung upside down, reaching for his daggers, but they were gone. One was still sticking out under the wyvern's jaw.

Kern stopped before he swung, knowing that the cargo would fall, dragging the wyvern to the ground. And if the creature still had Ty's leg, it would be ripped off.

"I can't! Throw my bow," he said, sheathing his sword. Galandrik's head disappeared for an instant, then reappeared next to Kern's bow. "Catch!" the dwarf shouted, dropping the bow.

Kern caught it and called, "Quiver! Quickly!"

Galandrik held it out and dropped it just as Draygore spun in the air, snapping at Ty. The sudden movement made Kern lurch, and he missed his quiver. It landed on the net next to him and the arrows all slid out, falling to the ground. Kern reached and grabbed it, looking inside. One arrow left. He notched it and aimed.

"Ty, show me his heart!" Kern shouted over to the upside-down thief. Ty heard and looked up at Draygore as its snarling, snapping jaws came toward him, close enough for him to grab his dagger—still protruding from under the wyvern's head—with both hands. With all his strength, he pushed the blade up into the beast's mouth, lifting its head. Kern unleashed his arrow; it flew straight and true, missing Ty's arms by inches and striking Draygore in the chest.

Instantly Ty dropped, pulling his dagger clear and swinging toward Kern, thudding into the remains of the cargo. Draygore flew up, flapping its mighty wings, then they stopped and its head rolled back. Body arching backward, the wyvern fell like a stone.

"Hold on!" Kern shouted, wrapping his arm in the net.

Draygore, still attached by the rope, swung back and forth under the net before coming to a stop. The balloon began to drop.

"Release the creature, it's too heavy!" the gnome shouted down.

Ty got to his feet and raised Kern's sword. "Time to drop off some unwanted cargo."

"Just cut it," Kern shouted.

Draygore swung its body round and snapped one last time at Ty—who fell backward with a scream—before the beast swung back down under the cargo net. Kern grabbed the sword from Ty. "You scream like a girl." He swung his sword and cut the rope.

Draygore dropped like a black stone towards Bodisha.

After a few moments to catch their breath, Ty and Kern climbed back up into the basket, which Galandrik and Lan'esra were trying to repair as best they could.

"What *was* that thing?" she asked, sitting down and wiping Draygore's black blood from her tunic.

"Just an old friend," Galandrik answered.

"You *knew* that?"

"Well, if it's the same one, then yes. We killed its partner last time we met," the dwarf said. He saw Ty's head twitch out of the corner of his eye and hastily added, "Well, young Master Ty here burnt it to a crisp, to be precise."

"You gained some valuable experience for the second fight then," she smiled.

"I can't believe I lost another dagger. Only had it a day," Ty said, cleaning the remaining blade.

"I lost all my arrows and quiver," Kern added.

"Backpacks!" Lan'esra said.

"Shit! They were in the first basket." Kern cursed. "Oh well, nothing important apart from the potion of teleportation," he added with a sly wink at the dwarf.

"Damn, that could have come in handy, too," Ty said, not looking up.

"I think we will be okay. Everything seems fine and steady," the gnome shouted across.

"Good. Just get us to Loft," Kern replied, lying back in the basket.

"How much cargo did we lose?" Lan'esra asked.

"There are two boxes and a few sacks left on here," Ty said, looking down. "We lost a lot. Well, *we* didn't, Heilo did."

"I wonder what's in those crates."

"No idea, but someone below is going to have a field day," Ty answered, sitting back down.

"Is there any food anywhere?" Galandrik said. "I am starving."

"What's new?" Ty laughed, closing his eyes.

Chapter Seventeen
The Green Dragon

The two balloons and the passengers hovered just above Loft and gradually descended down to an open yard where workers waited patiently with barrows and carts. It was mid-afternoon and the sky was clear blue. The seagulls that welcomed fishermen home after days at sea flew all around them, swooping and floating gracefully on the air currents. Their cries sounded like laughter, and the inquisitive ones often landed on the edge of the baskets, searching to steal their next meal.

The fresh, salty smell of the chilly sea was in the air as the easterly winds blew in from the harsh waters. The Voltic Isle stood proud in the distance, looking as menacing as its reputation. Many ships had been wrecked against the rocky coastline in the rough storms that surrounded the Isle. Historians said that the Voltic Isle had been created the day Theador, the ancient god of war, threw a fireball down into the sea in a rage against humans. When the icy waters froze the fireball, it formed the Voltic Isle. Others believed it to be an ancient volcanic isle, as the name suggested. Whatever the truth, the old volcanic rock that had spilled out hundreds of moons ago had formed its formidable defences, which made the coast line very hazardous.

In some ways, Loft was a fishing town like so many villages and towns dotted along the coastline, its residents priding themselves on the splendid variety of fish they caught and sold, but in other ways the city was in a class of its own. Loft was synonymous with bandits, pirates, thieves, cutthroats, bribery, and corruption. The man running the town was Lokin, an ex-naval man who had served in King Moriak's sea fleet. After Lokin lost an arm in battle, Moriak had posted him to Loft, mainly to tidy it up and suppress its notorious reputation, neither of which he had done. Lokin, the self-proclaimed Lord of Loft, had instead exploited the trading industry, and his financial gains through piracy had made him allegedly one of the richest men in Bodisha.

"Get ready for landing," the gnome pilot said when they hovered a few feet above the ground. The cargo gently touched down as groundworkers threw ropes up for the gnomes to tie off. Once the ropes on each balloon were tied, they fired up, lifting the balloons and making the ropes go taut. Two ladders were rested against the sides of the baskets and a human footed each ladder.

"Down you come, my lovelies!" a voice from the ground shouted. As they descended, they saw that the voice belonged to a fat human, who wore black leather leggings to match his dirty black boots. A red silk shirt was tucked into his leggings; a black silk sash was tied around his large midriff, keeping his sabre secure, and he had a red spotted bandana over his bald head.

"What the hell happened to the basket? It's ripped to shreds," the man said. "And where is the cargo and the other balloons—shouldn't there be four?"

"We lost two pilots, two balloons, and a load of cargo en route, Scoff. We were attacked in mid-flight," the gnome pilot explained.

"Attacked? Attacked by who?" Scoff asked.

"A dragon."

"There hasn't been a dragon around here in years."

"It wasn't a dragon, it was a wyvern," Kern interrupted.

"A wyvern, you say? Sorry, I am Scoff," he said, extending a hand which Kern shook.

"I am Kern and these are my friends, Ty, Galandrik, and Lan'esra."

"Kern the giant slayer, eh? Nice to make your acquaintance. It looks like trouble must just follow you around," he said, looking at the ripped basket.

"Yes, bad luck," Kern answered, raising an eyebrow at Ty. "We need a boat."

"You need a boat, do you, lad? What do you need a boat for? You don't look like sailors."

"Not to keep, just a ride to the Voltic Isle."

"Dangerous place, that isle. I have lost many a good friend to them rocky shores. Why do you head there?"

"Never mind that. Can you sort us out a ride or not?" Ty said, stepping forward.

"What do we have here? A brave little one who speaks his mind. You must be the Rat."

Ty smiled. "Yes, I am the Rat. You know of a vessel that can get us to the isle?" he said, full of self-importance.

"There will be someone who can take you. Go to the Dock Tavern Inn tonight and I will introduce you to someone. But be careful with that tongue of yours; you know they throw rats overboard."

"We will be there," Ty replied. "How much will it cost?"

"You'll have to ask the captain. It's a very dangerous journey."

"How hard can it be?" Ty shrugged.

"It seems a simple enough journey," Kern added.

"You landlubbers don't have the first clue what lurks out in them dark depths. The stories I could tell you would put you off ever stepping foot onto a boat. Then you have the storms and winds that rush around the Voltic Isle. It's a terrible place to try and get to, and getting back is just as bad. I know stories of people who went there and weren't able to return for months. When someone finally got to the isle to rescue them, they had been turned to rock. Three statues to serve as a warning to other fools—" he looked around at Lan'esra, Kern, Ty, and Galandrik— "who want to go there and loot the dungeon treasures."

"We aren't looking for treasure. We are after fighort leaf," Kern explained.

"Whatever you seek, hear my warnings: That isle is evil. Take precautions, and I wish you all the luck in Bodisha. By the gods, will you need it." Scoff turned to his men. "What are you waiting for? Get them boxes loaded up or you'll be sorry you woke up this morning!"

"This quest gets better and better," Galandrik said.

"Don't worry, it's never as bad as it seems. Trust me," Ty said.

"Better and better," Kern said, following and shaking his head.

"Do *they* ever get any better?" Lan'esra asked Galandrik.

"Nope. This is as good as it gets," Galandrik answered.

*

The waiting wagons were loaded with the boxes, barrels, and crates that had survived the journey from Wade. When the last of the cargo had been loaded and the workers had moved off, shouting and laughing, to their next task, one of the boxes shuddered and the lid was pushed open from within. A leather-clad hand appeared, and then another, as the lid opened more and more. Finally a head appeared from the darkness, eyes squinting to adjust to the light. When he was sure no one was watching, Bok climbed from his wooden home.

"Now, where is that Rat?"

*

Kern, Ty, Galandrik, and Lan'esra stood on the docks of Loft. Hundreds of boats lined the quayside, from small fishing boats to large cargo ships, all protected by the sea wall surrounding the harbour. The only way in was through the pier heads. Each pier had a tower with a beacon at the top; this was lit and used to guide the ships in through the pier heads when the seas were raging. Many a ship had sunk trying to get through there at night. They walked past a massive warehouse boasting hundreds of boxes full of different types of fish, being sold at auction. Seafood, fresh or dried, was a staple food for much of the coastal population.

Further along the quay was the Dock Tavern. It looked exactly as they had expected: rough. It was situated quite near the quay edge; sailors and fishermen could literally step off their vessel and into the tavern. They could hear the singing and shouting from where they stood.

"Fancy a pint?" Galandrik asked.

"Nope, I need to get another dagger and equipment," Ty mumbled. "Skint again."

"How can you be skint?" Kern asked. "I gave you one hundred gold coins two days ago."

"Well, you know, this and that. It soon goes," Ty lied, not wanting to admit he had given fifty gold pieces to Retch.

"No, I don't know 'this and that,'" Kern said. He knew Ty would never tell him the truth about his money, no matter how much of it he had.

"You have money from the horses. Just be happy we aren't completely skint. This time last year I was stealing our dinner," Ty said abruptly.

"You don't miss much, do you?" Kern said, smiling.

"It's just part of my charm," Ty smiled back.

Kern thought for a second or two. "Right. Ty is right—*before* we start drinking we need to get everything we need for the Dungeon of Dreams. We lost a lot on the balloon ride."

"All right. Meet back here as soon as we are all done. We will leave as soon as we can. What time did Scoff say be here?" Ty asked.

"He just said tonight, but I can't see us leaving in the dark," Galandrik explained.

"Remember, it will cost us to travel. If they charter a ship just for us, I dread to think what it'll cost. So don't spend everything—we may need it," Kern added.

"Also, everyone make sure to buy ranged weapons, too. I have a feeling we will all need them," Galandrik added.

The group parted ways, then headed off into Loft to purchase their supplies and weapons for the journey ahead.

*

Conn sat at his desk. His head jolted upward as Queen Cherian entered his study. "This better be important, Conn," the queen hissed. "Why bring me here?"

"I had a message back from Bok, my queen," Conn said, standing up. "Well, from Bok's ruby, that is."

"So? You could have come to me to tell me that!"

"No, these walls have no ears. I trust your halls and rooms have many."

"Very well. You said from Bok's ruby?"

"Well, it's… well… strange."

"Please stop with these riddles, wizard. Either tell me the message now or I will—"

"'Everybody is dead and I killed them. Ty the Rat killed them all!'" Conn said, waiting for Queen Cherian's reaction.

"Everybody is dead? Ty the Rat killed them all? How can this be?" The queen frowned.

"I don't know. Bok assured me that he killed the Rat, but now it seems he lied or he is playing a very silly game with me. I swore on my sister's life I would see that thief die for Solomon's death, and I thought it was done. Now this!" Conn said, looking out of his study window.

"So, the message, is it from Bok?"

"Sadly, I think not. I think it's from Ty."

"He is proving a very annoying halfling, this… Rat. What do you intend to do?"

"Well, he must have the other ruby, and if he has killed Bok then he must be reunited with Kern and Galandrik. So it's no major loss on our behalf; they will still be going to get the herbs. It just saves us killing Bok later. I will send a paperfinch telling them to continue with the quest."

"Where was the message sent from?"

"Wade. Lord Heilo also sent a message explaining they have taken a balloon ride across to Loft. His elite guard went with them for security, to make sure nothing happens."

"They are heading to the Dungeon of Dreams first then?"

"It looks that way. Then to Lake Fortune."

"Send Gorgon down to meet them after they have retrieved what we want."

"But I thought they were going to—"

"Plans change. Send Gorgon and the Black Guard to get what we need. By the time they get to the lake, the thieves should have gotten all the herbs."

"As you wish, my queen," Conn said, nodding.

"This is becoming a joke. Send Gorgon! Kill them and get the herbs, bring them back here, heal the king, and be done with all this nonsense. We have orc armies on our doorstep, growing by the minute, and we could do without these pathetic distractions."

"As I said, it will be done."

"One more thing, Conn."

"Yes? What is it, my queen?"

"Go with Gorgon and get the job done. Do not come back until you have those herbs, and the thieves are dead."

"Go…" Conn started to stutter. "Yes, of course."

"And when I say dead, I mean *dead*. Not 'he said so' or 'I thought he was.' Bring me their heads if you want, just don't fail me."

"Yes, my queen."

"Take those damn dragons, too."

"But the king wanted to—"

"Just take them. I will tell him we sacrificed them to the gods in exchange for his life. They are just another unwanted distraction I could do without. When Moriak is healed I need him to sort out this damn war, not worry about bloody dragons."

"I understand."

"Maybe you can find out what happened to Belton while you're traveling," she said with a wicked smile as she turned toward the door. Those words hurt Conn, and she knew it.

"I shall bring back what King Moriak needs."

Queen Cherian nodded as she left the study. Conn watched as the guard outside closed it behind her.

Conn sat down and picked up a paperfinch from his desk. "Just get the herbs and complete the quest. Thrane's life depends upon it and Bok's death has saved me a job." He held it in his cupped hands and whispered, "Fly, baby, fly." The finch flew out of his hands and through the window.

Conn spun round in his chair and gazed down at an old chest sat that sat on the floor. With a snap of his fingers the lock sparkled and exploded silently into hundreds of tiny blue fireflies; then, as quickly as they had come, they disappeared. He placed his hand on the lid. "Killing thieves. Is this what I have been reduced to?" the wizard said, shaking his head and flicking the chest lid open. His smile grew as he gazed at the contents.

Sitting on top of a set of robes was a pair of leather gloves and a pointy hat, both black apart from the grey band that ran around the hat. Conn removed them and placed them on his desk. He reached in and carefully picked up the black robes, placing them next to the other mage armour. Lastly, he pulled out a sack and a spell book—red leather with ancient runes scrawled all around the cover, gold trim lining the edges. He placed the sack on the table and let the spell book fall open. He began to mutter. "Identify, fool's gold," he said, as a hint of a smile appeared on his face. He turned the page. "Flame arrow, explosive runes, hold person." The wizard stood up and walked from his desk. "Summon monster, wall of ice, confusion." He looked at the mage armour on his desk and his smile broadened. He flicked over a few more pages. "Stone shape, polymorph self, fireball." He closed the book and held it to his chest. "I think I'm going to enjoy this."

*

The Dock Tavern was packed and very noisy. Most of the clients were humans, mainly fishermen and dock workers. They filled the bar, along with the odd group of adventurers, sitting in corners keeping themselves to themselves. Everyone in there had to raise their voice to be heard over the next person. Smoke filled the room, hanging like a fog. Drinks were thrown into the air as people sang and danced drunkenly.

Galandrik gazed out of the Dock Tavern window and watched as the fiery red orb of the sun disappeared beneath the line of the horizon. The last threads of light pierced the sky and bounced off the sea's waves, making them glisten and shine in the distance. Only a few birds flew over the docks, looking for the last scraps of food left on the quayside by the fishermen. The air was cooler now that the sun had gone, and the menacing sea looked like a lonely world, far away from the comforts of Bodisha. Galandrik's mind raced with thoughts of what lived beneath the water.

"Did you know, they reckon you could drop the tallest mountain in the world into the sea, in certain places, and it would disappear," Lan'esra said.

"Who said that?" Ty said, pushing his empty plate away.

"I don't know exactly *who* said it, but it was written down by scribes many years ago."

"If I wrote down 'a three-headed man lives under a mountain,' would people believe that in a hundred years?" Ty questioned.

"Now you are being silly," Lan'esra said, shaking her head.

Kern turned to the cleric. "No, I agree with Ty on this. Just because it's written in some book somewhere doesn't automatically make it right. I mean, how would anybody know how deep the sea is?"

"Exactly. And if they did, how could they measure a mountain in comparison to depth underwater?" Ty added.

"I don't know. Maybe they used magic to go down? What about the story you told me, Ty, about flying from a temple window?"

"What about it?"

"How do I know it's true? I wasn't there."

"No, but *I* was!" Ty laughed.

"So it's your word we rely on. If all the dragons disappear, do you think people will believe it in years to come that these flying beasts breathed fire, burnt towns, and ate people?"

"Dragons don't eat human," Ty grinned.

"See? How do you know?"

"One told me," Ty said, smiling at Kern.

"You're being silly again," the cleric said, crossing her arms.

"No, one actually did—"

"Look, the point I am trying to make is that people document things and that's how we learn. We *read* and learn," she interrupted.

Galandrik turned from the window. "It's all down to belief. If you believe something, it can be as real as the nose on your face. If you don't, then it can be as unbelievable as Ty getting a round of drinks in."

"Oi," Ty said, sitting up. "Who woke you up?"

"You lot did, with your stupid arguments! Bodisha is full of magic; anything is possible. If you believe a mountain could disappear in the sea, then you do. If not, then you don't. It is quite simple."

"But Lan'esra is saying it's true. Surely the burden of proof should be on her," Ty argued.

"Oh, hang on. I'll just go get a mountain and drop it in the sea," she said, pretending to get up.

"Now who's being silly?" Ty smiled.

"I never said it was true, I said they *reckon*."

"Well," Ty said, leaning on the table, "*I reckon* it's false!"

"Well *I reckon* you never flew out of that window," Lan'esra said, standing up. "Drinks?"

"Go on, one more, girl," Galandrik answered as she strode over to the bar.

"I *did* fly out of a window," Ty mumbled under his breath.

"So," Kern said, changing the subject, "did we all get what we need for the dungeon?"

"Yes. Lock picks, food, torches, rope, weapons, crossbow bolts—you name it, I got it."

"Me too. Backpack weighs a ton," Galandrik added.

"Good. It's going to be a tough journey. It's a hard dungeon and above our usual level."

"You mean pinching a bag of gems from the goblin cave is our level?" Galandrik sniggered.

"That was a good lead! Heldar told me." Ty frowned.

"Exactly," Kern and Galandrik said simultaneously.

"Whatever. Where the hell is that clown Scoff?" Ty said, looking around the pub and diverting the conversation away from Heldar. Lan'esra came back to the table. "The maid will bring them over."

"I think you talked him up, Ty," Galandrik said, nodding toward the door. Scoff and another man stood at the entrance, looking around the inn. Kern waved his hand and got their attention.

"There you are, my good fellows—and lady," Scoff said with a smile at Lan'esra. "This is Captain Blackshore."

"Nice to meet you all," Blackshore said, nodding. "I hear you want a lift to the Voltic Isle?"

Blackshore towered over the table, standing six inches taller even than

Kern. He looked as strong as he was tall, though his face was slender and lined with scars. His nose was as beaky as the parrot that should have sat on his shoulder. Thick black dreadlocks hung down over his shoulders, complete with the odd bead or bow. His green silk trousers were tucked into his black knee-high boots, and a red sash was wrapped around his middle, complete with sabre tucked in on the side. His muscular, tattooed chest could be seen through the open buttons of his blue silk shirt, and a thick gold necklace caught Ty's eye. The captain rested his hand on the hilt of his sword.

"Yes, Captain Blackshore, that is where we would like to go," Kern replied.

"Call me Blacky. Only my men call me captain," the pirate said with a smile, showing one golden tooth.

"When can we leave, Cap—Blacky?" Ty asked.

"We sail in one hour."

"One hour? One hour from *now*?" Galandrik stuttered.

"Yes, one hour from now. We leave for Bloodmoore and we can drop you en route at the Voltic Isle as we cross the channel. It'll be fifteen gold each, and you'll reach there at midnight."

"Fifteen gold pieces *each*?" Ty questioned.

"Did I stutter?" Blacky said coldly.

"I don't want to *buy* the bloody boat, just sail in it!"

"She's a ship. Boats have paddles, I have cannons. You want to board my *ship* or not?" he said, looking menacingly at Ty.

"Twenty for the group, and we have a deal," Ty said, holding his hand out.

Captain Blackshore glared at the thief for a second. "Call it forty and you board the *Green Dragon* very cheaply."

"Hmm… the *Green Dragon*. That's the name of your bo—ship?" Ty questioned.

"Aye, lad. She's the finest vessel from here to Bloodmoore," he said proudly.

"Are you by any chance missing your ship's bell?"

The tall pirate glared at Ty, anger etched all across his face. He drew his sword and pointed it at Ty where he stood between Kern and Galandrik.

"Whoa, hold up there, Blacky," Kern said, looking at the shining sabre only inches from his face.

"Speak, you little shit, or I'll cut you where you sit and feed your guts to the gulls!"

"I know where it is. I have seen it," Ty smiled.

Kern frowned at Galandrik, who shook his head.

"Let's just put the sword down, shall we? Before someone gets hurt," Galandrik said, resting his elbow on the handle of his great axe that leaned against the wall next to him. The captain hesitated. Although he knew he could raise a small pirate army within minutes, he also knew he wouldn't last five seconds against four. With a smile, he tucked his sword back in his red silk sash.

"Excuse me. The bell was very precious. It was on the ship when she was built, forty years ago. I sailed on her the day of her maiden voyage, and my father was the first man to ring it. So you see why I want it back."

"Oh, of course. Such a treasured item should be exactly where it belongs, and that is on the *Green Dragon*. Now, before I tell you where this precious bell can be found, did we say twenty gold pieces?" Ty said, leaning back in his chair, smiling from ear to ear.

The pirate knew Ty had him. "How do I know you are telling the truth?"

"Have I even stepped foot on your ship? How else would I know? I haven't even been in Loft before," Ty answered.

"Someone could have told you."

"Fine, we will pay forty, no problem," Ty said, grabbing his pouch from inside his tunic, knowing he had nowhere near that amount.

Blacky grimaced. "Twenty it is, and if it isn't where you say it is, by the sea god himself I will find you," he said with a snarl.

"Oh, it is definitely there. I rang it not ten moons ago."

"Tell me."

"It is behind the bar at the Factory Inn in Tonilla."

"I fucking *knew* Grego had taken it, the bastard. He talked about that town all the time when we were at sea."

"That thieving little shit! And after all we did for him!" Scoff added.

"Well, that's where it is, hanging on the wall, proud as punch," Ty said.

"I will be paying it a visit very shortly. My ship leaves soon. It's along the quay, about two hundred paces. Be there with your gold." Scoff and Captain Blackshore left the inn and headed up the quayside.

Kern, Galandrik, and Lan'esra all stared at Ty.

"What?" he said, with a shrug of his shoulders.

"It is really in the Factory Inn in Tonilla?" Kern asked, crossing his arms.

"Yes, I saw it. He said it was missing. I wasn't lying. It got us on cheap, didn't it?"

"I guess so," Kern said.

"Expensive, these boat rides, aren't they?" Galandrik said, picking up his backpack.

"It's not a boat, it's a *ship*," Ty said with a wink.

"You do push it, Ty," the cleric stated.

"You haven't seen anything yet," Kern laughed, slinging his bow across his shoulder.

"It gets worse?" she chuckled.

"It? Who's it?" Ty said, finishing off his drink.

"Here we go again," Galandrik said, rolling his eyes.

Chapter Eighteen
All at Sea

Bok stood hidden in the shadows of a shop doorway. The evening was getting colder and the dock was quiet. The usual hustle and bustle of this busy dockside had faded, and the town slept peacefully. Only a few drunken singing sailors wandered along the quay edge. The bright moonlight bounced off the waves, illuminating the sea like a magical display of watery ghosts dancing and jumping in and out of the water. Bok watched as Kern and the others walked up the gangplank and onto the *Green Dragon*. His mind raced.

Could I stow aboard? What good would it do? I'd still have to get off with them. I could kill him on board the ship, but I would have nowhere to run to. I could kill him, then jump in the little boat hanging from the side, but I'd only smash against the rocks and drown. That fucking Rat, he has escaped again. Think, Bok, think… Fortune. They will definitely go to town if they survive the dungeon, and they will… He always does. He won't die, can't be killed—he will be grinning in Fortune, bragging about the dungeon he just completed and the riches he found. I can picture his smug face now.

Bok touched the burnt skin on his cheek. It was hard to the touch and he couldn't bear to look in the mirror. A rat scurried past his feet along the path. Bok kicked out but missed, and it disappeared down a drain hole.

You did this to me, Rat—you, not Conn. It's your fault. Yes, Fortune; I will head there and prepare myself like never before and when he shows up—because he will, oh yes, bold as brass, slithering into the inn like a horrible snake, with a rat's head—I will be there, ready to cut the rat head off the snake's body… Bok will, you see if I don't. He will only escape you again. No! Not this time. Bok will be ready… ready and waiting.

He pulled his hood over his shoulders, taking one last look at Ty as he stepped onto the ship. Walking down the quayside, Bok slipped into the darkness of the night.

*

Kern, Galandrik, Ty, and Lan'esra stepped onto the ship. The crew rallied around as a slight drizzle started to fall. Hundreds of ropes hung down from the giant masts, creating a hemp web. Galandrik thought it inconceivable to fathom how they worked. The ship's decks creaked and groaned as it swayed gently back and forth in the dock.

Kern swallowed hard as his stomach did summersaults with the motion. The smell was a mixture of cooking, bad hygiene, pipe tobacco, and gunpowder, all mixed in a cauldron of sea air.

"There you are! Follow me down below, I'll show you where you can wait," Captain Blackshore said. They followed him along the side of the ship, passing crew members as they went who looked like the nastiest bunch of vagabonds ever gathered in one place. Not one smiled as they passed, and the glares they got were enough to scare the most hardened adventurer.

Eventually they climbed down a set of stairs at the back of the ship. They were all surprised at the space below, as the corridor that he led them down had many different doors and cupboards. He pushed a door open at the end of the corridor to reveal a square room. In its centre was a long wooden table with eight chairs surrounding it. Sofas lined two sides and the third wall had a bookshelf with hundreds of books filling it to the brim. A smaller table sat in the corner, covered in maps and navigation tools. A couple of chests sat in the other corner. Hanging above the table was a giant lantern that illuminated the room.

"Stay in here. The weather is getting up and it looks like we are in for a heavy night. Hopefully we can drop you off before it gets up too bad. We should be there in three to four hours, depending on the winds. I will have hot food brought down in an hour. Drink and bread will be here shortly. The bread will settle your land-loving stomachs. If you do want to throw up, please go topside and aim at the big wet bit that surrounds the ship. Make sure you call me and tell me before you leave this room, *and* go in pairs. People have been known to go missing."

"How can we call you?" Kern asked.

"You see that silver tube on the wall with the brass funnel? Whistle down that and we will come open the door," Blacky explained. "Is there anything else?"

"Yes, I have a question," Ty said. "Why leave now? Why not leave at first light?"

"The waters between Bodisha and Bloodmoore are deadly. Pirate ships patrol these waters like sharks circling an injured whale. It's easier at night. If you get caught by a couple of pirate ships, it is very hard to escape, and many have lost their ships to these people. At night you get the thick fog, especially this time of year with the changing of the seasons. The *Green Dragon* doesn't get much grief because they know how we operate. We once took out three attacking ships."

"So you wouldn't call yourself a pirate ship then?" Ty said, staring at Blacky, who locked his gaze for a couple of seconds.

"No, we take cargo for Lord Lokin across to Bloodmoore."

"What sort of cargo?" the thief asked.

"Fruit. We carry loads of fruit."

The door locked behind him.

"What is your game?" Kern said, laying his backpack on the sofa.

"Nothing, why?"

"What's with the hundred questions?"

"I just have a gut feeling about this guy. You cannot trust a pirate, and he *is* a pirate. I don't care what he says; he stinks of pirate."

"He is a strange one," Galandrik added.

"They all are. It's the damn sea air. I'm going to get a couple of hours sleep before we hit the Voltic Isle. I suggest you three do the same," Kern said, resting his head on his backpack and rolling over.

"Well, I am waiting for the food. I am famished," Galandrik said, sitting at the table.

"You are always hungry," Ty said, looking at the chests.

"There's so many nautical books here, it is unbelievable," Lan'esra said, holding one in her hands. Ty pushed a chest open; it was full of parchments and maps. Gently he lowered the lid and moved to the next.

"*How to Navigate Freebird Point. Ship's Hull Repairs. Sails, Snatch Blocks, and Rigging,*" she read aloud. "Everything you would ever need to know about boats."

"Ships," Ty smiled, "and don't believe everything you read." He lowered the second chest lid.

"Do not go there again," she said, replacing the book.

"I won't. I won the argument last time. I can't stay in here, it's like a floating prison."

"No, you didn't. Anyway, we are not to go out without his permission," Lan'esra said, sitting down next to Galandrik, who had nodded off in his chair. Ty sat at the table opposite Lan'esra, and they chatted while Galandrik and Kern softly snored. They could feel the movement of the ship as it slowly eased its way out of Loft's harbour. It gently rolled side to side and the cleric watched as the hanging lantern swayed with the ship's movements. They could hear rain hitting the ship's upper decks and the shouting of the crew as they battled against the rising storm.

"I'm going for a piss," Ty announced.

"We are not—"

"Listen, Lan'esra, please listen. People in life who act like sheep get treated like sheep. You were born original; don't die a copy."

Lan'esra folded her arms on the table and rested her head. "Whatever. I don't even know what that means."

"It means—never mind," Ty bent down and examined the lock. "Damn key is in from the other side," he muttered. He felt the bottom of the door. "Should be enough room." He jumped up and rummaged through the little table. "Perfect." He squatted down. Carefully, he slid an old map under the bottom of the door and unrolled his lock picks on his knee. Pulling out a long pick with two curved ends like a snake's tongue, he delicately placed it in the lock. With a twist and a turn, as carefully as he could, he pushed the key out. He heard the clink of the key landing outside the door, but it was muffled by the map.

After slipping his tools back into his tunic, he gently eased the map toward him. The key sat on top. "You never lose it," he said, turning his head, but no one was watching—nor even awake. He returned the map, then, as quietly as he could, unlocked the door and turned the handle. It clicked, and he opened the door slightly. The corridor was empty. He reached around and slipped the key back into the lock from the outside.

All of a sudden he felt a pain in his chest. He fell to his knees with his hand on his heart. His face twisted with pain and he couldn't breathe. For ten seconds the pain was immense, then it faded as if it had never been there. Ty rolled over on his side and gasped for breath, like a fresh-caught fish lying on a river bank. Beads of sweat rolled down his temple. He breathed slowly and rolled onto all fours, and finally got to his feet. He undid the leather laces on his tunic and opened the buttons of the shirt underneath.

"Dragon shielding." The scales had spread to middle of his chest and where they started, the skin was black like a fist-sized bruise. "Like I have time for this."

He felt the bruised-looking skin; it was hard—just what you would expect to feel when touching a dragon's scale. Shaking his head, he did up his tunic and peered down the corridor. It was still empty. Quietly he tiptoed through the doorway and stepped into the corridor, closing the door behind him. There were three doors on either side. The first door on his left had the name 'Captain Blackshore' on it in gold-encrusted lettering. The one dead opposite said 'Kitchen.' Ty quietly tiptoed to the next door and read 'Toilet.'

With his fingertips he gently pushed the door open; the room was empty. He stepped inside and closed the door behind him. His moment of relief was short-lived as he heard footsteps in the corridor. Quickly he reached round and slid the bolt, just before he heard somebody try it.

"Hurry ups, you scabby sea horse. I'm bursting outs here," Ty heard an unfamiliar voice with a slight lisp say. Holding his hand in front of his mouth he mumbled, "Give me a minute."

"Just be quick," was the reply.

The voice moved down the corridor and he heard a door creak open. As soon as nature had taken its course he undid the bolt and opened it up, peering through the tiniest of cracks. His heart was beating fast; he hadn't felt like this for ages. The adrenaline was coursing through his veins and he felt alive. He could see the kitchen door was ajar. Without hesitation, he stepped out into the corridor and darted down it. As he passed the slightly open door, he heard the name 'Kern,' so he stopped and backed up against the wall next to the door and listened.

"What does Captain want me to make?"

"A rabbit stew. Use any old shit; they won't knows and we can get rid of its. Shove a few more herbs in."

"Who's the bloody cook here? I know how to hide the taste of rotten meat. I've been cooking it for you for years."

"Yeah, I knows. Tastes like shit half the time."

"Thanks, I'll remember that the next time you ask for a steak."

"Listen, I needs a shit, so just slip some poison in there for ours guests and serve it up."

"What's the point in cooking a fresh stew, then, if they will die within minutes? I might as well use last night's leftovers." Ty swallowed hard.

"Not kills them, knock them out!"

"What? Then do what?"

"Then we strip them and throw them in the hold with the other slaves. 'Gold per heads,' Captain said, 'gold per heads.' Plus we wants to have some fun with the girl too. No good if she is dead, now, is it?"

Ty's eyes widened. *A slaver's ship,* he thought.

"Okay, I will give them this. Pass that bottle off the shelf there."

"What one?"

"The one with the cork; yes, that one. NO! The other one. Thanks. I reheated last night's so it's virtually ready."

"Right, I'm off. Ring the bell when they are sleeping. I wants to go first on the girl."

Before Ty could react, the door open inward and a fat pirate walked out into the corridor, luckily with his back to the thief. "I think I will have a steak, now you have mentioned it," the fat man shouted as he closed the door.

"Tastes like shit, remember, Skinny!"

"Whatever. Just do it."

Ty held his breath and searched for anything, any shadow that could help conceal him, but there was nothing. He thought of his invisibility ring. The fat man stepped towards the toilet and stopped outside; with a whistle he took off his jacket and hung it next to the door. Ty squinted, praying he wouldn't turn and spot him. His prayers were answered: He entered the toilet and the door closed behind him. Ty gave a massive sigh of relief and tiptoed as quietly as he could down the corridor toward their door. Just before he got there, he stopped and looked over his shoulder, remembering the fat man's jacket.

He quietly tiptoed back down the corridor toward the jacket. It was a leather waistcoat tunic with the arms cut off. Gently, he reached in the pocket and pulled out a key on a leather strap. In the other pocket were a couple of rings. They appeared to be nothing special, but he slipped them into his tunic. *It's not the loot, it's the looting,* Ty thought to himself as he skipped back toward his door. He heard talking from behind him, and quietly slipped inside the room with the others and closed the door.

"Kern! Wake up," Ty said, as loud as he dared. "Wake up, you fool," he said, shaking his friend.

"What…? What… Ty, where…?" Kern mumbled, trying to focus. The door to the room opened and Captain Blackshore entered, along with another member of his crew who was carrying a tray with knives, forks, bowls, and jugs. He placed them on the table, which woke Lan'esra and Galandrik, who both raised their heads from the table and began to rub their eyes.

"Food," Galandrik said, still half asleep.

"Yes, it's food time. And try this little beauty," Blacky said, pulling a bottle of rum from behind his back and placing it on the table. The captain walked to the back of the room and began sifting through an old crate.

"Thanks. I could do with a drop of that," Galandrik said, yawning.

"What was it, Ty?" Kern said, rolling his legs off the sofa.

"Nothing. I will tell you later," Ty said, watching Galandrik pick up the bottle of rum. "Allow me!" Ty said as he scurried over to the dwarf and virtually snatched the bottle from his hands.

"If you insist, lad."

"Oh, I do." Ty pretended to take interest in the label. "From Bloodmoore, five years old. It looks a nice vintage."

"It's a knock-out," the captain said, smiling. "By the way, I locked this door. How come it was open?"

"No idea. We have all been asleep," Ty quickly said.

"Strange. Maybe it is me in my old age," he added as the cook walked in and placed a pot of stew on the table. He was holding it by the handles with two cloths. "Careful now, it might hurt you."

"You can bet on that," Ty mumbled.

"What was that?" the cook asked.

"That looks lovely," Ty said with a smile.

"Don't just cuddle it, lad, pour me a drink," Galandrik said, ladling a spoonful of stew into a wooden bowl. Ty placed the bottle of rum down on the table, and picked up a mug and blew into it. "Can't have a dusty mug for such fine rum, now, can we?" He pretended to clean it.

"Hmm, I am starving," the dwarf said, picking up a spoon, as Kern sat down and the cook left the room. Captain Blackshore moved to the table and studied a map as Ty picked up the pepper pot as the dwarf lifted his first full spoonful. "Wait, Galandrik."

"What now?" the dwarf asked, frowning at being stopped.

"You need a snip of pepper in that. Stew is always better with pepper," Ty said, watching as Lan'esra and Kern each picked up a bowl.

"Please, Lan'esra, after you," Kern said.

"Thank you," she smiled back.

"Go on then, lad. Hurry it up, I am starving," he said, dropping the spoon back into his bowl. Ty surreptitiously unscrewed the top with his forefinger and thumb and tipped it into Galandrik's bowl. The lid—along with half the contents of the pepper pot—covered his stew.

"Oh shit, sorry," Ty said, picking the bowl up and blowing the pepper off.

"That's ruined. I can't eat that."

"Sorry! Take my bowl, I'm not hungry," Ty offered. Galandrik got up and reached for the last bowl as Kern passed the ladle to Lan'esra.

"Captain, I think you should come and see this," they heard a voice shout from down the corridor.

"Coming," he answered. "Enjoy your food," he said with a smile.

Kern's spoon was just about to touch his lips as Blacky closed the door. They heard it lock with a click. Ty threw the pepper pot across the table, knocking the spoon clean out of Kern's hand. Stew spattered his face.

"What the hell!" Kern shouted, jumping up, sending his chair flying backward and brushing the hot stew from his cheek.

"Shh! It's been poisoned," Ty said, holding a finger up to his lips. Lan'esra and Galandrik dropped their cutlery.

"How do you know?" Lan'esra whispered as she stared into the pot.

"Remember he said the door was unlocked? Well, that was me; I slipped out and overheard the cook talking to some bloke called Skinny. They are going to drug us and throw us in the hold… well, apart from you," Ty said, nodding at the cleric. "I think they had other plans for you."

"Those dirty, rotten scoundrels! How dare they!" she said angrily.

"Let's rip the place to shreds," Galandrik said, grabbing his great axe.

"Hold on. We wouldn't stand a chance against this many, and even if we did, what would we do then? None of us can captain a boat."

"He is right, Gal, far too many," Kern agreed.

"Are you sure that is what you heard?" Galandrik said, examining a spoonful of stew.

"Why not try it? Then we can wait and see," Ty said, folding his arms.

Galandrik dropped the spoon in the pot. "No, I believe you. It just looks so nice."

"Eat some rations then, if you're that hungry," Kern added.

"And the rum?" Galandrik said, picking up the bottle.

"Try it," Ty said, walking to the door and examining the lock. "He has taken the key this time. I can pick the lock."

"Then what?" Lan'esra asked, grabbing her mace.

"Sneak up and into one of those little boats on the side?" Ty suggested.

"We would be spotted for sure. Even if we didn't, we are in the middle of the channel. We could end up anywhere," Kern said with a curse.

"They think we are going to be knocked out, right?" Lan'esra questioned.

"It doesn't *look* poisoned," Galandrik said, pouring out a little of the rum out.

"Yes, all unconscious," Ty replied, ignoring Galandrik.

"Well, let's be unconscious when they come back. We will have the jump on them."

"You mean pretend?" Ty frowned.

"Yes," Kern agreed. "If we all lie around as if we are drugged when really we are ready to attack, they won't be expecting a thing."

"Smells all right," Galandrik said to himself.

"Yes, then we can take Captain Blacky hostage," the cleric said with added enthusiasm.

"I see. Good idea," Ty smiled. "Then what?"

"If we have their captain, they will let us mount the smaller boat. We can take it to the Voltic Isle and then release him back to his ship," Kern said, nodding at Lan'esra.

"Well, I'm taking it anyway," Galandrik mumbled, wrapping the rum up and tucking it into his already full backpack.

"Are you listening to a word we said?" Kern asked the dwarf.

"Yes, yes. Play dead, kidnap the captain, grab a boat, get to the island, and release the captain," he replied, pulling a piece of dried beef from his backpack.

"Right. Lan'esra will stay closest to the door, Ty opposite. I think they may just make a beeline for her anyway. I will be back here and if Ty gives Gal his crossbow, we can do the ranged attack. Sound good?" Kern suggested.

"Yes. Make sure you place a bowl on the floor as if spilt. Makes it look more authentic," Galandrik added.

"You *were* listening," Ty said, passing the dwarf his crossbow. "You do know how to use it?"

"I'll use it on you if you want," Galandrik snarled, loading the crossbow.

Lan'esra tipped a bowl over on the table, letting the stew spread over it.

Then, holding a dagger on her lap concealed under the table, she lay her head down. Ty sat opposite and let his head fall backward. Galandrik rested his head on his arms on top of the table, and Kern lay on the sofa with his longbow on the floor next to his spilt bowl of stew.

"Remember, these people are vicious. Don't give them an inch," Kern advised.

"I won't. If they want to see vicious, I'll give them dwarven vicious."

"Just don't hit me with a crossbow bolt," Ty sniggered.

They didn't wait long; they soon heard footsteps coming down the corridor.

"Remember, fast and aggressive," Kern whispered.

They heard the key turn in the lock and the door creaked open, "Look, they are all sleeping like babies." Ty recognised the voice of Skinny.

"Yes. Grab the backpacks and see what they have," Captain Blackshore said.

"My stew worked wonders. That poison could knock out an army," the cook said, laughing.

"Looks at this little princess. I'm goings to have some funs with her!"

"Just search the bags, worry about her later." Blacky said.

Skinny walked up to Lan'esra and pulled her head back from the table, sitting her back in the chair. He reached down and placed his hand on his breast. "She will be worth a few gold, too. Young, attractive, and—"

"Awake," Lan'esra said, pressing her dagger against his groin.

"What? Wait..."

Skinny shrieked as Kern rolled off the sofa, grabbing his bow and notching an arrow. Ty released his daggers and stood in front of the captain, poised to attack.

The cook grabbed the door to pull it open. No sooner had his hand touched it than a crossbow bolt thudded into it, pinning him to the door. The cook grabbed his wrist with his other hand and screamed.

"Just drop your sabres to the floor and no one else will be harmed," Kern said. The captain looked at Skinny and, as if a message had been relayed without speech, they both attacked. Skinny backhanded Lan'esra around the face, spinning her head round, and reached for his sabre. The captain also reached for his, crossing his hands and grabbing each hilt. Before he could draw, Kern unleashed an arrow, striking the pirate in the thigh and dropping him to his knees. Skinny was quick; he grabbed his sabre and raised it, but it never came down. Ty's dagger hit him plumb centre of his forehead. The sabre dropped to the floor and Skinny followed, dead.

The cook was still screaming and grabbing his wrist. Blood flowed from the crossbow bolt that protruded from his hand.

"Shut him up," Kern said, placing his bow on the sofa. Ty stepped forward to where the captain was sitting on the floor with his injured leg straight out, both hands around the arrow. "You'll never leave this ship alive!"

"I'll be the judge of that!" Ty said, punching the injured pirate straight in the face. His crooked nose broke instantly and blood splattered his face. He fell backward, now holding his broken nose. Ty grabbed both the captains' swords and stepped forward toward the cook, who was still screaming. With lightning speed he brought the first sabre down, cutting the cook's hand off at the wrist, leaving it pinned to the door, still twitching. The cook fell to his knees screaming even louder, holding his wrist as blood poured from the stump. With an upward arc, Ty swung the other sabre, slicing the cook's face from chin, though his nose and up between his eyes, opening it up like a melon. The cook's eyes rolled and he fell backward in a heap.

"I said silence him, not cut him in half," Kern said quietly.

"These are sharp as hell," Ty said, ignoring Kern's comment and examining the blades.

"Right, drag his body out of the way and lock the door. Galandrik, find some rope and we will tie this piece of shit up. Lan'esra, what happened? I said be ready."

"Sorry. He was too quick."

"Not anymore," Ty said, retrieving the dagger from Skinny's forehead.

"You'll never leave alive," Blacky said, sitting up, blood still flowing from his nose and Kern's arrow sticking out of his leg.

"Then you'll die with us," Galandrik said, bending down and gripping the arrow. As soon as he touched it, Blacky winced with the shooting pains that ripped through his leg.

"This might hurt a little," the dwarf said as Blacky lay back.

"Do your wor—"

He ripped the arrow out as the captain screamed in agony.

"My god, you pirates make a lot of noise," Ty said smugly.

"Noise! How many times?" Kern said in disbelief.

"I'm going to enjoy feeding you to the fish," Blacky said, tears streaming down his blood-spattered cheeks.

"Save it. Lan'esra, see to his wound after Galandrik has tied his arms. We don't want him bleeding out before we leave," Kern ordered.

Galandrik tied Blacky's hands behind his back and used another short piece of rope to tie both ankles, long enough for the captain to walk, but only one foot in front of the other, restricting his movement. Lan'esra dressed his wound as he sat on one of the chairs.

Ty walked over to their captive; even though the leggy captain was sitting down, they were at eye level. He drew a dagger and held it up to the captain's face, making the captain lean back apprehensively. Ty lifted the purse that hung from his belt and cut the strings. "Call this a poison payment." Ty smiled, tossing the bag in the air and catching it.

"You'd better kill me, because I will find you."

"Join the queue," the thief said, pressing the dagger into the pirate's chest.

"Go on, do it! I dare you. Then see how far you get."

Ty flipped the dagger upward, cutting the captain's shirt, then he grabbed each side and ripped it open, revealing an inch-thick gold necklace.

"My god, that's bigger than my belt!" Ty smiled as he removed it and held it in his hands. "Kern, come and feel the weight of this bad boy."

"Ty, now isn't the time to loot. Now is the time to work out how we are getting off this damn ship! There are more pressing matters at hand than the weight of some shit necklace."

"That necklace was given to me by my father, and his father before him. I will get it back. You know that, don't you?"

"Of course you will," Ty said, rolling his eyes.

They heard footsteps from down the corridor along with some voices. "What will you do now?" the captain asked.

"*We* are doing nothing. *You* will tell them to leave, everything is fine, and to come back and shout once we are anchored next to the Voltic Isle."

"And if I say no?"

"Then I will remove your tongue," the dwarf said, resting the great axe on his shoulder.

Ty jumped up onto the table and reached for one of the smaller oil tins that sat around the giant wooden lantern. He blew out the flame and, using his tunic to keep from burning his hands, he unscrewed the lid and dropped it onto the table. "And then we will burn the ship down and escape in the panic. No one will worry about us four when they are trying to put the flames out," Ty said, pouring the oil over the table.

The captain's face changed to horror. "You wouldn't!"

"He would. In fact, that's actually a better idea. Unscrew another and cover the book shelf," Kern said. Ty took another and jumped down, throwing oil over the books and parchments. There was a knock at the door and then someone tried the handle.

"Captain?" they heard from outside the door.

"The choice is yours," Kern whispered into his ear.

The captain looked at the two bodies on the floor and the oil on the table, and he knew they were serious. "Carry on heading to the Voltic Isle. Don't disturb me until you have anchored up."

"Aye aye. Skinny wasn't at the crew change, captain."

"He's in my room asleep. Don't bother him, Kell; he feels like shit. Tell Salim to take his place."

"Aye, Captain. Is that all?"

"Just look after the ship."

"Aye aye, Captain." The footsteps disappeared down the corridor.

"Wise choice, my friend," Kern smiled.

Chapter Nineteen
Balls and Orbs

Conn and Gorgon sat side by side on their mounts outside the main gate of King Moriak's castle. Twenty soldiers of the Black Guard sat saddled up behind. It was early morning as the yellow shining sun started rising over the horizon. It filled the sky with mighty colours of reds and splashed the clouds with rays of pink. The warm rays of the sun were welcome as Conn sat, ready to begin his journey.

"Why are we carrying these damn dragons all the way back?" Gorgon asked.

"Queen Cherian has ordered it so. She doesn't want them to distract the king from the war," Conn replied.

"Why not just kill them now?"

"No, we might need them. We told Kern we would release them. He will not just hand over the herbs without the illusion of his father and the dragons—that was the deal."

"So? Just kill them and then find Kern, kill him, and take what we want."

"Don't underestimate them, Gorgon. Look what damage they have caused already."

"You honestly think three petty thieves could take me on?"

"Like I said, Gorgon, don't underestimate them."

"Waste of time and effort."

"Look, we can kill them and the dragons as soon as we get what we need. It'll be killing two birds with one stone."

"Two birds with one stone, eh? I have heard that before," he said with a smile.

"Good, then you know what we want."

Behind them was a horse-drawn cart with the two dragons chained up inside. Covering the cart was a large leather sheet, strapped down on all four sides. Fucan rode up next to Gorgon.

"Everything is ready for our departure."

"Well done, Fucan. The route is to ride down past Raith's Wood and through the Double Dikes."

"How will we find them in the westlands?"

"They have a paperfinch ruby. I can speak to them," Conn said.

"Oh, I see. The sooner this is ended, the better. The troops are restless. They want battle, not babysitting dragons."

"They will get their battle, Fucan, as soon as we get the king back on his feet. I will address them when we camp next. How's the training with the new recruits?" Gorgon answered.

"All right. Found some good men, whittled out some shit."

"That's good. Shalamia depleted our numbers badly, and good men are what we need."

"By the time we come back we should know more. Kildrid is training them hard."

"He is good. He doesn't stand for time-wasters. Right, tell the men we are now moving out."

"Yes, Gorgon." Fucan rode back, shouting orders at the men.

"You lost a lot that night," Conn said.

"Indeed, some very good men," Gorgon said, kicking his mount into a canter.

"Yes, including Belton. He was a fine man," Conn said, following.

"I liked him. It is such a shame what happened. It goes to show, you must keep your wits about you every second of every hour of every day."

"Such a strange way to go though, falling off a mountain."

"It was very windy. Or maybe it could have been Shalamia. She killed half my troop; maybe she saw Belton and swooped down, grabbing him in her razor-sharp talons and squeezing the last ebbs of life from his body. A giant saw-eagle? Orcs? Whatever happened, he's dead and it's a shame."

"So you didn't see him die?"

Gorgon stared at Conn. Anger was building up inside his body and he could feel his rage in the warmth of the blood pumping though his face. His heart began to beat at double speed, and for an instant he imagined drawing his sword and removing the wizard's head. Instead, he bit his lip.

"Maybe he liked the dragon's lair that much, he decided to stay a little longer. Why don't we pop by on the way and say hello?"

"Don't mock me, Gorgon," Conn said sternly. "These men might be frightened of you but I have fought things you could only dream about."

"Then don't ask me about that fucking friend of yours again. He has gone. Where? I don't know. We all lost good friends that evening. These men are not scared of anything. They respect me, and this is something you might want to do."

"Like I said—"

"Yes, I heard. Well, if you ever dream about challenging me, you better wake up and apologise," Gorgon interrupted.

There was a few seconds' stare between the two men before Conn eventually smiled. "Let's go kill some thieves," Conn said, and trotted forward in front of the group.

"And maybe a wizard," Gorgon muttered under his breath.

*

Kern, Galandrik, Ty, Lan'esra, and the tied-up Captain Blackshore all sat at the table. Two hours had gone by since the knock on the door. They could hear the noises above them and the shouting of the men. The ship rocked back and forth, and the lantern swung with the motion.

"We have anchored up," Blacky said. "Nearly time for your masterful escape."

"Indeed. You will obviously be having a trip to the isle with us for security's sake; we wouldn't want you to fire cannons on us, now, would we?" Kern explained.

"I won't fire on you. Just take a boat and be gone. You have my word."

"We have your word? Your word was to bring us here safely, not drug us."

"That was an unfortunate decision on my behalf."

"Indeed, and two of your men have died for it already."

"I don't want any more deaths aboard my ship."

"To be honest, this is now *our* ship, and you would do well to remember that. In fact, don't most pirate ships have chests of bounty?" Ty said.

"*Your* ship?" The captain laughed. "These men wouldn't sail her for you. A common thief? They would rather die than have you control her."

"Maybe they will, then."

"I have forty hardened sailors who all will fight to the death to save the *Green Dragon*; do you honestly think you stand a chance? Where would you go? Sail into any harbour and you would be strung up for piracy and murder."

"I still like the idea of burning it," Ty smiled.

"That charge would be mass murder and sinking one of the king's cargo ships. Not a wise idea."

"Who would know it burned? Maybe it smashed against the rocks and sunk," Ty added.

"No one is burning anything or killing anyone. We will get off and let you go," Kern said, shaking his head at Ty.

"You would be wise to kill me. You know I won't stop hunting you."

"That can be arranged," Galandrik said, listening at the door. "People coming."

"Right, tell them to ready our boat, the closest one to the exit. Tell them to gather the men at the front of the boat near the wheelhouse; you want to address them all. Make sure it's the whole crew."

"Captain Blackshore, we are anchored off the Voltic Isle," they heard, accompanied by a knock at the door. Ty held a dagger to the captain's neck.

"Well done, Kell. Ready a boat for our guests' departure."

"But I thought we were—"

"Do as I say, man! Ready boat two and then gather the men at the wheelhouse. I have an announcement."

"All of them," Kern whispered.

"And make sure everyone is there," he added.

"Captain, is everything all right?" Kell questioned. Ty pressed the dagger into Blackshore's neck.

"Everything is fine. It's good news."

"Have you seen the weather? It is pouring down."

"Do as I say, man! Or I'll give you twenty lashes!"

"Aye aye, Captain, I will round up the crew. Should I wake Skinny?"

"No. He is aware of what I have to say."

They heard the footsteps disappear down the corridor. "Well done," Galandrik said, gathering his possessions.

"Right—everybody get ready. They might try and overpower us," Kern said, sheathing his sword.

Ty opened the lock and peered down the corridor. "All clear."

"I will lead the way. You lot stay behind him. We will get Lan'esra down onto the boat first, then Gal, Ty, the Captain, and lastly me."

"Chew these leaves," Lan'esra said, pulling a bag of herbs from her backpack. "It'll help us in the water."

"Leaves of water breathing?" Ty asked.

"No, you'd need a potion for that. These will help buoyancy. Stop you sinking with your armour, weapons, and backpack."

"I don't intend to go in!" Ty said, taking the leaf from Lan'esra.

"You never know; better to be safe than sorry." They each thanked her and ate a leaf.

"What about if they charge us?" Galandrik asked.

Kern stared at the captive for a few seconds. "Slit his throat and fight."

Blackshore swallowed hard.

"Oh, I hope they do. I haven't swung it in ages. It could do with a workout before we enter the dungeon."

Kern led the party down the corridor and up the stairs. He peered through the crack of the door and saw the gathering of men at the front of the ship. The night sky was black and rain poured down from the heavens; the ship rolled in the wind and the odd wave crashed over the handrails.

"Be aware," the ranger said, and strode through the double doors. The crew looked round and saw Kern with his bow drawn. Instantly they knew something was amiss; several swords were drawn. Captain Blackshore appeared next, with his hands tied behind his back. They could see the dried blood on his face and moved forward.

"Captain!" a crew member shouted.

"Stay back! There is nothing you can do here."

"What's happening?" Kell shouted from the front of the cluster of men.

"These guests are going to the isle and I will accompany them. Once they have landed I will return. Simple. Don't cause a fuss and no one else gets harmed."

They moved to the side of the ship where the boat was being lowered into the sea. It was bigger than they had expected, and could easily hold twenty men. Oars on either side were tucked onto the boat.

Captain Blackshore's men finished lowering the boat and backed off to the other sailors.

"Lan'esra, quick, climb down," Kern ordered, looking around as the crew crept forward. He unleashed an arrow and it struck Kell directly in the foot, pinning him the wooden deck. With a scream, he dropped his cutlass and fell, clutching his ankle. "The next arrow will be head height, so stay back!" Kern shouted.

Galandrik dropped his backpack, which Lan'esra caught, and climbed down the rope ladder. "You next, Ty. And keep your crossbow on him. We will need to untie him to let him climb down."

"Is it wise to untie him?" Ty asked, keeping a careful eye on the crew.

"How else is he going to climb down?" Kern shouted as the wind and rain pelted his face.

"There must be other ways of getting him down," Ty shouted back, as the captain peered over the handrail down at the boat.

"Hurry up!" they heard Lan'esra shout.

"What? Just untie—"

Ty dropped his crossbow and pushed the captain over the handrail. He watched as the pirate fell, landing in the boat below in a heap with an almighty groan. His landing rocked the boat side to side and Lan'esra struggled to stay upright.

"What the hell are you doing?" Kern shouted, stepping forward toward the crew with his bow raised and threatening to shoot.

"Fuck him," Ty shouted, swinging his leg over and beginning his descent. When Ty was finally settled in the boat Kern swung his leg over, still aiming his bow.

"Come on," Galandrik shouted from below, untying the ropes that secured the boat to the winches above. Kern swung his bow over his shoulder and climbed down into the boat.

"He's dead," Lan'esra shouted against the noise of the wind.

"Who is?" Kern replied, releasing the other rope.

"The captain. He broke his neck when he landed."

"I don't believe you, Ty. You are unbelievable! Prop him up. Galandrik, grab an oar and row!"

The boat moved away from the *Green Dragon* as Kern and Galandrik rowed with all their might. They could see the rocky coastline of the Voltic Isle in the distance, lit up by the moonlight. All the crew had now gathered, looking down as they escaped. Ty tried to pull the dead captain up, but his weight was too great and the body slumped back down, smashing its head on the side on the boat.

"The captain is dead!" a pirate shouted from above. "Load the cannons!"

"Shit! Row faster," Kern ordered as Ty and Lan'esra grabbed oars and began pulling back and forth in time with the others. An arrow thudded into the seat next to Kern. "Ty, kill him!"

The thief looked up and saw a pirate notching another arrow. He grabbed his crossbow and aimed it, taking note of the sails as they blew in the wind. He adjusted his crossbow to the right of the pirate, and up he fired. The bolt soared through the night sky, glistening in the moonlight as it spiralled toward its victim. With a sickening thud, it struck the pirate in the stomach, and he fell backward out of sight.

"Bullseye," Ty shouted, grabbing the oar again. They were a good fifty feet away when they heard the almighty boom of a cannon.

"Heads down!" Kern shouted, but before they could even flinch they heard the whoosh of the cannonball passing them and then saw the giant splash. "Row!" Kern shouted again.

The sky lit up, and they saw a small globe of fire falling toward them.

"They have a magic user?" Ty groaned as he heaved on the oar.

"It's not magic, it's oil orbs. If one hits us, it will cover us all," Lan'esra shouted. "It's sticky and very flammable, so don't try and pat it out if one does hit; it will just spread."

Boom! Boom! Another two cannons were fired. The rushing noise that accompanied the lead balls just before the massive splash, only ten feet away, was louder and their aim was getting closer. The sky was lit again with three orbs heading directly at them.

"Row!" Kern shouted again.

"It is close now! I can make out the rocks on the shoreline," Ty said, trying to see the coast through the barrage of rain.

"Look out!" Galandrik said as one of the oil orbs struck the front of the boat and ignited. The prow was covered in the fiery liquid, and it had also spattered the captain and his clothes. The flames took hold quickly, untroubled by the rain and seawater. The other two orbs ignited when they hit the water; not only was a direct hit lethal, but even the misses were dangerous, as they lit up the area like a beacon.

Boom! Another cannon sounded and they all ducked their heads again. This time the ball splashed only a few feet away and the power of the wave it created rolled the boat side to side.

"The next one will finish us. We need to jump," Ty shouted. "Look! We could make it to that gap there!" He pointed to a spot in between two rocks.

"The fire will engulf us all soon," Galandrik said as the flames travelled towards them.

Four more oil orbs were launched from the ship, and shone bright in the night sky as they began falling down toward them like small fiery comets. *Boom!* Another cannon shot was heard in the distance and the whistling of the ball followed.

"Jump!" Kern shouted as he launched himself off the side of the boat and into the freezing sea, followed by Galandrik and Lan'esra. Three of the orbs hit the sea around the boat, lighting up the rocks and the gap they swam for. The last orb struck the middle of the boat, sending the fiery oil all over. Some splattered on Ty's leather leggings as he jumped from the boat, just as the cannonball struck the side, smashing the boat in half and sending fiery wooden splinters into the air.

Ty stayed underwater and could see the sea alight above him. He knew his companions were ahead but they were too far away to see. He swam for all he was worth. His heart rate doubled and he longed to take a breath. He heard a splash above him and saw a cannonball soaring through the water in front of him, followed by a tail of bubbles as it descended out of sight to the sea bed.

Above him, the fire had gone and he pushed himself upward, breaking the surface and inhaling as he did. He spat out some sea water as he gasped again. He spun, looking behind him. Remnants of the fire still lingered in patches, and the front end of the boat was now pointing upward, still alight. It fizzled out as the boat disappeared. The *Green Dragon* still sat in the distance, and he could hear the shouting from her crew.

"Ty!"

He heard Kern's shout and he spun round, swimming as best he could. Luckily the tide was in their favour and pushed them directly into the gap between the rocks. He saw Kern, Galandrik, and Lan'esra all on the shore, then felt his feet touch the bottom. He struggled as he waded through the water the last ten feet to his friends.

"Quickly, follow me," Kern ordered as he jumped onto a rock and climbed up. "Look, they are launching an assault," Kern said, pointing at the ship.

"Why are they launching boats?"

"Let me think… maybe to kill us?" Kern said, raising an eyebrow.

"Persistent bunch," Ty said, looking at the men climbing into the boat, "but we did just kill their captain, I guess."

"Pardon me? *We* killed him? You mean *you* killed him."

"It was an accident," Ty protested.

"How is shoving a man to his death an accident?" Kern argued.

"I didn't know he would land on his head."

"His hands were tied. What did you think he would do?"

"Enough. We need to move," Galandrik interrupted.

The Voltic Mountains stood ahead of them, looking gloomy and menacing. The ground was unforgiving; not a blade of grass could be seen. It was rock and stones all the way from the shore leading up to the skirt of the giant mountains that rose high above them.

"Follow me," the dwarf shouted as he jumped from rock to rock. Soon they were at the base of the mountain. Caves and cracks were plentiful and Galandrik bent down, using his dwarfish skills to examine each one as they passed. Finally he said, "This one," and stepped into a cave entrance.

"Don't light a torch; they will see it from Loft," Galandrik said.

"Maybe I can help," Lan'esra said, stepping forward. She held out her hand and a dull blueish light emanated from her palm, enough to see ten steps ahead by.

"Good work. Walk with me, lassy," Galandrik said, holding his axe in front of him. They continued for about twenty paces before the found the back of the cave. There was a tunnel leading upward and twisting round in a circle. They followed it until they entered another cave, looking down onto the rocky ground below. Lan'esra closed her hand, extinguishing the light, and they squatted, looking down on the torchlights that were dotted about as small parties of pirates flooded the isle in a vain attempt to find them.

"Look, there is another corridor here," Kern said, trying to see in the darkness. "Lan'esra, light it up. Galandrik, keep an eye on them below. If any get close to the entrance below, let me know."

"Aye, lad."

Kern followed the corridor for another twenty paces. It curved deeper into the mountain, then came to a circular room. Lan'esra shone her light and they saw bedding that had been made up on the floor, and two torches hanging from the wall. A collection of rusty weapons and armour lay piled against a wall next to a stack of firewood, and the remains of a fire sat in the middle.

"I guess we are not the first to visit here," the cleric said.

"No, but the first in a while, it looks like," Kern said, dropping his backpack to the floor and searching for his flint and tinder.

Galandrik and Ty entered the room. "They are retreating," Galandrik said.

"Good. We'll have to get out of these wet clothes soon, before we die of the cold," Kern answered. "As soon as we're sure they're gone, we'll light some torches and that fire, and try to dry off."

It wasn't too much longer before the coast was clear and Kern soon had a fire crackling on the floor. The smoke rose up and out through a crack in the ceiling.

"Get out of your wet clothes and empty your packs. You'll need to dry the equipment. Mine was soaked," Kern said, pouring some water into a tin pot.

Soon all four were out of their wet clothes and into the spare driest clothing they had left. Their equipment was spread out over the cave floor to dry. Makeshift linen lines hung across the room with clothes, blankets, and leather armour hanging from them. Kern added some vegetables to the pot and hung it above the fire, while Galandrik and Ty looked through the pile of swords and armour; most had been largely consumed by rust. Sword hilts with only a few inches of blade left lay on the floor, amidst the leather straps that had once graced their handles. Galandrik held up a chainmail vest by the shoulders; the front was completely rusted away, and only the back remained. A shield that was more of a half-moon lay at his feet.

"Looks like these have been here a while," Ty said, holding up a dagger hilt. "Shame. This feels like a decent weight," he concluded, tossing it into the air and catching it.

"Here, throw this in the pot," Galandrik said, tossing Kern a sack.

"What is it?" Kern said, looking into the sack. "A rabbit? Where the hell did you get a rabbit?"

"I grabbed it from the kitchen as we passed by on the ship," the dwarf said sheepishly.

"And you call *me* the thief," Ty laughed.

As they warmed their cold bodies around the fire, Galandrik examined the rum from the ship and still debated trying it.

"So Lan'esra," Kern said, "do you know what fighort leaf looks like?"

"Yes, it's a white leafy weed. Grows in bunches. You can't miss it, it stinks of cat's piss."

"Great. You can carry it then," Ty said, feeling his still-wet hanging clothes.

"It isn't that bad, but that's how we tell," she explained.

"Finding it is going to be the hard part," Kern said.

"Do we actually know where the entrance to the dungeon is?" she asked.

"Nope, but Mr Sabrehargen here will surely find it," Kern smiled.

"First thing in the morning. I haven't had a good sleep for days," the dwarf said, making a bed of the driest blanket he had.

"I hate dungeons," Ty announced out of the blue.

"I thought you liked them. Riches and magic items to be found," Lan'esra asked.

"I like that part, but getting them is different."

"It could be worse, lad."

"True, we could be in the hull of that ship awaiting slavery like the oth—" Ty stopped mid-sentence and grimaced, knowing what was coming.

"Go on. You were saying, about others?" Kern asked sternly.

"The other slaves on the ship," Ty said reluctantly.

"Are you telling me that the *Green Dragon* was a slave-trade ship?"

"Yes. Why else would they want to throw us in the hold?"

"And you knew that the hold was full of men, women, and children awaiting their fate of being sold to some fat lord in Bloodmoore?"

"Not really, I just—"

"And you didn't want to mention it?" Kern interrupted.

"This is why! We are on a quest to save your father."

"We could have saved lives! We could have helped."

"How, by taking on the whole ship? It would have been suicide."

"Maybe, but it would have been *right*."

"Right or wrong, it would have been a whole new unwanted quest! If we had released them, then what? Sail the ship back to Loft and report it to Lord Lokin, the man who was making money on their sale? Think about it."

"I didn't get a *chance* to think about it, did I? You kept it a secret."

"It's none of our business. *This* is our business," Ty said, hitting the floor with his fist.

"We could have made it our business."

"Oh, sorry. I forgot. 'Kern the Dragon Tamer, the Slayer of Giants'—now you want to add 'the Slave Saver' to the list of false titles?"

"That's what this is about, isn't it? You're jealous."

"Jealous? Jealous of *you*? You're so far up your own arse we should report you missing!"

"I should have left you in the Spider Temple!"

"Then you would have been in the hold now, all drugged up."

"Enough already," Galandrik interrupted.

Kern and Ty both huffed like a couple of arguing school boys. Lan'esra didn't know where to look as the dwarf raised a knowing eyebrow. The uncomfortable silence lingered for several minutes before Kern finally spoke.

"Who's taking first watch?" he said, throwing a lump of wood on the fire.

"Do we need to? I could set a trap down the other corridor and that would alert us," Ty suggested, as if the argument had never happened.

"What if they can disarm them?" Kern asked.

"I'll make it a good one," Ty answered.

"No, you have done enough damage for one day. I'll take the first watch; then Galandrik, then you, then Lan'esra."

Ty agreed, mumbling something under his breath. The others nodded and made the best bedding they could. Soon the dwarf was snoring.

Chapter Twenty
Keep Awake

Kern rotated his backpack next to the open fire, drying the other side. He moved against the wall and wrapped his arms around his legs, placing his chin on his knees. He thought of his father—Thrane—and wondered how he would react after his release. He thought of the slaves on the ship, and tried to think of ways they could have released them and chartered the ship to another port. But the more he thought about it, the more he knew Ty was right. Lord Lokin—cousin of King Moriak, dealing in the slave trade. Who would he have gone to? Maybe just releasing them would have been enough.

He felt a chill and the wind howled down the corridor, the flames of the fire flickering and dancing to its voiceless song.

Kern heard a strange noise; he looked as the flickering fire lit the passageway, and placed his hand on the hilt of his sword and listened. "Must have been the wind," he mumbled to himself, still looking intently into the next cave. Quietly he got to his feet and walked to the exit, sword in hand. Suddenly he saw a shadow dart across the entrance inside the other room. He stepped back, raising his sword and squinting his eyes to help him see better.

"Kern…"

He thought he heard a female voice call from the room ahead. The wind blew his hair and dust blew into his eyes. He stepped back and silently placed his sword down and picked up his bow. Swinging the quiver over his shoulder, he notched an arrow and aimed it down the corridor.

"Kern…" he heard again in a windy, whispery voice.

Is that wind? the ranger thought in confusion. *My mind's playing tricks. Get a grip.* He took a step into the corridor and listened, and thought he could hear a faint crying from the room in front. Slowly and silently he stepped forward as the crying got louder and louder, until he saw where it was coming from. A little girl was standing with hands over her face, long dirty blonde hair hanging down to her waist. Her dress, which had once been white, was dirty and ripped, and her bare feet were black and bloody. Kern dropped his bow and ran over to the girl. Bending down, he placed his hands on her shoulders.

"Don't cry, little one," he said softly. "I am here. What is your name?"

"Katalina," she said between sniffles.

"Katalina is a lovely name. What are you doing here?"

"I escaped from the boat."

"Boat? Do you mean the big boat just out there?" Kern said, slightly confused.

"Yes, the big boat that you just left," she said, still covering her face.

"But how did you escape?"

"My mother held me up, and I climbed up onto a man's shoulders and squeezed through the bars."

"Clever girl. Where was—"

"My mother said, 'go call Kern and he will free us all,' but you ran off and left us to die."

"No, I never knew you were down there."

"Do you know what they do to little girls like me?"

"Listen, Katalina, I will wake the others and we can go—"

"Ty is right about you. You only care about what people think. If you truly cared, you would have helped us," she said, dropping her hands and staring at the ranger. Her upset demeanour slowly changed and her face was contorted by all-consuming anger. Her nostrils flared, her eyes closed into slits, her mouth tightened, and she raised one hand, pointing at Kern as he stood up and placed his hands on his head, turning round. She spewed the words like a snake spitting venom. "My mother is being raped as we speak, because of you."

"No, I couldn't do anything," he said, looking at the now-aggressive little girl.

"You may as well kill me, rape me too!"

"Stop saying these things! It's not my fault; Ty never told me you were there!"

"Don't blame Ty. He saved you, and you couldn't even save a little girl."

"She is right," Kern heard a man's voice say.

He spun round and saw his father, "Thrane, what are you doing here? How did—"

"I escaped, like she did; you could never have saved me. You're pathetic."

"But… but how did you find me?" Kern stuttered.

"How did I *find* you? You leave tracks like a clumsy mountain bear. You never were any good, not like your brother Noahk," Thrane said, stepping next to the girl and placing his hand on her shoulder.

"I don't… How did you escape the cage and… How did you get to—"

"Without your help, that's how I escaped!"

"As did I," the little girl said menacingly.

"I may as well kill this little bitch. She is dead anyway. You have seen to that," Thrane said as he gripped the girl's hair, pulling her head back.

Kern stepped forward and held his hands out, palms up. "No! Let me take her, let me save her! I will take her to her family"

"Don't make me laugh, you insignificant little fuck. It's far too late for that," his father replied, drawing a dagger and placing it against her neck.

"Stop! Why are you doing this?" Kern shouted.

"Do it! Before he rapes me!" Katalina screamed.

"Raping innocents now, are we? What have you become, you monster?"

"I haven't raped anybody! Please—just put the knife down."

"You have failed, Kern; you have failed me, your mother, and Noahk. You are a disgrace to the Ocarns," Thrane said, slicing the dagger through the girl's throat. Blood gushed out, covering her dress in a red waterfall.

"You killed me, Kern Ocarn," she gurgled before falling forward, her face smashing into the stone floor.

"Nooo!" Kern shouted and ran at Thrane, tackling him around his middle and throwing him back onto the floor. "You bastard! She didn't deserve to die!" Kern knelt on Thrane and held his hands down to the floor.

"You dare beat your father, your own flesh and blood?"

"You killed an innocent girl!" Kern shouted.

"Release me, Kern!"

Kern looked down at Thrane and remembered the respect he'd had for him as a child, but now he was kneeling over him holding his wrists, restraining him.

Does he hate me that much, to turn into this... thing?

Kern slowly let the pressure up off his father's wrists and leaned back. "What's happening? What is going on?" he whispered.

Kern felt a solid blow to his stomach and bent forward as the wind was knocked out of him. He opened his eyes just as a left hook from Thrane knocked him sideways onto the floor. He rolled onto his back and gasped for air. Looking up, he saw Katalina looming over him, her dress and hair drenched with blood, her eyes bloodshot red and her head tilted to one side.

"What's the matter, cat got your tongue?" she said. Her voice was a horrid gargling sound as more blood oozed from her mouth and neck. She slowly began to smile, but as her mouth opened he noticed she was toothless, and blood began to flow even more freely from her toothless smile. She screamed as she lunged forward, landing on top of the ranger. Her nose was only inches from his and she thrashed about, biting, clawing, and screaming. Blood poured from her neck and mouth and poured onto his face. He felt the warmth of her blood enter his mouth and he spat it out. Using all his strength, he threw the girl off. She rolled a couple of times and ended up lying face down, hands over her face, and the familiar crying was heard again.

Kern bent down and spat again on the floor, picking up a rusty short sword.

"Very courageous, hitting a little girl," Thrane said from behind him.

"Stop!" Kern shouted as he spun round, facing his father. "I don't know what's happening here, but she is not a little girl and my real father would never hit with his left hand!" Kern threw the short sword at his father, and it stuck, tip first, straight in the forehead. The figure stood dead still and the sword fell from his hand. The colour drained away and the figure of his father became almost transparent. It began to flicker and change, and in the blink of an eye the form changed from Thrane to the little girl and back. It flickered again between different figures: Bok, Conn, Joli, Thrane, Katalina, Solomon, Jarrow, and Svorn—all appeared and disappeared hundreds of times in a split second. He could see them all clearly then, in a flash, gone.

He was in the first room, and it was dark and damp. The cool night air gently blew through the opening. He glanced around for the girl or Thrane, but there was nothing, no sign of anything. He could see the fire flickering in the distance where his companions slept. He looked down for his bow, but it was also gone.

"Wake up. Kern, wake up!"

Kern opened his eyes and sat up straight. Sweat drenched his forehead and neck. "What… what time is it?" he asked, rubbing his eyes.

"It's time for my watch, lad. I woke up for a piss and you were sound asleep, making some funny noises."

"Asleep?" He felt his face for the blood, but nothing was there. He could still taste Katalina's blood in his mouth, and he spat onto the floor. "I had the strangest dream."

"Aye, lad. I thought you were having a fit."

"It was pretty rough, I admit."

"Best you get back to sleep, lad. There is still a long journey ahead of us."

"You are right. Be careful, Gal," Kern said, curling up on his bedroll.

*

Galandrik stoked the fire and watched as the red embers rose and skittered about like fireflies. He grabbed another chunk of wood and placed it on the top, and watched as the flames licked around it like a slobbering dog around a new bone. He rubbed his hands together at the new heat it was generating, and watched as Ty rolled over and Lan'esra flicked out her legs. "This must be why they call it The Dungeon of Dreams," he muttered to himself.

He walked over to his axe and picked it up, examining its beauty in the fire light. He held it in both hands and pointed it out straight, looking down the edge of the blade. *How many orcs will this kill before it rusts away?* he thought. He wandered down the corridor into the next room and stood looking out the entrance. Even though the moon was out, he couldn't make out the rocks lining the shore or the sea in the distance. He spun round with his axe as if there was an attacker behind him. His axe whistled through the air in an arc before he rested it down onto the floor with a smile. "You never lose it, lad," he whispered to himself with satisfaction, "you never lose it." He picked the axe up again and crouched, as though he was in an aggressive melee stance. Then he pounced forward, sweeping his axe upward and spinning around, swinging it in one hand and pivoting on one leg. The axe came round as he returned to his starting position, holding his axe in both hands.

Galandrik paused to catch his breath. "I'm too old for this." He picked up his axe and walked over to the entrance again, still breathing heavily. Even the weight of the axe in his hands made his muscles ache. His biceps burned as the blood pumped through his body. *I used to swing this all day for fun,* he thought, and with a shake of his head he lowered the axe to the floor. As it touched, he heard a metal-on-metal sound.

Laying his axe on the floor, he knelt down and brushed the dirt and stones away, revealing a metal hatch. After a few minutes it was clear it was a doorway down, complete with a metal ring to lift it. Galandrik thought about waking the others, but his curiosity got the better of him. *Let them sleep,* he thought. *I will just take a peek.*

He grabbed the ring with both hands and pulled, but it didn't budge. The dwarf jumped up and rolled his shoulders. "Come on, don't let this beat you," he said out loud and spat into his palms. He jerked his head side to side, making his neck crack, and rubbed his hands together. "This time, lad!"

Galandrik bent down again and grabbed the ring. Straightening his back, he counted: *One... two... three.* He heaved and groaned as slowly the door started to lift. "Come on, lad, lift!" He moaned under the strain of the door's weight. Eventually the iron trap door cracked free from the dirt that surrounded its edges, and he raised the door until its edge was at his waist. He repositioned his hands and edged his feet forward either side of the entrance until the door was at its tipping point. With one almighty shove, it fell backward and stopped. The hinges stopped it from falling all the way back.

Galandrik punched the air. "Yes!" he shouted, then remembered the others sleeping. He gingerly stepped to the corridor and peered to see if anyone had heard him. All was quiet, apart from the crackle of the fire.

Galandrik saw a set of steps which looked like they were carved into the mountain itself. He grabbed his axe and made his way down them. They looked surprisingly clean and dirt-free for something that hadn't been used for a long time. It was even well-lit, though there was no sign of torches. The steps led down about twenty feet and stopped at a solid-looking oak door.

He examined the door for a second, debating whether to go grab Ty to search for traps, but again his curiosity got the better of him. For some reason he relished this solo adventuring. He grabbed the door handle and slowly turned, looking to either side of him, half-expecting something to come jabbing out or the floor to disappear beneath his feet. But nothing happened as the door clicked open. He pushed it inward, and heard voices and the sound of swords clashing together. Looking down from the doorway, he could tell he was a good twenty feet up from the room's floor. It was a square room with one exit to his left. Ty and Lan'esra were backed against the right wall, fighting a half dozen orcs. The room was bare, other than three dead orcs lying face down.

"Get down here quick, Gal! We can't hold them off much longer," Ty shouted, dodging a thrust from an attacking orc and swiping a dagger across the orc's forearm.

Galandrik's heart raced and he searched around for some way down, but there wasn't any—apart from the obvious jump.

Holding her mace in two hands, Lan'esra parried a downward swing, the orc's sword burying itself deep into the mace's wooden shaft. The orc's strength was clearly greater as he pushed the sword closer to her head.

"Hold on, lassy," Galandrik shouted as he held the axe in both hands. He stepped as far forward as he could, then looked up to make sure he wouldn't knock himself out on the top of the door frame.

He shouted as he leapt from the doorway, landing on top of two orcs and sending them crashing to the ground with him, all three rolling and disorientated. He felt an indescribable pain in his right ankle as he lay on his back. He reached for his axe but it was out of reach, and he saw the two orcs shake their heads as they tried to rise. Galandrik sat up to get to his feet and saw his foot. It was twisted and pointing at a right angle, and the pain suddenly hit home like a thunderbolt. It raced through his body, burning every nerve ending he had. The two orcs stood and picked up their weapons. The dwarf tried to forget the pain and reach for his axe, but the burning pain was too great. He screamed in agony and reached for his broken ankle. The orc raised his sword as Galandrik saw Ty behind him shouting, "Galandrik! Galandrik! Your leg is on fire! *Galandrik!*"

Galandrik opened his eyes and saw Ty standing above him in the cave. He looked down and saw that his ankle was smoking. He could feel the heat through his leather boots, and he jumped to his feet.

"Ow! Ow!" he shouted as he hopped about, undoing the leather laces that tied his boot. He flicked it off and quickly removed his sock.

"Come here," Lan'esra shouted and the dwarf hopped over to her. She held his reddened ankle and trickled water over it.

"Oh, that's better. Don't stop."

"I can't believe you feel asleep with your foot in the fire," Ty scoffed.

"Did I? I can't remember falling asleep. Saying that, I can't remember sitting down either," he answered, leaning on Ty's shoulder as Lan'esra tended to his foot.

"I have something for this. I need to mix it. Keep a cold tin or something next to the burn to keep it cool. It'll help," Lan'esra explained.

Kern sat up, rubbing his eyes. "What's going on?"

"Dumbass here fell asleep with his foot in the fire," Ty answered, bending down and laughing.

Kern smiled. "Really? How did you manage that?" he replied with a snigger.

"I don't think I did. One minute I was in there opening a trap—"

"A trap what?" Ty asked, rubbing the tears away from his eyes.

"Nothing. I must have dreamt it," the grumpy dwarf said, folding his arms as Lan'esra rubbed cream onto his foot.

"I should think you did," Ty laughed, stretching.

"It should keep the heat away," Lan'esra said, wrapping a bandage around his foot. "It's not a bad burn, just minor. You'll be fine."

"Thanks, lassy," he replied, picking up his sock.

"I think something is definitely amiss here. I had a real bad dream earlier, and now Galandrik," Kern said, sitting against the wall.

"Well, we are searching for the Dungeon of Dreams," Lan'esra replied.

"It's a bit chilly in here now. Kern, do me a favour and throw another foot on the fire," Ty said, lying down on his bed laughing.

"I'll throw you on," Galandrik said angrily.

"Be serious for a minute. These dreams mean something, I am sure of it," Kern said.

"I agree, but what?" the cleric said, sitting down next to Kern.

"Well, I dreamt about a survivor from the boat and my father—one person that I *should* have rescued," he said with a dark look at Ty, "and one I am *trying* to rescue."

"What about your dream?" she asked the dwarf.

"I found a secret trapdoor through there and went down a flight of stairs. At the bottom, a door blocked my way, and when I opened it you and Ty were in a room below, outnumbered and fighting a troop of orcs. I jumped down to smash their skulls and save the day, but I landed badly and busted my ankle."

"Your subconscious must have felt the pain from the fire and transferred it into the dream as a broken ankle, I guess."

"Yeah. I could feel the pain in the dream like it was real."

"Well, what you felt *was* real. Your foot was on fire," Ty chuckled.

"But I don't know if they are connected dreams, or maybe just coincidence. Ty and I didn't have a dream."

"Who knows? I think we should eat, then look for the entrance," Kern said, walking through to the adjacent room. "I wonder if that ship has sailed yet," he added as Ty followed.

Kern and Ty stared out of the hole in the side of the mountain. The sun was rising on the horizon and there was no sign of any ships. Water crashed against the craggy rocks stretching along the unforgiving coast line; seagulls hovered above, swooping down and catching the stranded fish that had been washed onto the rocks by the waves. The slope that led down from the opening to the floor and along to the coast line was made up of rocks and stone. There was not a blade of grass in sight.

"Fancy sliding down this one?" Ty asked.

"No trees to break our fall this time," Kern smiled.

"Fish for breakfast?" Ty said as he watched the gulls feast on the easy morning meals.

"I'll heat the pan," Kern said, turning round and heading back toward the others.

"I guess I'll go gather some," Ty groaned.

Chapter Twenty-One
The Search for the Herb

All four sat eating their fish breakfast. "I can't remember the last time I ate fish," Galandrik said with a burp.

"No, I can't either. There's plenty down there. You have to fight the gulls for them; they swoop down and snatch them from your hands," Ty said.

"Better you than me. Those birds are vicious," the dwarf said.

"Where do we start looking for the entrance?" Lan'esra said, packing her bedroll up.

"We will just go out and head north around the curve of the mountain. It'll show up," Kern explained.

A finch flew through the corridor and made straight for Ty. The startled thief jumped as it landed on his shoulder.

"It's just the paperfinch returning," Lan'esra chuckled.

Ty cupped the bird in his hands and listened. "'Just get the herbs and complete the quest. Thrane's life depends upon it and Bok's death has saved me a job,'" he said to the party.

"What did it say about my father?" Kern said, springing to his feet.

"'Just get the herbs and complete the quest. Thrane's life depends upon it and Bok's death has saved me a job,'" Ty repeated.

"Wait a minute, 'Bok's death'? What the hell has that toad got to do with all this?" Kern said.

"This is getting more confusing than ever," Galandrik said scratching his ginger beard.

"I don't understand. Where did you get that paperfinch from again?" Kern asked, frowning.

"I bumped into some guy in the street, just before we had the brawl with Retch, and took the opportunity to relieve him of his purse. It was easy. See, when someone opens up to you and—"

"I know *how* you did it, but who was he?" Kern interrupted.

"I don't know," Ty said, slightly annoyed that he hadn't got to tell his story.

"Who was the finch from?" Lan'esra asked.

"A wizard named Conn," Galandrik said.

"There was a 'C' on the finch, if you remember," she reminded them.

"So the finch you stole belonged to Conn—but what has all this got to do with Bok?" Kern mused.

"How does Conn even know Bok?" Ty added.

"This is weird. And why would he think Bok is dead?" the ranger said, scratching his head.

"Well, if Bok had the finch, he wouldn't just give it to Ty, would he?" Lan'esra asked.

"Give it to me? He would sooner put a dagger through my heart."

"So the man you stole it from in Wade must have been this Bok character. Then when Conn got the message you sent, saying you had killed everyone, he assumed you killed Bok and stole it," she suggested.

"No, it wasn't Bok. This guy had real bad scarring down his left cheek. I couldn't make out much more. His hood was covering his head."

Kern and Galandrik stared at each other before saying simultaneously, "Kob!"

"Kob? The thief you hired to replace me?"

"Damn, how stupid are we? Kob is Bok. Get it? He reversed his name."

"So let me get this straight, you replaced me with the person who killed me?" Ty sniggered.

"Remember when we met Kob—or Bok or whoever—he said Ty was

dead. He said he'd heard a bounty hunter took him out with a single arrow to the chest," Galandrik said.

"Yes, he did! He must have been talking about himself. He didn't know Ty was still alive—the last thing he'd seen was the arrow sticking out of Ty's chest," Kern said.

"That's why he disappeared when he saw Ty in the Spider God's temple, remember?"

"Yes. He didn't want me to look through the spyhole in the door; he said it was 'only a sacrifice.' He knew that as soon as we saw Ty we would rescue him. No wonder he went as white as a sheet, that sneaky bastard," Kern growled.

"So Bok is now working for Conn, then?" Ty questioned.

"Yes, he must be. He must have followed us to Wade."

"Well, unless he hid in one of the balloon baskets and then snuck onto the boat he must still be there," Lan'esra pointed out.

"He won't give up until one of us is dead," Ty stated. "He will follow me to the ends of the earth."

"He can join the queue then," the dwarf sniggered.

"That was one hell of a disguise, though," Kern admitted.

"Oh come on, it doesn't take a lot to fool you two. I would have known him straight away," Ty said, smiling.

"Of course you would have," Kern said rolling his eyes.

"I would have definitely seen through it. His charisma versus my intelligence? No problem!"

"Yes, I'm sure if you had, say, *bumped into him,* you'd have seen straight through his disguise," Galandrik laughed.

"Well, but—" Ty began.

"Whatever. Come on, let's find this entrance. We can worry about Bok later," Kern said, getting up.

*

They made their way out of the cave and started heading north around the skirt of the mountain. The terrain was a combination of rock and loose stone, which made the ground rough under foot. The ring of staggered rocks that lined the coast protected them from the sea and wind, and hundreds of birds sat and watched them from their rocky homes. Fish bones and crab shells were scattered everywhere. They followed Galandrik as he led the way. After two hours they had reached the north end of the isle. "No tracks, no common signs of manmade trails," Kern said, kneeling down.

"Nor any difference in the rock formation," the dwarf added. "Nothing has been here for years, apart from a million seagulls."

They carried on around the northeast curve of the mountain. The coastline stayed just as rugged and challenging, but the distance between the shore and the mountain slowly started to widen.

"This is probably a wild goose chase," Ty mumbled as he negotiated the loose rocks.

"Nonsense. I know loads of people who have been here," Kern answered.

"Did Heldar tell you this?" Ty quipped.

"Only you listen to Heldar."

"Well, it's better than listening to Fat Mary."

"Who is this Fat Mary?" Lan'esra asked. "I keep hearing her name."

"She is a rather large woman with whom Kern got drunkenly locked in a cupboard one night," Ty laughed.

"Don't listen to him. Fat Mary is his comfort blanket," Kern said, dismissing the cupboard story.

"Maybe when we go back that way, I can ask her for the truth," Lan'esra laughed.

"Look!" Galandrik shouted. "There's a tower."

All four stood and looked in the direction that Galandrik was pointing. On the east side of the mountain, as the gap between the mountain and the shore line widened, stood a tower in the middle of a lake. The ground leading down to the lake got less stony and they could see grass in the distance.

"I guess there is your Dungeon of Dreams," Ty said.

"Only one way to find out, I guess," Kern replied.

They kept walking until they were within fifty yards of the lake. Only a few stones lay about in the luscious grass underfoot. The tower was one hundred fifty feet high and at least a hundred feet in diameter; random windows were dotted all around the circular structure. The walls were white-painted bricks, and on the top sat a brown thatched roof. The distance between the edge of the lake and the tower was a good three hundred feet; they knew a swim would be out of the question.

"Look down there, on the bank of the lake," Lan'esra said, pointing.

"What is it? It looks like a large rock," the dwarf said, squinting.

"No, it's a person," Kern disagreed.

"Let's go say hello, then," Ty said.

They got ten paces away and stopped. It was indeed a brown-cloaked figure hunched over at the edge of the lake.

"Hello, friend!" Kern said to the lone figure. With a jump like a startled rabbit, the figure spun round and got to his feet, revealing under the cloak a tall, skinny, young human wearing a set of brown robes, complete with a large leather belt with pouches along it. A fishing rod dropped to the ground as he sprang up. His face was pale and narrow, and his pointed nose made him look like a new-born chick. He pulled a gnarled foot-long wand from his belt and pointed it at the four adventurers.

"Don't make me fry you! I am powerful," the robed boy shouted, his hand shaking visibly.

"Whoa! Please don't hurt us," Ty said sarcastically. The man seemed as harmless as the new-born chick he resembled.

Kern gave a shake of his head and said, casting an eye at Ty, "Listen, we are not here to hurt you. We are just passing through."

"Well, just pass, unless you want—"

"To be fried?" Ty interrupted, sniggering.

"Don't push me!" the skinny man said loudly.

"If you're all-powerful, why are you fishing?" Ty said, folding his arms. "Why don't you just conjure some food?"

The man didn't answer; he just held the wand up higher and pointed it at Ty.

"Please ignore my friend. We are all friendly here… even him," Kern said, holding his hands up.

At that moment, Ty took a step forward. "BOO!" he shouted with a jolt of his small frame, as though he was going to lunge for the boy.

"*Hazan amor!*" the boy shouted, thrusting the wand forward at Ty. The wand fizzled and crackled, and a tiny puff of smoke rose from the tip. The boy hit the wand with his free hand. "Damn thing is still wet."

Ty laughed. "What?" he asked, after catching Kern's steely glare.

"You're a bad man, Mr Rat," Lan'esra said.

"He could have had a wand of lightning bolts, for all you knew," Galandrik added.

"I wish he had," Kern said, stepping closer to the boy.

"Oh, that's right—Pick On Ty Day, is it?" the thief said, his smile now gone.

Kern pulled the backpack off his shoulder and sat it on the ground. He delved inside and took out some dried beef rations and held them out to the boy. "Here you go, lad."

The boy tucked the wand back into his belt with a shaking hand, and reached for the food. He picked up a slice and chewed it like he hadn't eaten in many moons. Kern offered his water canteen and got the same response.

While the boy devoured the meat and drank half his canteen, Kern was examining him closely. When the boy had finished the rations, he asked, "Why are you here?"

"I came with a party of four trying to enter the tower. We were attacked by wargs that came down from the mountains at night, killing our leader. Another died swimming in the lake. He went diving, looking for the entrance, and never came back. We had him on a rope, but it became limp and just floated to the surface. My friend Polak went off to the south looking for firewood but also never returned. I have been here for four days."

"Why haven't the wargs eaten you, then?" Ty asked.

"Just up the mountain slightly, there is a small cave that I can just about crawl into. I had to kill a couple of snakes, but once inside it's big enough to sleep comfortably. Wargs can't get in; their heads are far too big."

"Did the wand fry the snakes?" Ty quipped.

"It wasn't wet then," the boy snapped.

"Ignore him. He had a bad experience in an alleyway once with a wand," Kern said, smiling at Ty. "My name is Kern, and these are Galandrik and Lan'esra. He is the Rat."

"Nice to meet you all, and how fitting your name is, sir," the boy said, smiling at Ty.

"What's yours?" Ty answered, raising an eyebrow.

"My name is Darkfire," the boy said proudly.

"Darkfire?" Ty said, laughing. "No, seriously, what's your real name?"

The young man's face reddened before finally answering, "It is Darkfire."

"Okay, Darkfire it is then," Ty said, stepping to the edge of the lake. "I only asked."

"Nice to meet you, Darkfire. What do you know of the temple?" Kern asked.

"Well, not a lot, apart from that people call it the Dungeon of Dreams. We heard rumours of a secret entrance under the water, but obviously we never got close to finding it."

"Well, there isn't going to be a front door, that's for sure, lad," Galandrik said, looking over the water and the mist-covered bottom of the tower.

"No shit," Ty mumbled.

"Right. Lan'esra, you come with me and walk around the lake this way. Ty and Galandrik, you go that way. Meet dead opposite."

"Why?" Ty grunted.

"See what we can find, stumble across. You never know—you may find a boat," Kern smiled sarcastically.

"Why can't Darkfire summon one?" Ty said, looking at the boy wizard.

"Why don't you just—" Darkfire started to say.

"Right! Let's walk, and hopefully we can find something," Galandrik interrupted, grabbing Ty's shoulder and spinning him around.

"See you on the other side," Lan'esra added.

"What about me?" Darkfire blurted out.

Without even turning round, Ty said, "No chance."

Kern rolled his eyes. "Come with us."

*

"Why do you always antagonise people, Mr Rat?" the dwarf asked as they wandered around the bank of the lake.

"I was just playing with him," he answered, wincing as he felt the hardened skin under his tunic.

"What's up with you?"

"Nothing, just an old wound," Ty lied. "This is going to take forever," he said, changing the conversation.

"Well, unless you want to swim across, lad, searching for a boat may be a blessing in disguise."

"True, but I can't see a boat being left here anywhere."

"That is yet to be seen."

*

Kern, Lan'esra, and Darkfire walked along on the opposite side.

"Why does Rat mock me, Mr Kern?"

"Don't take offence. It isn't you; he mocks everybody, until you get to know him," Kern explained.

"Yes, and then he mocks you more," Lan'esra smiled.

Kern smiled at her, "True. I don't think he will change much now."

"This wand does work. It just got wet, that's all," the boy wizard explained.

"I'm sure it does, and you will be able to show us soon. What's in the pouches on the belt?"

"It's herbs; herbs for my spells."

"Do you know much about herbs, other than your spell ingredients?"

"Yes, I studied alchemy and know enough. Why?"

"We are looking for fighort leaf."

"Really? Fighort leaf is rare—and I mean *rare*. I haven't seen any for ages."

"Well, is it supposed to grow in the Dungeon of Dreams."

"I wouldn't know, but if I see it I will know it," the young boy said, smiling.

"Lan, what was the other herb?"

"Willow rose," she replied.

"Ah, willow rose is more common, and is usually found down in Lake

Fortune. It all makes sense now—you are making a superior healing potion to cure buckthorn poison?"

"I don't really know, to be honest," Kern shrugged.

"Willow rose, fighort leaf, and sorrwell wood bark mixed make a cure for buckthorn poison. That's the only time I have heard of those two being mixed, apart from the treatment of troll bites."

"Troll bites?" Lan'esra asked.

"Yes. Their saliva isn't poisonous like a snake's venom is, but it will gradually rot your flesh away. When they eat animal bones, the saliva and acids in their stomachs is so powerful it decays the bones in days. Amazing creatures, evolved over centuries—"

"Okay, we get it," Kern interrupted.

"Sorry, I get carried away. But yes, unless you're mixing willow rose, fighort leaf, and sorrwell wood bark to cure buckthorn poison, you will mix willow rose, fighort leaf, and sourmash grapes to cure the flesh-rotting bite from a troll," Darkfire said with a knowledgeable smile.

"I think it's poison in this case. I can't see the king getting close to a troll," Lan'esra said.

"The king? You are on a quest for the *king*? King Moriak?" Darkfire said eagerly.

Kern glared at the cleric and she mouthed, 'Sorry.'

"Yes, we are on a mission for King Moriak. You must not tell a soul, because it is a very secret mission."

"If King Moriak has been poisoned by buckthorn, you better get your skates on. It kills very quickly."

Kern thought about this, remembering how they had been told to be hasty in the quest. Then he thought of his dad, locked in the cage, and how this boy knew of the king's illness and could spread it across the land of Bodisha. He knew their names and their quest. *Damn Lan'esra.*

"But I have been around this island many times and never seen a sign of fighort leaf," Darkfire continued.

"Well, it doesn't hurt to have another look," Kern replied.

"Of course not. Maybe things have changed since I last looked."

"If we cannot find a boat, what choices do we have?" Lan'esra asked.

"Getting wet, I guess," the ranger replied.

"I have some leaves that help you breathe underwater," the boy said, searching through one of his pouches.

"I believe you, no need to show me," Kern said, paying no attention as the boy fumbled in his pouch.

After an hour's walk, the party finally met on the south shore of the lake. "How many boats did you find?" Ty asked.

"About the same as you did," Lan'esra answered before Kern said anything.

"Looks like someone is getting wet then, lad," Galandrik added.

"Darkfire, when you and your party got here, where did you go in and what exactly did you find?" Kern questioned.

"Well, roughly where you met me. We tried a few things because we had no guidance, so we just guessed at it. First we lowered a rope down with a rock tied to it. The rope was at least fifty feet long, but it never touched the bottom. It's very deep."

"And you said your friend drowned?"

"Yes. The rope just went limp and we never saw him again."

Kern looked into the water, scratching his chin. Then he picked up the largest rock he could find, took a run-up, and launched the rock as far as he could. The rock hit the water, making a splash several feet high. From all around the area of impact, fish jumped out of the water—fish with wings like a dragon, a yellow lion-like mane, and a completely red body.

"Dragonfish!" Kern said. "That's why your friend never returned. The lake is full of them."

"I wish we had done that first," Darkfire muttered, swallowing hard.

"Well, best we make a boat then," Lan'esra said.

"Make a boat?" Ty replied. "Out of what?"

"If we walk along the coast I'm sure we will find wood and stuff."

"If you think I'm going to set sail on a boat made of scrap wood across a lake full of dragonfish you are sorely mistaken."

"Just an idea," she replied.

"And a good one," Kern agreed. "I can't see any other way of getting across."

"If we made a boat that actually floated, and made it across the lake, then what? We already said there isn't going to be a front door."

"Stay here then," Kern said, striding off toward the east coast of the island.

"Please tell me it isn't just me who thinks this is crazy," Ty asked.

"His father is a prisoner, Ty. He will do what he must do," Galandrik replied.

*

All five walked to the rocks that jutted upward around the eastern coastline of the island. This side wasn't as rugged as the west, and soon they found a path that led down through the rocks to the shore. The path was neat and curved downward. At the bottom of the path was a stone jetty that lurched out into the sea like a giant diving board. They could only make it out when the tide sucked itself out, leaving spinning whirlpools before crashing forward again. They could make out wooden posts buried in the slab that boats moored to when the vicious sea allowed them to. The sea was rough and there was no shore, just waves crashing up onto the rocks that surrounded the isle.

"Never going to find anything down there," Galandrik said.

"No, you're right. This path is being used. Look, no loose stones, all pushed to the side," Kern said, kneeling examining the ground, "I'd say this has been used recently."

"Really? I wonder by whom?" Darkfire asked.

"Whoever lives in that tower is my guess. Why else would you want to come here?" Lan'esra said.

"I'll take a look north and see what other pathways I can find," Ty said, walking back up the path.

"I'm hungry," Galandrik said, rubbing his belly.

"Come on," Kern said with a smile.

"Look at this!" Ty said, squatting down at the top of the slope.

The others gathered around the thief and glanced out over the lake. To their amazement, they saw a small boat coming out of the mist.

"Well, I'll be Fat Mary's uncle!" Galandrik laughed.

"Aye, lad, I think we have found our boat," Ty said, smiling over his shoulder at the dwarf.

The party hid in the rocks that surrounded the coastline next to the sloping path, and watched as the boat got closer. Four people rowed the boat, with one at the back guiding the tiller; another was standing at the front. All the crew were in brown cloaks, but the party couldn't make out what race they were. In the centre of the boat stood wooden crates and barrels stacked up.

"Do you think this is another party?" Galandrik whispered.

"Could be. Maybe they have the herbs we require. It'll save us going," Ty answered.

"I wouldn't think they would be stealing barrels," Kern said.

"Unless they are full of gold," Ty joked.

"Or full of herbs," Lan'esra smiled.

"The king would be pleased if they were," Darkfire added.

"Oh my god, you have told a complete stranger of our quest?" Ty snapped.

"He overheard," Kern said, glaring at Lan'esra, then turned to Darkfire. "And what did I tell you about keeping that a secret?"

"Sorry, I forgot," the boy said, looking down.

"Brilliant," Ty said, shaking his head.

"Now is not the time. They are nearly at the bank," Galandrik said, holding his axe in both hands. As the boat reached the edge of the lake, the first man jumped off and rammed a spear into the soft grass. Another threw him a rope, and he wrapped that around the spear. They began to unload the boat. First, two flat barrows were removed, then slowly they lifted the crates and barrels onto them.

"What's the plan then?" Galandrik asked.

"Sit and watch what they do," Kern said, studying their movements.

"If they lift the spear, then we must charge or they will be in the middle of the lake before we get to the water's edge," Ty suggested.

"Agreed," Kern replied, "I could take a couple down from here, too."

Once the barrows were full, the men began to pull them toward the slope that led down to the jetty next to the party, leaving only one man guarding the boat.

"Half-orcs," Galandrik hissed.

"Ty, do you think you can get to the boat if we attack these five?" Kern asked.

"Easy," the thief replied.

"Darkfire, you go with him."

"I don't need—" Ty started to say.

"And I don't care. This is how it's going to work," Kern ordered. "Galandrik, Lan'esra—you both go and I will cover from here. All understood?"

"Agreed," they all whispered.

Once the half-orcs were below them and to their left, Kern notched an arrow. "Now!" The ranger jumped up and fired, hitting one lead orc straight in the neck. Blood streamed like a fountain as he grabbed at the arrow's shaft and fell to his knees.

Galandrik and Lan'esra jumped down and ran at the others. Ty leapt down and sprinted towards the lone orc on the bank, followed by Darkfire. The closest orc drew his sword, but was cut down by Galandrik's mighty axe before the sword was out of its sheath—a devastating blow with a sickening crunch that hit the orc at waist height, cleaving him in two. Lan'esra dashed past and launched a flurry of attacks on the next orc. Sword clattered against mace and sparked as the furious thrust and parry proceeded.

Ty was halfway to the lake when he was spotted. The panicked half-orc started to untie the rope around the spear. Ty pulled his crossbow and aimed. There was a *click*—then nothing. The crossbow had jammed. "Damn!" He swore as he threw it to the ground and drew his daggers from his wrists.

Another orc ran at Galandrik, swinging his sword down in an arc, but it was blocked away by the dwarf's axe. Immediately Galandrik swung the axe back toward the orc's head, but the orc was as nimble as the dwarf was powerful and ducked under the blow, sweeping his sword across Galandrik's thigh and slashing through his leggings. Galandrik grunted and swung a fist at the orc, catching him square on the chin and spinning him around. With a kick from the dwarf's boot, the orc rolled to the ground and was swiftly finished as Galandrik's axe came down, crashing into the orc's chest and the ground beneath.

Lan'esra fought bravely against her assailant, but they were too evenly matched; the pair went blow for blow, parrying and riposting, with neither one gaining an advantage over the other. Behind her attacker, Lan'esra could see another half-orc coming towards her, and she knew she couldn't hold off two. But she needn't have worried—another one of Kern's arrows hit the orc in front of her straight in the eye socket, forcing the arrowhead out of the back of his head. Blood splattered her face as the orc dropped his sword and fell sideways in front of the oncoming orc, which gave her enough time to launch her mace, crashing into his face, smashing his skull, killing him.

"All good?" Kern shouted down to the pair.

Lan'esra nodded and Galandrik looked down at the orc he had killed with his axe. "Now that's what I call a half-orc!"

*

Ty was within a few feet of the orc, daggers readied, when he lost his footing and slid on the wet grass; he knew he couldn't stop himself as his legs went from under him. The orc saw his fall and pulled the spear from the ground. Ty dug a dagger into the wet turf in a vain attempt to slow himself down as he hurtled toward the orc. It worked slightly, and he stopped within three feet of the orc, who stepped forward. With a two-handed swing, the orc swung the spear, hitting the thief in the side of the head and forcing him to roll over, immediately dropping his daggers. Ty looked up in a daze. He saw the orc's mouth moving as he lifted the spear above his head with one hand, but Ty was deafened by the blow. Suddenly, from out of nowhere, a lightning bolt struck the orc, engulfing him in an electrical shower that sparkled and twisted all around his body. Dropping the spear, the orc stood shaking from head to toe as the lightning swirled around him, twisting upwards like a dust devil. Then it was gone. The orc's eyes rolled in his blackened, smoking head and he fell backward into the lake like a felled oak tree.

Ty rolled over and saw Darkfire standing there, holding the wand out in front of him, his hand shaking. He got to his feet, rubbing his ear and shaking the deafness out of his head.

"I guess it dried then?" he said to the boy wizard.

"Ye-yes… I guess it has," he replied.

"Have you actually used this before?" Ty said, examining the wand in the boy's still-shaking hand.

"No. It was given to me by my friend who died in the lake."

"And you aimed this at me?"

"I thought you were attacking me!"

"Oh my days. You would have already been dead if I were. Put it away and don't point it at anyone," Ty said, walking past the boy and toward the others.

*

Kern, Galandrik, and Lan'esra were stripping the cloaks from the half-orcs as Ty approached. "Did you see that?" he said angrily.

"See what?" Kern answered, with a brown cloak in his hands.

"That boy! He just fried the orc with his wand."

"So the wand worked then, lad?" Galandrik laughed.

"Don't laugh, he tried to fry *me* an hour ago! He's a menace and could cause more harm than good."

"Why did he do it? Surely you were there before him," Kern asked.

"Well, I… I just wanted him to have his moment, prove himself. It was all under control," Ty lied.

"Well, blame yourself then! If you had taken the orc down, he wouldn't have fried him," Kern smiled.

"That's not the point," Ty said, rubbing his bruised face.

"What's wrong with your face?" Lan'esra asked.

"Oh, nothing. Just… lockjaw," the thief lied again and bent down, emptying an orc's purse.

"That'll be too much talking. As my great-grandmother used to say, 'You have too much of what the cat licks his arse with,'" Galandrik said, putting on an orc cloak.

"What the hell does that mean?" Ty asked.

"Talk about his tongue later! Ty, remove that one's cloak and put it on; we will need to look like them as we go through the mist. It might give us an advantage," Kern said.

Ty bent down again and started removing a cloak. "Bloody wizards and wands. The next time someone pulls one on me, I'm dropping them, plain and simple. No 'ifs' or 'buts' about it, they are going down. It could be a five-year-old girl with a teddy bear in the other hand, I'm still cracking her skull in two. Could have fried me, bloody boy."

Soon they had stripped the half-orcs and pulled their bodies into the concealment of the rocks. They went back to the boy and saw him standing on the lake's edge, looking at something.

"What is it?" Galandrik asked as they stood next to the boy.

"Look out there," he answered and pointed at the corpse of the orc he had felled. It was a feeding frenzy for the dragonfish. The water around the body splashed and churned as hundreds of voracious dragonfish fought to get their share of his flesh, turning the water red with his blood. Eventually the splashes stopped and only ripped clothes remained floating on the lake's surface, surrounded by a tinge of red.

"Did they drag his body away from the shore to feed on him?" Galandrik asked.

"Yes, they are very powerful fish. Here's a little tip for you all: Try not to fall in," Ty said, raising an eyebrow.

"Right, let's get into the boat. Darkfire, put this on," Kern said, throwing the boy a cloak.

"Wait just a minute! Why is he going? How many times have I said it, we are not a traveling circus! We can't keep picking up every waif and stray we come across. Nuran, Jarrow, Pedlyn—" He glanced over to Lan'esra.

"Go on, say it!" she said, placing her hands on her hips.

Ty shook his head. "We do it every time."

"Wait a minute. The way I see it is that Nuran saved our lives against the skeletons. Jarrow saved *your* life! Pedlyn helped us escape from Breeze. Plus, we need more bodies in the boat to make it look the same as what left the tower. We are one short now."

"And I just killed that orc before he speared you like a kebab," Darkfire added.

"Oh, did you?" Kern said, raising an eyebrow at Ty. "Who had it under control?"

"Rat kebab, eh, lad?" The dwarf smiled.

"Oh, just get in the boat," Ty grumbled as he stepped in. "And I am not rowing," he grumbled, and took a seat up at the front with folded arms.

"All in. Time is upon us," Kern ordered.

"Hmmm… I could eat a rat kebab," Galandrik said, stepping in.

Chapter Twenty-Two
The Dungeon of Dreams

Kern, Galandrik, Lan'esra, and Darkfire rowed as Ty sat at the front of the boat. Halfway across the lake they could see how impressive the tower looked. They sat with hoods covering their bowed faces. Ty looked up as far as he dared, to try and see the arched windows, but could not make out a thing. The mist was within yards of them now and the temperature began to drop drastically. Ty pulled the cloak tighter as the others continued to row, which kept their chill away. Within minutes they were deep into the mist and couldn't see their hands in front of their faces.

"Can you see anything?" Kern said, as softly as he could.

"Nope, it's like pea soup. Just drift, don't row. We will hit the walls of the tower before we know it," Ty said, squinting and waving his hand in front of his face as if trying to clear the mist.

The boat drifted through the mist for what seemed like ten minutes. "Are we moving?" Ty asked.

"Lan'esra, row slowly, but keep in time with me. You two, stop on three… one, two, three," Kern instructed. Ty could feel the boat moving forward, he wanted to touch the water surface to see the speed they were traveling, but thought better of it. Gradually the mist thinned and Ty could make out the front of the boat and the rest of the party in the back.

"This can't be right. We should have hit the tower by now," he said.

"Maybe we missed it and will come out the other side," Galandrik suggested.

"No way. It was massive," the thief said dismissively.

"Maybe we are under it?" Lan'esra added.

"Wherever we are, we will find out soon enough. The mist is thinning; I can make out a light up ahead."

After another couple of minutes, the mist cleared and they were in a domed cavern, just on the other side of a half-moon entrance. It seemed as though the mist stopped at the entrance, creating a wall and not daring to come inside. Twenty yards in front of them was a jetty, with a stone stairway leading up to a door in the walls of the cavern.

"What the hell is this?" Ty spluttered.

"It looks like we are under the mountain," Galandrik replied.

"We can't be. And where has the tower gone?" Kern said, looking up at his new surroundings.

"It must be an illusion. No wonder it's called the Dungeon of Dreams; I feel like I am in one," Lan'esra added.

"Head over to those steps," Kern said as he gave his oar a pull.

They guided the boat in next to the jetty and Ty was first off. He quickly fashioned a noose and placed it around a rock. One by one, they stepped off the boat. Stone stairs arced upward in a spiral to a door in the side of the rocky cavern. Ty reached the door first and pulled his lockpicks from his tunic.

"Can't see any obvious traps," he said, examining the doorframe and lock.

"Do your stuff then, lad," the dwarf said from behind.

"Hmm. It's a double cylinder holte lock. Should be a doddle," Ty said, peering into the lock before cracking his fingers. He rubbed his forefinger and thumb together as his selected two picks from his pouch.

Twenty seconds went by, and then there was a *click*.

"Child's play," he said smugly, as he placed his picks back into his tunic. Then he sprang up another few steps and showed Kern the now-unlocked door.

"Oh, I'll open it, shall I?"

"Did my bit," Ty smiled, drawing his crossbow.

Kern carefully turned the handle and pushed the door. "Clear," he said, looking in. They stepped into a square room. To the north in front of them was a large iron door; on the west wall hung a large mirror that stood from floor to ceiling. Against the east wall was a table. Different items were scattered about the room; small pictures lined the walls and two small chests sat on the floor next to the north door.

"Remember, don't touch anything without Ty looking at it first. If there is a trap, it'll be in here. Remember what Gizzir, Gronli, and Gamrot said in Tonilla—full of traps."

They searched the room thoroughly. The table contained basic writing materials—paper, inks, and feather quills. Under the table were gardening tools, including a pickaxe, spade, shovel, and pitchfork. On the wall above was a picture of the Eastern Mountains with the sun rising above, and the chests were mostly full of old clothes. One chest also contained a small wooden club and a few pots, but there was nothing else of particular interest.

"The door isn't trapped, but there is no lock. It must work on a mechanism or something. I will search for levers," Ty said, then he smiled at Darkfire. "Magic it open!"

"I can't. I don't have the correct ingredients."

"Brilliant." The thief turned to Galandrik. "What about trying to lift it?"

"I had a good look, lad; there is nothing on the door to grip."

Kern looked on the table. "Keep looking. There must be a hidden button or lever or something."

After an hour Galandrik knelt on the floor and opened his backpack. "I don't know about you lot, but I am starving."

"You are always starving," Ty said, looking in the mirror.

"You must—"

"Feed the furnace. Yes, we know," Ty interrupted. "Do I look skinnier to you?" he asked, rubbing his chin.

"There is more meat on this piece of beef jerky!" The dwarf laughed.

Kern stood next to Ty and examined himself in the mirror. "I don't know about you, but I *am* losing weight," the ranger said, turning sideways. Kern whirled around to look behind him, then peered intently into the mirror, then back to the table. "Ty, look in the mirror. What do you see?"

"A handsome thief and—"

"Stop being a—stop being *you* and look at the table behind us." Ty spun round. "No, not *at* the table… look at the table in the mirror."

Ty peered into the mirror. "I see a… table."

"No, look closely at the items," Kern said, as Lan'esra stepped up and studied it too.

"Writing materials…quills. I don't get it."

Lan'esra looked into the mirror then back at the table. "The red shirt!" she said with delight.

"I'm glad it wasn't just me. I thought I was going mental," Kern said, smiling at Lan'esra. "See it, Ty?"

Ty looked into the mirror then back to the table. "Yes, it is in the reflection but not actually on the table. Hang on, I saw one in a chest." Ty stepped over to the chest and rummaged through the clothes. "Ah, here it is!" he said, pulling out the red shirt.

"Place it on the table, where it is in the reflection," Kern urged. Ty stepped to the table and checked in the mirror, and placed the red shirt onto the table.

"Back a bit," Kern said, turning his head back and forth from mirror to table.

"Toward the middle slightly," Lan'esra added.

As Ty moved the shirt, they heard a clicking and the large iron door that Galandrik was leaning against started lifting from the floor.

"What the—" Galandrik said, caught unawares. As the door lifted, it caught the back of the dwarf's helmet. As the door got higher than his head he fell backward into the room with a groan, his legs in the air. Quickly he sat back up and straightened his helmet. "What?"

Kern just shook his head and passed the hapless dwarf, walking into another square room with a corridor to the east and west. In front was another large iron door with no lock, but a lever on either side. There were four fist-sized diamonds in a line, encrusted in the wall next to the door. Nothing else of interest was in the room apart from a torch on each wall, which they lit.

Ty and Darkfire helped pick the dwarf up and they entered the room. Looking down the corridors to the east and west, all they could see was blackness. After Ty examined the diamonds and realised to his dismay that they were not coming out, he had a scout around for traps. He bent down on the floor next to the east corridor.

"Hello, what have we here?" he muttered. "Come stand behind me," he cautioned. Once all the others stood next to him, he pressed down on a square pressure pad that appeared just like a floor slab. The square centre slab in the middle of the room opened and four razor-sharp cone-shaped spikes flew upward. Ty fumbled with the mechanism, but the slab started to rise up and he pulled his fingers out before they were trapped. The spikes lowered and the centre slab closed.

"I can't disarm it. It is on a quick release timer."

"Are there any more?" Lan'esra said, looking around, afraid to move.

Ty had a good search. "Nothing else. I think we are good to go; just do not stand on that one!"

Kern turned to the thief. "What do you mean, 'you think'?"

"I can't find every trap; and there are those that are a higher level than even I can master. Just like I can't disarm that one. I suspect in time I will be able to, if there are any more."

"Something you can't do?" Kern said, raising an eyebrow.

"I'll do *you*, you keep this up," Ty said, pulling a torch from his backpack and lighting it with his flint and tinder. "I will check down the corridor; stay here." Ty held the torch out in front of him and checked the floor and walls as he went.

Darkfire gently nudged the dwarf. "Do they always argue?"

"Pretty much, lad," he replied.

Ty felt a slab under his foot click downward and he shut his eyes, waiting for the inevitable blade to slice his head clean off from the side wall, or a dozen darts to pepper him like a poisonous pin cushion. But nothing happened, other than the noise of gears and cogs turning and churning from behind.

The door to the room which held the mirror slowly started to lower. Instantly Kern and Galandrik ran and tried to stop the door from closing, but as much as they tried it wasn't enough and the door slammed shut.

"I told you not to touch anything," Ty shouted over his shoulder.

"We never touched anything," Darkfire shouted back.

"It must have been on a timer," Ty lied.

Ty carried on down the corridor, lighting wall torches as he went. He cursed himself for setting off the trapped slab, and knew this dungeon was going to be a tricky task. After fifty steps, the corridor ended in a portcullis. Ty peered through the bars and saw two paladins standing against the wall opposite, each leaning on a two-handed sword. He couldn't tell if they were human or statues; even when he tapped his dagger on the bars they never flinched. The room was small and empty, other than the two statue-like paladins. He made his way back to the centre room and explained the layout to the others, then did the same checks on the west corridor, which was identical to the east, along with two more statues.

"Well, either those levers open the main door or they open the portcullises," Kern said to the party. "Only one way to find out, I guess. Everybody get ready." He grabbed the left lever with both hands and pulled it downward. With a clunk, the portcullis to the west slowly started to rise. They looked down the corridor and waited as the portcullis disappeared into the ceiling with another clunk. As soon as it had, the two paladins stepped forward toward them down the corridor.

"We don't want any trouble!" Darkfire shouted at the oncoming foes.

Ty glared at Kern and shook his head. Galandrik rested his mighty axe against his leg and spat onto his hands. "Let me handle this," he grunted, picking it up and readying himself.

Ty, Lan'esra, and Darkfire all stepped back as Kern and Galandrik stood side by side. "Shall we?" Galandrik said.

With a wry smile, Kern replied, "We shall."

The first of the paladins stepped into the room and lifted his giant two-handed sword up. Galandrik wasted no time and swung his mighty axe at the paladin's side. The blow was fatal and his axe smashed through the armour with ease, then smashed against the wall—which shook Galandrik to his back teeth. The paladin crumbled into a pile of amour. The second paladin stepped forward and Kern struck with a straight lunge. The tip of his sword pieced through the eye socket of the paladin's helmet, knocking it off. The armour fell to the floor in a heap and only the helmet was left hanging on the ranger's longsword. Kern lowered his sword and the helmet slid to the floor.

"How easy?" Kern muttered.

"I'd say too easy, lad."

They walked down the corridor and into the paladins' room. It was completely empty apart from two slabs the paladins had been standing on, with a swirling rune sign on each. Ty searched for traps and examined the slabs. "I don't think they are traps. More like pressure pads."

Kern placed the tip of his sword onto the left slab. "Step back." He pushed down on the slab which moved slightly downward. "Yes, pressure pads. What's the betting there are two more in the other room?"

"I'll guarantee it. Push all four together and the main door opens?" Lan'esra suggested.

"Looks that way," Ty agreed.

Darkfire stared down at the paladin's remains and kicked through the armour. *What controlled them? How could they walk with nothing inside?* he wondered. He squatted down and picked up the paladin's helmet and examined it. He was about to throw it to the floor when he spotted a golden necklace just hanging out of the breast plate. With a quick glance over his shoulder he picked it up.

Kern and Galandrik approached the other two paladins in the room where they stood, and dispatched them in the same manner as they had the first two.

"What's the plan of action then?" Ty asked.

"Maybe the four of us need to stand on the pads," Kern replied.

"But the paladins were on the pads before?" Galandrik noted.

"I know, but it's worth a try," Kern shrugged.

"Lan'esra and the boy can take these two, and you and Galandrik take the east side. We may need more weight here, so I'll stay here."

Kern listened to Ty's suggestion. "Sounds sensible enough to me."

"Unless you get Gal to stick a leg on each and you stay here?" Ty laughed.

"Whatever," the dwarf replied and he strutted up the corridor.

"You have to be a clown. Always have and always will," Kern said with half a smile.

"If you don't laugh you'd cry," Ty replied as Kern followed up the corridor, being careful not to step on the trap.

"Step onto the pads!" Kern shouted down the corridor, and they followed the order. Darkfire, Lan'esra, Kern, and Galandrik all stepped onto a pad each, which sank down, but nothing happened.

"Let me step on with you," Ty said, stepping on Darkfire's pad. Still nothing happened, no noise or anything.

"Maybe it is mine?" Lan'esra asked. Ty stepped across, then tried with one foot on each.

"What's happening?" Kern shouted down the corridor.

"Hang on, we are trying a few things!" Ty shouted back.

"Let me stand on here, boy," Ty said, pushing Darkfire out of the way.

"What about the wall next to the door?" Lan'esra asked.

Ty turned to her. "What about it?"

"It had four diamonds on it, maybe we should go look?"

"Good idea. Darkfire, you come with me."

They both went down the corridor and examined the wall. It had two diamonds lit up. Ty looked down toward Kern. "One of you step off!" he shouted. Kern did and one of the lights went off. "The diamonds are lighting up when you are on the pads. Get back on!" As soon as he did, another diamond lit up. "Lan'esra, get back on," Ty shouted down the west corridor and the same result happened.

"Right, I'll go down there. Tell me what happens when I step on." Ty hurried himself down the corridor and stepped onto the pad.

"All the diamonds have lit up," Darkfire said, not realising they were trapped in the rooms.

"Try pushing them," Kern shouted.

One by one the diamonds sank into the wall. "They are clicking into place!" he shouted. As he pushed the last one, he added, "And the door is starting to lift."

"Darkfire, pull the levers," Kern shouted, but the boy stood motionless looking at the door slowly rising.

"Pull the damn levers," Ty shouted, clenching the bars.

"It's lifting; the door is lifting," Darkfire said, still staring. "Feet… I can see two feet… big feet." Kern threw a stone at the boy, trying to knock him out of his apparent daze-like state, but missed.

"Come on, lad, pull the damn levers," the dwarf bellowed down the corridor. This seemed to get his attention, and Darkfire shook his head, looking down the corridor.

"Pull the levers, now," Kern ordered, shaking the bars. With that, Darkfire stepped forward and placed two hands on the lever and pulled with all his might. Gradually the lever moved and clicked, and cogs and pulleys could be heard churning and turning. The portcullis started lifting as Galandrik stepped back. Kern squatted down, waiting for enough space to get under.

"Do ours, quickly!" Ty screamed. Darkfire stepped across the doorway just as a giant arm shot out and grabbed him by the throat. The boy was lifted two feet into the air, gripping the massive wrist that held him. A huge humanoid stepped forward, holding the boy. The ranger stood up slowly and turned to Galandrik. "An earth elemental!"

Galandrik shook his head. "This is going to take some work."

Ty's eyes widened. "Earth elemental… it's a bloody earth elemental."

"Can it pull levers?" Lan'esra asked, trying to make light of the situation.

"Let's hope not, I'd rather starve to death!"

"Kern's door is open!"

"Damn. Right, help me get through these bars," Ty said, stripping off his leather armour and shirt.

"How?"

"Push me! Kick me and punch me! Just get me through!"

The earth elemental threw Darkfire down to the ground like a rag doll and roared; the boy fumbled for his wand and pointed it at the elemental.

"*Hazan amor*!" he shouted and lighting flew from his wand, engulfing the monster. The elemental stepped back and gazed at the lightning as it twisted and spun around his body, sparkling and cracking.

Kern's portcullis had lifted enough to get through,

"You ready for this?"

"Aye, lad, let's plough some earth."

They both ran down the corridor toward the elemental as it reached down and slapped the wand out of Darkfire's hand. He tried to shuffle backward away from the beast, but its giant hand reached down and grabbed his ankle.

"Noooo!" the boy cried as he rolled onto his belly, digging his fingernails into the concrete floor. With one almighty swing, the earth elemental swung him round and smashed him against the west wall. He fell to the floor and lay still.

Kern reached the monster first and swung in an arc at his back, slicing through into the earth. Brown mud oozed from the slash. The beast swung its huge arm around toward Kern's head, but the ranger was too quick and rolled under, then regained his attacking stance.

Galandrik exited the corridor and brought his double-headed axe down into the elemental's thigh. With a scream that shook the room, the elemental swung his arm, knocking the dwarf to the floor; the axe stayed embedded into his leg. It looked tiny by comparison.

Kern lunged forward again, swinging at his other leg and catching his knee. Again brown mud trickled. The elemental swung and hit the ranger square in the back, knocking him to the floor. The monster stepped forward and lifted his huge foot to crush the ranger, but Kern was able to roll away. Again he came forward. Kern squatted and waited as the clumsy beast swung again. Kern managed to sidestep, but was now in the corner of the room.

Galandrik eventually got to his feet and shook his head, trying to clear his dazed mind. He bent down and picked up a sword from amongst the paladin plate mail and stepped forward, thrusting the sword into the elemental's side. The giant roared and reached round, grabbing the sword's hilt. With a quick twist he snapped the sword in two, leaving a few inches of blade under the hilt. Galandrik stepped backward. The elemental held both hands out. With another almighty roar, the ground beneath Galandrik's feet moved and shifted. Two hands came out of the ground and grabbed his ankles, tripping him backward. The stone hands gripped him, holding him as the earth elemental stepped forward. Galandrik leaned back and reached out his hand to grab the other paladin's sword, but it was just out of reach.

Kern picked up his sword and ran at the monster's back, slicing another blow down his spine. The elemental spun round and caught the ranger across the face with the hilt of the sword, slicing across his forehead and left eye.

Kern fell to the floor, blood streaming down his face, but the adrenalin was pumping and he sprung to his feet and grabbed the sword again. He tried wiping the blood away, but it was a deep wound and blood continued to pour into his eyes making him virtually blind. Galandrik stretched for the sword, but could only just touch the hilt with his fingertips; he looked over to the ranger and saw the blood flowing from his head wound.

*

Ty had his top half through the barred gate; his hips were jammed as he tried to wriggle through. "It's no good! The bars are too close together!"

"You can do it! Remember when we first met, in the cell? You said, 'I am Ty the Rat and no…' I know what you were going to say now: 'No dungeon can hold me!' Tell me I'm wrong."

Ty looked at the cleric and down the corridor at Galandrik lying down.

"Go help your companions!" she finished.

"Oil! Get the oil out of the backpack, quickly." Ty wriggled back into the room slightly. "Pour it all over my waist and the bars."

Lan'esra did as she was told and soaked Ty in the oil.

He gripped the bars and pushed with all his might. "Push me!"

As they pushed with all the effort they could muster, Ty slipped through the bars and landed in the corridor.

"Pass me my sword," he ordered, holding his hand out through the bars.

She bent down to pick up his short sword and stopped. She stared at him for a second.

"What are you waiting for? The sword! Now!"

"The trap! Use the trap!" she said, gripping the bars.

Ty stared in confusion for a moment, but then the penny dropped. "You genius!"

Without another word Ty ran down the corridor and stood next to the slab. He could see Galandrik reaching for the sword and Kern with his back against the wall, wiping blood from his eyes.

"The sword!" he heard Galandrik shout. He jumped over the dwarf and grabbed the sword, then back to behind the elemental. With all the strength he could muster, he swung the sword, hitting the beast just above the knee. It never even made a cut. With Ty's lack of experience and strength using the sword, combined with the natural armour, it was virtually a miss, but enough to get the elemental's attention, though not before swinging a blow at the blinded ranger, knocking him to the floor unconscious. Ty knew it would have to take three steps at least before it was on the middle trap slab.

"Come on, you big fuck!" he shouted as he stepped backwards, goading the creature on and dragging the sword as he went. "Come to daddy," he shouted.

The elemental raised his arms and roared.

Galandrik started to shout, "Feet! He is—"

It was too late. Two stone hands reached out from the floor and gripped the thief's ankles.

"No!" Ty screamed. He looked at the slab, out of arm's reach, and used the sword to tap it, but it was no good. The sword just wasn't enough weight to sink it.

The elemental lumbered forward, now nearly standing on the middle slab. "Ty, pull the lever," Lan'esra shouted from down the corridor.

"I can't reach that," he shouted as he tried to get his feet free, but the hands were like set concrete.

"Use the hilt of the sword!" she shouted.

Ty spun the sword around and, using all his strength, lifted it up by its tip, hooking the hilt over the lever. With a quick look at Galandrik, he said, "This is going to hurt." Then he pulled down on the sword with both hands, slicing his palms as he did.

click

The lever clicked down and the portcullis began to rise. Ty dropped the sword and looked at the slices in his palms as blood started to flow. The elemental stepped onto the middle slab.

"Hurry!" Ty shouted.

Lan'esra crawled under the bars, ran down the corridor, and stood next to the slab. "Stick around!" she shouted, and jumped onto the trap.

Nothing happened.

"What…? Why…" she spluttered.

The elemental held his arms up toward Lan'esra and roared.

"No!" She screamed, falling backward as the stones beneath her feet became alive and gripped her ankles. Ty looked around for some divine intervention, but there was nothing that could help him now—Galandrik still reaching for the sword, Kern unconscious, Darkfire in a heap, and Lan'esra screaming. This was it…

*

The elemental roared, seeing all his victims caught like flies in his stone shackles. Time to pound their bodies, break their bones up and please his maker. He stepped forward toward Ty and Lan'esra. As his weight shifted off the centre pad, it opened and the four spikes thrust up from the ground, skewering the earth elemental's trailing leg up into his torso and flipping him forward. Galandrik's axe dropped to the floor. The elemental roared with the pain as brown liquid poured from his skewered body. The stone hands that held them captive opened and slipped back into the floor.

Ty was first to his feet, and grabbed the axe. "Galandrik," he shouted, sliding the axe along the stone floor.

The dwarf got to his feet and picked it up. He stepped next to the elemental and lifted the axe high above his head. The elemental swung an arm, trying to grab Galandrik's leg, but couldn't reach. He brought the axe down on the back of the monster's neck. Again he lifted it up and repeated the blow, hitting the exact same spot. Brown muddy blood poured from the wound, but it was only quarter of the way through the creature's massive neck. Again he swung, and again.

Breathing heavily, he lifted the axe up again. "Die, you freak!" he shouted as he brought the axe crashing down onto the neck of the creature, decapitating its head from its gigantic shoulders. It stopped moving and hung still. Galandrik dropped the axe and bent to one knee.

The four spikes retracted and after a few seconds the trap reset. The elemental crackled as the structure of its body began to disintegrate, and within seconds it was a pile of granulated dirt. The door to the previous mirror room lifted.

"Go help Kern," Ty shouted as he jumped over the dirt to Darkfire. He felt for a pulse but could feel nothing. Blood trickled from the boy's mouth and Ty knew he was dead. Placing his hands on his eyelids, he closed them.

"How is he?" Ty said to Lan'esra.

"He will live, but his eye is badly damaged. Bring my backpack, quickly."

Ty grabbed the wand that sat on the floor before running down the corridor and, grabbing both backpacks, he ran back as fast as he could, blood dripping from his wounds.

"My hands need bandaging as soon as you have finished with Kern."

Lan'esra poured water from a canteen into a bowl and mixed it with some herbs, then started to clean the ranger's face. "Mix that into a paste and rub some on your wounds," she explained. Ty followed her instructions and applied the healing balm to his wounds before wrapping bandages around his hands.

"I think he could lose his eyesight," she said, examining his face.

"That's not good. Best you don't say anything, and let the physician in the next town tell him," Ty suggested.

"Agreed. How are you, Gal?" she asked as the dwarf walked into the room with his and Kern's equipment.

"I'm fine, lassy. We dwarfs are made of sturdy stuff," he grumbled.

Ty stood up and stretched. "One thing... can I ask one thing?"

Lan'esra looked up at the thief. "Sure, go for it."

"'Stick around'?"

She looked away slightly embarrassed. "Sorry, I don't know where that came from."

"It came from hanging around with you too much," Galandrik said, peering into the room ahead.

Ty shook his head. "Whatever. How is he?"

"He's okay. He's lost loads of blood and needs to wake up in his own time," she answered as she finished bandaging around the ranger's head and across his damaged eye. "Seriously, though, his eye is... bad," she finished, resting his head on a blanket.

"We can worry about that in town. We need to get these damn herbs and get out of this shithole," Ty said, putting his leather armour back on.

"Look in here, Ty," Galandrik said at the entrance to the room. Ty walked over and examined the square room. It had one door dead opposite. On the stone floor, four square tiles stood out. Each had a different symbol: red heart, black spade, red diamond and black club.

"At least there are no more elementals," Ty said, kicking the dirt that had been the creature's head.

"Shall we take the boy's body into one of those rooms?" Galandrik asked.

"Good idea," Ty replied.

They carried his corpse into the east room and covered his face with his cloak.

"I'm going to make some food," Galandrik said, sitting down.

"Another good idea," Lan'esra agreed, smiling. "I'll grab a couple of those torches from the west corridor and we can use them for firewood."

Ty moved next to Galandrik. "I honestly thought we'd had it then, you know."

"Oh, rubbish, lad! We have been in worse situations."

"I don't think so, Gal. This dungeon is too hard. It's above our level, if you ask me. The first... first... monster was an earth elemental! We should have come with elemental-slaying swords, not the shit we carry."

"Maybe so, but we are here now, lad."

Ty nodded at the mirror room. "We could leave and find the herbs elsewhere. Kern needs medical attention. This is nearly suicidal."

Galandrik processed Ty's words and his usually gung-ho attitude wavered. "I don't think we can convince him. His father is captured."

"We will talk to him when he wakes up. Even Kern must see sense here. He is blind and my hands are sliced. That only leaves you and Lan," the thief said with a cheeky grin.

"Your hands will heal quickly. That balm is the best in Bodisha. My family in the Midas Hills has made it for centuries," Lan'esra said, walking back into the room.

Ty examined his bandaged hands. "Even so, we are up against it in here."

"If the elemental is the hardest this dungeon has to offer, we should be fine," Lan'esra said, sitting down.

"We were lucky! Listen to me, I smell luck, I *am* luck—and this dungeon has none. Trust me, we are in a bad place."

They heard a groan from Kern. Ty and Lan'esra jumped up and squatted next to him.

"Easy, friend," Ty said calmingly.

"What happened to the elemental?" he said, sitting up.

"Oh, well. I slipped out from the cell, sprung off the wall, and landed a critical back stab," the thief lied.

"My head is pounding, and my eye is so sore." Kern turned to Lan'esra. "What really happened?"

"We used the trap to kill it."

"Ah, use the trap! Why didn't I think of that? Where's Gal?"

"I'm here, lad, making you some warm food."

Kern looked at Ty's bandaged hands and around the room. "So where's Darkfire, and what happened to your hands?"

Ty shook his head. "He is gone; the elemental killed him. And I have sliced my hands badly. Listen, Kern, Darkfire is dead, I can hardly hold a dagger, and you need treatment on your eye."

"What are you saying?" Kern said, getting to his feet with the help of Lan'esra.

"I'm saying, who will be next? Gal, me… you? You can hardly see. This is a bad place and I have bad feelings about it."

"You want to quit? Leave and walk away?"

"Yes, while we still can."

"You don't care about anything or anybody apart from yourself, do you?"

"Oh, here we go. I care about this party, and that's why I am asking you to think about it."

"What if it was your dad in the cage? Would you still want to leave?" Kern said angrily.

"Listen, we can get the herbs somehow. I will find a way. We could rescue your father. It would be easier than this place!"

"Go. Just go if you want to. We don't need a coward thief." Kern stepped over to Galandrik. "What about you, friend? What do you think?"

Galandrik stared Kern in the eye then glanced at Ty. He smiled at the ranger and placed his hand on his shoulder. "I am with you, brother."

Kern sat down next to the bubbling pot above the fire. "What are we cooking? It smells good."

"Just a vegetable stew, nothing major," the dwarf added, sitting next to Kern.

Ty looked at Lan'esra, who shrugged her shoulders.

He shook his head back. "Let's go die then."

"Let's," Kern replied, without looking back.

Chapter Twenty-Three
Heart of Gold

Queen Cherian sat next to her husband as Murtal wiped the sweat from the king's brow. "How is he, Murtal?"

"Surviving. We are controlling the fever well, but the poison still surges and time is pressing."

"Conn and Gorgon will get what we need. They should be halfway there now."

"But they still have to get back."

"Don't worry, Conn will be swift. Trust me—when a wizard wants to move quickly, he will."

"That's good news, my queen."

"I just hope he gets on his feet soon. There are so many pressing things to be discussed and the council is restless."

"Yes, I know. What about Guldir and his awful wife? Did they ever contact you about the war meeting?"

"Yes, they did. I fobbed them off. If they got wind of our king being ill they could, and probably would, take some northern territories. I know for a fact that some adjacent neutral lands are only that way because of a word-of-mouth treaty. They could walk through them and gain a valuable advantage along our borders."

"Can we send men to patrol the borders?"

"No, we cannot afford to send any more. We have scouts and all is well, but gods forbid the elves find out. It would weaken our defences massively. They would have a stronghold, splitting our troops from east to west. It would be a nightmare for transportation and trade routes. They would have so much bartering power, they could tax us to cross their lands. It would be war, I am sure of it. And it would let the orcs in if we fought with the elves; we couldn't possibly fight on both fronts."

"What about Moriak's cousin over the sea in Bloodmoore? I thought he was sending troops."

"Threliun is too worried about what mistress he has in his bed every night. He has been promising things for years. We never receive them."

"Maybe we could send a message to him, mention that Gorgon is coming to inspect them or something?"

"That may be a good idea. The mere mention of Gorgon would be enough—and at least when the king gets better he will know we have been proactive."

"Plus you can control your borders and stop those bloody elves from moving in."

"Oh, yes. If my husband woke and there were elves splitting our defensive line to the north, he would have a fit."

"That's exactly what he doesn't want."

"True, Murtal; that is very true."

*

Ty examined the room the elemental had come from and found no sign of traps. The only things in the room were the four floor tiles with the heart, spade, club, and diamond. The only exit on the north was another door without a lock. Ty and Lan'esra were talking, whilst Galandrik and Kern slept in the previous room.

"These dungeons do me no favours whatsoever."

"What do you mean?" Lan'esra said, staring at the slabs.

"Well, we get hired to go with parties and open doors by picking locks, search for traps, etc. These people who create dungeons with no locks are putting us out of business."

"There will always be traps to find and disarm," she smiled.

"Yeah, I guess so. What do you make of the slabs?"

"Not a lot, really. Have you got any playing cards on you?"

"Yes, I think I have an old pack somewhere." Ty walked into the adjacent room and rummaged through his pack. "Ah, I knew I had some."

"What do you think, one on each?"

Ty shuffled through the deck and pulled out the ace of each suit. "Aces all day long." Carefully he placed a card on each slab. Nothing happened. They tried kings, jacks, and queens; just the picture cards; holding all the hearts on the heart slab; one card, two cards; one card on one, two on the next—but nothing worked.

"Well, I am as lost as you," Lan'esra said, sitting down cross-legged.

Ty walked towards the four diamonds in the wall, "I have no idea. To be honest I hope we can't go through, then we could turn round and get out of here," he answered, placing the pack of cards back into his backpack and taking out a dagger.

"You don't like it here, do you?"

"That's an understatement! This place is cursed," he groaned as he tried to prise the first diamond out of the wall. It didn't budge, and he moved on to the second.

"Maybe the elemental was the big guy and it gets easier from here on in?"

Ty wedged his dagger under the second diamond. "It… doesn't normally… work like… that… ah-ha!" He smiled as the diamond fell into his palm. "There's one out!"

"It's a bit big for you to swallow isn't it?" She laughed.

Ty held the diamond up to his eye. "It isn't worth a lot either!" he moaned, throwing it to Lan'esra. He tried the last two, but they were set solid.

"Maybe someone will buy it," she said, spinning it on the floor.

Ty moved over to the door and placed his hands on his hips. "There must be a release lever around here somewhere," he said, rubbing his hands along the wall next to the door.

Lan'esra sat spinning the diamond on its tip. "How do you know it's not worth a lot?"

"Easy—look at the girdle in comparison to the crown. It's far too shallow and the angle is wrong. Also the facets are flawed and the culet is far too wide for the pavilion."

"What the hell did that mean?"

Ty chuckled to himself; he knew his knowledge of diamonds would lose even the cleverest of people. "You asked!"

"Yes, I know, but what does it mean?"

"It's just a shit piece of glass. A diamond all the same, but not very valuable."

Lan'esra repeatedly spun the diamond on its tip. "It spins well though."

"That's about all it's good for," he answered, still rubbing the stone wall. The diamond spun and spun until its speed slowed and it started to wobble. It fell onto its side, rolling round in an arc and landing on the diamond pad. With a click, the pad sank an inch and locked into place.

"I think I have found something else it's good for, Ty," she said, jumping to her feet.

Ty glanced over his shoulder at Lan'esra pointing to the diamond. "What?" he said, walking over to her. "You smart thing, you."

"It was more of an accident if I'm honest. It just landed on it."

"I won't tell the others. Right—a spade... Got it, under the table!" Ty ran into the other room and picked up the spade. Jumping over Kern, he ran back to Lan'esra. "Here goes," he said, placing it on the slab. The slab sank and clicked into position.

Lan'esra ran into the other room. "The chest!"

"Chest? We need a club, not a chest!"

She came back holding a small club. "I found it in the chest earlier!" she said, placing in on the third slab. Again they got the same result.

"Hmm, heart. I suppose we could rip Galandrik's out!" Ty said, but his smile didn't last long. He knew exactly what Lan'esra was thinking. "No way," he said, shaking his head.

"He was put here for a reason, Ty."

"He's just a boy! We can't go cutting people open!"

"Cut who open?" Kern said, entering the room.

Lan'esra looked down to the floor as Ty paced across the other side of the room. "It's wrong," he mumbled to himself.

"Look at the slabs, Kern! We have locked three down. We needed to place the relevant items on each one... so now we just need a heart," Lan'esra explained.

"A heart? Where are we going to conjure up a heart from?" Kern asked.

Lan'esra stared at Ty as if to ask for backup but the thief just shook his head. Then the penny dropped.

"Oh my God... you mean... cut the boy's heart out?" Kern said, shocked.

"Well, unless we can find a heart then... yes." She shrugged.

Kern rubbed his forehead. "That's just ruthless. There must be another way. Have we checked everywhere in the other rooms?"

"I am afraid so. I think she is right, my friend. We need to use his heart," Ty said, "As much as I don't like it, it's that or we go back into the boat."

Kern paced around the room scratching his head. "We can't go back. The boy is dead, and he would have wanted us to complete this dungeon... So let's use it."

"I won't be cutting anyone's heart out!" the thief said stubbornly.

Kern seemed to ignore Ty's statement. "We will draw straws to see who will do it."

"Will I fuck draw straws! If you want to cut a child's heart out, go do it. I don't want anything to do with it," Ty said firmly.

"You know what... I'll do it," Kern said, drawing his dagger from his belt. "Wouldn't expect a coward like you to do it anyway. Move out of my way," he said, pushing past the thief and heading down the corridor.

He stared down at the boy's body on the floor, his face covered up with a blanket. A fist-sized bloodstain had seeped through. *Come on, Kern, you can do this. His soul has gone and left just a carcass, a piece of meat.* Kern knelt down and took a deep breath. *Right—undo his tunic, make a three-inch cut, reach in, and rip it out. Think about Thrane locked up... do it for your father.*

Kern cut the leather tunic's strings and ripped open the shirt, revealing the boy's bare chest. It looked like it had never seen the sun. A small necklace hung round his neck. He held the dagger in his hand and hovered it just above where he thought the heart would be. He knew he would have to smash through the ribs, and he made ready to stab down then draw it down the boy's torso.

He shut his eyes, unable to really believe what he was about to do. Slowly he raised the dagger, ready to thrust it down, when he heard a noise which seemed to have come from the boy. Kern opened his eyes, and looked around and behind him. He was alone.

"Darkfire?" he said quietly, but there was no answer. "I am bloody hearing things now," he said, shaking his head. Again he raised the dagger and braced his other hand against the boy's chest, steadying himself. "Right—let's do this. On three… one… two… three!"

He rammed the dagger down into the boy's chest just above the heart. Darkfire sprang up and grabbed Kern's throat. In complete surprise, the ranger released the dagger and fell backward.

"Cut my fucking heart out?" Darkfire shouted now as he got on top of Kern, still gripping his neck, his nose only inches away from Kern's. Blood trickled from his mouth onto Kern's face and the ranger thrashed his head side to side, trying to stop the blood entering his mouth, whilst shouting, "Ty told me you were dead!"

"That's it, it's Ty's fault! Like the slaves on the boat! Why is it never your fault?"

"I'm sorry!" Kern thrashed and tried to push him away, but the boy's strength was too great.

The boy knelt on the ranger's shoulders. "Too late for sorry! You want my heart that badly, you can take it!" He grabbed the dagger protruding from his chest and started to slowly drag it down. His face screwed up with pain. Blood poured down his chest and Kern could feel the warmth of it on his body as it seeped through Darkfire's clothes.

"No! Stop, don't do it! Lan'esra can heal you!" Kern screamed, unable to push the youngster off him.

"Fuck Lan'esra!" he said as he pulled the dagger out of his chest. He squeezed his other hand into the cut on his chest until it was up to his wrist.

"Noooo!" Kern shouted as he watched this self-mutilation take place.

Blood poured from the gaping wound in the boy's chest, and the blood covered Kern's face. He could feel its warmth and taste it as it trickled into his mouth.

"Arrrgh!" Darkfire screamed, looking up as he ripped his hand from his chest, holding his still-beating heart.

"What… No, this can't be!" Kern said, trying with all his might to fling the boy off, but it felt like a giant was sitting on top of him.

Darkfire looked down at the ranger as blood dripped from his heart onto Kern's face. "Have it!" He turned his hand, dropping the heart, Kern could hear it beating as it fell toward his face, and above it he could see Darkfire laughing, eyes and mouth wide open.

*

Kern sat up. "Noooo!" he screamed, his eyes wide with terror.

Ty and Lan'esra ran through from the other room. "What's wrong?" Ty asked, bending down.

The ranger looked at the thief for a second and then around the room. Galandrik was asleep next to him and the fire was nearly burnt out.

"Where is Darkfire?" Kern asked, grabbing Ty's arm.

"Down there, covered up. We told you he died," Ty replied.

Kern used Ty for leverage and got to his feet. "I need to see him," he said as he hurried down the corridor.

"What is all this about?" Ty asked, following the ranger.

"I just ripped his heart out."

"What? But you were asleep! It must have been a dream," Ty replied.

"What do you need to complete the puzzle in the room?" Kern said as he stopped, standing over the boy's body.

"How did…? We need a heart. We were going to wait until you woke," Ty said with surprise.

Kern grabbed the blanket and ripped it from the boy's face. His ashen features appeared relaxed, as if he were having an afternoon sleep. The only colour was from the two silver coins Galandrik had left on the boy's eyes. Kern pulled his dagger from his belt and cut the leather shirt straps. Then, dropping his dagger, he grabbed the shirt and ripped it open. He stared for a second before ripping the necklace off the boy's neck.

Without even looking at it he swung it round. Ty could just see a few links hanging out the bottom of his fist.

"Take it," he shouted, and Ty did. Kern closed the boy's shirt and picked up his dagger, "May you be blessed and return with the thunder of the gods," Kern said before turning and striding past the thief. "I'll wake the dwarf. We leave through that door in ten minutes."

"What? But we still need a heart," Ty said, shaking his head. The ranger didn't answer, and disappeared into the next room. Ty looked down at the boy wizard and sighed. Slowly he opened his bandaged palm; there, shining resplendently, was a golden heart on the end of the necklace.

*

Lan'esra redressed Kern's eye and Ty's hands before the party got their equipment, armour, and weapons equipped and readied themselves. Galandrik stood holding his axe in both hands. Kern notched an arrow and Ty and Lan'esra loaded their crossbows.

"Drop the heart and let's do this," Kern said purposefully.

Ty stepped to the last slab and held the necklace over it before turning back to his friends, concern etched all over his face. Kern nodded and the thief dropped it before stepping back to join the party. The slab lowered and clicked into place.

"Be ready. Anything could be behind this door," Kern warned. Suddenly the door behind them slammed shut, making Ty jump. "Damn! This is it. No escaping now."

All four slabs slowly started to move simultaneously downward. Lan'esra stepped forward and looked down at the disappearing slabs. "What the hell is going on?"

"Get back here, woman! Anything could come out of there!" Galandrik said, pulling her back and slightly behind him.

The slabs were now out of sight and they could hear a strange bubbling, whooshing sound. "That sounds like running water," Ty said, tilting his head to one side.

"Quick! The door, Gal," Kern shouted, dropping his bow. They grabbed the door and tried to lift with all their strength, to no avail. The door sat solid.

Ty stepped forward and examined the trap. "Shit!" he shouted as water shot upward out of all four holes, like four fountains, and the room began to fill with water.

"Try the other door!" Kern shouted. All four ran over and grabbed any part of the door they could, but it wouldn't budge.

"Great! I knew we should have gone," Ty raged as he desperately searched the walls again for any loose stone that might conceal a lever.

"Don't even go there. Nothing made you stay," Kern shouted back over the noise of the rushing water, which was now at his knees.

"Arrrgh!" Galandrik crashed his axe against the door.

Lan'esra waded over and hit the same spot with her mace as the dwarf prepared another swing.

Crash! His mighty axe smashed against the door and chunks of wood fell to the floor. The water was now at his waist as he swung furiously.

"Give me your mace," Kern shouted, and took over hitting the door. The damage was clear to see as chunks of wood continued to rain down into the water.

"A few more Gal, we are nearly through!" Kern shouted as the water rose steadily. Galandrik swung again and a small hole appeared as another splinter of wood fell out.

"A few more!" Lan'esra shouted, but it was too late. The water was up to the dwarf's armpits and his swing was defeated by the cold liquid.

"The axe, pass me the axe!" Kern ordered and continued to pound the door with all his strength, but the water soon got the better of the ranger as well, and he groaned in defeat.

Ty treaded water, only just managing to keep his head above water with the weight of his equipment and weapons. "What now?"

"You think of something! You're the Rat! No prison can hold you! Pretend this is a prison!"

Ty examined the ceiling for anything, but it was hopeless. They were stuck in a watery coffin.

"Anybody got water-breathing potions?" Galandrik asked.

"Leaves, the boy had leaves!" Ty shouted.

"And how exactly are we going to get them?" Kern shouted with his hands in the air, now touching the ceiling.

Ty realised he was right: The door had slammed, stopping them going back to the boy. He thrust his head under the surface of the water and could almost make out the floor in the gloom beneath them.

"Go through the holes on the floor! Once the water has filled the room hit the holes!" he shouted, his lips only just below the ceiling.

They all took one last big gulp of air before the room was full. Kern opened his eyes under the water and could make out Ty pointing toward the holes. All four swam down and through the holes, passing their backpacks through first. Kern's hand appeared again and grabbed his bow, dragging it down. They swam along a tunnel that led under the door until they came to a metal grating in the next room. The light shone down, penetrating the water. Lan'esra pointed to her eyes and down the tunnel and carried on.

Kern pointed up at the grating to Galandrik, who knew exactly what he was saying. He grabbed his axe with both hands and hit the grating three times before Kern waved him to stop and examined it. He shook his head as Lan'esra swam back, sweeping her hand across her throat, indicating a dead-end. Kern grabbed the bars above him and shook, but nothing.

Ty, now beginning to struggle for breath, tapped the ranger to stop and he did. Ty reached through the bars and into the room and felt about before nodding at Kern. He reached inside his tunic pulling out his lock picks. After choosing two, he handed Galandrik his pouch and stretched both arms through the bars.

Lan'esra looked at Kern with her eyes wide, and slowly shook her head. Kern forced a smile and placed a reassuring hand on her shoulder. Still Ty fumbled, his eyes shut with a mixture of holding his breath and concentration.

Galandrik grabbed Kern's arm and shook him, his head shaking. Kern grabbed his arm and nodded as if to say 'you'll be all right.' Galandrik kicked and forced his way to where Ty was. Desperately he grabbed the bars and shook them wildly, nudging Ty as he did. The thief stopped and glared at

Galandrik as Kern pulled the dwarf away and spun him round. Facing his friend, Kern shook his head and held up two fingers, trying to encourage Galandrik to hang on for only a few moments more.

But Galandrik's eyes were wide, and his mouth opened as he tried to gulp for air; his oxygen levels had run out. He felt his brain fuzz with the onset of asphyxia. He tried to hold on for one last minute, but his heart was beating frantically, desperate for oxygen. It was no use. The breath he'd taken moments earlier was spent and he was left with a headache, then dizziness as his thoughts disappeared. The lock picks slowly floated to the bottom of the tunnel and his lifeless body began to float as his last ebb of strength disappeared.

He dropped his beloved axe. Galandrik was dead.

Kern grabbed the dwarf's shoulders and shook him as though it would wake him just as he heard the click of the lock above. Ty pushed the grating open and climbed up into the room. Kern looked to Lan'esra and pointed at the dwarf then upward. She grabbed the dwarf as Kern pulled himself up and into the room above.

"Ty, help me grab Galandrik." They both reached down and hauled the lifeless dwarf into the room, then Lan'esra climbed up and out, sprawling on her back, gasping for air.

Kern rested his hands on Galandrik's chest and pumped before breathing air into his mouth. Ty watched in horror as he sucked in precious air.

"Wake, you bastard," Kern shouted inbetween deep breaths as he pushed on his chest

"I told you we shouldn't have come," Ty said.

With frightening speed Kern grabbed the thief by his collar and pointed a finger into his face. "If he dies, so help me God, you'll follow!" he said through gritted teeth, saliva splattering Ty's face, his eye was wide and lost with anger. It wasn't the Kern Ty knew. After a few seconds he released his grip, pushing Ty back. He pushed down on Galandrik's chest again before breathing into his mouth. It seemed like an eternity before Kern finally stopped and looked upward with clenched fists and screamed, tears rolling down his cheeks. Ty fell backward and stared at the ceiling, unable to believe Galandrik was dead.

Kern brought his fists down on his dead companion's chest, shouting, "Noooo!"

As he did, the dwarf's head jolted up, his eyes opened wide, and, with a cough, a mouthful of water shot out.

"Gal!" Kern said, and held the back of his head as he coughed his lungs empty of water, trying to replace them with the sweet oxygen that they craved. Kern rolled him onto his side and watched as the dwarf came back to life. Ty sat up and crawled over to his friend, along with Lan'esra. After a few minutes the dwarf rolled back over and gazed up at Kern blinking. His breathing had subsided and he stuttered, "I'm… hungry."

Kern fell backward and, through a mixture of tears and laughter, replied, "You're always hungry."

Ty placed his hand on his friend's shoulder. "Good to have you back, lad."

"Back? I haven't been anywhere!" He sat up and looked around. "Where is my axe?"

"I'll go get it, it's below us in the tunnel of water," Kern said, sitting back up.

Lan'esra swung her legs into the water. "Don't worry, I'll get it," she said with a smile as she dropped into the water. She swam to the bottom and saw the giant axe next to Ty's leather pouch of lock picks. She placed the picks into her tunic and swam back up holding the axe. Galandrik grabbed the axe and helped her back out of the water.

"Thanks," the dwarf said, smiling.

"Any time, friend," she said, turning to Ty. "I believe these are yours?" She handed down the wet leather pouch.

Ty smiled back. "Thanks. I think I may need to dry these out."

"And thanks for opening the grate. That is some skill you have there, to be able pick a lock from underneath, blind, and back to front. With the added pressure of potentially drowning! How long did it take you to learn that?"

Ty paused for a second. "I never did. That was my first time."

"Really?"

"Well, not underwater, at least."

Lan'esra could see in the thief's eyes that they had got through by the skin of their teeth. "So you really are lucky," she said, stepping over to her backpack. "Better try and dry some of this out, I guess."

Kern and Ty locked stares and, after an uncomfortable few seconds, Kern said, "I agree. Thank you, Ty."

"We are a team; no problem," he answered, and dried his picks.

"Get the food out, and bin the wet blankets and torches. They will be no good to us now; nor will the wet clothes. Remove everything that can't be wrung out. We don't have time to sit here and wait around for stuff to dry. We need to get moving," Kern said, removing his leather armour and wet shirt.

Ty faced away when he removed his shirt, not wanting to show his blackened hardened chest. It went nearly from shoulder to shoulder across his chest now, only a few small areas still covered with his flesh.

The room featured a door to the north and another to the south, which Galandrik tried to smash through. Water trickled down the door through the hole he made. The door to the north was a double door, barred with a large wooden block. A large sun covered the door, half on each. The room was bright without any torches. It must have been magically lit Kern thought.

Ty glared up at the sun. "Ironic… We could do with some heat."

"Everybody get prepared again," Kern ordered. "Ty, search for traps… please."

The thief nodded in agreement and went to work.

Kern, Ty, and Lan'esra stood in a line with crossbows and longbow ready to fire. Galandrik grabbed the wooden block and glanced back at Kern, who in turn looked at Ty and Lan'esra. They both nodded.

"Let's do this," Kern said.

Galandrik lifted the block and heaved it to the floor. He grabbed the two iron rings and pulled the door open. It revealed a corridor—and at the end stood a fire elemental.

"Fire!" Kern shouted, unleashing a volley of arrows.

"No shit!" Ty replied.

"No—*fire*—shoot it!"

The arrows struck the back of the elemental. It spun round and roared as more arrows and bolts hit the monster and disappeared in the flames that twisted and crackled around it. It held its flaming arm out and a fireball flew down the corridor, Galandrik only just managing to duck under it. Kern and Lan'esra jumped sideways as the fireball stuck the door behind them, engulfing it and then disappearing, leaving a circle of black and a few fragments of wood still alight.

"Get ready for melee, here it comes!" Galandrik shouted as the fire elemental floated down the corridor toward them like a ghost. A sword made of flame grew from its hand.

Ty stepped next to Galandrik and dropped his crossbow, drawing his short sword. Lan'esra stood next to Kern on the opposite side and drew her mace. The fire elemental entered the room. All the party attacked simultaneously and stuck the elemental. Their weapons swept straight through the flames of the beast, leaving a bright trail behind their weapons. The elemental screamed and swung his sword at Galandrik, striking his upper arm, cutting through his hardened leather armour and doing some burn damage. The smell of burning flesh instantly filled the room.

Kern swung his longsword at the side of the elemental, slicing straight through. The trail of flame that followed it hung in the air before balling up and dropping to the floor, where it split into three mini-elementals. They flew toward the ranger.

Lan'esra stepped forward to attack. The elemental raised his swordless hand, firing a web of flame that surrounded her, twisting and turning before forming a flame cage, trapping her.

Ty knew that his sword would be useless. He looked around the room and saw the far door with the trickle of water coming through the hole that Galandrik created. *Water!* The thief thought for a moment, then ran to his backpack and rummaged through until he found his last flask of oil. He threw it at the door, smashing it and covering the door in a thick liquid. He grabbed his crossbow and ran to the door.

Galandrik swung again, catching the elemental in its midriff. Again the flame that followed his swing gathered and fell to the floor, splitting into three mini elementals. Kern and Galandrik swung and retreated as the smaller ones pushed them back. The main elemental raised his hand and launched a fireball at Kern, who managed to dive out of the way, narrowly avoiding it as it crashed against the wall and exploded but dropping his sword as he did. The smaller elementals attacked. Kern jumped up and grabbed Lan'esra's mace, swinging it wildly. The elemental raised his hands in the air and roared.

Ty aimed his crossbow and fired. It caught the monster directly in its throat. It never flinched; instead it brought its hands down, and fire streamed from its fingers and spread across the floor before splitting into seven more mini-elementals.

Galandrik swung his axe at one, and it disintegrated and disappeared. Another attacked, burning and scorching his leather armour. The heat was intense and sweat began to trickle into his eyes. Two more floated toward the dwarf.

Kern swung the mace as Lan'esra looked on, helpless. He fought off two as three more approached, and she knew they couldn't hold off for long. She tried to touch the bars, but the heat was unbearable. Ty fired another bolt, catching the elemental in the chest. It looked directly at him and lifted a hand. "Fire then you piece of shit!" Ty shouted as a fireball flew from its hand.

Ty jumped, but slipped on the oily floor. The fireball caught his shoulder, knocking him to the floor. He banged his head as he fell, rendering himself unconscious, and flames mingled around his shoulder as the door was engulfed in flame.

Kern noticed the door ablaze, and saw the water that was flowing through it. "Galandrik!" The dwarf turned and looked. "Hit the door, hit the door hard!" Kern shouted as he continued to swing.

The elemental fired another fireball at Kern. It only just missed as he rolled out of the way, crashing against the wall behind him. The smaller ones raced toward him as he backed away on his behind, hands, and feet.

Galandrik waited for his moment and ran, taking a fiery blow to the back of his legs. He could feel the burn and intense pain, and the burning leather sticking to his flesh. He raised the axe above his head and brought it down on the burning door.

—*Crash!*—

The door split, and the pressure of the water behind it was enough to burst it open. The water crashed into the room, taking Galandrik, Kern, and Ty with it. The tidal wave swept through the room, eating the mini elementals at it went. It crashed through the cage and Lan'esra's legs went from under her, forcing her along on the tidal wave. The fire elemental fled down the corridor, but the water caught it in seconds. It smoked and fizzled as it got sucked into the water. The party were spinning and crashing down the corridor until they smashed into the door at the end.

Ty had come round in all the watery confusion and didn't know what was going on. All four fought hard to reach the surface and grab that valuable breath.

After a couple of minutes, the water had levelled out and Kern, Galandrik, and Lan'esra stood up; Ty was still treading water. "What the hell just happened?" the thief asked, spitting a mouthful of water out.

"Galandrik burst the door and it flooded, extinguishing the fire elemental," Kern said, shaking water out of his ear. Ty felt the floor with his toes as the water slowly drained away.

Suddenly a head burst out of the water, gasping for air. It was a gnome; his head looked too big for his body and wisps of hair above his ears were all that were left on his bald dome.

Kern grabbed him by the back of his neck and lifted him out of the water; he was naked apart from a loin cloth. "Please don't hurt me!" he squealed.

"Hurt you! From the man who was throwing fireballs about like no tomorrow, that's a bit rich!" Kern shouted.

"I thought you were here to kill me!" the gnome wailed. The water had all but gone now and the backpacks and equipment lay strewn all over the floor.

"We might be, and still might kill you!" Ty said, rubbing the cut on his forehead.

"I can… I *will* make sure you get out alive with no more injuries!"

"What's to stop us killing you and just carrying on? We defeated everything you have thrown at us so far," Galandrik added, looking at his burnt and ripped armour.

"You don't understand," the gnome said, begging for his life.

"Oh, we understand just about right, my friend," Kern said, dropping the gnome on the floor and drawing a dagger. "You killed a friend of ours, blinded me, burnt everyone, drowned him—" he pointed at the dwarf— "and nearly killed us all with an earth elemental! Give me one good reason not to," the ranger said, pointing the dagger at the frightened gnome.

"Because… if you kill me, you will never get out of here. Without my help you'll be fighting elementals until they knock you into dust."

"Why would we need your help?" Ty asked, folding his arms.

"Because I created this. It's a self-regenerating dungeon; if I die it'll never end," he said, shivering.

"How do we know you are not just making this up to save your skin?" Kern questioned.

The gnome looked at Kern for a few seconds and then turned to Ty. "Very well, reach the brick behind you, the one with the scratch across the middle, and push it," he said to the thief.

Ty studied the brick. "And it does what?"

"It'll open the door behind me. Nothing will hurt you… I promise," he said, standing up.

Kern stepped closer to the gnome and held his dagger across his throat. "You better pray nothing does, or you'll die long before me." He nodded at Ty.

Lan'esra and Galandrik picked up their weapons. Ty pushed the brick in, and they heard cogs and gears churning. The door slowly lifted, revealing another square room. It was empty apart from two doors, one on each of the east and west walls, and in the middle of the room on a big red pentagram was an air elemental.

"Kill me and it will attack. If you manage to kill it, there are creatures just as nasty behind the other doors. Let me go and I will get you out of here safe and sound."

The party all knew they had been lucky with the first two elementals, and didn't have the weapons to defeat this one. "Very well, I will let you go and we won't harm you, but we need what we came for," Kern said.

"I don't have hordes of treasure and I wish people would—"

"We haven't come for gold," Kern interrupted.

"Well, if there *is* any…" Ty said.

"No, we have come for fighort leaf," Lan'esra said calmly. The gnome looked at her, then around at the others. A smile appeared on his face and then he erupted into laughter.

"Careful, gnome, we could change our minds," Kern said, raising an eyebrow and pressing the dagger harder into his flesh.

The gnome stopped laughing, but couldn't get the smile off of his face. "Fighort leaf doesn't grow in here! Only what *I* say grows in here. What you need is up on top of the Voltic Mountain. I think I have some in my study."

Kern looked at the others in disbelief. "But we were told—"

"Sorry friend, you were told wrongly."

Kern released the pressure of the dagger slightly, "If you are lying to us, gnome…"

"I am not. You'll see. The brick two above the first one you pushed? Give that a go, too."

Ty did and the door began to close. When it was down, he asked Ty to push another brick below the first one and when he did, the door rose again, revealing another square room. This time it had a glowing blue oval hovering in the middle, and electrical lights spun all around it like a million blue fireflies.

"What the hell is that?" Galandrik asked.

"That, my friend, is a teleport gate to my house in the mountains. You have two choices: You can kill me and fight forever, or step through with me, grab your fighort leaf, and be gone."

Kern looked at the others and shrugged his shoulders. Ty nodded back in agreement.

"Right, grab what you want to take. The food, torches, clothes, and blankets are ruined. Leave them and take what's salvageable. This better not be a trap," he said, looking at the gnome.

"It's not. You are here for the herb and I protect my family with this elaborate dungeon. Follow me." He stepped forward and waited for Kern's nod of approval.

"Wait, I want to go with you," Kern said.

"You can't. It's one at a time," the gnome said, rubbing his cold bare arms.

"Fine. I'll go first," Kern said.

The gnome stared at Kern for a few seconds and then agreed. "Sure. I will follow."

Chapter Twenty-Four
A Dignity of Dragons

Kern gathered his belongings—those he could save—and stepped into the glowing blue oval of lights. Before his head was even through, he could feel his foot touch the ground on the other side. It felt like he was still in the room. He took a deep breath and pushed his head through. He was in what looked like a study, a square room with one door to his left. Above it was a stuffed orc's head. At the far end was a massive bookshelf covering the whole wall from floor to ceiling; in front of this was a desk, cluttered with paper and books. To his right was a leather sofa, facing away, and he could hear voices coming from it. He stepped out of the light and stood in the room. "Hello," he said quietly.

"Father!" he heard a voice shout as a little girl's head appeared from behind the chair. She had big blue eyes and long blonde hair. "You're not my father! What have you done?"

"I haven't done anything, sweetie. He's right behind me," the ranger said, taking a step forward.

"Don't you come any closer!"

"I won't hurt you," he said, stepping forward.

"I warned you. King, Princess, up!" she shouted, and two large black dogs appeared at each end of the sofa, slowly walking round until they stood in front of the girl. Their razor-sharp teeth showed as their snarling top lips lifted up; their ears were pinned back and they each had a stump for a tail. They squatted slightly on their back legs, ready to pounce at the girl's command. Their growl was fierce and Kern knew if they attacked him, he wouldn't stand much of a chance.

"Whoa," Kern said, raising both hands. "Calm down. Your father will be through any second—we are friends."

"How come I have never met you then?" the little girl said, folding her arms.

"I'm an old friend," Kern said calmingly.

"I don't believe you," she sung in a nursery-rhyme style. "King, Princess, forward…" The two dogs edged toward the ranger, never talking their eyes off him.

"Just go easy, sweetie; I am not here to hurt you, your father, King, or Princess."

"I don't believe you," she sang again as the dogs advanced.

Kern stepped backward past the teleport; silently he begged for the gnome to come through. "Look, your father—my friend—will come through there any second. Just pull your dogs back and we can wait," he said as he backed up against the wall with nowhere else to go.

"Okay—tell me his name and they will go back to their chair. Get it wrong and…" The little girl placed her hand on her mouth and giggled.

Kern thought for a second. *Did he say his name? …Damn, he didn't*. He stared at the little girl and placed his hand on the dagger in his belt. "His name was…"

"You don't know it," the girl sang as she skipped around in a circle. "King, Princess—"

At that moment the gnome appeared behind her. "Daddy!" she shouted and ran to her father.

"King, Princess, come," he said, and the dogs did, one sitting on either side of the gnome.

Kern breathed a sigh of relief. "Thanks," he smiled. The gnome smiled back before bending down and making a fuss over the dogs. "Go sit," he commanded and they did, both jumping up onto the chair and curling up.

"They won't hurt you, soft as anything."

"Yeah, just very protective. We had four when I was a lad. Anybody went near my brother Noahk, they would snarl and bite."

"Yes, these are protective of Annet, too. Ever since—" He stepped closer to Kern and glanced over his shoulder at his daughter, sitting and stroking one of the dogs. "—her mother died, they are her best friends and sometimes her only companions. I'm away a lot and she needs them."

"Sorry to hear that. Yes, I can see that they are great company for her," Kern replied just as Lan'esra stepped through the teleport.

"Hello. What's your name?" Annet said, sitting up and looking at Lan'esra.

"Hello, little one. I am Lan'esra. What's yours?"

"Annet. Daddy calls me Netty, but when I am naughty it's always Annet."

"I'll call you Netty, then, if that's okay."

"Yes. Want to come see my drawings? I did them today."

"I will in a second, Netty. I need to bandage Kern's poorly eye first. Have you any clean webbing we could use?" Lan'esra asked the gnome.

"Yes. Netty, bring the brown bag from the bottom drawer please." The girl ran off and returned with a brown leather sack. Lan'esra redressed his eye. After she had finished, the little girl drummed her hands on the table from the chair she was kneeling on. "Come see, Lan'esra."

"Netty, leave Lan'esra alone."

"She's fine, honestly," Lan'esra said, following the little girl to the table.

"Well, I must admit you are the first group to come through here and defeat two elementals. After the first, I was surprised. Using the trap was a good idea; I never thought of that. So I became the fire elemental to get the job done, as it were. When I saw the dwarf hit the door I just knew it was game over. Brilliant questing."

"Thanks... sorry, what was your name?" Kern asked.

"Bodlin, Bodlin Cryfoot," the gnome said, extending a hand, and Kern shook it.

"I am Kern. This is Lan'esra, and this is Galandrik." The Ranger said as Galandrik entered the room and stood with his axe in his hands. "Where is this place?" he said to Kern and Bodlin. Both dogs got up and moved the end of the sofa next to the dwarf and snarled.

"King, Princess, stay! Put the axe down, Galandrik," Bodlin said. Galandrik leaned it against the wall.

"This is my home, the tower you saw," Boldin answered.

"So how did we float straight through it?" Kern asked.

"The mist is a teleport—just instead of the usual flickering lights, it's a mist. Genius, eh?" Bodlin said smugly.

"Well, it certainly had us fooled. Can I ask one question?" Kern said sheepishly.

"Sure, but I bet I know what it is," Bodlin replied, grabbing some cloth trousers and shirt from a chest.

"Why kill all those adventurers? Why go to all that trouble? Why can't you just live here in peace with your daughter?"

"You answered it; I can't live here in peace. Adventurers will come like they always have, seeking their riches. Some big groups come, and some smaller groups; some get rust monsters and orcs, some get elementals. It all depends on the power stones. Look, it is very complicated. There is a reward if completed; if they die then their items get put to good use—metal melted down and anything magic will be drained to re-power the stones," Bodlin explained as Ty entered the room.

"But I'm still missing something. If people come here, then why not move? Go somewhere where adventurers won't bother you," Kern questioned.

The two dogs had jumped straight down when Ty had arrived, and were excitedly sniffing his legs. Bodlin watched them from the corner of his eye as he answered. "Because I work here. I farm minerals—and that's all I can say. My Mistress would not like it if I said more, and you wouldn't want to upset her," he said with a smile. "Oi, King, Princess, get up!"

The dogs didn't move, nor did Ty; they were up to his waist and weighed more than him.

"King, Princess!" Bodlin shouted again. Still the dogs didn't move.

Netty jumped down from the table and walked over. She stood a couple of feet away and stared at the thief. "They can smell it on you."

"Annet, don't be rude! Go draw and call them off," he shouted pointing at the table. "I am sorry, Ty. She gets a bit daydreamy sometimes."

The little girl clicked her fingers and pointed at the chair and the dogs instantly jumped up. "They know…" she said as she skipped back to Lan'esra.

Ty frowned at Bodlin. "That's all right. I just have a fear of strange dogs, especially when they're as big as those ones," he said, watching as the dogs lay back down.

"Must have been chased and bitten by a few then?" Kern sniggered.

"Part and parcel of the game," Ty agreed, looking at the little girl. He felt like he knew her.

"Right, who wants feeding? It's not usual I have guests, but to hell with it—have you got time?"

Before anyone else could answer, Galandrik's head turned. "Aye, lad, we have time for that!"

Kern smiled and nodded. "Sure, we would love to."

"Good. I will get the table sorted." Bodlin walked to the door and rang a bell that was attached to the wall on a bronze wall bracket.

Within a minute, the door opened and two gnome women stood there, "Yes, Mr Bodlin?"

"Go set the table for—" He quickly glanced around the room, counting. "—six, and plenty of my wine."

"Yes, Mr Bodlin, sir," they said, closing the door behind them.

"If you need dry things, look in that chest over there. You will find loads of clothes, and I'm sure I may be able to accommodate you with some armour tomorrow."

"That is very kind, thanks," Kern answered. They all thanked him and changed into whatever they could find. They left their weapons there, too—apart from Ty, who would rather die than leave his daggers.

Kern walked back to the gnome after changing. "Don't take this the wrong way, Bodlin, but you don't know us, yet you seem fine with us being here, offering us clothes and food—how do you know we won't try anything?"

"You won't," he answered as he puttered about in the room, grabbing a belt from a shelf and a hat from off the hat stand.

"You are sure of this?" Kern questioned.

"Quite sure. Mr Galandrik is hoping for beef; you want to get the herbs and to be gone; young Miss Lan'esra misses her family; and Mr Rat there has already opened every drawer and chest in this room with his eyes," he said, smiling.

"You're a mind-reader?" Lan'esra said from the table.

"No, I am just a good judge of character."

"I haven't even noticed a chest!" Ty said, frowning.

"You don't have to be a mind-reader to know that's a lie," Kern laughed.

"I was thinking more pork, to be honest," Galandrik added, which made them all laugh.

*

"Right, follow me. Netty, pack your pens and books away now. It's dinnertime."

"Can't I tidy up after dinner?" she asked sweetly.

"Annet, you know the rules," he said with his hands on his hips.

The little girl frowned and her bottom lip came out. "Okay, daddy."

Lan'esra smiled and said, "Let me help you."

"Thanks!" Annet said, smiling.

Bodlin shook his head and opened the door. "Bring Lan'esra up to the master dining room when you have finished."

"Okay," Annet answered.

They walked out the door into a corridor leading around in a circle. The room was one of a few in the centre of the tower, and the corridor led around the circumference to a set of stairs leading upward. At the top of them was another door, not too dissimilar from the one they'd just left.

Bodlin pushed it open to reveal yet another square room. There was a massive table in the middle lined with a typical banquet. A huge lump of beef was the centrepiece and around it were vegetables, breads, and fruits. Pictures and tapestries depicting battles and landscapes lined the walls. On the far wall sat a massive leather armchair with a small table in front of it. A couple of Annet's toy dolls rested on it.

"Take a seat, anywhere you like," Bodlin offered, pulling out the closest chair.

"I'll take this one," Kern said, selecting the chair opposite the gnome, facing the door.

"I think I'll sit here," Galandrik said, sitting next to the huge side of beef in the middle of the table. "Smells good."

"Tuck in, Mr Dwarf, no need to wait for the others. Where is Mr Ty?" Bodlin asked just as Ty entered.

"I was just looking out the window. You can see for miles," he said, sitting next to Kern.

"Yes, on a clear night you can see the coastline of Bloodmoore," he answered, ladling some potatoes onto his plate.

"Really? That is interesting," Kern said as Lan'esra and Netty walked into the room. The little girl jumped up onto a chair next to Bodlin, and Lan'esra sat at the end of the table. King and Princess trotted around and lay on the floor behind Annet.

Soon they all were eating and drinking and chatting. "So Bodlin, your… Mistress isn't here, then?" Kern asked, breaking fresh bread.

"No, she has important business elsewhere. Troubled times, I am afraid."

"Shal—"

"Annet, please! This is big people talk. Eat your dinner."

"Sorry, Daddy," she replied, hanging her head.

"Sorry, Kern. As I said." He looked down at his daughter and shook his head. "Troubled times."

Kern smiled at the little girl. "That's not good. It seems Bodisha is full of troubled times," Kern replied.

"Yes, not good at all. Orcs to the north and appearing in smaller troops all over. Mankind and elves just cannot get on; it's ludicrous. So where is it that you are heading to next?"

"We will travel down to Lake Fortune as soon as we have eaten and rested."

"You do know there is no way off this island? The next boat will be in two weeks," Bodlin said, draining a goblet of wine. "Oh my, that is the best wine in Bodisha!" He finished with an exaggerated smack of his lips.

Ty's head turned. "Two weeks!"

"Yes, my halfling friend, two whole weeks. Unless there is an uncharted boat bringing the next wave of adventurers—and sometimes there is; just like the one you came on. And unless they are coming from Bloodmoore, you'll be heading in the wrong direction."

"We haven't got two weeks," Kern said with a serious edge to his voice.

Bodlin poured another glass of wine. "I can't help you, I'm afraid."

"My father's life depends upon these herbs; you must have a boat we could… borrow."

"Mr Kern, firstly, if—and I haven't, but *if*—I had a boat, how would you bring it back, and when? And secondly, do you honestly think a rowing boat could get you to the mainland? The tide would take you miles out of the way. Gods know where you would end up." He looked around the room. "Can any of you navigate nautically?"

After a few seconds of uncomfortable silence, Lan'esra spoke. "Couldn't we send a paperfinch explaining our delay?"

"It won't help; he'll die before they get the herbs. Damn! There must be a way," Kern said, standing up. Both dogs sat up at the sound of Kern's raised voice.

Annet rubbed King on his head. "He won't hurt you, boy."

"Have you finished, Netty?" Bodlin asked, and Annet nodded her head. "Go take them up for some air please."

"Okay, Daddy. Can I give them some beef?" she asked, with an angelic look on her face.

"Go on, then," he smiled back.

She grabbed two lumps and stood in front of the dogs. "Paw," she said, and they lifted one each into her tiny hands. "Down!" she commanded, and both dogs went down instantly. "Play dead," she said, holding the beef behind her back as both dogs rolled over with their legs in the air. "Good dogs!" she said. They jumped up and sat down. She threw both pieces in the air and they were gone, each dog claiming its prize before being led from the room. "You coming?" Annet said, looking at Lan'esra and holding out a hand.

"Miss Lan'esra hasn't finished her dinner, Netty; stop being rude."

Lan'esra wiped her chin and placed the cloth next to her plate. "It's okay, honestly. You have a break from looking after her, and I'll have a break from my kids," she smiled, gesturing towards Kern, Ty, and Galandrik.

Bodlin smiled back. "Thank you. It's nice for her to have female company."

Lan'esra grabbed her hand and the door shut behind them.

"What did she mean, kids?" Ty said, wiping spilt gravy from his tunic.

"No idea," Galandrik smiled.

Kern was still pacing the room, oblivious to the last two minutes. "There must be a way, there is *always* a way."

Bodlin wiped his face and picked up his goblet. "Smoke, anyone?" he asked as he got up from his chair and walked to the leather sofa.

"Don't mind if I do," Ty said, following him.

"You like Stonecrop leaf?"

Ty smiled and sat next to the gnome. "Who doesn't?"

"I know why you came here, but what is it you go to Lake Fortune for?" Bodlin asked, passing a spare pipe and tobacco to the thief.

"Willow rose," Ty replied.

"Ah, I see, more herbs. I think you'll be able to buy that in Fortune Town."

"It's all for nothing if we can't leave here for two weeks," Kern said, draining a goblet of wine.

Bodlin blew a large smoke ring. "What's the hurry?"

"We need the herbs to heal the… heal someone and, unfortunately, as a means of persuading us to take this herb-gathering quest, they imprisoned my father. If we don't get the herbs and the… person dies, I fear my father will too," Kern explained.

"I am truly sorry to hear that, but I can't help you. I really wish I could," he answered.

Galandrik burped loudly and got up from the table, wiping the grease from his beard.

"You look like you have been dragged through Hades and back," Ty said, looking at the dwarf, his armour ripped and burnt.

"I feel like it, too. Give me some of that, lad," the dwarf said, sitting down. Ty passed him the pipe.

Within twenty minutes Galandrik and Ty were asleep, Bodlin walked back to the table and sat opposite Kern as gnomes scurried about cleaning up the leftovers. He handed Kern the pipe, and he forced a smile in return.

*

Annet and Lan'esra walked up three flights of stairs before reaching the top. The pointed roof they saw from the floor was tied up in the middle like a folded umbrella. The area was huge; chairs and tables, a wooden shed, a swing, and dog bones and toys littered the roof. Annet kicked a ball and the dogs ran together after the ball. Annet led Lan'esra to some steps and peered up over the wall. "This is my favourite place," she said, standing on the third step to see over.

"Be you careful there," Lan'esra said, standing next to the little girl, concerned she might fall.

"Don't worry. I come here all the time. My mother and I sat here a lot. She used to read me stories."

"Ah, bless you."

"Go on, ask me," Annet said out of the blue.

"Ask you what?" Lan'esra said, pushing a loose strand of the girl's blonde hair back from her face.

"How she died."

"You don't want to talk about that. Bringing up the past isn't nice."

Annet jumped down and threw the ball, and King and Princess chased it. "But you want to know."

Lan'esra stared out over the Voltic Isle. The mountains looked awesome against the sea, which sparkled in the distance like a million diamonds as moonlight bounced off the waves. She could hear the crashing of the waves on the rocks and the cry of the seagulls in the distance.

"Well, only tell me if you really want to, Netty," she said, sitting on the wall.

"We were up in the mountains searching for flowers and got attacked by wargs. Mum fought bravely and even killed one, but they got the better of us. We died and father was devastated. He'd only left us for a minute."

"I'm sure you mother did all she could. And yes, your father would have been devastated; when we lose someone we love, it is always hard, but it wasn't his fault that… hang on, you said 'we' died?"

"Yes. The wargs killed mummy and me, but my mother couldn't be saved. She could only save me," she said, smiling and pointing upward.

"I'm sure she did what she could," Lan'esra said, looking up.

"Yes. If she could have saved mummy, I'm sure she would have."

"I'm sure too," Lan'esra smiled. "Come on, let's play with the dogs."

"One of your friends knows her, I am sure of it," Annet said, throwing the ball across the rooftop.

"What makes you think that?"

"I just know. It's a gift she gave me."

"Oh, I see. So she saved you and gave you a gift… What is her name?"

"Father told me not to tell anyone, but I never see anyone. It's so unfair," she said, folding her arms and stamping a foot.

"I am a friend and I promise not to tell anyone," Lan'esra said, moving over to the other side of the roof and looking out to sea.

"I call her Mia for short."

"It is always nice to shorten names. My mother called me Esra."

"Mia is like a mum to me now, but she only comes now and again. People are scared of her but I am not scared. She is lovely."

"When is Mia here next?"

"Soon. She should have been here weeks ago, but something happened and daddy won't tell me what."

"Well, hopefully she will be here soon."

"Yes, but she never stays long. She just flies in and goes again, and always at night," she said, looking up into the sky.

"Fly in? What does she fly in on?"

Annet giggled as she skipped around in a circle. "Silly Billy, she is—"

"Annet! It's your bedtime," they heard a voice call from the stairs.

"Oh, I must go. Will you be here in the morning?"

"Yes, I expect so. See you in the morning."

"Bye Esra! Come on, you two," she shouted as she ran off down the stairs with the dogs in close pursuit.

Lan'esra leaned on the wall and thought about what the girl had said. *She is just a child with a hell of an imagination. Her mother's death must have been bad and this how she deals with it.* She felt a cool breeze and wrapped the cloak tighter around her.

*

Kern sat facing Bodlin. "You know I must leave this isle, don't you?"

"Yes, I can see your pain, but it is impossible," he answered. Just then the door burst open and Annet ran in, throwing her arms around her dad.

"Good night, Daddy," she said, kissing his cheek.

"Good night, Netty. Get Lorina to read to you, I am busy with my friends."

"Okay, Daddy. Good night, Mr Kern," she said, extending a hand, which Kern shook.

"Good night, Netty," Kern replied. She tiptoed over to Galandrik and Ty, and stood looking down at the thief; she gently touched his hand and closed her eyes. She saw hundreds of flickering images in just a few seconds, and released his hand.

"Netty, get away from them, now." She skipped back to Bodlin, wrapped her arms around his neck, and whispered something.

"That's enough of that talk, go to bed!" Bodlin said, no longer smiling.

"Good night," she said, and skipped out of the room.

Kern could see that whatever she whispered had disturbed Bodlin. "What did she say?" he asked, lighting the pipe up.

"Oh, nothing. Ever since her mother died, she makes stuff up. I just hate to hear her lie."

"It must be hard for her," Kern said as Lan'esra entered.

"Hey, any wine left?"

"Sure," Bodlin said, lifting the bottle up. "Damn. Hang on—I'll go fetch some from the cellar."

"You don't have to, Bodlin, I am—"

"No, it's no trouble," he said with a smile as he left the room.

Lan'esra got up and closed the door. "Netty is a lovely girl, but she said some really weird things to me upstairs."

Kern frowned at Lan'esra. "Like what?"

"Well, she said she died when her mother did, but she was saved."

"You think it is shock?"

"I don't know. She also said that the woman who saved her, who's called Mia, comes to visit now and again."

"What's so weird about that?"

"She flies in because people are scared of her."

"Flies in? I think she has lost her marbles. I bet it's the shock of her mother dying. She just whispered something to Bodlin and it freaked him out. He said she lies all the time since the death."

"It got weirder. She also said that one of you three knew the woman, and that she had given Netty a gift."

Kern stared at Lan'esra. "Mia had given her a gift?"

"Here we go," Bodlin said as the door opened. "Strange, I can't remember closing the door."

"Sorry, that was me; I felt a chill coming through," Lan'esra lied.

"Oh, it's probably the windows open down the hallway," Bodlin said, as he filled three goblets with wine.

"Cheers," Kern said, lifting his goblet. They toasted and Bodlin filled his pipe again.

"Bodlin, can I ask a question please?" Lan'esra asked. Kern knocked her knee with his under the table.

"Yes, of course, Lan'esra." He smiled, putting the goblet to his lips.

"Who is Mia?"

Bodlin nearly choked on his wine, and put the goblet down on the table and wiped his mouth, "No one," he answered looking away.

"Well, Netty seems to think this 'Mia' saved her and gave her a gift."

"Netty says too much," he answered, shaking his head.

"She also said –"

"Listen, you are talking, so that means you think you know—you should try and listen, and maybe you'll learn something instead," he said, standing up. "She makes these things up. Ever since her mother died, she has done this. Mia is a figment of her imagination. That is the end of it."

"Sorry, Bodlin, I never meant to—"

"Don't apologize. Just don't listen to her stories anymore," Bodlin said, sitting back down.

"I won't. I don't know what I was thinking," she replied, slightly embarrassed.

Kern stared at the gnome and knew that if he was going to get off this island, he had to say what he was thinking. "Do you know what I think, Bodlin?"

The gnome stared at Kern, dreading where this was leading. "What does Kern think?" he asked solemnly.

"I think she was killed and resurrected, the side effect of which is her gift."

Bodlin didn't flinch. "Go on."

"I think she was saved by a dragon named Shalamia. She called her Mia to Lan'esra, and earlier, when you were speaking about your Mistress, she nearly let it slip."

"Ty was saved by her, too, wasn't he?" Bodlin asked as he leant back into his chair.

"Yes, he was. That's what she whispered to you before she went to bed, wasn't it?"

"Yes, I am afraid it was. So I guess now you go and tell the whole of Bodisha and we get tenfold more adventurers attack us. Damn. I knew this day would come."

"You haven't heard a word I've said, have you? Ty was healed by Shalamia. We saved her eggs, we returned them to her, and now we are gathering these herbs to save them again, along with my father!"

"That was you lot?" he said, sitting back up.

"Yes—well, nearly all of us," he answered, flashing a smile at Lan'esra.

"Yes, of course! It all makes sense now! She told me about you three, and even described you! Why didn't you say earlier?"

"Well, it isn't the sort of thing one just shouts out."

"I guess not! Oh my word, this is amazing. I know all about the capture of her young and how she narrowly escaped, too. Does she know what you are doing?"

"I don't think so; we haven't seen her since she healed Ty."

"She should be here tomorrow night. You can tell her and she will probably be able to get you off this Island," he said, clapping his hands. "She will be so pleased."

"Where is she now?" Lan'esra asked.

"She flew south to see some other dragons; I think they may be planning an attack on the king."

"Attack the king? Other dragons? I thought she was the last," Kern stuttered.

"Poppycock. There are loads, they just hide well nowadays."

"Damn. If they attack the king it'll be bad for everyone. He will probably pull troops back from the war in the north with the orcs. That would let the orcs walk right into the heart of Bodisha."

"Do you think she cares about that? She is peaceful and never attacks men of any race." Bodlin looked at Lan'esra and added, "Or women. That's how she healed Netty; Shalamia was feeding on mountain wargs and goats and came across her by chance. Unfortunately, the day her babies were taken, a whirlwind of destruction was set in motion."

"Well, perhaps it may not come to that. If we can get these herbs and trade them for her young and my father, all might be good."

"It would be better than a dignity of angry dragons descending on the king's castle and Raith. That—as you said—could be devastating for all concerned."

"Indeed. When will she get here?"

"Sometime tomorrow night. I will show you something in the morning that I think you will like."

"Very well. We need some rest anyway. My eye is throbbing, too; can you take another look, Lan'esra?"

"Sure," she replied, and started removing the bandages from the ranger's face.

"I'll grab some blankets, are you happy to stay in here? Unfortunately we don't have any spare beds because no one visits, so you don't have much choice, I am afraid."

"This will be fine. One question: What minerals do you farm for her?"

"Fire stone, mainly, but there are others. Now you are going to ask why?"

"Well, I was kind of…"

"I have no idea! That's the truth. She saved Netty and this is how I repay her, no questions asked. Be right back with those blankets." He left the room.

Lan'esra finished removing the bandages. "Shut the good eye. Can you see this?" she asked waving her hand in front of his face.

"It's just a blur; I can see something moving back and forth, but no idea what it is."

"Well, that's not the worst news. I'd be more concerned if you couldn't see out of it, but honestly, Kern, as a friend I'm telling you, you need to see a healer and get it looked at. You could lose it otherwise."

"How can I see a healer?" Kern smiled as she re-bandaged his head.

She shook her head. "Everything is a big joke. You and Ty are so similar; laugh in the face of death and poke danger in the eye!"

"Don't ever compare me to him! Thanks for that," Kern said, sitting down on the leather chair.

"No problem," she answered, lying next to Galandrik and resting her head on his side.

Bodlin walked back into the room with an armful of blankets. All four were already asleep, and Galandrik had begun to snore. He gently covered them all up and blew out the torches.

*

Kern swung his sword in a wild arc in front of him. "Come out and fight me, you little whore!" He spun around, his sword again circling and slicing through the air. "Show yourself, you bastard," he cried as he swung his sword wildly, turning round and round like a blind man. A small cloaked figure holding two daggers stepped out from behind a tree stump and crouched in front of him, ready to attack. Kern swung again and the small figure rolled under the arc of the sword then lunged forward, stabbing Kern in the thigh. Kern swung to the side where the attack had come from but sliced thin air as his attacker rolled under the sword and squatted, holding his daggers up, ready to attack again… "You never beat me! Fight me like a man and not like the cowardly little whoredog you are!" The cloaked figure picked up a small stone and threw it past Kern. It landed behind him and, without any hesitation, Kern swung at where the noise had come from. The cloaked figure lunged forward and sliced through the back of Kern's armour. Instantly he spun round again, swinging the blade through the air, but, to his dismay, hitting nothing. He could feel the warm blood running down his back. "I'll catch you, thief!"...

Ty woke up, his face and neck covered in sweat. His breathing was heavy. He wiped the sweat from his eyes and tried to focus. All the others were asleep on the chairs next to him. He could feel the warmth in his chest, and placed his hands on the hardened skin. He lay back down and heard a little girl's voice say, "I told you I knew…"

Chapter Twenty-Five
Old Friends and New Acquaintances

Kern woke up and stretched. He winced as he yawned, the pain of his eye coming back to him. Galandrik and Ty were sitting up at the table eating, and Kern could smell the fresh bread and bacon. "Morning," he said, folding the cover up after he rose.

"It's nearly afternoon!" Galandrik said around a mouthful of bread and bacon.

Ty looked at the dwarf. "It's like a pig searching for truffles in the dirt, watching you eat."

"Where's Lan'esra?" Kern asked, pulling out the chair next to Ty.

"She's gone off with Annet," Ty answered.

"Did she tell you about last night?" Kern asked, forking some bacon onto his plate.

"No, but she was all happy to tell us you had something to say. She quoted me, saying 'Can't say, loose lips sink ships!'"

Kern laughed. "Well, you have said that to her. It turns out that Bodlin's Mistress is none other than… Shalamia!"

Ty spun round. "You're kidding me!"

"Nope. Apparently his wife and Annet were picking flowers in the mountains and got attacked by wargs, and they both died. Shalamia found them as she was searching for wargs and mountain goats to eat, and she healed Annet, but the mother couldn't be saved."

"That's why she said the things she did! I knew something was amiss. I thought I was dreaming last night," Ty said, shaking his head.

"She also has a 'gift.' Shalamia will be here tonight, and we can explain where Sleeper is and what we are doing. But the scary thing is, she is so damn angry she is rounding up some other dragon friends to pay the king a visit," Kern explained.

"Oh my. That could be devastating to everyone, lad," Galandrik said, wiping his chin.

"That's exactly what I said. We need to tell her we can get Sleeper back without her needing to go to war."

"Let them go. Fuck the king," Ty said, lighting Bodlin's pipe.

"It's isn't just the king, Ty, it's the war as a whole. Imagine the king bringing his armies back to fend off the dragons. The orcs would run riot through Bodisha," the ranger explained. "All the northern towns—Tonilla, Phebon, Leopards Town, Raith—they would all be in danger."

"We could stay down here," Ty said, leaning back. "It isn't our war."

"Sorry, but it *is* our war. Your views are completely different to mine on this. I have family and friends up there—and even if I didn't, I wouldn't stand by and let the orcs rule us. You want to run forever? Be enslaved by them?" Kern argued.

"It'll never happen. The orcs are clueless," Ty said, admiring a tapestry.

"Without a defensive force to stop them, a clueless army can still walk in and take over."

"Best we put Shalamia off the idea then," Galandrik said, picking up the pipe.

Ty groaned as he stretched his aching limbs. "Say whatever you like, but I'm not fighting in any bloody war."

"Theoretically, you'll be doing your bit if we can persuade her not to attack," Kern said with a smug smile.

"There you go, then. I'm doing my bit. If anybody asks me to help, that's what I will tell them." Ty smiled back.

Kern rolled his eyes and turned to the dwarf. "Where's Bodlin?"

"He said he would be back after he took care of some business."

"I hope Shalamia can get us off this island. Do you know it never even crossed my mind that we might get stuck?" Kern dropped his fork onto his plate. "Bodlin sure does spoil you. I may have to visit here again," the ranger said, finishing with a burp.

"You'll be coming on your own, then, because I cannot think of anywhere I'd rather *not* be," Ty said, picking up a book from the table.

"When this is all over, I'd like to live somewhere like this—collecting wood for the fire, fishing for your dinner, peaceful without a care," Kern said, daydreaming.

Ty put the book down and laughed, "This will never be over, Kern, O Slayer of Giants."

The door opened and Bodlin walked in carrying an armload of scrolls. "Here, let me help you," Ty said, stepping forward.

"No need, sir, I'm just putting them on here," Bodlin said as he scurried past and let all the scrolls roll onto the table. "Right! I have got in contact with Shalamia, and she has agreed to get you off the island. I mentioned you had some news about her young, too. She is most interested to hear what you have to say."

Galandrik nodded. "I bet she is. She must be worried sick."

"Oh, she is in a foul mood, I can tell you. Anyway, I do feel a bit guilty for damaging your armour and other things, so," he explained, "with Shalamia's blessing I—*we* would like to replace some things. Please follow me." He turned and left the room.

Galandrik, Kern, and Ty were all confused, but followed Bodlin out of the door. They went around the curving corridor and down some stairs, then through another corridor and down more stairs. Finally they reached a set of double doors. Bodlin fumbled in his pocket, then pulled out some keys on a small ring. He fiddled with the lock for a few seconds before the lock opened with a *click*.

"I knew it was this key," he muttered. "Before we go in here, remember this isn't *all* for you, and stealing from a dragon can be a very risky business… even for the best of thieves." He cast an eye at Ty. "So please don't take kindness as a weakness." With those words, Bodlin pushed the double doors open and said, "Welcome to Shalamia's hoard."

The circular room was filled with every weapon imaginable: swords, shields, and axes; plate armour, leather armour, and chain armour; bows and crossbows, quivers and potions, wands, staffs, and everything else an adventurer might need to carry as he quests.

"By the love of…" Ty whispered.

"I have never seen so many weapons," Kern added, staring at the abundance of swords. "You could arm a garrison with all this!"

"I think I just woke up in heaven, lad," Galandrik said, his mouth still wide open.

Bodlin stepped into the room, "Well, don't just stand there—come on in and see what fits!"

They entered the room, each heading in a different direction. Some tables were lined with potions, and others with scrolls, wands, rings, and necklaces. Sword rack after sword rack stood against the edges of the room, and suits of armour lined up in rows, from soft leather to hardened leather, chain mail to plate. Helmets sat in rows on the floor—golden, silver, some with spikes, others full-face or with leather caps.

Ty stood looking down at a table full of knives and daggers. Some had double blades that twisted into a point; runes adorned some and others pulsed and glowed with magic in shades of blues, greens, and reds.

Kern stared in amazement at the twenty or more bows hanging horizontally on nails—white wood, red wood, brown wood; some had double strings while others sparkled with magic. Quivers filled with arrows leaned up against the wall beneath the bows. When Kern took a closer look, there were little flames dancing around the wooden shafts of some of the arrows while hundreds of different-coloured feathers adorned others, and the odd few appeared to have wisps of smoke twisting round and round the shafts. "Breath-taking," he said, scratching his chin.

Galandrik looked down a table that had a half-dozen double-headed axes laid out on it; other tables boasted one-handed axes, throwing axes, dagger axes, battle axes, halberds—

"There must be thousands of gold worth of weapons here."

"Yes, it's surprising what adventurers leave behind," Bodlin said.

"Shalamia is a generous dragon. She has agreed to give you each one set of armour; one weapon, complete with accessories; and one magical item. Unfortunately, most of the magical items you see here—such as the rings, wands, potions, and necklaces—are not identified. However, I do have some identification scrolls, so choose your items wisely and I will identify them for you when I get back."

Bodlin turned and backed out of the room, pulling the door handles with him. "Oh—and remember my words," he added. "Only a fool would steal from a dragon. That includes swallowing."

The doors clicked shut behind him.

Ty placed his hands on his hips. "Was that aimed at me?"

"Nah. Why would he?" Kern laughed, pulling a bow from the wall.

"Well, I think it's very judgmental, You know, not all thieves… Fine. I get his point, but even so!"

They all laughed, but were quickly absorbed in considering their options.

The dwarf picked up a two-handed axe, silver with golden runes covering the blades. The handle was wrapped in deerskin and felt like nothing he had picked up before. As he turned it, it seemed to glimmer and change colours before his very eyes. "This is mine," he declared. "The craftsmanship is out of this world! It feels light as a feather."

Kern smiled at the dwarf and said, "Take your time, Gal. Don't be hasty—there are quite a few to choose from here." He held up a bow and pretended to fire. "I agree, though. There are some high-level items in here."

"You need them against the elementals," Ty chuckled, picking up a ring and examining it. "Hey, what if I just *wear* the rings? He will never know."

Kern spun on his heel and saw Ty holding the ring, threatening to put it on. "Wait, Ty! No—"

But it was too late. Ty slipped the ring onto his index finger and he was gone.

"You absolute fool halfling!" Kern shouted, taking a step forward.

"Give us your gold!"

Kern jumped at the voice and felt a prod in the back. He twisted around and saw Ty with a big grin on his face. "What are you doing, you clown?" Kern said angrily.

"What's up with you? It's only a teleportation ring."

"How did *you* know? He said nothing was identified!" Kern snapped, stepping past the thief and hanging the bow back up.

"Calm down," Ty said. "We used these on high-risk operations back in the day." He placed the ring back on the table.

"'High-risk operations'—don't make me laugh. What 'high-risk operations' did you ever do?" Kern chuckled as he examined another bow.

"Plenty, but if you're going to mock me I won't bother telling you," Ty said, throwing a dagger into the air.

"Oh, come on. Tell us of these 'high-risk operations,'" Kern mocked.

"Go to hell," Ty answered.

"Listen, you two," Galandrik spoke up. "We are in adventurer's heaven here, and you still want to argue? We will never get a better chance of free equipment without killing two dozen monsters to get to it, so let's leave the squabbling for later." He picked up some metal wrist bracers. "Always the same. Ever since I've known you two, always arguing and moaning."

After a few minutes of busy silence, Kern risked a glance over his shoulder. Ty was going through a rack of leather armour. "Found anything yet?"

"I can hardly believe it," Ty said, pulling out a set of black light-leather armour and holding it up to the light. "It's only a set of stealth armour of the Assassins! I would pay one thousand in gold for this!"

"You'd part with that much money for those? Why?" Kern asked, looking over at the happy thief.

"Why? Because it's a rare set! There are not many sets left in Bodisha."

"I gathered that, but leather is leather, no?"

"Far from it. In these you will move quieter, run faster, hide better in shadow, attack better—hell, you'll even pick locks quicker!" Ty said, like an excited schoolboy.

Kern walked over to the swords. "Glad you have found something you like."

"'Like'? I have *dreamt* about one day owning a set of these," Ty said, stripping out of his old leggings and dropping them onto the floor.

"I don't know if we should necessarily get dressed before we ask," Kern said dubiously, watching as the thief squirmed into the black leather leggings.

"He said we could have a set, so I am taking a set. These are coming with me. He could say no and I'd still take them."

"I think Shalamia would have something to say about it, lad," Galandrik said, placing a golden helm on his head.

"She would have to catch me first, and her head wouldn't fit in between the rock outside." Ty smiled smugly. "Oh my god, there are even the leather boots, gloves, and cap! It's a full set of stealth armour! Unbelievable."

"She might not fit, but her fire would. She would heat them so hot you would be part of this island forever," Kern said, looking through the hardened leather armour.

Ty stood in the full set of armour, admiring his new attire and hopping from foot to foot with excitement. "I feel so much better, I'm never taking it off!"

Kern laughed. "What's new?" He opened up a chest next to the rack of leather armour. "Hello! What have we here?" He reached in and pulled out two one-handed katanas, a type of traditional sword made in Helkini, a land far to the east of Bloodmoore. The blades had a distinctive appearance—a curved, slender, single-edged blade with a circular or squared guard. Runes lined the blade from guard to tip. Kern held both, twisting and turning them in the air, and exclaimed, "These are mine!"

"Dual wielding now, are we?" Galandrik asked.

"I used to dual wield all the time, and these little babies are too good not do it again. I think I'll get him to identify them too."

"Well, I am keeping the armour; I know what it is. I think I will keep the daggers I have and choose something different. I can't see anything that catches my eye."

"What about the magic item?" Kern asked, pulling out a set of brown armour.

"I think I'll keep the teleportation ring, maybe get him to identify it to see how many charges it has left. If I have to pick another I'd probably end up choosing a ring of cartography," Ty said with a laugh as he looked through the crossbows.

Galandrik stepped into the centre of the room, dressed in a set of dwarven armour, a mixture of golden chainmail and blue hardened leather. The shoulders were elongated like wings and protruded outwards into three tiers. A glorious golden eagle was embossed on the chest. The armour hung down to his knees and was finished off with an edging of gold. "How do I look?"

"Like a dwarf ready for battle," Ty said, nodding his approval.

"Well, this is staying on. Now, do I keep the two-handed axe, or this one?" He picked up a one-handed axe with matching shield.

Kern sifted through the rings and necklaces. "Choice is yours, Gal. I'm keeping the katanas and I think this ranger's armour here. There's not a lot to choose from, really—still, it's a lot better than the rubbish I have. I just don't know what magic item to choose."

"This is me," Ty said, holding a short sword; the same shade of black as his armour, it had silver runes running along one side. "It feels good."

"You just picked it because it matches your armour," Kern said, trying on his new brown leather armour. "Actually, this feels good."

"No, not at all," Ty said. He was doing up the scabbard on his belt when the door opened and Bodlin and Lan'esra strolled in. She was dressed in a striking set of light green leather armour with matching hat and boots, with a silver mace hanging by her side.

"I see you have picked, then?" Ty smiled.

Lan'esra did a turn, swishing her cloak around. "You like?"

"Very nice, lassy," Galandrik answered.

"Well, have you all picked?" Bodlin asked.

"I would like the armour I'm wearing and this sword please," Ty said, tapping the short sword. "Oh, and this ring of teleportation. Could you identify the sword, please?"

"Are you sure this is your choice?" Bodlin asked, picking up a couple of scrolls.

"I'm not a greedy man," Ty said, smiling.

"Very well," Bodlin said, unravelling the scroll. "*Cort van murd!*" A yellowish light swirled around the sword Ty held, then disappeared as fast as it had come. "You choose wisely," Bodlin said. "That is a short sword of shadows. It is a type of sword once used by necromancers, who enchanted their swords to do extra damage, commonly called damage of the dead. The extra damage isn't instant; it accumulates over time. That's why they are called 'dot weapons,' standing for 'damage over time'."

"Excellent. Thank you, Bodlin," Ty said with an enormous grin on his face.

Bodlin turned to the ranger. "Kern, what about you?"

"The armour I have on, these katanas, and this necklace please."

Bodlin read his scrolls again; the same yellow light swirled around Kern and vanished. "The armour is elven—hardened leather armour. It's as strong as chain, but no more. The necklace is spot invisibility—but it only has one charge, so use it wisely. And the swords are katanas of vanquishing." Kern smiled at that news. He had heard of the weapons and knew how sought-after they were for their fine craftsmanship. Furthermore, any weapon with the title 'vanquishing' would inflict more damage than the standard. "Thank you," he said with a nod, placing the necklace inside his tunic.

"And what about you, Sir Dwarf?"

"This armour, two-handed axe, and ring please," Galandrik said, showing the golden ring in his palm.

Bodlin's yellow light swirled again and he announced, "The armour is Horbit's dwarven armour of heroism. A two-handed axe of orc slaying and… hmm… a very nice ring; it's high level and anyone can use it. It is a ring of magic protection. Once placed on the finger, it will create a magic shield that will protect you and your party, as long as they stay within the radius of the ring's protection—usually a few paces distant from the wearer. It has two charges which will last for five minutes each, but unlike some rings that become empty of magic this recharges after one week." Galandrik nodded, taking all the information in.

"So, is everybody happy?" Bodlin looked around.

Ty and Galandrik both nodded, admiring their new equipment. "You have been more than generous, Bodlin," Kern said, placing his hand on the gnome's shoulder.

"Don't thank me; I was ready to drain the magic out of all of them. Thank Shalamia."

"We will, lad," Galandrik said.

"That we will," Ty added.

At a signal from Bodlin, Lan'esra tossed him a sack, which he handed to the ranger. "Please put all your unwanted things in the sack and bring them upstairs. I have prepared baths; I'm sure you would like to clean up before Shalamia gets here."

"I sure do!" Galandrik said, sniffing himself exaggeratedly.

"Yes, that would be nice," Kern agreed.

"Meet me in the study, then, and I'll show you where they are. Oh, and Mr Ty? Put the ring back," Bodlin said, not bothering to turn round as he left the room.

The thief smiled sheepishly and reached inside his new armour, pulling out a diamond ring. With a shrug of his shoulders, he placed it back onto the table.

"And the amulet," Bodlin called from the corridor.

Kern shook his head. "Unbelievable!" he said as the amulet appeared from the other side of the thief's tunic.

Galandrik just stared without saying a word.

"What?" Ty asked angrily.

Galandrik shook his head and began gathering his old armour.

"When are you two ever going to realise, it's not me! I have a kleptomaniac living inside me and I can't control him," Ty said as the ranger and dwarf walked out of the room. "Oh, silent treatment now, is it? I'll remember that the next time a fire elemental is kicking your arses!" he shouted at their backs.

Ty looked around the haul of items in the room, and itched to place something else into his pocket.

What a waste, melted down and destroyed. Suddenly, he doubled up in pain, dropping to his knees with the intensity of the burning in his chest. He knew it was his flesh ripping, being replaced by the blackening dragon scales.

Once the pain had subsided, he opened his new black armour and shirt. The scales had spread almost completely across his chest. He flexed his shoulders backwards and forwards, feeling his chest tighten with the movements. He remembered Klay's words: *The scales will cause restricted movement, bringing agony for the bearer.*

Then he did up his shirt and got to his feet.

*

It was nearing midnight and Kern, Galandrik, Ty, Lan'esra, and Bodlin all stood on the flat roof of the tower. All members of the party had bathed and eaten, and Bodlin had given them all new backpacks and what moderate supplies he could find amongst the heaps of stockpiled equipment.

"What time did she say she would arrive?" Ty asked Bodlin.

"Dragons don't do 'on time.' She will be here when she arrives."

"Sooner the better. We need to find the other herb and get them to the king," Kern said, pacing anxiously back and forth.

"She will be here, don't worry. In fact, I think that's her." Bodlin pointed out over the sea to the east. In the distance they could make out the large black shape of Shalamia over the sea, and the beating of her wings could be heard even from where they stood. "I'd move back here if I were you. Dragons are not butterflies," Bodlin said as he backed up to the edge of the stairs.

Within moments the dragon circled above them, making a few passes before landing on the roof and making the whole tower shake. She folded her wings back and stretched and rolled her neck before looking at the party. "These long flights are so tiring."

Bodlin stepped forward, saying, "Shalamia, these are the—"

"I know who these people are. These are the ones who returned my young, only for me to see them taken again," she said, a wisp of smoke leaving her nostrils.

Kern stepped forward. "We had nothing to do with this, Shalamia. In fact, they have something of mine as well, and are using me—" Kern looked at the others— "using *us* to get things in return for releasing my father and your children."

"Don't talk nonsense! They have Sleeper and Erella. They created an illusion of your father to make you do their bidding," she said angrily.

Kern's mouth fell open, and he shook his head in disbelief. "No—it can't be! I spoke with him; he was but a few feet away."

"Do not doubt me, ranger. It was an illusion. You father hasn't been touched. They needed a way to get you to do as they wished, and pretending to have your father worked," she hissed.

Kern leant on the wall of the roof and stared out into the dark of the night.

Ty walked up behind him and said, "You may have been tricked, but at least your father is safe and well."

Kern turned to the thief. "But it all seemed so real."

"That's exactly what Bok thought after I drank that disguise potion, remember?" Ty smiled.

Kern looked blankly at Ty, then turned to Galandrik. "Gal, you were there, you saw him."

Galandrik shook his head. "Sorry, lad, I was looking at the two dragons under the net."

"He couldn't have seen the illusion, Kern. They couldn't let Gal look because he hasn't ever seen your father; therefore he wouldn't have been able to imagine him being there," Lan'esra added.

"Damn! I can't believe I have been fooled," Kern seethed.

Shalamia arched her head forward, now only a few feet from Kern and Ty. The moonlight lit up the lines of the jade scales, rippling along her jawline with the movements of the muscles underneath. The razor-sharp teeth shone white and her huge cat-like eyes narrowed as she drew nearer. "It is only a fool who thinks he cannot be fooled."

Kern stared at the dragon for a few seconds, then said, "It's easy to fool the eye, but hard to fool the heart. We will free Sleeper and Erella."

"What do you have in mind?" the dragon asked, two trails of smoke rising from her nostrils.

"Well, they have us chasing herbs, so if we get them, we will simply swap them for Sleeper and Erella," Kern said.

"I don't think it will be that simple, my friend. They have no intention of releasing them, and they want you three dead. They attacked me with a monster called the Gorgon. Do not underestimate him. And don't think that just because I am a dragon I can simply fly down and roast him. He has killed many of my kind, and has every trick up his sleeve to defeat me."

"They want—no, they *need* these herbs far more than they want us killed. Without them, the king dies," Ty said with a smirk.

"We shall see. I planned to attack them myself with a few friends, but I cannot risk the lives of my children. You are my only hope. If you fail, I will attack the king and burn his castle to the ground—along with every woman, man, child, dog, and cat within a mile," Shalamia snarled.

"Remember, Shalamia: An eye for an eye, and the world will eventually go blind," Kern said.

Shalamia moved her huge head forward, now only inches from Kern's face. "All humans are blind! Blind people who *can* see but choose not to. Free my children and the blind will carry on seeing."

Kern could smell her dragon-breath and knew that with one sneeze she could destroy all of them. Her immense power was on full display, the muscles rippling in her legs and neck, the sheer size of the teeth and claws. How Gorgon could possibly have a prayer of defeating such an awesome creature was beyond Kern's understanding.

"Can you get us back to the mainland?" he asked, trying to be appear unfazed.

Shalamia slowly drew her head back, her eyes never leaving Kern's. "Yes. My friends will carry you to Fortune. Gorgon and his troop are currently passing Raith's Wood, heading towards the Double Dikes to pass through the mountains. Whatever you have in mind, you need to do it soon. They will be upon you within four days."

"We will get Sleeper and Erella back," Kern said, nodding. "And you have our thanks for the items."

Shalamia looked down at the ranger, fighter, cleric, and thief in their new armour. "I hope you are right. If these items help bring my children back, you are more than welcome to them. Bodlin, is everything else well?"

"Everything is fine. Netty wanted to see you, but—"

"I will come back and see her. These aren't matters for her delicate ears," the dragon interrupted.

"Very well. Everything else is fine," Bodlin said, bowing.

"When we met last time," Ty said with a smile, "you told us that dragons don't sleep on a bed of gold. You forgot to mention they store it elsewhere."

"All… men crave fortune and fame. They want my scales to make armour, my heart for spell ingredients—even my teeth as trophies. The lure of the treasure is for the thieves and bandits… all men want to destroy us somehow. So if I keep the fortune that you all so desperately crave somewhere other than my lair, perhaps it might somehow defer some of those *men*."

"Not all men wish to harm you Shalamia," Kern quickly said.

The dragon stretched out her giant wings. "Let's leave this for now. Your ride will be here very shortly and I need to pay a visit to another friend."

"When we recover your children, how will we find you?" Ty asked.

Shalamia looked at the thief. "Just release them. They will know where I am." With a few flaps of her giant wings, she rose elegantly above them. "Be safe, little ones," she called, "and get my children."

"We will, trust us," Kern said, placing his hands on the hilts of his swords.

"One last thing," Shamalia said, looking down. "Beware the red eagle." And with another mighty flap of her wings she was gone, the wind of her flight buffeting them as she went.

"Beware the red eagle?" Kern asked, turning to the others. Galandrik shrugged his shoulders.

"Well, that was very cryptic. You realize I will spend the rest of my life killing every red eagle I come across," Ty said, picking up his backpack and swinging it over his shoulder.

Lan'esra was looking over the wall to the north. "Look," she said, pointing, "four flying foes!"

"Very poetic! Quick, ranged weapons!" Kern said, and picked up his bow.

"At ease, soldiers," Bodlin said, holding his hands aloft. "This is your ride."

"*This* is our ride?" Kern said, as the new arrivals got closer.

"Yes, that is your ride. Please welcome Red Jai and some of her sisters," Bodlin announced.

"My life just gets stranger and stranger," Ty muttered under his breath as four beautiful giant dragonflies landed without a trace of sound.

The lead dragonfly was a beautiful wash of reds, a pair of transparent wings on either side, their transparency glistening with blues and greens. All six legs touched the ground, and her elongated body stretched nearly the whole length of the rooftop. The insectoid face with enormous eyes that they expected to see wasn't there—in its place was a woman's face, looking almost elven, complete with long blonde hair. Her wings flickered as she stepped forward. "Bodlin, my good friend, please introduce us to Kern, the Slayer of Giants and friend of Shalamia."

Bodlin stepped up next to the ranger. "This is Kern and his party. I have already told them your name, Jai."

"Pleased to make your acquaintance," Kern nodded. "This is Galandrik, Ty, and Lan'esra," he added, indicating each of the others in turn.

"Pleased to meet you. Now, time is upon us and we need to move. We are very conspicuous during daylight hours, so we must return to our home before sunrise," she said.

"We are ready to go," Kern said, picking up his backpack.

"Choose your ride; there are saddles between our wings. Please wrap the leather straps around the body and hold on tight—but don't yank or choke. We wouldn't want to throw you off to gain breath, now, would we? We travel fast, so make sure everything is tied on and safe. If it falls, you won't see it again. Oh, and wrap your cloaks tightly. It'll be chilly up there."

They all thanked Bodlin for his hospitality and said their goodbyes, then climbed up on the small leather saddles buckled to the middle of each dragonfly's back, between the wings.

As Lan'esra climbed up onto her dragonfly ride and gripped the reins, she called, "Say goodbye to Netty for me! Tell her I will come visit."

Bodlin stood and watched as they lifted into the air. "I will!" he shouted. "Be safe all!" He watched as they flew off to the south.

Chapter Twenty-Six
The Walls Have Ears

The party flew from the tower on the dragonflies at speeds they could only have imagined. The wind blew through their hair and against their faces, making it hard to catch a breath. At times the dragonflies would drop down to just above the water, their feet skimming the surface, leaving four distinct watery trails behind them and frightening the fish that jumped out of the water all around them. They moved through the air with all the grace and beauty of sharks gliding through the water.

The dragonflies breathed through spiracles—tiny holes in their abdomens that let them travel at unrivalled speeds without trying to catch a breath. Their wings could beat together or separately, making them easily able to turn, twist, and tilt at high speed—all of which was done at around seventy beats per second, so rapidly that to the human eye the wings looked stationary, as if the creatures were gliding through the sky. These creatures were true masters of speed and aerial manoeuvres.

As the dragonflies approached the coastline, their riders could make out little fires dotting the shores of the two small islands just beyond, and the beach huts made of straw. These were the huts of Fishmonks, a vicious bunch of mutants with toad-like bodies as big as a dwarf. They retained the scaly, slimy green skin, bulbous eyes, and big mouths of their amphibian ancestors, and their mouths were lined with rows of tiny razor-sharp teeth. The leader of the Fishmonks always carried a three-pronged trident, while the others used whatever weapons they could find to attack, kill, and eat anything that neared their camp. Individually they were reasonably weak, but they lived in groups of up to forty and together they were a force to be reckoned with. High-level fighters often set upon and slaughtered entire Fishmonk camps to practice their swordsmanship.

The dragonflies flew through the Fishmonk camp, keeping low and making their campfires crackle and flicker as they passed. Sand blew up into the air in their wake and roused the guards in their small watch towers. Within seconds, they had reached the other side of the camp and were whizzing through the trees dotting the isle.

Ty wanted to laugh with the rush of pure adrenaline that was flowing through his body. He kept his head down, but watched in awe as the trees and rocks flew past him. He glanced over to Kern and the others—everyone was in the same position, hunched over and seeming to hold on for dear life.

Soon they were back over the water again, and the coastline of Eastern Bodisha was coming up fast. As they skimmed the water, they could see the lights of Loft shining in the distance to their right. After a few more minutes, they were soaring over boggy marshland and the trees were starting to thicken. The dragonflies rose up, skimming the tops of the trees that grew there. The riders could smell the stench of the marshes. It passed quickly, however, and soon they were soaring over open grassland, with Fortune forest coming up fast. Suddenly all four dragonflies pulled steeply upwards, and the riders gripped tight to stop themselves falling backwards and plummeting to the earth. Once at a certain height, the dragonflies levelled out again and flew towards the town of Fortune.

Kern squinted as they flew. "Why such height?" he shouted against the noise of the onrushing wind.

"Tree trolls are exceptionally skilled with nets, and love the taste of dragonfly," Red Jai answered.

"I see. How far until we reach Fortune?" Kern shouted.

"It's there in the distance, that group of lights just past this forest."

In another few minutes, the forest had disappeared into the distance behind them, and in front of them lay the town of Fortune. A giant wall encircled it, guard turrets stationed all the way around the wall. The small lanterns hanging in the turrets shone out into the darkness of the night. The high buildings inside the wall were visible even from a distance, and the town looked as big as any town or city they had previously visited.

They were still a hundred yards away when the dragons flew down and landed gently. The four adventurers all climbed off, stretching their aching legs and arms.

"Thank you all for the ride," Kern said, and the others all nodded.

"It was our pleasure. Any friend of Shalamia's is a friend of ours," the dragonfly answered. "We must be gone now. Is this close enough for you?"

"This is fine. We couldn't be more thankful," Kern said for them all.

The dragonflies hovered briefly in the night sky, then they were gone. Ty kicked his feet and stretched his arms and said, "Well that was… quick."

"Tell me about it. They certainly know how to soar!" Galandrik said, rolling his neck.

"Come on, let's get to Fortune and get a room before it's too late," Kern said. He swung his backpack over one shoulder and they set off.

They walked around the eastern curve of the city's great wall until they finally came to the main gates—two massive wooden doors that stood fifty feet tall, with six town guards standing outside the gates. As they approached, two of the guards stepped forward, and Ty also noticed a few archers covering them from the top of the wall.

"Who wants entry to Fortune at this unholy hour?" one of the guards said, his sword pointed at the ground.

Kern looked at the others, then turned to the guard. "Just a weary party in need of a hot meal and a good night's sleep."

The guard looked him up and down. "Where have you travelled from?"

"We have travelled from…" Kern paused for a second, "Loft, and we are very tired."

"Loft is a week away on foot. Where are your mounts?" the guard questioned, peering into the darkness behind them.

Kern raised an eyebrow at Ty, and began, "We—"

"We lost our horses on the way down. Attacked at night, two ran, two died in the fight, now can we come in or do you need to know what colour they were?" Ty interrupted.

The guard glared at Ty. "We are all tired, sir," Kern interrupted, trying to defuse the guard's anger, "and just need a room. Please excuse my friend."

The guard waited for another outburst from the halfling, but nothing came, "Go through—but it'll be two gold each."

Ty had just opened his mouth to say something when Kern gave him a look, and the thief knew exactly what he was thinking.

"Thank you, good sir," the ranger said, before walking past the guard to the gates. A small door opened to another guard's knock, and finally the four walked into the town of Fortune.

"Why are all guards such dicks?" Ty said after a few moments of silence. "Every one you meet either wants to fight you or get as much money out of you as humanly possible."

"Maybe it's you," Kern replied. "Maybe you antagonize them."

"Whatever. You know exactly how they act," Ty answered. "And it seems that we attract them everywhere we go."

Kern glanced at Galandrik, but didn't remark on Ty's 'we' comment.

*

They walked through the main gates of Fortune; on either side were lines and lines of stables, and the stable lads rushed about tending to the horses. Guards patrolled up and down the area, watching out for opportunistic horse thieves.

"Why patrol? Horse thieves can't exactly steal one and ride out of the gates," Ty said with a shrug.

"The town is big enough to hide one, though," Galandrik said.

"I guess so, but the grief to sell a stolen horse inside a town that's locked down? That's not for me," Ty stated.

"Just try not to steal anything, please, for the sake of… everything! Let's just find an inn and make a plan for freeing the dragons before Shalamia destroys the king," Kern suggested.

"Are you trying to make it out as though I steal at every given moment?"

Lan'esra pointed to their right. "Look, an inn sign. Shall we have a look?"

Smoke flowed from the inn's chimney. Most of its windows were open, and they could hear the music and noise from fifty feet away.

"This looks like exactly what we want," Ty said with a smile.

"Will we be able to hear ourselves talk in here?" Kern asked, shaking his head.

"Of course we will, lad," Galandrik said, excited at the prospect of a good meal.

Kern gave a half smile. "Best we take a look then."

They made their way into the Blind Unicorn Inn. It was a typical busy, bustling inn. Music played in the corner and folk of all races danced and sang, enjoying the night's festivities. Other customers sat around tables, some eating, others playing cards or dice, arm wrestling, or just talking about their day's events.

"Look over there," Lan'esra said, and pointed at a large square table in the corner. A man with a hood covering his face was face down across the table, his goblet of ale spilt around him and four bone dice spread across the table.

"Looks like someone couldn't handle their beer," Ty said, sitting next to the hooded man, "Oi, wake up!" he shouted. He prodded the man in the head through his hood, but got only a change of snoring in response.

"He stinks of lavender pipe tobacco. My father smoked that shit." Lan'esra waved her hand in front of her face.

"Leave him. He isn't doing any harm," Kern said, flagging down a maid. A few minutes later, the maid brought back four ales and placed them on the table. "Want anything else?" she asked, wiping the man's spilt ale onto her apron.

"Have you got a couple of rooms for the night?" Kern asked.

"I will see the innkeeper. I think you are in luck," she said, smiling at the dwarf. "What about you, is there anything you need?" She stroked his beard.

"Just keep the ales coming, lassy," Galandrik said, smiling up at the barmaid as she turned to go back to the bar.

"She wanted you," Ty smiled, emptying half his goblet in a gulp.

Galandrik laughed. "She's only human!"

"All right, what's the plan?" Ty asked, untying his cloak and hanging it on the chair.

"Well, we will buy the other herb tomorrow and head back to Tonilla, I guess. We need to get a message to Conn the wizard. We need to get some sort of an advantage here," Kern said.

"What do you have in mind, lad?"

"We need to meet somewhere neutral and close, somewhere we have the advantage. If they want us dead, we need all the help we can get. Conn is now passing Raith's Wood so… hmm."

"When we meet them, we could hang the herbs over a fire and threaten to burn them unless the dragons are released," Lan'esra suggested.

"Good idea, but what then?" Kern said, holding four fingers up to the maid. "We threaten, and if they do release the dragons, then what?"

"We throw the herbs towards them and it's done. The dragons fly, we walk, they walk, and the king gets healed," she said leaning back and folding her arms.

"I wish it was that simple. I think they will attack. As soon as the dragons are released and they have the herbs, they will attack. We need to be somewhere we can defend ourselves—and even better, we need help."

The maid had brought their second round, and after the ranger thanked her she said, "We have two rooms. The innkeeper will keep them for you; just pay when you next go to the bar."

"Thanks," Kern said, smiling as she collected the empty goblets and turned away. He looked at Lan'esra. "So, where do we go, or who do we ask?"

"Why doesn't Shalamia help? After all, they are her children," Ty said harshly, "and to be completely honest, now that your father isn't involved, what is keeping us interested? We aren't doing this for a bag of gold now, are we?"

"You have certainly changed your tune," Kern noted.

"Well, not really. I don't like it that dragons are treated rather harshly, but why are we now going to take on the fight of our lives, when surely she could just fly down and burn them all?"

Kern looked at the thief and thought about his statements. "We are doing this for what is right. They have tricked me and manipulated us into getting these blasted herbs for the king; they have entrapped Shalamia's children and probably intend to sacrifice them—everything they have done is wrong and I won't back down without a fight," Kern addressed the table.

"And if we don't free the dragons, Shalamia will cause havoc in the north, too," Lan'esra added.

"Besides… what else we got to do?" Galandrik laughed.

Ty looked one by one at his friends around the table, and realized that trying to persuade any of them to change their minds was impossible. He raised his goblet in the air and stared at Kern. "Here's to fighting Conn and Gorgon, because that should be easy enough!"

They all laughed, clunked goblets, and drank.

"You are right, though; we will need help," Kern said, slamming his goblet down.

The thief sighed. "Need help? We will need an army!"

"Then we shall get one," Lan'esra said sternly.

They all turned and looked at the cleric. "Do you know where there is an army close by, lassy, and willing to take on the Gorgon?" Galandrik asked.

"Yes, as a matter of fact I do," she answered smugly.

Kern rolled his eyes. "Oh, pray tell then, young lady," he said, placing his elbows onto the table and folding his hands under his chin. "Where is this army in waiting?"

"The army waits in the Midas Hills," she said proudly.

"The Midas… isn't that where you live?" Ty asked.

"It sure is. All my life," she answered with a smile.

Ty started to laugh into his goblet. "We need an army of fighting men! Not carrot-pickers!"

Lan'esra stared at the laughing thief and her face reddened. "How do you think we get on when orcs attack?" She got angrier as Ty continued to laugh. "How do you think we get on when common thieves and bandits attack, the pathetic excuses for men who use daggers and hide in shadows? We destroy them!" She was almost shouting by the time she finished.

"I'm sorry," Ty said, trying to stop himself laughing, "I just pictured famers throwing cabbages at Gorgon as he attacked." He set himself off again and got up from his chair, crying with laughter and holding his stomach. "I need a wee, maybe you can sort out an attack 'plan…t'!"

"Just go," Kern said, seeing how upset Lan'esra was. "I am sorry about that. He hasn't had a drink in ages and it's gone to his head."

"Not much else in there! I won't mention it again," she said angrily.

"It was a good idea. How many men does your village have?" Kern asked sincerely.

She looked away before meeting the ranger's eyes. "You honestly want to know?"

Kern said sombrely, "Yes. It is a good idea. How many?"

"We have twenty-five to thirty men. They all fight—not to the level of Gorgon and his soldiers, granted, but who does?"

"Ignore Ty; his mouth moves before his brain sometimes," Kern smiled, "but he is right in saying that thirty farmers are no match for thirty of Gorgon's highly trained men. There are tales about his exploits versus three hundred *trained* men."

"I know that, and I hope you didn't think for one minute that I didn't!" Lan'esra snapped.

"No, calm down. I never thought that—but you did say you had an army, and that army is thirty farmers," Kern said softly.

"Yes, thirty farmers in the hills. Their hills… they blend in, disappear, they become their surroundings, they *are* the hills. There are tunnels, traps, caves, and superb ambush spots. One hundred and thirty *trained* men would struggle against my thirty farmers."

Kern stared at Lan'esra as she called the maid over. "I see where you are coming from now. How long would it take us to get there and convince them to act on our side?"

"It's only around the top of Lake Fortune and through the Grey Towers."

Ty walked back to the table. "It's all good, I have stopped laughing now."

"Good, how do we get Gorgon to head there?" Kern asked.

Ty leant forward. "What have I missed?"

Kern smiled at Lan'esra. "She was right. Her people don't fight toe-to-toe; they use the Midas Hills as their weapons. Tunnels, caves and traps. We could use it to our advantage. Fighting his men alone would be suicidal—and that's without Gorgon and Conn."

Ty nodded. "I'm not going to argue; you're the boss."

"I think it's a splendid idea," Galandrik said, "but first you need to sort your eye out, lad. It doesn't matter how many you have or how good they are if you cannot see the enemy coming."

"I will go in the morning."

"And if in the morning he cannot do anything?" Ty asked.

"I'll get a patch," Kern snapped.

"You'll have to cut a hole in it, or you won't be able to see out of it," Ty said, trying to keep a straight face.

"It'll be fine. For now, I think a good night's rest—then we'll meet here for breakfast at dawn," Kern suggested.

"Sounds good, lad. I am knackered."

"So we need to send a message to Conn by paperfinch, sort your eye, and get those herbs," Ty smiled, standing up.

"Then get to the Midas Hills and hopefully get Lan'esra's people to help," the dwarf added.

"*And* fight thirty of the Black Guard, a dragon-slaying daemon, and a wizard," Kern smiled.

Ty raised an eyebrow and smiled. "Then what are we doing after dinner?"

*

They finished their drinks amidst laugher before heading over to the bar to pay for their rooms. The hooded man at the table they left behind reached up a hand from underneath and lifted his hood up slightly, watching the party as they were escorted to a side door by the innkeeper. Once they were out of sight, he lifted his head up from the table top.

Ambush at the Midas Hills, eh? I wonder what Conn would have to say about this. He will probably forget to punish me for telling him the Rat was dead, Bok thought, standing up from the table. *Just need the paperfinch stone. I'll never get there on horseback in time. Tomorrow; I will get it tomorrow and tell Conn of his plans... the Rat's dirty plans. I could sneak upstairs tonight and steal the stone, but if I saw him lying there I would stab him... stab him, then I would be free, free to go and live happily without Conn or him... the Rat... stab him, cut off his little ratty tail.* Bok left the inn and made his way into the night, muttering.

Chapter Twenty-Seven
An Eye for an Eye

Kern sat in the healer's shop the next morning, while Lan'esra stood in the front looking at healing ingredients. The gnome physician removed the bandages Lan'esra had put on and examined Kern's wound.

"My, my; you took a good one there. I don't think it has penetrated the actual eye but it has definitely scratched it." He picked up a crude-looking magnifying glass and examined further. "Oh yes, hmmm, my, my."

"'My, my' what?" Kern asked impatiently.

The gnome continued his examination. "It's a nasty one. Only time will tell, but my honest opinion is that you need magical help. Don't get me wrong—in time it could heal, but I think you will always be partially-sighted in that eye," he explained, placing the magnifying glass down on the table.

Kern sat up, looking at his hand through his bad eye. "It's all blurry."

"It will be until it heals, but usually a scratch like that damages it beyond natural repair. It will get better, but never perfect."

"So what can I do then?" Kern asked, standing up straight.

"Well, good Sir Ranger, I will give you eye drops and a patch that will speed up the healing phase. But if you really want to get it back to perfect vision, I suggest you go visit a friend of mind named Veloin. He runs a shop in Tonilla called The All-Seeing Eye—he could help you."

"We don't have time to get to Tonilla and back to where we are going. We only have a couple of days," Kern explained.

"Oh my, you seem to misunderstand me. He will not be able to fix you on the spot—he will probably send you to the Bracon Ash Dungeon in north Bodisha to retrieve some… *ingredients*. It all depends on what you want."

"My vision. I just want my vision back."

"Then I suggest you speak with Veloin. He can make you see like an eagle, through walls or… well, I better let him explain," the gnome said as he searched through an old chest. "Ah, here it is," he said, holding up a potion bottle. After blowing the dust off, he handing it to the ranger. "Two drops a day until the whole bottle has gone, unless you reach Tonilla first."

Kern took the bottle. "Thanks. Bracon Ash Dungeon—why there?"

"Oh, I can't remember, but that's the usual place he sends people. You'll need to speak to him—and make sure you tell him Jamfoot sent you. He may even give you a discount, but I doubt it; he isn't known for his generosity." Jamfoot handed the ranger the eyepatch.

Kern took it, but looked at it sceptically. "Really?"

"Yes, really. It'll never heal without it, you'll just overstrain it trying to focus. It'll be painful and ten times worse. But you're a big boy, and I can't force you," he replied, smiling.

Kern smiled back and nodded, knowing that the words Jamfoot spoke were the truth. He slipped the patch over his head and covered his eye.

"Suits you!" Jamfoot said, making light of the situation.

"Leave it," Kern replied with a laugh.

*

Later that afternoon, Ty and Galandrik sat in the Blind Unicorn Inn waiting for Lan'esra and Kern. "Did you manage to find the herbs, lad?"

"No, I left that to Lan'esra. I had a mooch around the market place," Ty answered.

"I found a lovely bathhouse just down the road. Bath and full shave for one silver."

"Really? That is cheap. I thought you looked trimmer and smelt a bit *fragrant*." The thief gave him a wink.

"Nonsense, lad, I never had any fragrance put on."

Ty pushed his nose forward and, with an over-elaborate sniff, said, "Well, someone does."

"Whatever," the dwarf answered, draining his goblet. "Maid!"

"What about the horses?" Ty asked, forgetting in an instant his attempts to wind the dwarf up about fragrance. "Find any?"

"I did, but they are not the best. The money we pooled from the spider temple haul just about covered them."

"I take it we are skint again?" Ty said, pulling out his purse.

"Yeah. By the time Kern gets his eye sorted and we buy herbs, we probably will be."

"See, this is what I don't understand. We went to Raith to find work. Instead we found you."

Galandrik's head turned at that, and he frowned at the thief's words.

Ty smiled cheekily and said, "I'm not saying it was a bad meeting, but the work we found was a dirty quest for a dirty king. Now, what, six months later? and we are still pooling together to buy scabby horses! No better off than we were six months ago. I stood in the top of the orc tower surrounded by gold—there was enough treasure there to build another tower!"

"Why didn't you take a load, lad?"

"I don't know. Solomon, finding the dragon's eggs, carrying all your equipment—oh, and being chased by a dozen guards!"

"A dozen now!" Galandrik laughed, remembering the first time he had heard the story.

Ty's face reddened. "I… I just guessed. It was so long ago."

"Aye, lad, it was too. Why not go back? You know the way in and out."

Ty looked at the dwarf and thought about his words for a second before shaking his head. "Nah, it'll never work."

"Why?" The dwarf's question was mostly in jest, as he knew Ty hated admitting that he couldn't steal something.

"Well, don't get me wrong, here—I could easily get in and up to the treasure, no problem," Ty explained.

Galandrik leaned forward, stroking his chin through his beard. He always knew when Ty was trying to talk his way out of a situation, because he would never make eye contact. Ty always said, 'you can tell a liar by his eyes.'

"So if you can get in and up to it, what's the problem?" Galandrik prompted the thief.

"It's getting it *out*. A backpack full of gold weighs more than we both could carry. If I was to go, the loot isn't worth the risk, you see?"

"If you take someone with you, double the load…?"

Ty finally looked at the dwarf before saying with a calm smile, "But when you split it, you end up with the same."

"Ah, but isn't it…" Galandrik hesitated and smiled back at the thief, "*Not the loot, but the looting?*"

"I could walk over to the bar and pickpocket anybody—you never know what you will find. Law of averages are telling me that in this shitty little inn I'm not going to pull ten platinum pieces—more than likely, four copper pieces—but…the *rush* is the same. The buzz you get when your hand is in that pocket, the thrill of the ride—you just never know what the loot will be, and you always hope for that bag of platinum."

"Something I never have and probably never will experience, lad."

"You don't know what you're missing, Sir. I know people frown upon burglars, but we never stole off the likes of you or me. We only stole off those who could afford it. We took back from the machine what it had been ripping from us for years. But when I was in those posh stately houses creeping through the corridors and rooms, hiding in the shadows when the butler walked by, heart beating out of my skin—it wasn't whatever necklace I could find or what box of rings, it was the buzz of doing it. I didn't give a damn about riches and wealth. We never got it anyway; the guild did. No, I just liked the job… doing the job."

"It's a lonely world though, lad, and high risk."

"After I… *left* the guild, I loved it. I spent years living only at night, never speaking to anybody for weeks on end—and I absolutely loved it. I didn't exist. The dark was my playground, my peaceful, beautiful playground."

"So why stop? Why change if you loved it so much?"

"I don't know really. The quest for fortune, that one dungeon that'll set you up. There are only so many dungeons you can tackle solo, without a fighter's help. I met Kern and the rest is history—we have been skint ever since," Ty laughed.

"Maybe one day you'll hit the jackpot, lad."

"Hopefully you are right, and sooner rather than later. Let's get these damn herbs to Conn, release those dragons, and find some decent work."

"I don't think it's going to be as easy as that."

"No, I agree, but as long as we get the dragons released before we hand over the herbs, what damage can they do? The king will get healed and everybody is happy."

"Let me see... kill us?" the dwarf said, shrugging his shoulders.

"They can try, I guess. They can try."

"Have you seen Gorgon? He is a man mountain! Even Shalamia is scared of him! Then we have his highly-trained soldiers—oh, and not forgetting Conn the wizard... Should be a breeze."

"We have Kern," Ty said, taking a sip of his ale. "We will be fine."

Galandrik saw the look on Ty's face. "It almost seems like you want him to fail."

Ty stared back at the dwarf for an instant before smiling. "Don't be ridiculous! If he fails, we all fail—and probably die, too."

"Your face tells a different story."

"Nonsense. Here he comes now," Ty said, nodding at Kern and Lan'esra who were walking towards them. "Aye, aye!" Ty said with a smile, looking at Kern's patch.

"Yeah, yeah, very funny," Kern replied.

"What did they say?" Galandrik asked as he beckoned the maid over.

Kern adjusted the patch. "Well it may come back all right, but probably not. My vision will be impaired unless I do something about it."

"Like what?" Ty asked.

"I need to speak to Veloin in Tonilla, and he will probably send me to Bracon Ash Dungeon for some *stuff* to get my sight back."

"Seems long-winded. Why can't he just heal you?" Ty shrugged.

"Well, I think he can, but if you get whatever it is he needs, he can repair the eye and give you extra vision—like, eye of an eagle or see through walls. I don't really know."

Ty's head twitched at this. "Eyes of an eagle. Hmm. Can we all get this?"

"I don't know, but if my eyes were all right I wouldn't want them messed with. Unfortunately I have no choice."

Ty leaned back in his chair. "What about the willow rose? Did we get the herb?"

Lan'esra reached into her tunic, pulled out a small sack, and placed it onto the table, "Yes, and it was expensive! This was all he had, and he said he didn't know when the next batch would pass through here. It is farmed from the bottom of Lake Fortune. Well, that's what he said."

"I can't believe they sent us shopping," Ty moaned.

"Yes, it is slightly ridiculous. The dungeon, yes, but this one…? Oh, well. We have it now," the ranger replied.

"Paperfinch?" Galandrik asked as the maid set some more drinks down.

Lan'esra reached into her tunic again. "Yes, it is here," she said, pulling out the piece of paper and offering it to Ty.

"I don't want it," the thief said grumpily, getting up and walking towards the toilet.

"What's up with him?" she asked, looking at Galandrik.

"I don't know. He started on about how he lived alone and loved his work at night, and how now he is always skint. I think he is just in one of those moods."

"He could soon go back to it. Nobody keeps him here," Kern replied. "Lan'esra, maybe it's better that you send the bird. You know where they need to meet us."

"Should I just say 'go to Midas'? We can watch as they move through the hills."

"You know best," Kern smiled.

"All right," she said, standing up and placing the small bag of herbs in her tunic. "I'll go outside, where it's quieter."

"We will eat, then probably leave straight away. Did you get—"

"Yes, they are in the stables," Galandrik interrupted.

Kern smiled and nodded at the dwarf. "You're a good man."

*

Outside the Blind Unicorn Inn, the street was its usual busy self, all manner of people going about their daily business. Carts and barrows were being moved to and from as traders headed towards the market with new stock. Lan'esra quickly stepped down the alley next to the inn and pulled the paper from her pocket. Before she had a chance to say a word, she felt a sharp point stick into her back.

"Move and you die. Scream and you die," she heard from behind her.

"I have nothing to give you," Lan'esra said, not daring to turn.

"Oh, but you do, sweetheart, you have *so much* to give me," the voice behind her said. "Now move on."

"All right. Just go easy."

They moved further down the alley until they were fifty feet away from the busy street. Lan'esra was shoved, her right shoulder up against the wall.

"Don't move. I swear I will kill you. Just drop the stone and paperfinch into my hand."

"But… but it's worthless unless you have the paired stone! It's just a stone, it—"

"I'll be the judge of that. Drop it," he interrupted.

Lan'esra cursed under her breath. "I'm telling you, it is worthless—" She felt the sharp point dig deeper into her back. "All right! Fine, you're the judge." She dropped the stone and piece of paper, then felt a hand near her left breast. She looked down as the hand slid into her tunic, pulling out the bag of herbs. "That's just spices, I grow them in my—"

"Shut that pretty little mouth of yours before I fill it with something you won't like," the voice said, jabbing the point in deeper.

"All right! Just leave those spices, please! You don't know who they belong to."

Lan'esra felt his face near the side of hers; she shut her eyes as she felt his tongue lick the side of her cheek. She could smell his revolting breath, and she recognized the smell of stale beer and lavender pipe tobacco. In a gravelly tone next to her ear he whispered, "They belong to me now, and I will return them to where they belong. I will just first have to decide whether or not to kill you."

Lan'esra trembled with fear. "Just take what you want and leave. You are in enough trouble already without killing me as well."

"I don't think Kern will help you now," he growled.

Upon hearing Kern's name, Lan'esra immediately turned her head, only to be met by Bok's forehead. She slumped to the alley floor, unconscious, as Bok stood above her.

"Stupid girl."

He cupped the paperfinch in his hands and whispered, "*Conn, this is Bok. Please forgive me—I was wrong about Ty. I have followed them for you ever since I learned of my error. They head to the Midas Hills, and intend to use the locals and the surrounds there to help them against you. They should be there in two days. I also have one of the herbs that you require.*" He stretched out his hand. "Fly my baby, fly."

*

Kern craned his neck looking out the window and into the street. "She has been ages."

"She may have gone to get some more of her healing supplies. Want me to go look again?" Galandrik asked.

"No, you looked once. She's a big girl now," Kern said reluctantly.

"I think this is her," Ty said, nodding to the door.

Lan'esra walked towards them holding her nose, dried blood covered her face and the top half of her tunic. The locals in the inn all stared as she walked through. Kern stood up and took her arm, guiding her to her seat. "What the hell happened, woman?" he asked.

"He got it all, paperfinch, stone, and herbs," she replied, touching her swollen nose.

"Who has it all? What are you talking about?" Kern pressed.

"Your bloody friend! He must have been following us for days."

Kern frowned and looked at Ty, who shrugged his shoulders. "Who?"

"The one Ty bumped into in Wade, behind the arena, and pickpocketed him."

Kern, Galandrik, and Ty looked at each other and, in virtual synchrony, said, "Bok!"

Ty stood up and paced. "But how…?"

"There is no way he could have followed us, unless he was in your backpack. We got a lift here on bloody dragonflies!" Kern smacked the table with his fist.

"How would he know about the herbs and—"

"Lavender pipe tobacco!" Lan'esra suddenly said.

"Lavender pipe tobacco? Stop speaking in riddles, woman," Kern said angrily.

"Last night, we sat over there at that table, next to the drunk who stank of lavender pipe tobacco. Remember? I said it smelt like the shit my father smokes. Well, just before he knocked me out, he was close enough for me to smell that exact smell."

"Loads of people smoke it though, it could be coincidence," Kern said, shaking his head.

"Could be. But he mentioned your name. That's when I turned my head and saw his half-burnt-off face. Then it all went black."

"That's a very old thief's trick; we call it 'the Drunken Ear.' In the Thieves' Guild Wars years ago, they would place a 'drunken ear' in rival inns to see what they could find out. They'd usually pay an older outsider. It's not an uncommon thing to see someone asleep at the bar or a table, you know? You just don't think anything of it."

"I feel sick. What do we do now?" Kern said, shaking his head.

"Well, if Bok was the 'drunken ear,' then he knows exactly where we are heading, *and* that we intend to use the villages in the Midas Hills to help us. If he tells Conn all this, I think they will go there—and that will put everyone in the area in danger. We need to get to them before Conn does," Lan'esra said sternly.

Kern stared at her. He could see she feared for her village and for those who lived there. "I agree—and as we can't get any message to Conn now, we may as well head in that direction. It's on the way back."

"Thank you. I think they will need all the help they can get. I'm going to get myself sorted; I think that bastard broke my nose," Lan'esra said, standing up.

"He did me like that, too, back in Raith," Ty said.

"So why isn't he dead yet?" she asked, clearly still feeling the pain in her face.

"I was just thinking that. The chances we have had to get rid of him, yet he still comes back like a bad smell," Galandrik said, shaking his head.

"No more. Next time we bump into him, he is dead," Kern said, watching as Lan'esra left. "Should somebody go with her?"

"No point. If he wanted her dead, she would still be laying in the street with a dagger in her back. He wanted her to tell us. He wants us to go to Midas and he wants us to die there," Ty said.

"Yes indeed, lad."

"We leave as soon as she returns. Time is well and truly upon us now," Kern said, standing up. "I'll go see to the horses and make sure they are ready."

"I'll come with you, lad. You never know—Bok might be lurking," the dwarf said with a sly wink at Ty.

"Don't you start. You'll end up as bad as him," Kern answered, with a nod at the thief.

"I'll stay here and wait for Lan'esra," Ty said, smiling.

*

A few hours later, all four stood with their mounts in the stable of the Blind Unicorn, Kern with his eyepatch and Lan'esra with a white gauze covering her nose. The beginnings of black underneath her eye could be seen as the swelling around it grew.

"He caught you a good one there," Galandrik said as he buckled up his saddle.

"He certainly did, and trust me, he will have more than just a scarred face when we meet again. I only just realised he stole the mace that I got from Shalamia."

"He's a gutter pig. He will steal the fillings from inside your mouth," Ty added.

"Opportunity makes a thief. He did miss the ring I got, though."

"Really? A ring of what?" Ty asked as he jumped into his saddle.

"I will show you when I meet Bok again," she answered as she mounted.

"I pity Bok when you meet him again!" Kern laughed, kicking his mount into a trot.

"Don't pity the weak and foolish; pity the people they infect," Lan'esra said, trotting next to Kern.

"Revenge will be yours, I am sure," Kern said, as they headed towards the main gates of the town.

*

Bok entered the Glowing Staff, a magic-users' shop, selling most magical items you could think of. A tall human wearing the traditional long purple cloak covered in half-moons and stars stood behind the counter. "Hello there. What can we do for you today, good sir?"

Bok stepped forward with his hood up to cover his grotesqueness. "I have to get north—I'd say it's two days' travel on horseback, and I need to do it quicker. Have you anything that could help me?"

The mage rubbed his chin and pondered Bok's question. "Hmm, two days' travel you say… What about a ring of polymorph self?"

"Polymorph into what?" Bok asked.

"An eagle? You could fly directly over Lake Fortune. That would save you half a day; you'd be where you need to be in half the time."

"Sounds good. How long does it last?" Bok asked.

"Let me see, an eagle can fly a maximum of maybe three hours before landing, and this ring has four charges. So yes, this will keep you in form for roughly up to twelve hours. After that, you will fall from the skies in human form."

"How do I break it, if I want to land before it runs out?"

"Just think about taking the ring off. Be careful though."

"All right. How much?"

"Now, let me see. Polymorph-self times four charges—"

Bok placed Lan'esra's silver mace onto the table. "I will swap for this."

The shop owner raised an eyebrow at Bok, and looked down at the fine weapon. "Kiggo, come here."

Another human walked in from the back of the shop, this one wearing silver chainmail, his blond hair swept back into a ponytail. "What is it?" he asked, one hand on the hilt of his sword.

"This good man wants to swap this mace for a ring of polymorph. Just take a look and tell me what you think."

The blond man picked up the mace and spun it around. "Where did you get it?"

"A dungeon. It was loot," Bok said without looking up.

The man looked at the shop owner and eventually nodded. "We have a deal. Take it in the back, Kiggo, and place it with the other weapons." He dropped the ring into a little leather sack and handed it to Bok. "If you get any more of these silver weapons, please do not hesitate to bring them here. We will always give you a good price."

"I will do. Thank you," Bok said, turning and walking out of the shop, ringing the bell as the door shut.

"Kiggo, what sort of mace was it?"

"A silver Mace of Mercy. Probably worth a hundred gold. You made a killing, boss!"

"*He* probably made a killing to get it and that's why he wanted the polymorph ring—to get out of here. Better keep it hidden for a few days before you shift it."

Chapter Twenty-Eight
Change of Plan

Conn sat next to Gorgon as they journeyed through the Double Dikes. Two massive statues sat to either side of the entrance to the path that split the Eastern Mountains from the west. Both statues were of human warriors and stood over one hundred feet tall. No one really knew who they were or how the statues came to be, but ancient scripts identified them as Theador, the God of War, and his twin brother Thryon, the God of Justice. They had been sent down by their father Thrand to guard the pass as a punishment.

"I wonder how Kildred is getting on with the training of your troops?" Conn asked Gorgon as they rode.

"He will do fine. He will weed out the quitters and the weak, and bring the rest through. Tough and hard men is what I am after, not these cloth-wearing girls."

Conn raised an eyebrow but Gorgon didn't turn around. "I'm sure that the cloth-wearing girls could cause you a fair few problems."

"I doubt that. I'll be glad when we have killed these thieves and I can move up north and get into the orc."

"You and me both. I can't believe the grief these thieves have caused us already."

"When you play in the thieves' world, be prepared to play dirty," Gorgon grumbled. "I would sometimes rather fight a dragon than three good thieves."

"These aren't thieves. They are just three bloody chancers!"

Gorgon turned and looked at Conn. "These three chancers have killed a wyvern, given the king's guard the run-around, then killed a score of *your* guards, escaped an orc tower, and currently hold the king's life in a cloth sack—if they have the herbs we require, that is. I think they are a little more than chancers, don't you?"

"I could crush all three in a heartbeat. They wouldn't get near me," Conn said, waving one hand as if swatting a fly.

"No doubt you can, but sometimes they have protection against magic, along with smoke screens, invisibility, and every other dirty, sneaky little trick that can help keep them alive. Trust me, I have fought the smallest thief to the biggest fighters, and it's hard to fight when the fight isn't fair."

"We shall see. To me, it sounds like you are scared of our little thieves," Conn joked.

Gorgon never turned, just smiled. "I have fought dragons, ogres, orc generals, trolls, and even giants, and I was never afraid. The only people afraid of dying are those who haven't lived."

"We shall see what these three have in store. Maybe—"

Conn was stopped midsentence by a paperfinch landing on his arm. Gently he picked it up and cupped it to his ear and listened.

"Conn, this is Bok. Please forgive me—I was wrong about Ty. I have followed them for you ever since I learned of my error. They head to the Midas Hills, and intend to use the locals and the surrounds there to help them against you. They should be there in two days. I also have one of the herbs that you require."

Conn repeated the message for Gorgon, then demanded, "How the hell is he still alive? How has he got the paired stone back?"

"I tried to tell you, these little thieves are resilient."

"Resilient! They are like cockroaches—doesn't matter how many times you stand on them, they always seem to crawl away!"

"Best way is to remove the head."

"I am beginning to believe that too. We need to speed up if we are going to get to the Midas Hills before them."

Gorgon looked over his shoulder and shouted, "Fucan, come!"

Fucan rode up next to Gorgon. "Yes sir?"

"Get the men ready. It seems our little friends are heading to the Midas Hills and it would be advantageous to get there before they do."

"Yes sir. Where are the thieves now?" Fucan asked.

"We don't know, but they are expected to arrive in two days," Conn answered.

"We should easily get there before them, sir. If my memory serves me correctly the Midas Hills are just on the other side of the mountains."

"Let the troops know we will be at full pace. We will stop now for ten; then we move and we will not stop until we reach the Hills."

"Yes sir."

"And make sure those dragons get fed some rabbits. I don't want them dying."

"They have been maintained, sir, but they grow fast and these cages are too small. I think if they wanted to, they could break free with ease."

"They're just babies, they won't do anything. Just keep them fed. Once we have the herbs, they are on the end of my lance anyway."

"Yes sir, it shall be done." Fucan turned and started barking orders at the troop.

Gorgon and Conn dismounted. "So once we have the herb, the dragons and thieves all need to be destroyed?" Gorgon asked, holding out an apple to his mount.

"The main priority is the king. Once we have the herb, I intend to get it back to Murtal as fast as I can—and trust me, my horse and I can fly when we need to. What you do after that is up to you. They won't be back around us, nor will those dragons. So dead or alive, it doesn't matter. It ends there and then."

"Best to tie up all lose ends, Conn. We wouldn't want them to come back and haunt us, now would we?"

"Like I said, I will be leaving once those herbs are in my hand… unless you need me to kill those thieves for you?" Conn said with a hint of a smile.

"No, you keep your smoke and mirrors, and make your horse run faster home. Leave the fighting to the fighters," Gorgon smiled back.

"Just make sure you bring their heads back to parade in front of your king.

You never know—he may send you to another war as a reward."

They rested for ten minutes, and when they headed off towards the Midas Hills, their pace was quickened.

*

Kern, Galandrik, Ty, and Lan'esra headed north around the lake, passing only a few travellers heading towards Fortune. Even Fortune Wood looked quiet, but uninviting all the same. They kept up a good pace, against Galandrik's wishes and moans of belly rumbles, even refusing to stop and buy fresh fish caught from the lake by the fishermen who sold their catch on the side of the road.

After a full day's ride, the darkness of night cloaked the sky and a bitter chill filled the air. They were on the north side of the lake and could see the Grey Towers in the distance to the west. Both towers had fires alight at the top, an age-old tradition that was kept alive by the Grey Keepers, a group of monks that lit the towers for generations. These towers were originally used as warning towers during the Battle of Blood, a war that had taken place between Bodisha and Bloodmoore centuries ago. The Grey Towers alerted the whole of Eastern Bodisha that the 'Moores' had landed their many warships on Bodisha's soil. In the old testimonies, the town of Fortune was nearly razed to the ground on more than one occasion. Its original name had been Fortina, but the locals changed it to Fortune after the numerous fruitless attempts to destroy it.

After an uneventful night's sleep on the north shore of Lake Fortune and a ham and bread breakfast, the group moved on towards the Grey Towers.

"We loved these towers as children. They were so magical. Our parents would tell us horror stories—that the fires on top contained children being burnt for being naughty, or stories about them being the towers of the gods of the harvest. My father would call them Power Towers."

"Sounds lovely," Ty said, raising an eyebrow to Kern.

"They do look magnificent," Galandrik said, looking up as they got closer.

"They remind me of Queen Valla's Tower," Kern replied.

Ty laughed as he remembered the Tower of Sanorgk. "You mean where you two were chained up and destined to spend the rest of your life breaking rocks until I rescued you?"

Kern looked at Galandrik and shook his head slightly.

"We would have escaped, lad, it was just a matter of time," Galandrik answered. "Anyway, wasn't that just before that shopkeeper kicked your head in down that alleyway?"

Ty turned and glanced at Lan'esra before turning back to the dwarf. "He hardly 'kicked my head in'—he had a bloody Staff of Lightning bolts! It was hard to get out of the way of, in a three-foot-wide alley. You would have struggled to even fit down there."

"Enough! I think we should be on the lookout. There are many bandits around these parts and we *all* should be vigilant," Lan'esra said, breaking in to defuse the minor argument.

Kern smiled to himself. "Well said, Lan'esra. We should reach your home by mid-morning, all going well."

"Yes. Hopefully my father will be happy to see me," she said, looking up at the giant towers.

Galandrik frowned at Ty. "Why wouldn't he be? His daughter returns after months away? He will be delighted."

"You don't know my father... well, I'm sure he will be all right."

"Yeah, I am sure, too. What father can resist a sweet-talking daughter?" Kern said, smiling.

"We shall see," Lan'esra replied as the two towers rose above them.

*

The flatlands of Bodisha slowly turned into the rolling foothills of the Eastern Mountains as the party rode on. The area surrounding the Midas Hills had innumerable paths leading through its enormous span, to the extent that some people disbelieved the small village of Midas actually existed: Traders claimed to have gone searching for it, following dozens or even hundreds of paths through the hills, yet never finding the village.

Some of the hills reached heights of fifty feet, but climbing them was easy in comparison to the craggy slopes of a mountain. This land was green and luscious, and small clumps of trees were scattered all around the Midas Hills, fed by the freshwater stream that snaked its way down from the snowmelt of the peaks of Wade Mountains. All types of vegetation grew here, along with many insects, birds, reptiles, and, of course, humans. The conditions were almost perfect, as was the soil—with all the natural minerals and nutrients required to grow abundant crops—and many history books claimed that life in Bodisha had begun around the Midas Hills because of its ideal environment.

"Which way, Lan'esra?" Ty asked, looking at the pathways leading between the many hills that slowly rose around them.

Lan'esra felt in her element. She smiled as she kicked her horse into a canter and said, "Follow me!"

She led the party through the web of paths, past the clumps of trees and water pools that were dotted all around the landscape.

"It's like being somewhere else completely, as if we have walked into another world," Kern marvelled.

"I agree, lad. It's like a natural maze made by the gods," the dwarf said.

"It's the best place ever," Lan'esra said excitedly. "It can be dangerous, fun, and fruitful all at the same time. From an early age, we were taught what to eat and what not to eat; most things here are edible, but a lot can do serious damage. We were taught what rocks to lift to catch scorpions and what rocks not to lift for snakes, what pools to drink from and what pools have Shire leaf growing in them—drinking from that pool would make your hands ball up tight never to be opened again."

"Why catch scorpions?" Kern asked.

"Before you can treat the sting you have to be stung!"

"And people volunteered for this?" he questioned.

Lan'esra laughed. "Only in tiny doses."

"It certainly looks a fruitful landscape," Ty said as they rode past a pool with a clump of trees growing around one side of it.

"Yes, the fresh water that comes down from the Wade Mountains has a natural goodness that helps everything grow here… good or bad," she smiled.

"How far is your village?" Kern asked.

"Oh, it's close, it's only—"

"I'm surprised you remember!" a voice interrupted.

They all looked up, and saw three men standing on a hill looking down. Kern reached over his shoulder and grabbed an arrow, ready to notch it, just as Ty reached for his crossbow. But Lan'esra held both her arms out wide, indicating that the danger was minimal.

"Migaan, my old friend, how very nice to see you," she said, bowing her head.

All three men carried spears and were dressed in light green leather; bows were slung across their backs, and each man had a sword hanging at his side. "How very nice to see you again, young Lady Lan'esra."

All three companions turned to the girl, who just stared up at the three men.

"Lead us to my father. We need to speak with him."

"As you wish. I'm sure he will be delighted to see you," Migaan said with half a smile. All three men disappeared down behind the hill before reappearing in front of them on horseback. "Who are these... people?" Migaan said, looking at Kern and the others.

"These *people* are the ones who rescued me and brought me home. Now please take us to my father. I have some very important news."

"As you wish, Lan'esra."

They trotted behind the three men, who led them through the maze of hills until finally it opened up into a clearing. From where they stood looking down, they could see the lines of wooden huts and the river that ran parallel to the village. Two little bridges crossed the river, separating the many huts from the fields of vegetables. They could see children playing and women working in the fields, and a couple of people fished along the wider banks of the river. The Eastern Mountains rose high up in the distance and the woods to the west of the huts provided them with supplies.

"*Lady* Lan'esra, eh? Is there something you haven't told us?" Ty said, raising his eyebrows.

"Oh, nothing... apart from the fact that my father is Lord Lan'sukra of Midas."

"Nothing? I really think you should have told us, Lady Lan'esra," Kern laughed.

"That is exactly why I didn't," Lan'esra answered.

The three men leading them made their way down the slope of the hill towards the village. As they got closer to the locals, they could hear the whispers of 'Lan'esra' as villagers ran around alerting each other. Quite a gathering had formed by the time they reached the far side of the village and stood in front of a larger hut. The three local men dismounted, as did Lan'esra. Migaan disappeared into the hut briefly before reappearing and standing in a line with other men of the village. Lan'esra stood in front of the hut and waited, and it wasn't long before her father appeared in the doorway of the hut. He was a withered old man, and leaned on a staff that was a foot taller than him. A tangled explosion of roots twisted and writhed around each other at the top, reminding Ty of an upside-down tree. He wore a black bear-head headdress, and his robe was of a black and white animal skin, though it was no animal Ty recognized. A golden sash wrapped around his middle and leather sandals finished off Lan'sukra's outfit.

"Lan'esra, my girl, where in Hades have you been?" the old man said in a croak.

"It's a very long story, Father, but the summary of it is that I was gathering herbs and got kidnapped by a cult to the north." She turned and looked at her friends, who were still on horseback. "These are my friends. They rescued me and, in return, I have been helping them."

The old man looked up at Kern, Galandrik, and Ty, and said, "I thank you for saving my daughter. What are your names?"

Kern dismounted and stepped forward, "I am Kern Ocarn. These are Galandrik Sabrehargen and Ty Quickpick," he added as the others dismounted.

"I have heard of Kern and his party of thieves."

"We are not thieves," Kern said, without so much as a glance at Ty. "We are just adventurers, trying to survive like anybody else."

Lan'sukra stared at the ranger for a few seconds. "So Kern the giant slayer has tired of slaying giants and moved on to rescuing kidnapped women?" the Lord of Midas asked.

"I am honoured that you have heard of me, Lord Lan'sukra, but unfortunately we have come here to ask for your help, not praise."

"Is that *all* you have come for?"

"We are in a dire situation and need your support, nothing more," Kern continued.

"Not you, ranger." The old man turned to Lan'esra. "You, my own flesh and blood—have you come to your father only for help?"

Lan'esra looked at the floor for a few seconds before saying, "I came to seek your help for my friends."

Lan'sukra stared at his daughter. "Speak the truth here, girl. Are you telling me that if you didn't need my help, you would still be lost and I would still be mourning the loss of my daughter? Every day grieving inside until I have no more tears to fall?"

Lan'esra looked at Kern as if asking for help, then turned back to her father. "I never wanted to leave. I was kidnapped."

"Damn you, Esra!" he shouted. "Would you have come back?"

Lan'esra looked around at the faces of the people she had been brought up with, then back to her father. "It isn't as if I ran away!"

"Answer the damn question, girl! *Would you have come back?*" Lan'sukra raged.

"*NO!* Never!" Lan'esra screamed back at her father.

His eyes widened and he stepped back, holding onto his staff. Migaan stepped forward and took the lord's arm. After a minute of uncomfortable silence, Lan'sukra spoke. "You are no longer welcome here. Your brother Kulo will be the next ruler of Midas. I unburden you of your high-born name—*Lan*—you are now Esra as I named you. Kulo will be Lan'kulo, next in line to lead us. We shall have the ceremony as soon as he is back from the hunt."

Lan'esra stepped forward and dropped to one knee. "Father, please... you are right, I have failed you. And Kulo will make a stronger and far better leader for Midas than I. But we need your help. I am begging you. After this, I will go—go far away, never to return. I will never bring dishonour to your doorstep again."

Lan'sukra looked down at his daughter, seeing the memory of his dead wife in her face. "You bring humiliation to your father, then have the nerve to ask for help?"

"Please, Father. I have never asked you for anything. Do this one thing, and I will leave here. You will no longer be encumbered with my betrayal."

For all Lan'sukra's strong-headedness, he still loved his daughter dearly; banishing her from Midas was the hardest decision he had ever made. Deep down, he longed to reach down and pick Esra up and cradle her in his arms as he had done when she was a child—his first child—but he knew he must lead by example. If the people thought he was weak, they would take advantage, and he couldn't afford a rebellion in his village. He knew his wording would be crucial if he was to help his daughter.

"What is it you require of us, the village you left behind?"

Lan'esra stood up and smiled, saying, "Thank you, Father. I will let Kern explain."

"Not out here. Come inside," he said, and turned and walked into his hut with Migaan at his side.

Kern, Galandrik, and Ty all followed them into the circular hut, which looked nothing like what they expected. Instead of the signs of poverty—poorly-constructed rustic homemade furniture, a dirt floor—they were greeted by the sight of a large table with eight chairs sitting in the middle of the hut, papers and maps scattered across the table. A weapons rack to their left was filled with spears and swords, and on their right was a long desk, again filled with parchments and books.

As they looked around, Kern spoke. "We were tricked into doing a quest for Conn, wizard to King Moriak. They created an illusion that they had my father and if we didn't do as they asked, they would kill him. Since then, I have learnt it was only illusion."

"What was the quest?"

"Gathering some herbs."

Lan'sukra took a seat in one of the chairs, and Migaan stood at his side. "Herbs? He got Kern the giant slayer to gather herbs?" His croaky laugh echoed around the hut. "What nonsense is this?"

"The herbs were in the Dungeon of Dreams—he didn't need an herbalist to retrieve them, he needed adventurers."

The old man looked up at Kern. "Dungeon of Dreams, eh? So why does he need these herbs, and what do you need from me?"

Kern looked at Ty and Galandrik before answering. "The king is dying. These herbs will save him. They need them back as soon as possible. As for the help from you, well—"

"Speak up, man!" the old man interrupted.

"The king has a wizard named Conn, who travels here now to get these herbs, with the king's Black Guard for company."

"So give him the herbs and it's finished."

"It's not that easy. They have also captured two dragons from their mother—Shalamia—from the Eastern Mountains. It's a long story, but we returned these young dragons to her a few months ago and saved them from a sacrifice by King Moriak. His men then returned and re-captured the dragons with the sacrifice in mind, but since the king has fallen ill, they used the dragons—along with the illusion of my father—as leverage to make us take their damn quest."

"Then swap the herbs in exchange for the release of the dragons. What's the difficulty?"

Kern shook his head. "That is how simple it *should* be, but unfortunately we have got on the wrong side of the king and—well, he wants us dead also."

"Well, send a messenger to them now with the herbs, and forget about the damn dragons."

Galandrik stepped forward. "We would—trust me, we really would, but if those dragons die, the mother dragon will rain down fiery hell upon King Moriak."

"Let her! The king is an old fool anyway!" Lan'sukra roared.

"Yes, we also agree," Kern answered, "but if the king loses interest in the war with orcs in favour of fighting a damn dragon, the orcs will flood in from the north. Then *you* will have a lot more to worry about than a wizard with an attitude."

Lan'sukra looked at the four adventurers for a few seconds, his mind working overtime to process all the permutations of what he was hearing. Eventually he spoke. "Agreed. You need to make sure the dragons are freed;

the herbs and everything else all comes secondary to that. So what do you have in mind?"

Lan'esra stepped forward and said, "We were hoping for backup. I know you don't have an army but our... *your* people know these hills. We could use the tunnels to our advantage against them. There will be bloodshed, and I am desperately sorry for bringing this to you, but you must see why we did. If these dragons are not released, Bodisha could fall to the orc army."

"Which way do they come?" Lan'sukra asked.

"They are heading through the Double Dikes pass in the Eastern Mountains," Kern answered.

"How long until they get here?"

"We don't know, but 'soon' is our guess."

Lan'sukra turned to Migaan. "Get the men ready. They will head down and through the old horse passage, so make sure the archers use the tunnels that line the hills along the pass, along with the boulders... yes, drag the boulders up, too. We will be on the flat top next to old Mrs Hickory with the best ten we have, shields and swords at the ready."

Migaan nodded. "Yes, my lord," he said, and left the tent.

Lan'sukra looked at Ty. "You've been quiet. Surely you must have something to say, little one?"

"Yes, one question... who is old Mrs Hickory?"

"It's a tree," Lan'sukra answered. "A very old tree which has stood in these hills since time began. It is just a vantage point. Conn and his army will be below us."

"There is one more thing, Lan'sukra," Kern added.

"Yes? Go ahead, it can't get much worse than it already is."

"It can, I am afraid. The leader of the Black Guard is a mountain of a man who goes by the name of..." Kern took a deep breath, hoping the old man hadn't heard the name before. "...Gorgon."

"*The* Gorgon? The man who slays dragons, the man who beats three hundred orcs with thirty... that Gorgon?" Lan'sukra said.

Kern smiled and raised an eyebrow. "Yes, *that* Gorgon."

"For the love of... any other things coming this way that I need to know about? Giants and ogres, or maybe some trolls?"

"No. Just one wizard, and Gorgon and his twenty or so men," Kern said almost apologetically.

At that point a young lad came in the hut. "My lord, I have a message from Migaan."

"Well, what is it lad?" Lan'sukra shouted, obviously still angry about Kern's news of the Gorgon.

"He says the army of men are about an hour away from the old horse passage," the young messenger said between deep breaths.

"Tell Migaan to have the men ready, but first take these four to old Mrs Hickory." Lan'sukra turned to Kern and said, "Get ready for their arrival. I will have both sides waiting."

"Where will you be?"

"I will make myself seen. Just wave a torch in the air; this will be our signal."

"Thank you, Lan'sukra," Kern said. "We will not forget you for this." Kern bowed and followed the lad from the tent, along with Galandrik and Ty.

Lan'esra smiled at her father before nodding. "Thank you, Lord Lan'sukra. You are and always will be the best father a daughter could ever have. Again, I am sorry for my actions."

"Don't worry. Just save those dragons."

"I will, Father. When will Kulo be back?"

"Soon. He will be back soon."

"Good. I'd like to see him before I go," she said with a smile, and walked out of the hut.

Lan'sukra dropped his head into his hands. "Why come back and ask this? Why now, why me…"

Chapter Twenty-Nine
The Battle of Old Mrs Hickory

Kern, Galandrik, Ty, and Lan'esra all stood on the flat-topped hill. The branches of the old tree next to them towered over them and up into the sky, twisting like distorted limbs reaching for the sun. Below them was the pathway leading towards the Eastern Mountains. On either side of the path were hills, making this more like a valley. It was easy to see that this was the perfect spot for an ambush. They could see, along the lengths of the hills, the movement of the people from Lan'sukra's village.

Ty looked up at old Mrs Hickory and said, "She may have been here for hundreds of years, but I think she died long ago. It's almost eerie."

"I agree, lad. Spooky," Galandrik answered.

Ty stabbed three torches into the ground and lit each one before loading his crossbow and hooking it onto his belt. Kern stuck twenty arrows into the ground to his right, ready for notching.

"Listen," Kern said holding up a hand. They all stood still and in the silence they could hear the thudding of hooves in the distance. "They are close. Get ready; where are the herbs?"

Ty dropped the hemp sack onto the ground. "Here."

Kern nodded. "Right, I don't know how this is going to play out, but just be ready—and good luck," he said.

"Look," Lan'esra said, and pointed down at the oncoming army.

"Get down," Kern said. They all squatted next to a line of the bushes that dotted the entire area of the Midas Hills and waited.

When Conn was twenty feet away from being directly below them, Kern stood up and unleashed an arrow. It struck the ground just in front of Conn and Gorgon. Behind them were twenty men and a cart carrying something covered with a brown leather sheet.

Conn's horse reared, and he held up a hand to his troops. "Halt, men!" he shouted.

In a whisper, Gorgon said, "Looks like your friend beat us here."

"Looks that way," Conn replied. "Well, well. Kern, how are you?"

"Quite well. We have what you want; let me see the dragons."

Gorgon nodded to one of his men, who unfastened the sheet covering the cart and pulled it off to reveal an iron cage with the two dragons inside. Both dragons hissed and screamed as the daylight hit their eyes.

"Now, where are my herbs?" Conn shouted up at Kern.

Ty stood up and lifted the sack above his head. "In here. Don't worry, it is what you want."

"Good to see you, Ty. I thought you were dead!"

"You wish! Don't listen to all you hear, Conn, and only believe half what you see!"

"Wise words, thief. Now bring those herbs down to me, there's a good boy."

"Nah, how about you release those dragons into the air? Then I will gladly hand them over."

"How about I come up there and take them, then shove your head up a dragon's arse!" Gorgon shouted.

Conn turned his head and murmured, "Very tactful."

Ty held the bag over the top of the torches. "How about I burn them, and you can shove your own head up the dragon's arse?" he shouted back.

Kern shook his head. "Just let me talk!"

Conn held his hands up. "Everyone just calm down. Look around you: We have twenty of the king's Black Guard here. You can burn the herbs and the king dies, but so do you. Just hand them over and we will leave peacefully."

"Last chance. Let the dragons go, or my friend here will burn your precious herbs!" Kern shouted as Ty shook the bag above the flames.

At that moment, an eagle came swooping down and grabbed the bag from Ty's grip, then soared off into the air.

"What the hell!" Ty shouted as he stumbled back, falling onto his behind from the shock of the bird snatching the bag.

As the eagle circled up above them, Kern grabbed another arrow from next to him and fired. The arrow struck the eagle in the wing and, with a puff of feathers, the great bird fell from the sky. It landed next to Conn, and no sooner had it hit the floor than it started to morph.

"Kill it!" Gorgon said, but Conn raised his hands.

"No, wait!"

The two Black Guards stopped their advance, but kept their swords drawn. A man's figure slowly began to take shape, and within a minute a cloaked man lay on the ground before them, an arrow through his forearm. With his uninjured hand, he reached for his hood and flicked it back.

"Bok!" Conn said with a smile.

"*Bok!*" Galandrik, Kern, and Ty said simultaneously.

"Yes, Bok. Here are your herbs," he said, tossing the bag up to Conn.

"Well, well. You have outdone yourself," the wizard said, looking into the sack.

Ty stood up. "That dirty thieving pigdog!"

Kern shook his head and looked at Ty. "We shall see now what their plans were. They hold all the cards." He looked down at Conn and called, "You have the herbs, now keep your side of the deal: Release the dragons."

Conn looked up at Kern, then at Gorgon, who smiled coldly. "See, I would love to do that," Conn said, "but unfortunately my friend here has other orders, and releasing the dragons isn't among them."

"You have what you want! The king will never know if you slay them or not," Kern shouted down.

Conn turned to Gorgon. "Did he just say what I think he said?"

"Aye. I think he is asking us to lie to our king," Gorgon said, shaking his head.

"Sod this," Kern said, ripping a torch out of the ground and waving it above his head.

"What's he doing now?" Conn said, as two guards helped Bok up to his feet.

"He has some help—look," Gorgon said, nodding towards the hills on either side of them. Men appeared, lining both hills, and Gorgon shouted, "Ambush! Side flank defence!" His men dismounted and made a line of horses on either side of them. Two lines of men held position behind the horses with shields above them, while the remaining men created a line in front of them with their shields up, creating a barrier of steel and horses almost completely encircling the soldiers.

"Very impressive. Looks like we are going to war, lad," Galandrik said, holding his two-handed axe.

"Looks that way," Kern answered. "Look—there is Lan'sukra. I think it's now going to kick off."

To the right of the Black Guard, a door opened from the side of the hill, falling out and down like a drawbridge. Two raising-chains made of rope held the door in a horizontal position as Lan'sukra walked out, holding his hands out in front of him in a gesture of surrender.

"Greetings, Conn and Gorgon," he said, bowing his head.

"That two-timing, double-crossing piece of shit!" Kern growled.

"I just don't believe what I am seeing," Lan'esra said, stepping forward.

"And you are?" Conn shouted up.

"I am Lord Lan'sukra of the Midas Hills. We wish you no harm, and do not want any part of these troubles. Those people," he said, pointing towards the party, "are common bandits and should be hanged! Hanged by the throat until dead!"

"Father! How could you?" Lan'esra shouted.

Lan'sukra looked at his daughter, and slowly turned away.

"That dirty—" Kern began to say as he notched an arrow.

"No, don't! If you kill him, we'll have fifty more men attacking us," Lan'esra said, holding her hand over Kern's bow.

"She is right," Ty said, "and there's something else. We are in a bad place.

Our horses are behind us; we would never get there before they got to us."

Conn and Gorgon both laughed.

"It looks like your plan has backfired! How about dropping your weapons and walking down? It'll save me coming up there to get you," Gorgon shouted.

Kern watched as all the people disappeared and the hatch in the hill closed, then he turned back to his companions. "If we get through this," he said, looking at Lan'esra, "your father will be the first person I visit."

"Not before me," Ty hissed. "I don't know who I'd like to kill more, him or Bok!"

"I think we need to fight these first, lad," Galandrik added.

Kern smiled at the dwarf. "You are right, as always. What do you have in mind?"

"Charge them?"

Kern sniggered. "Always joking, even in the face of adversity."

"I wasn't," Galandrik said, stony-faced.

"You must be kidding! Us four running at that lot? We wouldn't even break through the first row of shields!" Ty argued.

"I have a summon-earth-elemental ring," Lan'esra said.

"Oh, I suppose you have a better idea?" the dwarf growled at Ty.

"Anything would be better than suicide!" Ty continued to argue his case.

"I got it from the Dungeon of Dreams," Lan'esra said.

"It may be suicide, lad, but it's still better than running away!"

"Running? Who said anything about running? I haven't even—"

"SHUT UP!" Kern interrupted. "Lan'esra, what did you say?"

"I have a summon-earth-elemental ring, with two charges. I got it from the Dungeon of Dreams," she explained.

"The Dungeon of Dreams! I got a teleport ring—I could get down there and cause havoc!"

"I have the magic protection ring," Galandrik said, pulling it from his pocket.

"You have ten seconds," Gorgon shouted, "then I will come up! Ten… nine… eight…"

The party stood up and looked down at their opponents. "Very well, we are coming," Kern called. To Lan'esra he added, "Summon whenever you like," in a whisper.

Lan'esra slipped the ring onto her finger, and pointed down to the ground in front of the line of guards. A bright light flashed and fired out, striking the ground. The earth began to bubble and spit like a hot spring, and slowly the head and shoulders of an earth elemental began to rise, as if it were pushing itself from the ground.

"Earth elemental! Stand your ground," Gorgon shouted as his men formed a V-shaped formation.

"I am sick of this," Conn said as he opened his spell book. "*Fizure de Nam*!" he shouted, and a fireball shot from his hand and flew towards the party.

"Gal, the ring!" Ty shouted. Galandrik held the ring between two fingers. As he tried to slip it on a finger of his other hand, he fumbled and the ring fell. Ty jumped towards Galandrik and, reaching down, caught the ring as it fell, slipping it onto his finger in the same movement. Just as the fireball was virtually upon them, a circular globe of protection appeared around all four of them, and the fire engulfed it like fiery rain falling onto an umbrella.

"Lan'esra, create the other earth elemental!" Kern ordered.

She removed the ring, then slipped it on again, and as she repeated the action another earth elemental began to grow from the ground.

"I don't believe it! They have magic protection?" Conn shouted, over the commotion of the Black Guard fighting the two elementals.

"You forgot elementals! I told you these thieves are troublesome," Gorgon shouted as he dismounted. He picked up his massive shield and a spear, saying, "If you want a job done right, do it yourself! Fucan, come, and bring three more."

Kern looked down and saw Gorgon walking up the hill towards them, along with four men. Behind him the rest of the Black Guard was fighting the two elementals, while Conn sat on his horse watching over the battle.

"Ty, can you teleport down there and free those dragons?" Kern asked.

"Most definitely. What about him?" he replied, nodding towards the giant man walking towards them.

"Leave him to us. Just free those dragons—Bodisha is relying on it."

"All right. Good luck," Ty said, holding out his hand and smiling.

"We'll shake when it is over." Kern smiled back as Ty slipped the ring on and disappeared.

"I think this may be difficult," Lan'esra said, holding her mace.

"Just stay away from Gorgon," Kern answered, then looked at Galandrik. "Shall we?"

Galandrik smiled back. "Thought you were never going to ask."

Kern notched an arrow and sent it flying towards Gorgon, who simply raised his shield, blocking the arrow as it thudded in. Again Kern let fly, but struck only the giant shield. Even the men behind Gorgon were covered.

"Sod this," Kern said, drawing his new katanas of vanquishing. "Let's play with these babies, then." All three of them stepped back towards the mighty tree to wait for the inevitable arrival of Gorgon.

"Who is taking whom?" Lan'esra asked.

"I will go for Gorgon," Galandrik said. "You two hit the guards."

"Sounds like a plan," Kern agreed, knowing the dwarf's armour could withstand more damage than his own.

"Need a hand?" said a voice from behind them.

"Kulo!" Lan'esra said, springing forward to wrap her arms around her brother's neck.

"All right, all right. Let's do this first, then we can catch up," Kulo answered.

"Kern, Galandrik, this is Kulo, my brother."

"Pleased to meet you both. These are my good friends," Kulo said, gesturing to six men behind him. "What's the plan?"

"Your worst nightmare—but I am glad you're here. Get ready, there are four soldiers and a massive human called Gorgon coming up that hill. Galandrik is heading for the big man, and we are taking the rest."

"Josha, Flathuim, Gourtin," Kulo called, "go with Galandrik. Petre, Drollon, and Toure—with me and Lan'esra."

All ten of them stood ready, and waited for Gorgon to reach the top of the hill with his four guards. "Well, would you look at what we have here,"

Gorgon growled when he came into sight. "Lambs for the slaughter!"

"Just walk away. This doesn't have to end like this," Kern said, bracing himself.

"You have disobeyed the king. It ends now!"

"It will never end," Kern replied.

"Oh, it will end. If you kill enough of them, they stop fighting eventually. Now *die*!" Gorgon screamed, and launched his spear with frightening speed.

The weapon struck Josha's shield, completely penetrating it and piercing his chest. Josha grabbed the spear; a trickle of blood appeared at his lip as he fell backwards. With a scream, Kulo raised his sword and attacked, along with the rest of his men and Kern, Galandrik, and Lan'esra.

*

Ty appeared next to the wheel of the cart. Conn sat on his horse in front of the cart, casting spells at the earth elemental. Five guards were fighting each elemental, and three guards lay motionless on the ground. Ty could see that the guards had the upper hand, and before long they would be charging Kern. Further in front of them was the hill where he had teleported from, and all around him were horses. Without any further hesitation, Ty set to work on the lock of the cage.

When Sleeper and Erella saw Ty, they turned their noses towards him and smelt the air. "Shhh… you'll be out of here soon," Ty said, placing a finger to his lips, then went back to work on the lock. At the same moment the lock clicked open, Ty heard a twig breaking behind him. He quickly removed the lock and spun on his heel, throwing it at his opponent and drawing his two daggers. The lock flew over Bok's shoulder as he ducked.

"The eagle has landed, then?" Ty sneered as they began to circle each other.

"I have waited for this for such a long time. I'm actually gutted that it's finally here and you're going to die—my life will seem so empty," Bok said.

"Your life *is* empty, like your head."

"You always were the clown, the joker… the imbecile."

Ty looked at Bok's scarred face and bandaged arm, and he could see that

Bok struggled to hold the dagger up. "You have been through hell to get revenge," he said, shaking his head. "You really want more?"

Bok's eyes were those of a madman; his face was twisted with rage, an irresistible craving to spill the blood of his nemesis. "What's up, Rat? Don't quit on me now, little boy," he spat venomously.

They circled each other slowly, cross-stepping—left leg over right, just as they had been taught in the guild—and Ty said, "Oh, I won't quit on you. I just wish I'd killed you long ago."

"Why wait!" Bok shouted. He lunged forward and their blades crashed together. Tiny sparks surrounded their battle in the twilight as they swiped and crossed, stabbed and lunged. After a melee of attacks and blocks, they split and began the circling again. A small trickle of blood ran down Ty's cheek from a nick above his ear.

"I'm sure you're getting slower, Rat-boy."

Ty wiped the blood onto his sleeve. "Lucky hit, that's all." Ty jumped and struck first, his blades slicing around Bok's face. Bok parried his attacks and riposted with his own, both blades slicing left and right until all four blades were interlocked. Bok's face was inches away from Ty's, and his strength was evident as he pressed his weight down on the smaller thief. With gritted teeth, Ty pulled his right arm away, knowing Bok's dagger would slip harmlessly past his shoulder; in the same movement, he punched Bok in the arm, exactly where Kern's arrow had penetrated. Bok stumbled back, groaning and holding his now-aching wound. Blood dripped from his fingers as he wobbled, bent over, holding his arm.

"You bastard," Bok hissed through gritted teeth.

"Walk away now, disappear forever, and that will be that. The end of it, no more, finished," Ty said, rocking from one foot to the other.

"Never!" Bok shouted as he swung round. His wound was obviously not as bad as he had made out; their blades struck together, more ferociously than ever.

Ty ducked one swing and stabbed Bok's thigh, and he stumbled back, one hand on his wounded arm, the other on his thigh.

"Run, Bok… last chance," Ty said, flipping a dagger and catching it.

"We all must die," Bok said as he straightened up. Ty could tell by his face that Bok's pride was stronger than the pain his wounds dished out.

"Let's go die then," Ty said and stepped forward.

*

Galandrik's mighty axe swung at Gorgon, who sidestepped the attack even as he blocked another from Gourtin. For such a huge man, his swordsmanship was graceful—more like a dancer than a brutish warrior. Gorgon parried another blow and sliced Flathuim across the face, sending him reeling backwards, screaming in agony. Galandrik swung again as Gourtin lunged, but the giant man sidestepped the dwarf's blow once more. Gourtin's stab caught him in the forearm, but he riposted, pushing Gourtin back as he frantically tried to block the attacks.

*

Kern knelt and blocked a downward swing above his head as he sliced a guard's stomach with his other katana. Petre and Drollon fended off the largest guard, who swung, jabbed, and sliced, attacking like a berserker and sending both backwards. Lan'esra dodged an attack but took the hilt of the sword to her jaw, sending her spinning and crashing dazed into the dirt. But before the guard could finish her, Toure stepped in and took over the assault.

Kulo was a skilled swordsman; he fought almost as if he were fencing. He swung his two swords, arcing and prodding at his opponent's weak spots. The guard managed to parry the blows on the back foot, counter-attacking at every opportunity. The people of the Midas Hills were warriors at heart and they fought with the courage of a mountain lion—dying in battle was a proud way to go—but none had the skill of Kulo. His natural grace and ability with the sword was clear for all to see, and had been so from an early age.

Kern looked over his shoulder, and spied the larger guard pushing Petre and Drollon back as they struggled to defend against his blistering speed. Kern spun and jumped, slicing the guard down his back. The guard screamed and turned, aiming a downwards blow at Kern's shoulder. With a quick turn of the heel, the guard's sword whistled past. He raised his other sword, but the blow never came—Petre and Drollon both lunged, their swords sinking deep into the guard's side, and the man fell and died.

"Help the others," Kern shouted, as he turned in time to see Gorgon thrust his sword deep into Gourtin's stomach.

Galandrik stepped back, holding his axe with both hands. "Come on then, lad, let's have it."

Gorgon pulled his sword free, letting Gourtin's body fall face-first into the dirt, then stepped forward swinging his two swords. Galandrik blocked with both ends of his axe and his forearm shield, managing to swing a counter-blow. His axe was devastating when it connected, but for duelling he knew he wouldn't fend off Gorgon for long. Eventually Gorgon landed a blow that sliced into the dwarf's thigh, dropping him to one knee. Blows rained down from the giant man's weapons like a blacksmith beating an anvil.

Kern leapt forward from Gorgon's side; he only just managed to spot the attack, and swung round to parry. Gorgon and Kern fought like two tigers, stopping after a couple of minutes to gain a breath. Kern had a slice across his forearm, cheek, and shoulder where Gorgon had caught him, but the giant man himself wasn't unscathed either—his chest ran with blood from two cuts down the centre of it.

Leaning on his axe, Galandrik tried to get to his feet; blood was now pouring from the leg wound. Gorgon stepped forward and kicked the dwarf square in the chest, sending him rolling backwards down the side of the hill. Kern screamed and jumped forward, and his katanas whistled as they arced and sliced through the air.

But Gorgon was just too good, parrying every move the ranger had in his repertoire, and using his elbow to catch Kern in the jaw, spinning him round so that he ended up on his knees. Kern swung his sword but Gorgon parried, knocking the sword out of the dazed ranger's hand. He stepped on Kern's other sword, trapping his hand under the hilt, and reached down to grab Kern by his throat.

Kern angled his head upwards and looked at the beast's eyes as he struggled to focus.

"Time to die, thief," Gorgon growled.

Gorgon lifted Kern up by the throat and pushed him up against the tree. Dropping his sword, he drew his dagger from his belt and raised it above his head, thrusting it into Kern's shoulder and pinning him to the tree. Kern screamed in agony as the blade penetrated his flesh.

*

Kulo finished off his guard by spinning round and slicing through his neck. The guard dropped his weapon and grabbed his throat, blood pouring through his fingers as he fell down into the dirt. Kulo turned to see the last guard stabbing his friend Toure in the side. Petre and Drollon jumped in to continue the fight as Toure fell down, clutching his side. Kulo jumped over to Lan'esra and lifted her head; she tried to speak, but he touched her mouth and said, "Shhh, sweet sister."

Looking up, he saw Kern against the tree and Gorgon stepping back, picking up his sword, and holding both swords out from his sides. Just as the giant man was about to swing both swords at once, decapitating the helpless ranger, Kulo jumped forward; screaming, he lunged in and attacked, cutting through the flesh above the knee. Gorgon spun round and parried the onslaught, and gradually he began to counter and make his own attacks. It was like one of the choreographed sword fights that played out in arenas around Bodisha, both men well-skilled and almost evenly matched, their swords dancing in the air, clashing and sparking.

*

Conn watched as the final elemental was sent crashing to the ground; only four guards remained from the epic battle. Looking up, he saw Kern and Galandrik's fight with the giant man on the hill.

"Go help Gorgon!" he bellowed, and the guards ran to help their general. Looking to his left, Conn saw thirty or forty men running towards them, led by Lan'sukra. "Damn!"

He looked up at Gorgon and reached for his spell book—then stopped. Looking at the bag of herbs that hung by his side and the men running towards the hill, he thought of his friend Belton… and closed the book.

"Fuck you, Gorgon," he whispered, and turned his horse around.

He saw Ty and Bok circling each other with daggers drawn. Ty's back was to him, and he kicked his horse forward. Hearing the noise, Ty spun, but the horse knocked him to the ground. Skidding to a halt in the dirt, Conn came to a stop next to Bok. He pulled his staff from his back and aimed it forward, and lightning shot from the end towards the thief.

Ty saw what was happening and remembered the ring. He rolled onto his side and pulled it off, then replaced it, creating a semicircle of magic protection all around him. The lightning sparkled as it engulfed the shield.

Ty looked up; through the shield, he saw Gorgon lifting Kern up and forcing him against the tree. He watched as the Beast raised his dagger, pinned his friend to the tree, and stepped backwards to pick up his sword. Ty knew he had to get up and help. He got up into a squat and pulled the teleportation ring from his finger.

"If there is a God, now would be the time to show yourself," he whispered, and slipped the ring back on his finger—but nothing happened. 'Damn you!' he muttered.

Just then he heard something like a whisper, inside his head.

Release us! We will help your friend!

He looked up at the cage and saw that Sleeper was looking at him. Ty could see that, even though he had removed the lock, the catch still sat over the metal loop. He knew that stepping out from the magical circle of protection could be fatal. He turned, looking at Gorgon again, and saw him extend his arms out to either side, holding a sword in each hand.

"Why me?" he said, shaking his head, then jumped up and flicked the catch.

Both dragons shot up into the air, twisting and turning, screeching as they went.

Ty reached for his short sword of shadows, but his hand never even reached the hilt.

His world was plunged into darkness.

*

Kulo dodged and parried, but Gorgon's attacks were coming thick and fast. Frantically he tried to parry the onslaught of attacks, but it was useless. Finally Gorgon's strength won through, and the sword was sent flying from Kulo's hand. With a forearm smash to the face, Kulo fell to the floor, the other sword falling from his grip. He looked up and saw Drollon and Petre also being cut down, as four more guards appeared on the hill. His friends fell to the ground; Drollon slumped and reached for his sword, then he glanced sideways and forced a smile just as a guard stuck a sword into the back on his neck.

"Nooo!" he screamed and pushed himself up. Gorgon grabbed the back of his hair and pulled his head backwards, lifting him up so he was kneeling. Kulo thrashed and swung his arms.

*

Kern opened his one good eye as the pain flowed through his body from his injured shoulder. He saw Gorgon holding Kulo's head from behind as he ran his sword across his throat, and saw Kulo fall forward into the dirt.

Gorgon turned to the ranger and looked into his eyes. "Don't worry, you're next," he said, wiping Kulo's blood off on Kern's ripped and tattered armour.

"Fuck you," Kern said. He spat into the face of the Beast, wincing with pain as he did.

The big man stepped back and blinked, wiping the spit from his cheek. "Still a little fight, I see," he said, lifting one sword up. "I like it when someone who is seconds from death has that much spirit! Now, if there isn't anything else… please just die."

Suddenly Kern heard a screech and felt a huge surge of heat as Sleeper blasted Gorgon with flame while Erella ripped at his arm, making him drop his sword. Gorgon stepped back screaming, holding his head—which was now engulfed in flames, as was everything from his belt upwards. Turning and spinning, he ran blindly, still screaming as he fell and tumbled down the side of the hill, rolling like a fire ball. Then the dragons turned to the guards, ripping the men with their razor-sharp talons and blasting them with fire. Within seconds all the guards were dead.

An arrow whizzed up, just missing Sleeper. He turned round and saw the men running up towards them, and with a quick glance at Kern the dragons were gone, soaring up into the air as more arrows flew past them. Kern saw this and tried to speak, but his head dropped still.

Chapter Thirty
Aches and Pains

Kern opened his eye. He could smell the fragrances of flowers and herbs, but everything was blurry. "Where am I?" he muttered to himself.

"You're in the Midas Hills, lad," came the reply in Galandrik's familiar voice.

"How long have I been out?"

"Just two days," the dwarf answered.

"Two days! Where is Lan'esra?"

"I'm here, Kern," she answered.

"And Ty? Where is Ty?" There was a pause, an awkward silence as his vision slowly regained focus. He could make out Galandrik and Lan'esra standing in front of him. "I asked, where is he?"

"We don't know," the dwarf answered. Kern saw he was leaning on a stick, wearing a white cloth gown. Then Kern looked down at himself, and realised he was in bed, bandages covering his chest and shoulder. "Then we must go find him," he said, trying to sit up in bed. But the pain in his body was too great, and he winced as he lay back down.

"All in good time, friend. You have serious injuries, as have we all. We need to rest."

Kern looked at Lan'esra. "I didn't think you were welcome back here."

"Things have changed." She paused and took a deep breath. "My brother died in the battle. I will be next in line to rule."

"But—"

"I know what I said before, and what my father said, but it's in the past. I am Lan'esra of the Midas Hills."

"What changed your mind?"

"That battle. I dragged you here promising things I shouldn't have. My brother was killed because of me. If nothing else, I owe my father and the people here."

"It's your choice, Lan'esra."

"I have been talking to my family and friends while you slept, and this is where I belong—not fighting elementals and wyverns. These are my people and they need a strong leader. Father isn't getting any younger."

"Nonsense! I thought you—"

She held a finger up to her mouth. "Shhh… I have made my decision."

Kern smiled as she held his hand. "I am glad you found peace with your father."

"Me too. Now get some rest." She smiled and kissed his forehead before walking off.

"Rest well, Kern, for you will need all your strength to find our missing friend," Galandrik said softly.

"Bloody Ty, I knew he would get us in trouble one day," Kern said with a smile, but even that made his face contort and wince. "I wonder where he is?"

"You can be sure that wherever he is, he will be causing chaos for someone."

"I can just imagine. What happened to Gorgon? I seem to remember fire and heat."

"Well, good and bad, to be honest," Galandrik said hobbling to a chair.

"What do you mean good *and* bad?"

"Ty must have released the dragons, and apparently, when you were last man standing—or pinned I should say—" the dwarf broke off into a laugh.

"Not funny! But go on," Kern said, looking at his bandaged shoulder.

"He was just about to skewer you when Sleeper and Erella appeared and burned him, setting him on fire. He stumbled about and ended up in a heap at the bottom of the hill."

"Aye, I remember now."

"Lan'sukra had a change of heart and came back with his men—a little late, to be honest—and didn't realise about the dragons. They scared them off with some arrow shots."

"Well, at least they got away. So what's bad? It all seems good to me, apart from the obvious," Kern said, nodding at his wounds.

"This is the thing: Lan'esra sent two men out to load up the dead onto a cart for burial… but they never returned."

"What? You mean… I don't understand," Kern said, confused.

"Nor do I, lad. When those two didn't return, they sent others. They found the first two dead, with their heads turned completely around—and Gorgon's body was gone."

"He's alive?"

"It looks that way. He took the cart and *all* the dead guards."

"So he took his men home, which would be Gorgon all day long."

"Exactly. And he will not be happy with his face burnt off. I should imagine he will be pretty angry, in fact."

"Sod him. Let's just hope he doesn't take it out on Ty."

"Yes, let's hope so," Galandrik agreed.

"And Conn? What about that slimy wizard?"

"No idea. He and Bok both vanished into thin air."

"So the king gets his herbs, and Shalamia is reunited *again* with Sleeper and Erella, preventing the Orc invasion—we just need to find Ty and it will have all worked out well."

"Seems that way, but we need to talk about this later," Galandrik said, standing up and hobbling to the door. "Rest well, lad."

*

Kern swung his sword in a wild arc in front of him. "Come out and fight me, you little whore!" He spun around, his sword again circling and slicing through the air. "Show yourself, you bastard," he cried as he swung his sword wildly, turning round and round like a blind man. A small cloaked figure holding two daggers stepped out from behind a tree stump and crouched in front of him, ready to attack. Kern swung again and the small figure rolled under the arc of the sword then lunged forward, stabbing Kern in the thigh. Kern swung to the side where the attack had come from but sliced thin air as his attacker rolled under the sword and squatted, holding his daggers up, ready to attack again…"You never beat me! Fight me like a man and not like the cowardly little whoredog you are!" The cloaked figure picked up a small stone and threw it past Kern. It landed behind him and, without any hesitation, Kern swung at where the noise had come from. The cloaked figure lunged forward and sliced through the back of Kern's armour. Instantly he spun round again, swinging the blade through the air, but, to his dismay, hitting nothing. He could feel the warm blood running down his back. "I'll catch you, thief!"…

"Maybe in the afterlife," the voice replied. Kern swung round to where the voice came from and made contact. The thief stepped back as another attack swung inches from his face. He looked down and saw the cut above his knee starting to ooze blood. "You like that?" Kern asked, looking around wildly. "Come get some more!"…

Ty woke from the dream, sweat drenching his face. As he opened his eyes, he felt the pain in the back of his head. Slowly he rotated his head, feeling the aches and pains. When he tried to reach up he realised his hands were tied in front of him. When his sight cleared, he saw a length of rope which ran from his hands to his tied feet, keeping them only one foot apart. He looked around and realised he was in the cage that the dragons had been in. Spinning on his side, he looked through a hole in the leather sheet that covered his moving prison. He could see Bok sitting in the front of the wagon, Conn on horseback trotting next to him. Slowly he edged against the side of the cage and pushed himself up into a sitting position, then began to undo his leather boot. When he finally kicked it off, he reached inside and pulled out a small leather pouch and unrolled it. His lock picks lay in a line. He carefully pulled out a small file and went to work on the rope that tied his hands. It was laborious, but eventually he cut through the knot, slipped his hand out of the ropes, and untied his feet.

Stretching, he rubbed his neck and rolled his wrists around in circles. Then he placed the small file back into the pouch and pulled out two small lock picks, placing them between his teeth. He got his boot back on and tucked the leather pouch in his belt. Reaching out through the bars, he felt for the lock.

"*No prison can hold me…*" he whispered.

Chapter Thirty-One
No Dungeon Can Hold Me

Ty knew the only way out of this metal cage was to pick the lock on the outside, a sheet covered the cage and the only light piercing the darkness came from the gap between the bottom of the sheet and the wagon base, and the fine streams that shone through the tiny holes in the fabric. *Even if I can open this damn lock, the sheet will stop me lifting the lid; it's tied down on either side of the wagon.* He held the picks in his hand and studied the hemp ropes that blocked his escape. All were too far away; even if he could reach to somehow cut them, the sheet would flap around, and Conn and Bok would surely see it and be on to him. *Damn! Do I risk it or sit tight and face what's coming to me? Damn! Those bars aren't that strong. Maybe I could… yes, just maybe.*

Ty placed the lockpicks on the floor, then spat onto his hands and rubbed them together. *Come on—bend bars or lift a gate, it's all the same. Come on.* Ty grabbed the bars, counted to three, and pulled with all his might—but they never budged. *Damn!* He knew the only thing for it was to pick the lock and lift the cage lid. Maybe he could squeeze through; maybe the sheet had enough slack in it.

Ty reached up and began wielding his lockpicking skill. He closed his eyes and felt the workings of the lock through the picks. *One more turn…*

But just as he was about to make the final twist, the wagon came to an abrupt stop and he fell into the side of the cage, dropping the picks and jarring his wrist. *Damn!*

*

"How long are we going to sit here, Jojo?"

"Listen, have I ever let us down?"

"We've been sitting up here for four hours and there hasn't been a soul come along the path. I think the traders know this route is full of bandits and are using another pathway. We have over-farmed it."

"Rubbish. This is still the only route though the Eastern Mountains. How else are they going to get through, fly over?"

"I don't know, but how many hits have we had lately?"

"Listen, Grud, you haven't been a day without a meal for months. Just be patient."

"I am being, but this is just so boring. Sitting, waiting, sitting, waiting—it's all we do, and for what? A wagon full of rotten fruit and a few horses!"

"Shhh... listen."

"Horses!" Grud said, looking over the edge of the rock they hid behind.

"Only two men, too. This should be a doddle! I'll alert Peahead and Calin." Jojo whistled and two faces appeared from behind another rock across the pathway. He signalled and they signalled back, then he said, "Right, Grud, load your crossbow. You know what to do." Jojo picked up a fist-sized rock and loaded his slingshot.

"Really?" Grud asked.

"Yes, really!"

"Have you actually ever hit anybody with it?"

"Yes, last week! You know I did!"

"You can't count that—it hit his leg."

"Oh, shut up and just be ready!" Jojo held the slingshot down behind him and watched as his two companions across on the other side readied themselves.

The wagon was nearly directly below them now. Jojo began to swing his sling in a circle, gradually raising it until it was above his head. The man closest to him was wearing a black cloak with his hood up, and another man rode on the cart behind, but he was blocked by the first.

Jojo swung the sling around his head and took aim. *Whoosh*—the stone flew from Jojo's sling and straight at the man on the horse. *Smack!*—it struck him straight on the side of the head, knocking him from his horse.

"You fucking hit him! Straight in the head!" Grud exclaimed.

"Not now! Move! Kill that driver!" Jojo shouted as he picked up his crude, rusty sword and jumped down, bounding from one boulder to another, followed by Grud.

Bok saw Conn fall from his horse, and pulled up on the reins. Stopping the wagon with a lurch, he jumped down and raced over to his fallen companion. He rolled Conn over and saw the blood covering his face and the inch-long gash on his temple; glancing up and to his right, he saw the two men jumping from rock to rock, and the two men on the other side.

No time to waste.

Bok ran, not looking back; he could hear the whistling of arrows as they flew past him, but he didn't stop. He ran as fast as his legs could carry him, until the sound of the arrows had stopped. He didn't know how far he had run, but his heart was nearly bursting from his chest. He spotted a small path to his right that led up into the mountains, and wasted no time. He sprinted with every ounce of energy he had left in his aching limbs, jumping and scrambling up the cliff until he found a small alcove. He dived in—there could have been a bear inside, but he didn't care. Sitting with his back to a wall, he tried to breathe as quietly as possible, as quietly as his pounding heart would allow. He could hear footsteps and voices in the distance below, could felt the sweat running down his face, and could taste the saltiness as it passed over his lips. He shut his eyes and prayed.

"Fuck me, Grud, one bastard job! One little job! Kill the wagon driver, that's all you had to do!" Jojo shouted.

"What about Peahead and Calin?" Grud answered.

"What about them?"

"Well, in case you haven't noticed, there are four of us in the gang."

"I never told them to kill him, I told *you!*"

"Whatever! Always my fault," Grud grumbled.

THE KING'S PROMISE

"Let's get back before that driver reaches Breeze and tells the world," Jojo said, jogging back up the path.

"Breeze is three days away, and that's on a horse," Grud said, catching Jojo up.

"Did you see him run? He was like a mountain lion."

"He did go a fair pace, but so would I with four bandits chasing me."

Jojo and Grud reached the wagon just as Conn was being thrown on the back of it. "What we got?" Jojo asked.

"You will not be happy, Jojo," Peahead answered. "We hit a dud."

"You are joking? Please tell me you're joking."

"Nope. Roughly five gold, a staff, spell book, some herbs, and a couple of nice weapons."

"Not a total dud, then," Jojo said, examining one of Ty's short swords of shadows. "This should fetch a few gold."

"There is a pair, too. Come on, let's take the wagon back to camp."

"Hang on, what's under the sheet?" Grud asked.

"Just some skinny halfling with a big mouth locked in a cage. Said his name was Ty the Prat or something."

"Ty the Rat, actually!" they heard from under the sheet.

"Let's leave him here," Calin said. "Just unwanted hassle, if you ask me."

"No, if he is a prisoner, there may be a reward on his head. Let's get to camp and see what the man in black has to say," Jojo said.

The bandits led the wagon and Conn's horse west towards the Double Dikes. The two giant statues loomed above them as they turned south onto a path that led to a small clearing. The bandits untied the horses and removed the harnesses. Ty was led at swordpoint to sit next to a wooden stake, and his hands were tied around his back and around the post. He watched as they did the same with Conn. On the far side of the clearing was a small cave entrance, and Ty could see an extinguished fire and very crude bedding. Pots and pans lay all around; this was a typical bandit camp, primitive and very untidy. The bandits heaved the wagon to the opposite side, then removed the cage and sat it next to the cave along with the large sheet. The bandits wasted nothing; the sheet would be perfect for protecting the cave from the winter snow and winds, and the cage would undoubtedly harbour some poor captured trader in the upcoming days.

They lit the fire and examined their newfound loot, and Ty cursed under his breath as he watched Jojo spin *his* swords around. Jojo was a tall, skinny, scruffy bandit with mismatched clothes—all leather, all different colours, and all probably stolen. His black greasy hair was in a ponytail and a near toothless grin completed his grubby face.

"I hope you know what you are doing," Ty shouted across the clearing as a gentle rain started to fall.

"Know what we are doing?" Jojo frowned as he approached the captured thief, pulling his hood up protecting himself from the rain. "Is there something I should know?"

"The man you knocked out," Ty said, nodding at Conn, "is a very important person and will be very displeased when he awakes."

Jojo stared at Ty for a moment, then burst into a fit of laughter, "Oh my, we'd better let him go before he breaks the rope and kicks our butts! Quickly, Grud, cut this man free!" All four bandits laughed.

"Don't say I didn't warn you," Ty replied, shaking his head.

"So why were you in a cage then? Did you piss off this *important person*?" Jojo said, gesturing to Conn.

"You could say that, you could also say that you rescued me from a most probable excruciating death."

"What makes you think you won't be getting one anyway?" Jojo said with a sinister smile.

"Trust me, whatever you have in mind won't be as bad as what *he* had in mind."

"Oh, pray tell, what do you call 'excruciating death'?" the bandit, asked folding his arms.

Ty thought for a second, then remembered Lord Heilo from the town of Wade, and his infamous torture method. "Ever heard of the Sleeping Balrog?"

Jojo glanced over his shoulder at his friends, who shrugged their shoulders. "No, but do tell."

"Well, it's a torture device consisting of a cast iron statue of a balrog lying on its side. There's a hinged door on the back and the victim is forced to get in the iron balrog with the door locked behind him. Wood and coals are lit under the balrog, heating the iron to an unimaginable heat. There are only two holes, positioned to look like the balrog's nostrils, so when the victim screams as he melts to his death it echoes out, giving the impression that the balrog is roaring. Now that's excruciating."

Jojo's face was expressionless as he pondered how terrible a death the Sleeping Balrog would actually be: melted alive in a cast-iron coffin. "That would be bad. Maybe you will die in comfort, then."

"I tried to tell you."

"Very well, let's see what this *important man* has to say. Peahead, bring me the piss bucket."

Peahead disappeared into the cave and reappeared carrying a bucket. He handed it to Jojo, who took a step to the side and emptied the contents of the bucket straight into Conn's face. Some of the urine splattered Ty's leg, and he grimaced at the smell.

Conn tossed his head from side to side. His eyes opened, then squinted shut against the pain and the new light that hit his eyes.

"Wakey wakey," Jojo said, dropping the bucket and squatting down next to the urine-drenched wizard.

"What... where... who..." Conn muttered as his jumbled-up senses slowly came back to him. His eyes focused on Jojo only a few feet from his face, then he looked at his surroundings and saw Ty tied next to him.

"Morning," the thief said with a big grin.

Conn shook his head again and winced at the throbbing in his temple. He lifted his head and stared at Jojo, who lifted one hand and waved it at the wizard, smiling. "Hello." Finally Conn regained the rest of his senses and realised his hands were tied. He pulled with both arms before saying, "Untie me now and I will kill you gently."

"I told you he would be pissed off," Ty mumbled.

Jojo glanced at Ty and then turned back to the wizard. "Promises, promises."

"I am Conn, wizard and advisor to King Moriak. You need to untie me now or I swear I will—"

"Shhh, Conn, wizard to King Moriak," Jojo said, standing up, "and let me speak. I am Jojo, bandit king of the Eastern Mountains, and no one is coming to help you. King Moriak is a cock, and the reason I am here is because of him and his taxes, so *fuck* your king and fuck you, Conn, wizard to the king."

"He has a point," Ty added, smiling at Conn.

"And you can shut the fuck up before I cut out that slimy evil tongue of yours which never stops wagging," the bandit said, drawing his dagger. Ty noticed it was actually *his* dagger, and looked away in disgust. "That's better. Now where was I… ah yes. So where were you taking this toad and why?"

"He is my prisoner and I was taking him back to King Moriak. You don't understand—I need to get—"

"Stop! Please show me some respect here. You are not leaving here, so shut that begging mouth of yours and answer my fucking questions. If I have to tell you once more I'll cut your throat."

Conn stared into the bandit's eyes and nodded.

"Thank you! Now, why are you taking him? What has he done?"

"Killed numerous numbers of the king's guard, killed my nephew—" Conn stared at Ty before turning back to Jojo—"killed the king's pet wyverns, and stole precious gold."

"Really, this little street urchin did all that? I find that very hard to believe."

"Well, not entirely on his own. He had two friends, a ranger named Kern and a dwarf called Galandrik; between the three of them, they did all that."

"Kern the giant slayer? Kern the tamer of dragons?" Jojo asked.

Ty rolled his eyes and shook his head. "You must be kidding me! You have heard of Kern, but not Ty the Rat?"

"No, should I have?"

"*I* killed the giant and *I* tamed the dragon. I even bloody *named* the damned thing!" Ty scolded. All four bandits laughed and Ty could feel his anger brewing, his face reddening.

Conn smiled at Ty and said, "Morning."

"Fuck you," Ty said turning away, filled with anger.

"So where are the others now, his two companions?" the bandit asked.

"Dead. When I left them, Kern was about to be beheaded."

"Left where?"

Conn sighed at all the questions. "In the Midas Hills. We caught up with them there and had a battle with his party plus some local hillmen."

"All those against you?"

"No. I had Gorgon and his Black Guard."

Jojo's eyes widened. "The Gorgon?"

"Yes, *the* Gorgon."

"Gorgon—*the Beast from the East*—that Gorgon?"

"Is there another? Yes! That Gorgon!"

"Well, lads," Jojo said to his friends, "we are in good company. Kern the dragon slayer and Gorgon are all part of the daily lives of these two. I think that *dud* has just turned into a haul."

"So now that you know who we are, are you going to let us go?" Conn asked.

"Oh no, wizard, on the contrary. If you want to make it back to your precious King Moriak with your little prisoner, he will have to pay—and pay handsomely indeed," Jojo smiled.

"We don't have time for this!" Conn raged.

"He will have to make time, if he wants his wizard Conn back," Jojo said, returning to the others. The bandits sat around their newly-lit fire discussing their plans for Conn and Ty.

"Well, that went well," Ty said quietly.

"I can't believe this shit. And where the hell is that weasel Bok?"

"I don't know, but I never saw his body. He probably ran like the wind. You just can't trust these thieves, you know." Ty smiled.

"We are as good as dead."

"Nonsense. I'm sure the king will pay for you and the herbs."

"How long will that take, to get a message there and back? And then we have to make the journey with the herbs. If the king dies, I die. I cannot win."

"I have a question for you. When you told him about me, you said something about me killing your nephew?"

"You remember your guide Solomon? Well, he was my sister's son. I vowed to kill you for her, so even if we both die in this camp, I'll have kept my promise."

"But I never killed him! After he knocked me out I would have liked to, but sorry, wizard—it wasn't me."

"Rubbish! Bok told me it was you."

"Bok told you I killed him? That lying piece of shit!"

"Explain then, how did he die?"

"I don't know. Sol and I got 'the king's gold' from the orc temple and escaped. We hid in a cave and he explained to me about the eggs. I told him I was going to return them to their mother and he agreed—"

"Agreed? Now I know you are lying, because he sent a paperfinch when he was on his way back to me, telling me he had the *gold* and that you were dead."

"Let me finish! He agreed and I foolishly believed him, then when I had my back turned he rendered me unconscious and fled. He even took my cloak."

"I'm lost. But you had the chests; you returned them. If he had fled, how did you get them back?"

"He left with the chests—and left me with a lump the size of an egg on the back of my head, I didn't honestly think I would see the chests again. So I went on to rescue Kern and Galandrik. Long story short, when we got to Forkvain, I spotted Bok in a shop with the chests. It nearly killed me getting them back."

"This is too confusing. Where did Bok come into all this?"

"Bok and I were in the same guild years ago, and I bumped into him in Raith—actually just after we took your quest to find 'the king's gold'—which wasn't even gold. *And* there was no one thousand gold reward!"

"Get on with it."

"Well, in the Orc's Armpit we had a little altercation and he ended up getting arrested because of me. I think he followed me, trying to get revenge. I think he still is."

"So if he was following you, how the hell did he end up with the chests?"

"No idea, but that is the truth. Whether you believe me or not, that is exactly what happened."

"Hang on—you said Solomon stole your cloak?"

"Yes, after he knocked me out he—"

"That's it!" Conn interrupted.

"What's it?"

"Bok was chasing you, right? He must have seen Solomon wearing your cloak and—"

"He thought Solomon was me, that mangy dog!"

"How could I have not seen through his lies? Damn that thieving pig!"

"It all makes sense now. So where does that leave you and me?"

Conn looked at the floor, deep in thought. "I don't know that this has changed things."

"All I am guilty of is returning the eggs to their mother, where you stole them from in the first place."

"I know, I know, but the king won't see it like that."

"I got the damn herbs that *might* save his life," Ty said, trying not to raise his voice too much.

"That is your only hope. If the king lives, I can maybe explain how you got the herbs and saved his life. He might just let you off the hook. But if he dies and his son gets the throne, we are both dead. Remember, you killed his men and one of his wyverns."

"Well, actually I killed both wyverns."

"Both?"

"Yes, the second one attacked us as we travelled over the Eastern Mountains."

"Attacked you over the Eastern Mountains?"

"Yes—nearly did us, too. Plus Lord Heilo tried to get two guards on board to kill us."

"Kill you? He was instructed to help you!"

"He thought he had a claim to the throne if the king died. He didn't want the king healed."

Conn shook his head in disbelief. "I'm sure that tale is for another day. I have so many questions, but for now, how are we going to escape?"

"How are *we?* You're the wizard! Magic yourself out!"

"I'm not a self-prod wizard. I need my staff, spell book, etc."

"Self-prod wizard?"

"Yes, yes—a self-producing magic supply, using mana. I can't do this; I can't produce mana. I need ingredients like herbs or armour sets that hold the mana, or the spell book. Anyway, you're the thief—I thought this sort of situation would be easy for you."

"Let me think," Ty said, looking around.

"You survived two wyverns and numerous battles against my armies, but four bandits have you done? Maybe I should have hired them to kill you," Conn sniggered.

"Maybe you should have."

"Damn these ropes," Conn said, struggling.

"I've got it. When it gets darker, I will kick my boot off. Inside is my pouch of thieves' tools. I will kick them to you, and try and turn around this post. Then when I am facing away from you, you will have to try and kick them towards my hands. Once I can reach the pouch, I can take out the file and go to work on my ropes."

"That simple, eh?"

"Life is as simple as you make it, my friend."

"Tell that to Solomon."

"I liked Solomon. Maybe one day I will tell you of his courage and the adventure we went on."

"Don't pretend he was your best mate. You hardly knew the boy."

"Listen, you said he told you my party and I were dead."

"He did indeed."

"Why do you think he did that?"

"No idea."

"It was because we were friends and he didn't want any harm to come to us. We went through a lot."

Conn thought about Ty's words. "Maybe. I guess we will never know."

"Maybe we will see him sooner than you think."

"That's very possible," Conn answered, then, "what in Hades is that awful smell?"

"You don't want to know," Ty smiled.

Chapter Thirty-Two
All in a Day's Work

Kern looked out the hut door and watched as the Midas Hills children ran around in play. The boys fought with wooden sticks as the girls picked flowers and skipped happily, without a care in the world. How different things would have been if he had been born a farmer, his only worry was making sure the potatoes got harvested on time! He could be married with a couple of kids, coming home to a warm pot of stew in the winter, not having to think of where the next coin was coming from.

He pondered how close he had come, on occasion, to taking drastic action for food. There had been times when he and Ty had had nothing, had contemplated all sorts of acts just to get one meal. Things had always worked out though—they'd always got something, usually after Ty disappeared and reappeared with a few coins that he had 'won at cards' or in a 'dice game.' Kern knew they'd been stolen, that Ty had robbed some unsuspecting person in the inn or market place, but had usually been too hungry to care. The thief had hardly ever told him the truth, as if he would have been shocked at the dreadful deed, but what did he expect a thief to do? Go work for the money? No, he knew exactly who Ty the Rat Quickpick was and what he did.

His mind drifted to thoughts of where his companion could possibly be now, and he shuddered to think of the horrors that could be awaiting him. *He will turn up. He always turns up, like a bad penny.*

His attention turned to his faithful friend Galandrik walking towards him, still not wearing armour and not limping half as badly as he did even with a stick. Even though they hadn't been friends for many moons, Kern felt like he had known the dwarf all his life, and loved him like a brother.

"All right, lad?" Galandrik asked as he entered the hut.

Kern smiled at his abruptness. *Same old dwarf.* "I'm fine. Any news?" he answered.

"Nothing. Lan'sukra sent men out, but there's no sign of anybody."

"They can't just disappear," Kern replied, raised his arm in its sling as high as he could before wincing.

"I know. We will find him, don't worry."

"I'm not worried, Gal, but it's been three days since they left. They could be nearly back to the king by now. He could have been hung, drawn, and quartered already."

"This is Ty we are talking about, lad. Knowing him, he has irritated them so much they will make his pain last a lot longer than that."

"I don't know if I hope you are right or not."

"Trust me—and you know him a lot better than I do. No prison can hold him and all that."

Kern tried to force a smile. "I guess you're right. So how long until we leave here? We can't sit and sulk forever."

"I love your enthusiasm, but just three days ago you were pinned to a tree and Gorgon nearly cut my leg off. Not to mention that you're blind in one eye."

"Oh yeah. We need to visit Veloin in Tonilla and then head to the Bracon Ash Dungeon anyway. I can see all right, to be honest," the ranger said, removing the eye patch.

Galandrik could see the nasty scar going straight up across his eye. "Put the patch on the other eye."

"Don't be absurd, I can see you fine."

"Do it then," Galandrik ordered.

Kern covered his good eye with the patch. "I can still see you fine!" he said, pointing directly at the dwarf.

"Catch, then," Galandrik said, flipping a silver coin into the air. Kern grabbed wildly, but was nowhere near it.

"Damn it! All right, so it's slightly blurry, but it'll be fine," Kern ranted as he switched the patch to his bad eye.

"I am just saying, Kern, you can't do everything. You're not invincible. None of us are."

"I know. Sorry, but the eye will have to wait. We need to go and we need to go soon—to find Ty."

"It's not the eye I am concerned about; you can't even fire an arrow. It's going to be a good couple of days, maybe a week."

"You're talking shit, man—a week? We don't have a week."

"I'm telling you we need to—"

"And I'm telling you, dwarf, I will leave this place in the next few days with or without you," Kern said, turning from his friend and looking out the doorway.

Galandrik sighed. "Have it your way, you know best," he answered as he left the hut and hobbled off through the gardens.

"And send Lan'esra to me!" Kern shouted. Galandrik waved a hand without turning. "Can't fire a bow, who is he kidding," Kern muttered and picked up his bow from where it leaned against the wall. "We shall see who can't fire a bow!" He laid the longbow on the bed and grimaced as he gently eased his left arm from its sling. Turning his body to aid his arm, he picked up the bow. He shut his eyes and began to stretch his arm out. The pain shot down his arm and into his fingertips, but he didn't stop. Through gritted teeth and closed eyes, he kept going as the pain grew and grew. His arm had begun to shake, but still wasn't straightened out, when Lan'esra entered the hut.

"What the hell are you doing, you bloody fool?" she yelled from the doorway. Kern let go of the bow; it rattled as it hit the floor. He sat back onto the bed holding his left arm against his chest, his face contorted with pain as he rolled onto his side. "You had Gorgon's dagger pierce through your shoulder and stick you to a tree, remember?"

"Not really," he replied.

"Well, I do! You were minutes from death!"

"Like I was with the wyvern… twice; like I was with the elemental… twice; like I was with the giant, like I—"

"Enough of all that hero shit with me. What do you want, a medal? You need to stop believing your own hype. Galandrik is right—you are not invincible."

Kern rolled over onto his back. "I see he has been bumping his gums, telling you I need a week's rest, has he?"

She shut her eyes in disbelief, then stared down at the injured ranger lying on the bed. "He mentioned something, yes. Yes, because he cares! Like I do. You will not be leaving these hills until you can fire that bow and Galandrik can walk, even if I have to cage you," she said as calmly as she could.

"Listen, Lan'esra, Ty is my friend. He needs my help and I would rather die trying than not try at all."

"Try is all you *could* do, Kern. You wouldn't make it through the Double Dikes path; the bandits would eat you for breakfast. You couldn't even defend yourself from me, let alone hardened criminals."

"Oh, I'm sick of all this bullshit! Bring me my armour!" Kern said, sitting up from the bed.

"Fine, if you want to go, go! The armour is there—you get it. I'm not your slave. There are also a few bits you had left in your backpack."

"Thanks. That's all I wanted to hear," Kern said, striding over to his equipment and picking up his leggings.

"Your horse is stabled around the back of this hut. You'll have to saddle it up."

"No problem," Kern said as he fumbled with his leggings, trying to hold them with one hand.

"There is a fine line—"

"Between bravery and stupidity. Save the quotes for your farmers, I've heard them all before," Kern said as he slipped his right leg into the leggings. With a tug and a hop he tried to pull them up, but his foot was caught halfway down the leggings and he tumbled over, only just letting go of them before he crashed onto the floor, protecting his shoulder with his good hand. "Damn you!"

"Kern!" Lan'esra shouted, and helped him to his feet. He never said a word through the embarrassment, just sat on the bed with his head in his hand. She sat next to him and placed her arm around his shoulder.

Then Kern said, with a level of emotion she hadn't heard from him before, "I can't see out of one eye or fire an arrow… I can't even get my fucking leggings on." He shook his head and even managed a small smile at the thought. "Kern the Giant Slayer—ha! More like Kern the Useless!"

"You're being too hard on yourself. You need to heal. Think what you have been through."

"That won't help Ty."

"If you left now, you would die before you even reached him. This is Ty we are talking about—let him fend for himself for a week. You get healed, *then* go steaming into the king's castle and rescue him," she said with a smile.

Kern smiled back. "The trouble is I know you are right. I knew Galandrik was right earlier on, and I even know you are both only doing this because you care—but I can't just sit here and do nothing."

"You can and you will. Remember where I met Ty? We were tied up, captured by the spider guild, we were thrown in that giant spider's liar, it was terrifying. He fought it off with me, a pathetic, scared little girl, in tow, and with only a leg bone as a weapon!"

Kern forced a chuckle at that picture. "If he can do that, then he will be all right." He turned and looked deep into her eyes. "Thank you, Lan'esra, you are so right."

She stared back, holding his gaze for that second in time. "I know I am," she said, and blushed.

Kern studied her face for a few seconds. "I think you—"

"Right, lad, you up for a visitor or shall I leave you two alone?" Galandrik said, interrupting them from the doorway. Lan'esra quickly pulled her arm away, like a schoolgirl caught kissing her boyfriend.

Kern eased himself up. "Of course, good friend. Who is it?"

"I think you'll be surprised," Galandrik said, lifting the leather sheet that hung down and covered the door.

A tall elven man ducked under the sheet and stood up in the hut. His long green cloak hung just above the floor and matched his hardened leather armour perfectly; his boots and belt were black leather and shone like they had been waxed only minutes before. His blonde hair hung down to his shoulders and his handsome face wore a grin from ear to ear.

Kern studied the man for a second, then jokingly lifted his patch. "Well, I'll be! That *is* a blast from the past!"

"Is that it? Not even a handshake for an old friend?" the elven man asked. Kern stepped forward and they gripped forearms, and he said, "It's good to see you, Kern Ocarn."

"It's even better to see you, Lord Jarrow."

"Don't start with all that 'lord' rubbish!" Jarrow said, releasing his grip. "You look like you have been stampeded by a group of mountain trolls. What happened?"

"Where do I start?"

"So you are going to ignore me then?" Lan'esra said, with her hands on her hips.

Kern spun his head round. "Oh, I'm sorry—how rude of me! Jarrow, this is—"

"Not you, you fool," she said cutting him off.

"Sorry, Esra. Come here," Jarrow said, opening his arms.

Lan'esra hugged the elf. "Good to see you, Jarrow."

"Likewise. It's been ages."

"Too long." She let go of him, but held on to his hands. "I will go prepare for a dinner—father will be pleased to see you."

"I'm not too sure about that—the price of gold has dropped," he said with a smile.

"We shall see. I will send someone to bring you all when it's ready," she said before leaving the hut.

"I take it you know her, then?" Galandrik laughed.

"Never seen her before," Jarrow answered with a wink. "Anyway, you lot have been making some big noises throughout Bodisha."

"Big noises?" Kern asked.

"Kern the dragon tamer, Kern the giant slayer—I even heard a song that you fought off three wyverns while flying over the Eastern Mountains! You are becoming quite a name, my friend. What's with the eye patch?"

"Oh, an earth elemental tried to remove it. But those stories—it's all nonsense, just bar gossip and storytelling. Any little tale gets made into a song and dance. You know how it goes… *Lord* Jarrow."

"Yes, I do, but there is never any smoke without fire, and in your case it's like a forest blaze. You see, you say 'earth elemental' like it's just in a day's work. You wait; before you know it, it'll be 'Kern the elemental crusher'!"

"Whatever. We don't go looking for trouble you know."

"Ah, but trouble only sticks to those who like its company. Speaking of trouble, where's Ty? Still hiding from the town guards?"

There was a pause before Galandrik answered, "Lost. We think he has been taken to King Moriak."

"Taken to the king! Why? What's he done?"

"Nothing. It's a long story," Kern said sadly.

"Give me the short version, then. I am all ears."

"When we left you, we eventually got the dragon eggs to their mother—Shalamia—then we went to Tonilla, thinking it was all over. But a few weeks later we get a message saying the dragon babies had been captured *again*, along with my father."

"But why take your father? This is awfully confusing," Jarrow said, scratching his head.

"It gets better. They trick me into thinking my father is caught, but it's an illusion, and in exchange for his release, we needed to obtain some herbs from far and wide around Bodisha."

"Herbs? The king must have a hundred farmers! Why ask you?"

"I'm getting to that. Some of the herbs grow in dark and wonderful places, so they needed adventurers to seek them, not farmers."

"I see. But what for?"

"The king is ill, and they need them to heal his sickness."

"And in return your father gets released, along with the dragons—I see now. But, don't tell me—they kept the dragons!"

"Oh, no. Ty released the dragons—they even saved my life, just before Gorgon was about to—"

"Wait up—*the* Gorgon?"

"Yes, Gorgon the beast."

"Well, stone me! You must have really upset the apple cart this time."

"As I was saying, just before he was going to cut my head off, the dragons flew down and set him on fire. He ended up at the bottom of the hill smouldering. The trouble is, no one thought to go down and stick a blade through the back of his neck!"

"What do you mean?"

"Well, his body disappeared, and the two men who went to clear the mess up can now see behind them."

"Oh dear. You've flicked a very nasty ants' nest there, my friend."

"I know—and while Galandrik, some townsfolk, and I were fighting Gorgon, Ty went to free the dragons. Unfortunately he had to deal with Conn and Bok."

"Conn is the king's wizard, right? And Bok… where do I know his name from?" Jarrow squinted and gazed at Galandrik. "What is it?"

"Sorry, Jarrow. Bok was the cretin who killed Ltyh."

"That sack of shit," Jarrow cursed.

"And that very same sack of shit has joined forces with Conn to help kill Ty," the dwarf explained.

"He's still about then, sneaky dog," Jarrow said, shaking his head.

"He even joined *us* once!" Kern said.

"What? Joined you? I don't get it."

"Let's just say his face has changed," Kern laughed. "In a nutshell, that is it, really: We got the herbs, met them here, lost the herbs, released the dragons, had a fight, and lost a rat."

"Speaking of the Rat—remember in my house, when the guards entered looking for him but never found him? And then, when we went into his room, he was lying on the bed all calm, as though nothing had happened?"

"Yes, come to think of it, I do. We wondered how the guards missed him."

"I know how he did it. After you left, all the stories came out about what happened in the alley with him and Xioven."

Kern and Galandrik exchanged a glance. "And…?"

"He used an invisibility ring!"

"Invisibility ring?!" Kern and Galandrik said simultaneously. "Where did he ever get the gold for that?" Kern added.

"He didn't. He stole it; he knew the shopkeeper had it in his pocket because he had enquired about buying it moments earlier, before he ambushed him in the alley."

"I wonder how many other times he got out of trouble with it and never told us, making us think he was all mysterious," Galandrik said.

"Probably plenty. He's one strange halfling. You'd think he'd tell me, his oldest friend!" Kern said.

"The guys in the alley who saw him robbing Xioven said that when they spooked him, he stood up and shouted 'Be gone!' just before he disappeared."

"That is him all over. On death's door, but dramatic to the last second," Kern said, shaking his head.

"So are you heading to hold council with the king about your friend?"

Kern and Galandrik looked at each other for a second before bursting into a fit of laughter.

"Oh, stop! My arm hurts," Kern said though the hysterics.

"Hold council with a king!" Galandrik added, as they continued to laugh.

Jarrow folded his arms and looked to the ceiling, waiting for the laughter to finish. Finally it did, and Kern wiped the tears from his cheek.

"And why is that such a stupid idea?" Jarrow asked.

"We don't hold councils with kings! *You* do that—we don't!" Kern said, still smiling at the thought.

"Well, I think you should do. Remember, news travels fast and you aren't just Kern Ocarn—you are Kern the dragon tamer, slayer of giants, sky-fighter of wyverns. Your reputation will follow you forever now, and anyone with those titles can call council with a king—*especially* after obtaining his medicinal herbs and saving his life."

"You think, eh, lad?"

"Galandrik, I know. Reputation goes a long way. If two you walk into that palace with your balls on your shoulder, bold as brass, they will listen to *Kern the Giant Slayer* and *Galandrik the Great!*"

"I like 'the Great,'" the dwarf smiled.

"I'm telling you, it's true."

"You flatter me, but there is a slight problem with all of this," the ranger noted.

"Go on, knock me down in flames," Jarrow said, sitting down.

"On route to where we are at present, I have helped in the killing of two of the king's wyverns and about forty of his men, returned his sacrificial dragons to their mother, and burnt the face of his top warrior. That isn't the best audition to get an invite."

"Hmmm. I disagree; anyone who can do all that and then have the guts to walk into his backyard shows strength."

"Shows stupid, you mean?" Kern answered.

"Let's talk about this later. I'm starving, where is that dinner call?" the dwarf said, looking out of the door.

Kern and Jarrow both chuckled. "Yes, he is right. Let's talk about your next move over a nice glass of Verona wine and a smoke of Vinedale tobacco later tonight. For now, you can tell me some more of your stories, especially the sky battle with three wyverns!"

They both stood up and Jarrow placed his arm around Kern's shoulder.

"Three wyverns, you say?" Kern replied.

"Why, were there more?" Jarrow laughed. "Come on. I'll take you to the great hut."

Chapter Thirty-Three
Rabbit Anyone?

Queen Cherian stood next to her sick husband. His face was a deathly grey and his breathing was more of a growl. Sweat beads formed and the maid gently dabbed his head, but no sooner had she dried one than another formed.

"He looks worse than ever, Murtal. Do you think he will make it?"

"I don't know, my queen. It just can't be predicted. He has a strong heart, but we desperately need those herbs."

"He is going grey, Murtal. Is that normal?"

"It's the lack of minerals and all the natural goodness he isn't getting. That is why he is rapidly losing weight. The injections we are giving him keep him alive, but his life is draining."

"Give him a double dose!"

"It doesn't work like that, I am afraid. One more might do more damage than good. His body is beginning to reject it."

"Damn! Have we heard from Conn recently?"

"No, I am afraid not. His messages have dried up—hopefully because he is racing to get here. Or maybe he has used all the paperfinches?"

The queen turned to the guard on the door. "Go fetch Reddoc and bring him here," she ordered.

"Yes, Queen Cherian," he said, and with a click of a heel he disappeared.

"What are you thinking?" Murtal asked.

"I will see if Reddoc can contact Conn. We can't wait—we need to know."

"I couldn't agree more. Very wise, my queen," Murtal snivelled.

The door opened and Reddoc strode into the room. He was a tall robed man with a completely bald head, not a hair in sight—not even at nose or eyebrow. A brown belt was fitted around his waist with a small leather sack hanging from it, and sandals completed his look—more of a monk than a magic user. His skinny face, pointy nose, and pointy front teeth made him look like a rat—but no one had ever said it to his face.

Reddoc was the second-highest mage in the king's council, behind Conn. Some people thought he was a better mage than Conn, but Moriak favoured his longtime friend.

"Yes, Queen Cherian? You called for me. Please tell me, what can I do?" Reddoc said, bowing.

"Can you contact Conn? Yes or no—don't give me any of your mage rubbish. Yes or no?" she said, folding her arms.

"Well, if Conn has—"

"By the heavens above! Murtal, did *you* understand what I said?"

"Yes, my Queen, 'yes or no.'"

"Right, I will ask you one more time: Can you contact Conn, *yes or no*?"

Reddoc knew that the only possible chance he had to succeed was if Conn had created level seven paperfinches, a truly difficult creation spell that took years. Those finches would be extremely fast, and could fly to the maker and back again in one flight. Some mages had to create hundreds and hundreds of level six paperfinches for practice before being able to do level seven. The process often took several years, so many mages never managed it—level six were good enough, though they were not as fast and, although they flew straight to the creator, would never return to the sender.

Reddoc hoped to the gods that Conn had some made up. "Yes, my queen." He swallowed hard.

"See? That wasn't so hard, was it?" She rolled her eyes. "Right—now, is it by paperfinch?"

"Yes, my queen. You see, if you send—"

"Stop! I am really not interested in magic paper birds," she said condescendingly. "Do what it is you have to do, and ask Conn what's going on, where he is, and when he will be back with the damn herbs."

Reddoc bowed. "Yes, Queen Cherian."

"Then when he replies, come and tell me at once what was said. Do you understand?"

"Yes, Queen Cherian."

"Conn's study will be guarded. If they refuse you entry, tell them to come to me at once."

"Yes, Queen Cherian."

"And stop bloody saying 'Yes, Queen Cherian'!"

"Yes—" Reddoc barely managed to stop himself from saying it.

"Well? Don't just stand there like a wet whelk, go!"

"Yes, my queen," he replied as he scuttled out of the king's chamber.

Queen Cherian shook her head at Murtal. "Why do wizards and magic users always want to explain magic to everyone? As if anyone is interested."

"I don't know, my queen. Strange breed they are, indeed."

*

Reddoc hurried himself down the corridor towards Conn's chamber. *I'll give you 'yes, Queen Cherian,' you moody old cow! I'd like to punch you right in the throat—that'll stop your wicked tongue from scolding me every time you see me, just because Conn is the king's favourite, you horrible bitch.*

Reddoc reached the two guards outside Conn's study. "By orders of Queen Cherian, I need to enter Conn's study. It is a matter of grave importance."

The guards looked at each other. "When did she say this?" one of them asked.

"What does it matter? About three minutes ago, the bloody time it has taken me to get from the king's chamber."

"We are under strict orders not to—"

"Fine! Go ask her. And she's in a foul mood, so good luck." The guards looked at each other again. "Go on then, ask her!" Reddoc added.

One of the guards pulled a set of keys from his pocket and opened the door, saying, "I'll go in with you."

"Be my guest," Reddoc said, walking into the study. "Right—now, where would you put them?" he murmured as he looked around the room.

Papers and scrolls were scattered all over Conn's desk and table, and bookshelves and chests lined the walls. Reddoc searched for over an hour until he eventually lifted a velvet pouch from a small wooden box that sat on a shelf behind Conn's desk. He opened it carefully.

"You little beauty!" he said aloud, wiping the sweat from his brow. "Now what was it she wanted? Ah yes, I remember." Reddoc pushed the window open slightly and cupped the piece of paper in his hands, then whispered, *"Where are you? What's happening and how long will you be with the herbs? The king's health is fading fast."* Then he murmured, "Fly to Conn as quickly as possible, little one," and opened his hands. The finch sprung to life, flapping its wings as it shot from his hands and out of the window.

*

Jojo stared at his two captives, their heads both bowed and hanging down. He kicked Conn's foot. "Wake up!" he shouted. Conn opened his eyes and squinted in the early moonlight. Ty did the same. "I thought gobshite here was too quiet," Jojo finished.

"Ah, you've changed your mind and you are going to let us go?" Ty said, yawning.

"Hmmm, no, we thought we would roast you on a spit and have halfling pie," Jojo said, squatting down.

"Even you aren't that hungry," Conn said.

"What are you trying to say?" Ty said, glaring at the wizard.

"Nothing, but I wouldn't have thought that eating—"

"Shut the fuck up. It never stops. We are going to feed you, if you keep your mouth shut," the bandit said to Ty.

"How can I eat with my mouth shut?" Ty asked.

Jojo leaned forward and backhanded him across the face, twisting Ty's head. A trickle of blood dribbled from his nose as he spat out a mouthful of red.

"You did deserve that," Conn said, and Jojo did the same to him. Conn's head also twisted with the blow, but there was no blood. He glared at Jojo as his cheek reddened, and the bandit felt strangely scared. He could see anger in the wizard's deathly black eyes.

"Right. The next time you speak, I will take my sword and cut your tongue out. If you think I am kidding, try me," he said, looking first at Conn, then Ty. "Good. Now we know where we stand, I will continue. We are going to feed you, and this is how it works. We are going to release you one by one and take you over to the cage—you can eat in there. Without speaking, remember. You aren't going to try and kill each other, are you?" Both Ty and Conn shook their heads, and Jojo said, "Good boys."

One at a time, they were led at sword-point into the cage. Conn felt the lump on the side of his head; it was as big as a boiled egg. The door to the cage faced the cave entrance, with a rusty old lock keeping it shut.

All four bandits sat around the fire eating what looked like rabbit and boiled vegetables; they swigged wine from the bottle, and crammed meat and carrots into their mouths with their hands. Rabbit grease and red wine stained their chins and tunics.

"What about them?" Calin asked.

"Fuck me sideways, I forget our guests. How damn rude," Jojo answered. He ripped the rabbit in half and threw the back half it into the cage; it slammed against the bars and fell to the ground in the dirt. Grease splatted both prisoners, and Conn wiped some from his cheeks.

"Animals," he muttered under his breath.

"Veg?" Jojo asked. Conn just shook his head. "Didn't think so," the bandit leader said, and all four bandits laughed and slapped palms.

Ty picked some rabbit meat off the side that had landed upwards, out of the dirt, and began to eat. He handed a piece to Conn, who simply shook his head.

"You need to eat, keep your strength up," Ty whispered, pushing the meat closer to Conn.

Conn didn't want to eat rancid rabbit off a dirty cave floor any more than he wanted to fly, but he knew Ty was right. He took the meat and, with a nod, placed it into his mouth. To his surprise, it wasn't all that bad.

Ty ripped some leg meat off and sat next to the wizard. He knew if he could get Conn on his side, everything would be fine—no more quests for the king or being chased by his men. Peace at last.

"Did I tell you how Solomon saved my life?" Ty asked.

"Of course you haven't. We've barely spoken a dozen words to each other," Conn said angrily.

"We had found the chests in the top of the orc tower and realised there was no way out. Orcs were coming up in lifts and we were trapped—one window and a hundred-foot drop was our only option. He gave me a featherfall potion and we both escaped."

"He was a good kid."

"Yes, he was. He didn't have to rescue me. He could have left me there, but he didn't. Doesn't that tell you anything?"

Conn thought for a second. "Like I said, he was a good kid."

"No, he was our friend. I told you before, the only thing I am guilty of is wanting to do the right thing and return the eggs to their owner. Everything that happened—the people who were killed only died because they were trying to kill us. It was a matter of survival."

"A lot of good men died."

"Yes, it is unfortunate, but look at it from our point of view! There was no reward for us, no homecoming parade. Solomon did *exactly* what you told him to do: Get the eggs in his hands, then run, taking them back to you as fast as possible and leaving us behind. That's what he did."

"Pity he never made it. We wouldn't be here now."

"Maybe if you had told us what we were really doing, we could have helped him bring the eggs back to you, and protected him on the way."

These words devastated Conn. *Was it my fault Solomon died?* He tried to shake the blame from his head. "That's gone. Let's talk about the future. How are we getting out of here?"

"Well, I have been thinking about that." Ty opened his hand, showing Conn the small file. "If they move us back over there, I will get through the ropes with this—*eventually*."

"And if they leave us in here?"

Jojo threw a stone at the cage, and it clattered against the bars. "Shut it, you two! Quiet!"

They stopped talking until the bandits were deep in conversation again.

"We could start fighting in here," Ty whispered.

"What? Why would we?" Conn questioned.

"Well, they won't want us dead, so they would have to open the cage to split us up. When they do, we attack them."

"All those swords against us—hardly a fair fight, is it?"

"I see your point. Should we wait until there are more of them?" Ty joked.

"You know what I mean!" Conn hissed quietly.

"That's a good point. Where is the other one?" Ty asked. "I think they called him Peahead."

"Oh yes. I didn't notice he had gone. Well, better odds for us then."

"True. I guess we will have to wait and see what they do with us."

Jojo picked up a pot from the fire and looked through the bars of the cage, "Here you go. We are full now so you might as well enjoy what is left," the bandit said, and emptied the contents of the pot in through the top of the cage.

Conn and Ty moved their legs as it splashed onto the ground. The bandits all laughed as Jojo rejoined his friends.

Ty saw a rabbit's head in among the carrots and sweet potato that lay in the dirt in between the bars on the bottom of the cage. "Hungry?"

"Lost my appetite," Conn answered.

"Conn, look! The herbs!" The wizard looked up and saw Grud open the bag of herbs and look inside.

"What are these, Jojo? Can we cook with them?" the bandit asked.

"Let me see," he said, pulling out a small handful of fighort leaf and smelling it. "I don't know, smells like cat piss if you ask me." He threw it onto the floor.

"Damn! If they throw the rest, the king dies… and so do we," Conn said, looking on anxiously.

"Taste it," Jojo said to Grud, holding the bag out.

"No chance. Could be anything. I don't trust wizards. They carry some right shit."

Ty leaned forward and gripped the bars. "It's mine!" he called.

"What are you doing?" Conn whispered.

"Trust me," the thief answered.

Jojo spun round, then got to his feet. He bent down and looked into the cage. "And why would you be carrying herbs around?"

"Because... Poisons! I make poison for my blades."

"Poisons, eh?"

"Yes, I am a keen herbalist."

"Hmm. So why tell us? Why not let us eat it? I think you lie!" Jojo said, as Conn dug a fist into Ty's ribs.

"It wouldn't kill you. I need to mash it up and mix it with others to make it toxic. Besides, if you died, we would have been stuck here. I wouldn't want that, would I?" The thief tried to dig his way out of the verbal hole his was in.

The bandit thought for a second, then threw the sack behind him without looking. It snagged on a branch of an old bush growing above the cave entrance and swung there in the moonlight. "Well, you won't be needing it then, will you?" He smiled and returned to sit down with his friends.

"You fool!" Conn muttered.

"What? He was going to boil, eat, or bin it. At least we know where it is!"

Conn sighed and folded his arms. "Stuck in a cage with Ty the Rat. This time last week, I would have ripped your eyes out of their sockets at the drop of a hat, and now I am relying on you for help. Unbelievable."

"This time last week, I was fighting a fire elemental, killing a wyvern, and nearly drowning just to get those damn herbs for you. *And* this time last week, you didn't know I didn't kill Solomon."

Conn didn't answer; he just sat in silence. But the quiet didn't last long.

Conn leaped against Ty, squashing him against the bars as a vicious mountain dog stuck its head through the bars. Saliva dripped from its razor-sharp teeth as it snarled and snapped at the captured pair.

"Fuck me!" Conn said, pushing away from the beast against the thief.

"Hound! Here!" they heard from behind.

The dog backed off and sat next to Peahead and another large human man. He was dressed not too differently from the others, though he was a much larger man, and two shiny swords hung from his belt. His hair hung down his back, long and matted up. His face was filthy and scarred from years of battle.

"So what do we have here, then?"

"Welcome, Tor," Jojo said, greeting the new addition to the bandit camp.

"So these are the ones Peahead told me about?"

"Yes. The large man is Conn, the king's personal wizard. The other one was his prisoner—apparently he was in Kern the giant slayer's group, that killed some of the king's men. The wizard was taking him back. There was a wagon driver too, but he ran like the wind."

"The name is Ty the Rat," Ty said, pushing Conn off him.

Tor stepped forward and bent down. "So *you* are Ty the Rat?" he asked, looking surprised.

Ty smiled at Conn. "Yes. So you have heard of me, then?"

"Hmm… no," Tor said, shaking his head to a roar of laughter from behind him. Even Conn raised a grin.

Jojo stepped forward. "So, any ideas on how to ransom these two?"

"We will take them up near Raith, and join Frolin's camp. We can hide them there and get a message to the king. If he wants them, he will pay; if not, we introduce them to Marny Four-Fingers. He'll just cut their fingers, toes, and limbs off and send one every day until there is nothing left. They always pay."

"I like it, Tor," Jojo agreed.

"Right. No time like the present! Get them loaded up on the wagon. We leave now; we can make tracks to Raith's wood."

The cage was loaded onto the wagon; Ty and Conn were tied and forced inside at sword point while dodging the hound's snapping jaws. Conn caught one last glance of the hanging bag of herbs before the leather sheet covered them, engulfing them in darkness. The wagon began to move, and they could hear the horses' hooves and the muffled talk from the bandits.

"Well, we are done for," the wizard said.

"When we escape, your best chance is to just disappear."

"Disappear, to where?"

"Use your imagination. If you go back and the king is dead, you *are* done for, and that's the most likely outcome now, with the herbs hanging in that tree."

"This is a shit show. I cannot believe we have ended up like this, captured by bloody bandits."

"We could come clean about the herbs to them?"

"No. I am not putting the king's life in their hands. Common cutthroats."

"It may be the only chance he has."

Conn didn't answer for a few minutes, his mind working overtime going over all the permutations. If they didn't mention the herbs, it would probably be far too late to save the king—and that would be possible only if they paid the ransom anyway. And if the king was already dead, why would they? If they mentioned the herbs, the bandits would hold Moriak's life in their hands, trading it for a bag of gold, which the Queen would surely pay. If they could escape in the next few hours, they could get back to the herbs and still make it to the king, but if they died trying, the king would die. *Damn! What to do?*

"Can you pick this lock?" Conn asked.

"Of course I can. I did it two days ago when you sat up front," Ty answered.

"Yeah, and that did you a world of good, didn't it?"

"I was about to make my escape when the bandits attacked!"

"Of course you were. Well, pick it again and let's see this dramatic escape."

"What do you think I'm doing?"

"Absolutely nothing, from where I am sitting."

"I am filing the rope around my wrist; I should have it through soon."

"Well, do it faster!"

Chapter Thirty-Four
A Touch of Gold

Kern, Galandrik, Jarrow, Migaan, Lan'esra, and Lan'sukra all sat around the large table in the main hut. Used by the hierarchy only for important meetings, the table was now full of meats, pork ribs, hot slices of beef, strips of duck, vegetables, fruit, breads, potatoes, and three bottles of Verona wine supplied by Jarrow.

Lan'sukra stood up to address the table. "May you all feast well and fill your stomachs. The Midas Hills are as much your home as ours! Enjoy."

"I'll drink to that!" Jarrow said, lifting his glass, followed by the others and a chorus of agreement.

"So, Kern, when are you planning on leaving?" Jarrow asked, scooping some potatoes onto his plate. Kern gave Lan'esra a sideways glance, then looked across the table at Galandrik, who was waiting patiently for his answer.

"When I am healed," he finally said, reluctantly.

"Why don't you travel with me? I'm heading that way after I do my trading with Lan'sukra. It'll be more comfy on a cart and we have armed guards with us. You are more than welcome."

Kern looked around the table, but no one seemed to disagree. "Thanks, Jarrow. That is awfully kind of you. How long are you here for?"

"I won't be leaving until mid-afternoon tomorrow—but if Esra promises to make turkey pot pie, it could be the following morning."

Lan'esra laughed at the comment before saying, "Deal!"

Kern knew she'd said yes to keep him there another night. He didn't argue, though; he just smiled at the dwarf and asked, "Are you happy with that, my good friend?"

"Over the moon, lad. I couldn't stay here, I'd get too fat!"

"If Ty were here, he would have definitely said, 'Oops, too late!'"

"Oi! We will have less of your cheek, you!" He grinned. "But yes, you are right—he would have."

"So what are you trading in up here, Jarrow?" Kern said, changing the subject.

Jarrow looked at Lan'sukra and he nodded back. "Gold," the elf answered.

"Gold? You mine for gold here?"

"Yes. I trust you two can keep a secret?" Lan'sukra asked. They both nodded. "We have been trading gold here for years, finest gold in all Bodisha."

"If you have a rich gold supply, why live in… don't take offence, but—huts?"

Lan'sukra laughed. "We have enough gold here to build them out of it! We take what we need from the land and buy limited supplies. We farm all our own food and raise all our own livestock. Sometimes we have floods, or the animals get a disease, or even the odd giant or troll might take a fancy to some pigs or sheep—but we never get greedy or call attention to ourselves. We just restock what is lost and, with the likes of Jarrow there—" Lan'sukra gestured to the elf and got a bow of the head in reply— "we can buy what we need with coins. No one is any the wiser. If we do need anything substantial, like a gift for my daughter's wedding, Jarrow will bring it to us."

"I'm not interested, Father! I told you," she answered, blushing and flashing a cheeky look at Kern.

"I take the gold up north and far away to Raith, where they pay handsomely for it. Everybody is happy."

"See, Galandrik—such a simple system! Why can't we do that? Instead of wyverns, dragons, dungeons, and everything else that wants to kill us!"

"Aye, lad, it seems too good to be true," Galandrik answered, wiping duck grease from his chin.

"It would be far too boring for you, Kern the dragon tamer," Jarrow mocked.

"Do you know what? Galandrik and I were locked up in a cell for a few days after we left your house. The king's guards caught us up and… Well, it's a long story but we lost Ty—and not for the first time. Then when he rescued us, *he* had tamed—well, no, not *tamed* the dragon, but let's just say *raised* it. He was the one who even named it!"

"Maybe so, but history will not be rewritten now. I am afraid those songs will be sung long into the night with your name in them, not his. It's a gift; use it."

"Even so—oh, never mind."

The evening passed pleasantly as they chatted for hours about their adventures: fighting Dago in the Spider Temple, the Dungeon of Dreams, explaining to Lan'sukra what his daughter had been through. Jarrow told of their meeting in the mines under the orc tower, and they drank—they drank a lot.

*

The next day, Kern's arm was healing well. He still couldn't hold it out straight, but he had made a vast improvement. Galandrik's leg was also healing well; the healers in the Midas Hills knew their trade. That night they ate Lan'esra's turkey pot pie and talked of flying on the backs of dragonflies and fighting the giant that made its mark in song.

The following morning, Jarrow's wagon was sitting outside Kern and Galandrik's hut. It was pulled by two horses, with their mounts saddled and tethered behind. Jarrow's horse stood proud behind it, held by the wagon driver, and two mercenaries sat mounted in front, fully and identically dressed in chain mail with bright silver helmets, two long swords hanging down on either side of each man.

"You ready to go, ranger?" Jarrow said, entering the hut.

"Of course. I was born ready."

"What about you, Galandrik? How's the leg?"

"It's good, lad. Still a bit stiff in the mornings, but I'll survive."

"Great news. Trisok, bring the sack," Jarrow shouted. A young man entered the hut with a sack and handed it to Jarrow, who emptied the contents onto the floor. "Not much, but if they fit, have them," he said.

Kern and Galandrik looked at the pile of armour on the floor—nothing magical, but good hardened leather sets. Both sets of armour were light brown and in very good condition.

"Thanks, where did you get this lot?"

"I was going to sell it up in Raith. I have a couple of chests full on the wagon. I went through it earlier and these two sets are probably the only things you'll be able to use."

"We will buy it. How much do you want?"

"Don't be ridiculous, man. I don't want your gold," Jarrow replied, embarrassed.

"I'm going to keep with what I have, lad. It's Horbit's dwarven armour of Heroism, and I got a lass a few huts down to stitch up the rips."

"No worries," Jarrow said. "Take what you need and I will sell the rest."

After Kern and Galandrik were fully dressed, Lan'esra walked in carrying their backpacks. "There isn't a lot of your usual magical stuff," she said, "but they have everything you need—bedding, spare clothes, torches, oil, flint and tinder, dried meats, water, some water-breathing leaves. Your healing balm is in the leather orange sack. Oh, and there is even rope with a small grappling hook."

"Thanks, Lan'esra, that's very kind." Kern smiled.

"Come on, lass, give them here. I will throw them on the wagon."

"I'll come tie them down, you'll never reach," Jarrow laughed as they left the hut.

Lan'esra gripped Kern's good hand. "Please be careful, won't you?"

"I am always careful, you know that."

"And make sure you find me a rat."

"I will, don't worry. I will bring him back for turkey pot pie," Kern said, smiling.

Lan'esra released his hand, pulled her necklace off, and placed it over his head. On the end of the leather strap was what looked like a crystal; it was shaped like a shark's tooth that shone blue, but it appeared to be filled with a blue smoke, twisting and turning inside.

"What is it?" Kern asked, holding it in his palm.

"It was my mother's," Lan'esra said. "She made me wear it when I was a little girl. She always told me if I was in grave danger to just crush it in my hand and I would be fine. Only the wearer can crush it, and it can't be broken accidentally."

"I can't take this," he said.

"You can," she said sternly.

"It was your mother's!"

"Take it!" Lan'esra said, placing her hands on her hips.

"All right," Kern said after a long silence. He tucked it in his tunic and said, "Thank you."

"You are most welcome. I do have a question for you," she said, staring into his eyes.

"Go for it, Lan'esra."

"Well, the other day you were about to say something, but Galandrik came in and stopped you mid-sentence. What was it?"

They held each other's gaze for a few seconds before finally Kern said, "I was going to say, 'I think you—'"

"All loaded and ready, sir!" Jarrow bellowed as he entered the hut.

Lan'esra gently held his face and kissed his cheek. She whispered, "Another time, Kern the dragon slayer, another time." Then she spun on her heel and wrapped her arms around Jarrow's neck.

"Whoa! Easy, you'll do me damage," he mocked.

"Just look after my boys," she said, releasing her grip and wagging a finger at him before leaving the hut.

Kern picked up his longbow and swung his quiver onto his good shoulder. "Let's go."

Kern and Jarrow climbed up onto the wagon and sat next to the driver. "Where's Galandrik?" Kern asked as he looked around.

"I'm here, lad," Kern heard from behind. Twisting round, he saw the dwarf laid out on the back of the wagon, in between boxes and barrels.

"Get comfy, won't you?" the ranger laughed.

"Need to keep my leg straight. Sitting up front will stiffen it right up!"

"Any excuse," Kern said with a laugh, facing the front.

The wagon gently made its way from the village. Lan'sukra, Migaan, and Lan'esra all waved as they left, and the children ran next to the wagon, shouting and screaming, until it was on the outskirts, then turned and ran back.

"How long is it to Raith?" Kern asked the driver.

"Never can tell—five days, seven days. All depends on the weather and bandits. Three years I have been ferrying Mr Jarrow around, and one thing I have learnt is, never expect to be anywhere when you expect to get there."

"Wise words," Kern said, glancing over his shoulder for one last look as he thought of how life might be if he were to stop this and settle down.

"Game of dice?" he said to Jarrow with a sigh.

*

"I think I am halfway through," Ty said, "but I don't think it's wise to cut all the way through the rope. We have been travelling for a few hours now, so we are bound to stop soon—if they see it's nearly through…" He trailed off, trying to wriggle his wrist so the split rope was covered.

"Yes, good idea," Conn agreed. "Can I just ask, do you *like* what you do?"

"Like what do I do?"

"Well, you know, having to steal to eat, picking honest people's pockets."

Ty laughed. "I don't steal to eat—well, not all the time. It's just something to fall back on. Mostly we quest to dungeons and loot monsters' horded treasure."

Conn stared at the thief and raised his eyebrows.

"All right, maybe Heldar's tip-offs haven't been the best so far but—"

"Wait, who is Heldar?" Conn frowned.

"He's a local gossip, knows where some good loot is. But the last tip he gave us was the goblin cave, and that was a disaster. I thought Kern was going to throw me out of the end of the tunnel, then loads of goblins turned up so we had to jump and then—" Ty fell silent as he noticed that Conn was shaking his head, completely lost at his story.

"Goblins and jumping out of tunnels. Sounds like a fun night out!" Conn laughed.

"I wouldn't say 'fun.' The trees broke our fall but I still nearly broke my back."

"So you enjoy the thrill of the ride, then, is that it?"

"I think it's just looking for that big hit—that super loot, the moment when you can stop and think, '*yes!* I made it.'"

Conn was about to reply when a paperfinch flew up underneath the leather cover and sat on his shoulder.

"*Where are you? What's happening and how long will you be with the herbs? The king's health is fading fast.*" Conn nodded, and the finch flew down and nestled behind a bar of the cage, out of sight.

"The king's health is fading. Damn! They want answers. They want to know where we are and how long we will be."

"Don't tell them anything," Ty shrugged.

"I must or they could give up hope. I must tell them we are on our way back and will be three days."

"Three days? We will be lucky if we make it to Raith by then!"

"No, you fool, we'll have escaped by then!"

Ty's grin gradually appeared and he nodded. "I see. Make sure you tell them Ty the Rat is helping you!"

"Or should I tell them to send an army to destroy these kidnapping brigands?"

"That could take a while to assemble, get to us, get back to the herbs, *then* back to the king. Better off sticking with Plan A."

"Yes, you are right."

"And make sure you tell them about me."

"Or I could get Reddoc to portal down—no, I don't know where we are."

"Me, tell them about me!"

Conn shook his head and looked at Ty as if he had forgotten he was there. "Sorry, what?"

"Me! Make sure you tell them!"

"Tell them what?"

Ty blew his cheeks out. "Tell them I am not the murdering ogre people think I am, and I got the herbs!"

"Yes, yes…" Conn answered, staring at nothing, deep in thought.

"Go on then," Ty said. Conn still stared blankly at the floor, so Ty kicked his foot. "Oi!"

"What now?"

"Send it back, then!"

"I need to cup it in my hands! Why did you think I hid it?"

"I thought you were just thinking about what to say."

"No, I need to hold it in my hands," Conn explained.

Just then the wagon rolled to a stop. Then pulled off again, slowly sloped upwards, then levelled out and finally stopped again. The prisoners were untied, but the cage stayed on the wagon. They could smell the food being cooked and they both felt famished.

"I hope it isn't rabbit and dirt again," Ty said rubbing his wrists.

"What would you prefer: chicken and grass, or beef and tree bark?" Conn joked.

"I'll take the beef and bark, please, sir."

It wasn't long before Calin lifted the sheet covering the cage. They noticed that they were in a clearing surrounded by trees, set off from the path that they had come in on. They could see the bandits all sat around a newly-made fire. Food, pots, pans were all being readied.

Finally Calin approached and pushed his hand between the bars to set down two bowls of broth, spilling most as he tipped them to get them through. "There you go, enjoy!" he said, black teeth showing.

"Waiter service has gone downhill, too," Conn said, trying to make light of the situation, as the sheet was pulled back down.

"What about some light!" Ty shouted.

"One more word out of you, and you'll have light between your head and your body!" Jojo shouted.

Ty picked up the pot and pulled out the wooden spoon. "Oh well," he said, sipping, "it's not that bad."

"I'll take your word for it," Conn replied, as the paperfinch flew up and into his hands.

"Remember to tell them about me!"

"I know," Conn growled.

"Just reminding you," Ty added, spooning in a mouthful of broth.

Conn held his cupped hands up to his lips. *"We have the herbs and on our way back. Caught up in something and should be there in four days."* He paused, and Ty kicked his foot. Conn gave a scolding look to the thief and shook his head, but Ty kept pointing to his own chest and mouthing the word *me*. *"I've found out Ty and company are not what they seem, and have helped us no end. I suggest a pardon for their efforts. We will speak more on this when I am back."* Then he whispered, "Fly my baby, fly." The bird shot down and under the bottom edge of the leather sheet, and disappeared.

Conn stared across, and saw the enormous grin on Ty's face. He rolled his eyes and picked up the bowl of broth. *Ty was right, it's not too bad.* Then they both finished off their food and sat listening to the bandits laughing and talking.

"I've been thinking," Conn said some minutes later. "They will never put that rope back on your hands in the exact same position as before. You may not even get that same rope, and you'll have to start all over again," he explained.

Ty felt stupid thinking of what he had said earlier, and couldn't come up with anything to say, so he simply nodded.

Conn continued, "But you will have plenty of time to do it; I can't see us stopping here long."

"No, you are right. I wasn't thinking straight. I'll just have to do it again."

"Yes, indeed. Well, I think I will try to get some sleep. It seems ages since I last slept."

Ty agreed, and each man nestled into a corner of the cage and shut his eyes. Both prisoners nodded off, but for how long couldn't be gauged.

They woke up some time later to the clatter of swords, screams and shouts. The hound was barking.

"What the hell is going on?" Conn shouted, spinning around trying to find a hole in the sheet to see through.

Ty was doing the same, and answered, "No idea! I think we are being attacked or attacking."

The sounds of fighting continued, accompanied by the clash of blades and the screams of men, until finally the only sound was the dog's barking—then it, too, gave a cry and a whimper and fell silent.

It was dead quiet, literally.

"Can you see anything?" Ty asked.

"I can't see shit!"

"What the hell is happening?" Ty shouted.

"Shhh! Orcs could have taken the bandits on!"

Ty winced and nodded in agreement.

"Just be quiet," Conn whispered, holding one finger up to his mouth. There was light on the floor of their cage, coming in under the bottom of the sheet, and the two men watched as a shadow moved slowly closer until it stopped adjacent with them.

Then the cover of their cage was ripped upwards and the sunlight shone in, nearly blinding them. A large figure stood in front of them, and they shielded their eyes from the sun behind it. Once they regained their day vision and took in the sight before them, they stared at each other in complete shock.

Chapter Thirty-Five
Don't Lose Your Head

Jarrow's wagon rolled on and up through the path on its uneventful journey towards the Double Dikes exit on the western side of the Eastern Mountains. Every now and again, Kern jumped off to examine the marks in the dirt road. He knew that Ty had been near the wagon that had carried the dragons and, as that had disappeared when Ty did, there was a good chance he was on it.

"The wagon definitely came through here. Lucky we haven't had rain or much traffic; the tracks could have easily been washed away," Kern said as he climbed back up onto the seat.

"You think he is with the wagon?" Jarrow asked.

"I really don't know, but it's the only lead I have to go on."

"He can look after himself though, can't he?"

"Yes, he can, but Conn is powerful and the king wants us all dead, I am sure of it. So he is in dangerous company. Not many people can compete with the might of a king."

"That is true, my friend. Let's hope he is all right."

"All we can do, I guess," Kern answered as Galandrik started to snore.

"So, you like Lan'esra, then?" Jarrow asked.

"Yeah. She is a good friend."

"You know what I mean. You *like* her."

"What? Don't be absurd, she's just a kid!"

"She hasn't been a kid for many moons, and you know it."

"She's a cleric and was a member of our party, and that's it."

"Then why did she give you her mother's necklace?"

"How did you know she did?"

"It doesn't matter. She is a good girl and will make a fine leader of the Midas Hills. It's a good place to settle down, and with all that gold waiting to be harvested…"

Kern laughed. "I know what you're getting at, and don't go there!" he said with a smile.

"I can think of worse places to live."

"So can I. Let's just concentrate on finding Ty, shall we?"

"All right, but if you want to talk I am—"

"STOP! Look, the tracks!" Kern jumped from the wagon and squatted down, examining the ground. "The wagon stopped suddenly, footprints over here—maybe five sets—and there is blood. Whoever was on the wagon was ambushed." He picked up the stone that had knocked Conn out, and flipped it in the air, catching it as it came back down. Kern studied the area thoroughly, and decided that the wagon had moved on up the slope, but before that, someone had run down and away from whatever was attacking them, and two had given chase.

They followed the tracks until they veered off the road and up a slope curving around to the southern side of the mountains, then Jarrow and Galandrik got down and accompanied Kern. Jarrow told the rest to stay and cautioned them to be vigilant, then they followed the path until it came to a small clearing with a cave entrance. Kern squatted and studied the clearing floor, flicking over a rabbit's head.

"Look at these," Galandrik said, standing next to two wooden posts. Kern walked over and looked at the ground, then said, "Ty was here definitely here. The cage was sat over there, and they were tied to the post and moved to the cage." After inspecting the other tracks and the old campfire, he added, "They left maybe two days ago. Five men, two captives, and a dog."

"Five men and a dog? I didn't think Conn had a dog with him."

"Neither did I, but that's what it is."

"Maybe he had men waiting for him after the battle?"

"Very possible, but who knows. At least we know Ty was alive two days ago. Let's go—there is nothing else to see here," Kern said, glancing around.

They had begun to move back down the track when something caught Galandrik's eye. "Hey wait—look up there."

Kern spun around. "What?" he replied.

"Hanging in that tree, look," he said, pointing.

"Well, I'll be a—Jarrow, let me get on your shoulders."

Jarrow squatted down and Kern climbed on. Then, with a heave, Jarrow stood up straight. He wobbled a bit, and Kern said, "Whoa! Steady," as he tried to balance himself. "Forward, move forward," he said, then reached up and grabbed the leather pouch. "Got it!" Jarrow bent back down and Kern stepped off, said, "Thanks," and opened it.

Jarrow took a deep breath. "The king's herbs."

"The two captives were Ty and Conn," Kern revealed.

Galandrik said, "And the one that ran away?"

"Bok!" they said simultaneously.

"So they bundled Ty onto the wagon, came through the pass, and got ambushed?" Jarrow asked.

"Most likely, yes. You wouldn't come all this way for the herbs to save your precious king, then leave them hanging in a tree," Kern said.

"The bandits could have done us a massive favour then. Hopefully this will slow them down and we can catch them up," the dwarf added.

They climbed back onto the wagon and headed on towards the Double Dikes, Kern watching closely for tracks on the pathway.

*

Ty and Conn stared at the bodies of the dead bandits littering the camp; the dog lay on its side with one of Ty's swords piercing it, sticking it to the ground. The giant man in front of them dropped his hood back, revealing his black burnt face. Half his hair and beard had gone and were replaced by black charred skin.

"Not even a hello?" Gorgon said with a wicked smile.

"You look terrible!" Conn said, squinting at the burnt face of the warrior.

"I'm in disguise," he replied in his deep gravelly voice.

"What as, a piece of coal?" Ty said, straight-faced.

Gorgon didn't so much as flinch at the remark; his dead eyes just flicked from Conn to Ty and back again.

"How did it happen?" Conn asked.

"Dragon fire. Lucky for me I have a high resistance to it, especially young dragon fire. A mature dragon would have melted me into my boots."

Pity it didn't, Ty thought.

"Well, it's good you are all right—apart from the burns, of course. Now open this damn cage," Conn ordered.

"All in good time. I have a question first."

Conn frowned. He glanced at Ty and then back to the big man, and said, "Fire away."

"What I want to know is, why did you leave me and my men to die?"

Ty noticed that Conn suddenly looked mightily nervous. "What? I… I didn't leave you."

"Answer me this, then: Why are all my men dead, my face is burnt half off, yet you are sitting here, all jolly and unhurt? Answer me that."

"I wouldn't say that; we've suffered quite a bit. The rabbit broth was awful," Ty said, much to Conn's dismay.

"Ty, shut up. For once, just be quiet," he said with a grave look on his face.

"Wise words, wizard."

"Listen, Gorgon, when I left, your men had—*with my help*—just finished off the two elementals and they were running to help you."

"So you never saw the two dragons escape from the cage you were standing next to?"

Conn's face sagged and he just stared at Gorgon, who continued, "And you never saw the forty men running down the hill to help Kern?"

Still Conn looked horrified, as if every one of Gorgon's words was a punch to the stomach. The colour in his cheeks had drained to his boots, and Ty knew he was scared.

"He couldn't see anything, he was fighting me," Ty interrupted.

"Well, stone me fucking dead where I stand. I never thought I would live to see the day when *the Great Conn* needed a little halfling girl to talk for him. How sweet."

Conn sighed and extended an arm across Ty's chest, pushing him back. "I didn't see either, Gorgon. I had the herbs and was thinking of King Moriak. You looked to be in control."

"'In control,' was I? Well, that's not how I see it."

"You must believe me, Gorgon; we are on the same side."

"If we were, you would have helped me and my men."

"If I had known you were in trouble I would have sprinted up! I would have crawled up the hill through hot coals had I known."

The Beast paced back and forth with one hand across his chest and the other holding his chin, "So if I was to say to you something like '*Fuck you, Gorgon,*' that wouldn't ring any bells, then?"

Conn sat back, looking like he had seen a ghost. "Wh-wha… what?"

"Think long and hard now," Gorgon said with a cold smile. "I will ask you again: You did indeed tell my men to go help me, then you said, '*Fuck you, Gorgon,*' isn't that right? And be careful how you answer this, because I do hate a liar, don't you?"

Conn knew he had said something, but was it that? He couldn't remember—but anyway, how could Gorgon have possibly heard? He'd been thirty feet away!

"No! I never said anything of the sort. That's just absurd."

"Well, let me bring in my first witness," he said, folding his arms. A cloaked figure stepped out from behind a tree and came to stand next to Gorgon. Raising both hands to his head, he flicked his hood back and said, "Surprise!"

"BOK!" Conn and Ty shouted simultaneously.

"What have you said?" Conn said, grabbing the bars and staring at the thief.

"Just what happened. I would never lie to Gorgon. I have always been told to be honest," Bok said grinning.

"Tell him I never said that! Bok, tell Gorgon I never said that!"

"But you *did* say that. We could both have helped, but you ordered me to drive the wagon."

Conn's head dropped against the bars he was still gripping.

"What's up? Feeling sick, wizard?" Gorgon said, and Conn looked up.

"Bok is a liar. Remember Solomon? *He* killed him and told me it was Ty. He's a snake, Gorgon, don't listen to him."

"Did you kill Solomon, Bok?" Gorgon asked.

Bok didn't know where this was going, and he tried to think quickly: Should he say *yes* hoping Gorgon would ignore it and salute his honesty, or say *no* and risk Gorgon thinking he was lying? He made a quick decision and took a deep breath. "Yes sir, I did."

Bok tried to look as calm as possible, but waited for Gorgon's sword to decapitate him.

"Arrrgh!" Conn screamed, reaching through the bars at Bok.

"I don't think he liked that answer, Bok," Gorgon said grinning, watching Conn.

"I'm going to fucking kill you, you snivelling little dog!" the wizard said, spraying saliva as tears of anger rolled down his face.

Deciding Gorgon wouldn't care about the details of Solomon's death, Bok added, "And when I stamped on his head, he screamed like a little girl crying for his mummy."

"That's enough, Bok. You'll upset Conn. Now go fetch some more firewood." The thief walked off, but not before taking one last glance at Conn and pushing his bottom lip out, like a crying baby. Conn slumped back down and stared at the ground. Ty patted his shoulder.

"You will die very soon," Ty said calmly to Bok's retreating back.

"Yeah, right," he said, not bothering to turn around.

"I like you," Gorgon said, pointing at the halfling. "You've got balls."

"So have you. Pity they're in your head," Ty answered.

Gorgon roared with laughter. "We will get on just fine, you and me—well, until you hang. But up to that point, we should get along just fine." He grabbed one of the bars with his enormous hand. "Let's get you out of this horrid cage, then," he said.

Conn looked up at that. "Thank you, Gorgon. King Moriak will hear about this. I will see to it that you are made a lord."

"Well, that's too kind," Gorgon said. Then, with a jerk, he pulled the cage off the wagon and into the dirt.

Conn and Ty crashed down inside of it as it fell. The wizard smashed his head against the bars and a trickle of blood ran down between his eyes.

Gorgon picked up a rock and smashed the lock, and the gate fell open. Reaching in, he grabbed Conn and dragged him out by his collar. Grabbing the wizard by the leg, Gorgon lifted him and threw him five feet against a tree. Conn struck side on and landed in a heap with a groan, as Gorgon flipped the cage over so the door was downwards, against the ground. "I'll see you in a minute," the Beast growled.

He spun around, saying, "Right, now where was I? Ah yes, killing Conn."

Ty immediately began struggling to right the cage and gain access to its door, but it was far too heavy.

Gorgon marched forward and kicked the wizard in the ribs. He was lifted into the air and fell onto his back with another groan.

"Remember your friend Belton?" Gorgon said. Conn looked up at the fighter, eyes suddenly wide. "Let me tell you how that little bitch died." Reaching down, he grabbed Conn by the throat and lifted him up like a rag doll so they were eye to eye. "I held him just like this on the edge of the mountain."

Conn swung a punch. It connected with Gorgon's jaw but it hardly even moved his head, and the second punch was no more effective. It was like hitting stone.

Gorgon tittered, then head-butted Conn straight on the bridge of the nose, breaking it instantly. Blood streamed down his face as Gorgon released him, and he landed on his back in the dirt.

"Then, after a few seconds, that bitch Belton pissed his leggings," Gorgon said, grabbing Conn's head with one hand and backhanding him with the other. Conn rolled over with the force of the blow a couple of times. "He was so scared, he was begging me not to let go of him. I think he even shit his leggings."

From the corner of his eye, Conn spied his staff, an arm's length away. He scrambled for it and grabbed it, then swung it around to face Gorgon, but it was met with the giant's mighty boot kicking it out Conn's hand. The staff landed a few feet from the cage.

Ty reached out for it, his fingertips almost touching the end. "Reach it, damn it!" the thief muttered.

Using both hands, Gorgon grabbed Conn by the ankle and swung him round, then released him. The wizard landed and rolled a good ten feet away. "After he shit and pissed his leggings, he begged me for his life. He said he would do anything," he continued as he marched over to the wizard.

Ty pressed so hard against the bars that his shoulder dislocated, but he gritted his teeth against the scream and grabbed the staff, dragging it back into the cage.

Gorgon took hold of Conn's hair and dragged him for several paces, as the wizard gripped Gorgon's wrist and tried to break his hold, his feet kicking out wildly. The Beast grabbed a rock with his free hand, then smashed it into the wizard's forehead with so much force that the rock shattered. Conn rolled onto all fours as blood poured from his head wound and into the dirt.

Ty grabbed the top of the bars and counted. *One... two...* On *three,* he used his body weight to force his shoulder back into place. He let go of the bar with a scream and lay holding his shoulder, tears rolling down his cheeks. His shoulder hadn't slipped back in as it normally did, and the pain was excruciating. He watched as Gorgon smashed the rock into Conn's face. He gingerly got up to his knees, trying to ignore the pain from his shoulder, and rested the staff on the top bar of the cage, ready to use his good hand to launch it at Conn.

Gorgon moved to Conn's side, then took a couple of steps back, rubbing his chin. "Yes, 'anything,' he said—no, *begged*—but I didn't want anything. He started to put up a little fight and all that begging got on my nerves. Seeing a grown man cry, shit and piss himself, and beg was sad, so I began to crush his windpipe." He took a step forward and kicked Conn in the ribs again, rolling him over three times.

When Conn came to a halt, spitting a mouth of blood out, he opened one eye and saw Ty holding his staff. Ty nodded and, after a struggle to get his hand out from under him, Conn gave the thief a thumbs-up.

"Then he went green—no, blue… no, wait, sorry: Purple! That's it, he went purple and his eye popped out," Gorgon said, continuing his taunts.

"Wait!" Conn said using every last inch of strength to get onto all fours, "Let me get up and fight you like a man, I can't die on all fours."

Gorgon looked down at the wizard spitting another mouthful of blood out. "The next time you go down, you will stay down," he answered. "Anyway, then Belton's other eye popped out so, as he was looking down anyway, I dropped him off the mountain. It made a horrible sound when he was bouncing off the rocks down the side. Made my skin crawl," he said coldly.

Conn was on his feet now, but bent over, holding his ribs. "How do you want to do this, fists or daggers?"

"You are serious! You actually want to fight me? Brave, I will give you that—but, can I just say, a tad stupid." Gorgon pulled a dagger from his belt and flipped it. Catching it by the tip, he threw it into the dirt a few feet away from Conn.

Conn used his shirt to wipe the blood from his eyes, stumbling as he did, like a drunken man heading for the exit of an inn.

"Pick the damn dagger up, or I'll end this right now."

"Very well," Conn said, taking a step toward the dagger. Then he lunged forward, throwing the dirt and dust he had concealed in his hand into Gorgon's eyes. He spun and stretched out his hands to Ty, shouting "Now!"

Ty obliged by launching the staff, which Conn caught perfectly. He aimed it just as Gorgon regained his vision, and the huge man shouted "No!" and began to run at Conn.

Ty punched the air, then groaned at his shoulder pain.

"*Bournea itvatica calkum*!" Conn shouted, and a wave of lighting shot out of the staff, gripping the Beast around the middle in the shape of a giant fist. He screamed as it constricted him, but he gripped the top finger and pushed down with all his might.

"*Kalia valcium*!"

Gorgon flew backwards and up into the air, smashing against a tree. Leaves and branches fell down like rain as the fist squeezed him tighter, the lighting flowing like an endless stream of electricity. He continued to push the giant finger through gritted teeth but it was no good: The magic was overpowering and for the first time Gorgon was beginning to lose a battle.

"Pissed his pants, did he? Bounced off the rocks, did he? Well, this is his payback! *Modreum balilum*—"

Ty shouted, "Conn, watch out!" as he saw Bok running into the clearing, daggers drawn, behind the wizard—but it was too late.

Conn's head spun around, but Bok's daggers were already buried in his sides, and then the thief pulled them out and thrust them in again. Conn arched his neck and screamed as the daggers punctured his organs a second time. He dropped his staff, and Gorgon fell to the ground as Bok stepped back, blood dripping from each dagger.

Ty lay in the cage and gripped a bar with his good hand. Resting his head on his arm, he watched as Conn slowly turned around, step by step like an old man, to face the backstabbing Bok.

Conn felt his side with his hand, looked down at his blood-drenched palm, then glanced at Ty with a look of complete disbelief written all over his face. He stared at Bok, his eyes open wide and bulging, blood covering his face. Then he raised his arm, bringing the staff up to face Bok.

Bok could feel the sweat forming on his forehead, and wished now that he had stabbed the wizard a third time. Then he saw Gorgon standing up behind the wizard, raising his sword out wide.

"This is for Solomon," Conn said quietly, but as he finished saying the name, with a whoosh of flashing steel Gorgon's sword sent Conn's head spinning into the air. The head landed before Conn's body even began to fall, but it did; like a felled oak tree, it toppled down into the dirt.

In the cage, Ty buried his head in the crease of his arm and shed a tear for the wizard that was.

Gorgon dropped his swords and bent over, holding his sides. "Damn that hurt!"

"YES!" Bok shouted, feeling his face with both hands. "It's gone! My scars are gone!" As he jumped into the air with delight, he shouted, "No more staring people!" He looked down at Conn's head, then drew back his leg and kicked it, making a sickening thud. "Sod you, wizard." The head rolled to the cage and hit Ty's hand, making him jump up and scurry back to the opposite side of the cage. Conn's eyes were still open, and Ty felt like they were still alive and looking at him.

"You are sick. I can't believe you killed the king's wizard," Ty said.

"We didn't kill him. *You* did," Gorgon said, standing upright, still holding his waist. "That's what we saw, right, Bok?"

With a devilish grin, Bok stared at Ty. "Yes, I saw everything. He stabbed him from behind."

"Whatever, like I give a shit," Ty answered.

"Tell that to the hangman when he places the rope around your neck," Gorgon said, picking up a random backpack and looking inside.

"I will, don't worry—and I'll say you sent me," Ty replied, grabbing the bars with both hands. He looked through the bars, watching as Gorgon tossed the backpack to one side and picked up another, tipping its contents out onto the ground. He kicked through the them, then picked up another pack, looking more agitated then before. Hurriedly he opened it and tipped it out, muttering, "It's got to be here somewhere!"

"What has?" Bok asked, but he was ignored. Gorgon went through all the bags and backpacks before turning to Ty and clenching his fists. "Fuck!" he shouted, then demanded, "Where is it?"

Ty gave a knowing smile. "Where's what?"

"Don't mess with me, thief! Where are the herbs?" he replied, walking towards the cage.

"No idea. Why don't you ask—" he glanced at the wizard's face— "oh, right, you can't! You chopped his head off."

"Where are the herbs? Tell me now."

Ty sat back away from the bars, folded his arms and crossed his legs, and said, "What herbs?"

Gorgon pushed the cage over, rolling Ty with it, and pulled the door open. He reached inside and grabbed the thief by his collar, dragging him out and throwing him down into the dirt. He loomed above Ty, staring down at his victim, fists still clenched.

"Tell me were the herbs are!" he growled.

"Conn had them! How would I know?"

Gorgon reached down and gripped Ty by the leather armour over his shoulder of his recently dislocated arm. "Thief, this isn't a game. You can die now, it doesn't bother me one bit. Now where are they?"

Grimacing through the pain of his gripped shoulder, Ty shouted, "I don't know!"

Gorgon could see that Ty's shoulder was injured, and punched him in his collar bone. Ty screamed in agony, and Gorgon said, "Again: The herbs, where are they?"

Through tears of agony and gritted teeth, Ty cried, "Please, Conn had them."

"Arrrgh!" Gorgon shouted and swung Ty around, throwing him into the dirt.

Ty rolled several times until he came to rest lying face down next to the bandits' empty backpacks and equipment. He spat out some dirt and held his shoulder. He felt faint from the agonizing pain that was shooting down his arm and up his neck. He could sense the giant man stepping up behind him, and before he knew what was happening, he felt the Beast's boot on the back of his neck, forcing his head into the dirt. The weight was unbearable and Ty felt sure his neck would break at any second.

"Last chance. Tell me now or die, like your friend Kern did when I stuck him to the tree!"

As Gorgon shouted down at the hapless thief, Ty's whole life flashed before him. He knew he was only moments from death and made a split-second decision. Tapping the ground, he tried to speak, but only managed a gurgle that kicked up some dust around his mouth. The boot was released from his neck and Ty coughed, spitting out dirt as he tried to draw breath. "Wa… water," he said, clutching his throat and trying to buy valuable seconds to get his story straight. He couldn't believe Kern was dead.

"Bring me that flask," Gorgon shouted to Bok, shaking his head. Ty sat up and drank from the flask, spitting out the first few mouthfuls before finally swallowing some of the cool fresh water.

"Enough," Gorgon said, knocking the flask from Ty's hands. He gripped the thief's leather armour and hoisted him up to eye level. "Speak!"

Ty's chest was killing him as it constricted due to the amount of leather and skin Gorgon had rolled up in his giant hands. "A bandit took them," he said, trying to act convincing.

"A bandit took them? Took them where?"

"He has taken them up to a camp near Raith, a bandit camp."

"If you lie—"

"It's true," Ty interrupted. "They were going to throw the herbs away and Conn knew he had to save them."

"Go on, I'm listening."

"So... so... he told them they were for the king. He knew the bandits would keep them safe because they are worth gold— They're going to demand money from Queen Cherian if she wants the herbs."

"So why did the bandits let the herbs go?"

"To get the ball rolling," Ty said. He suddenly remembered something from the bandit camp, and said, "Frolin's camp! That's what he said: 'Take the herbs to Frolin's camp.'"

"You lie!"

"No! He said they would cut our fingers and toes off until the queen pays up! He said they always pay."

"I have never heard of Frolin's camp. You are making this up," Gorgon said, drawing his dagger.

Ty thought he had blown it. *Should I tell him they are in a tree, a day's ride away? That sounds even more ridiculous than the lie.* "No! It's the truth. He said someone... Marny, that's it! Erm, Marny..." Ty racked his brain trying to remember the name, then it hit him like lightning bolt of luck. "*Yes!* Marny Four-Fingers! That's right! He said he would chop our fingers and toes off!"

Upon hearing that name, Gorgon slid his dagger away, saying, "I know of this Marny and I know of the camp he is rumoured to live in. It's just north of Death's Wood near Raith."

"Yes, near Raith! That's what he said," Ty said anxiously.

Gorgon stared at the thief, looking for a tell, but the thief's high charisma won. "All right," he said, and dropped the thief, saying, "Bok, collect everything we can use, and throw it all in the backpacks and on the wagon."

Ty landed in a heap and just lay there for several moments, holding his shoulder and grimacing. *I can't believe he bought it*, he thought to himself. He watched as Bok pulled his short sword of shadows out of the dead dog and admired its quality. *That'll be in your heart soon enough*, he thought.

Gorgon picked up the cage and threw it onto the wagon; his strength was all too plain to see. He stepped over to Conn's corpse and chucked it over his shoulder before throwing it onto the back of the wagon as well, like a butcher would handle a pig's carcass. Then he grabbed Ty by an arm and a leg, and tossed him in the cage.

Ty's shoulder banged against the bars and brought a tear to his eye again. The giant man walked away as Ty stared at the opening. *I haven't even got the strength to run,* he thought.

Ty watched as Gorgon picked up an old sack and then place Conn's head into it. He came back to Ty and swung the bag onto Ty's lap, saying, "There you go, someone to keep you company." He laughed as he then dragged the cage towards him before pushing it over onto its gate. All the while, Ty was battered about inside.

Once the leather cover was placed on top of the cage, Ty pushed the head into the corner and turned away, lying in the dark and trying to work out which part of his body hurt the most. Reaching into his leggings, he pulled out the small knife that he had picked up when he lay next to the bandits' equipment. He smiled and tucked it back away, and shut his eyes.

Chapter Thirty-Six
The Trail to Friendship

Jarrow sat up front in the wagon next to the driver; Kern and Galandrik sat in the back, applying Lan'esra's healing ointment to their wounds.

"I tell you what, Gal, this ointment is superb. I nearly have full movement back, and the scar is looking good. How's the leg?"

"The same, lad. It can get a little stiff, but other than that it's healing really well."

"We will be back to our best in no time," the ranger said, rolling his shoulder.

"I wouldn't say that, but we'll be ok. Kern, what are we going to do after we get Ty back?"

"Depending on how this works out, I'd like to visit Veloin in Tonilla, then head to the Bracon Ash Dungeon and sort my sight out. Other than that, I don't mind, as long as it doesn't involve any looting tips from any of Ty's friends."

Galandrik laughed. "Sounds good to me, lad."

The wagon stopped a couple of times, and Kern looked for tracks, then reported that another horse had come through here after Ty. When they passed between the massive Double Dikes statues, Jarrow sniggered, "One day they might be replaced with Kern and Galandrik!"

"One day you might stop trying to wind me up," Kern answered.

"I am not, good friend—the complete opposite. I've seen it all before. Remember one-armed Mad Murgan, the Butcher of Bodisha?"

"I have heard the songs and stories; he killed over three thousand people on his campaign of slaughter. He wanted to rule Bodisha and overthrow the king."

"That's him. Well, apparently it was his brother, Bertol, who was the sadistic one. *He* was the one who wanted to rule Bodisha, not Murgan—Murgan had no interest. He only ever killed one person, in Raith over a game of dice—caught him cheating or something."

"So what are you saying?"

"His one act was the seed, his brother's actions were the food, and the people's song was the water. In the end, that one killing made him the most feared man in the whole of Bodisha." Jarrow looked at Kern's blank expression. "What I am saying is that your reputation will grow. Imagine it as a fire: It has already been lit, and every deed you do will be like throwing wood onto it. Bigger and bigger it will become."

"Listen, people can believe whatever they want; all I care about is me and my party. The reputation is what *they* want me to be."

"I know that, but the fire has started, so use it to your advantage. Look, when we went to Breeze and those people called me *Lord Jarrow*—they love to make up stories and rumours. I did a few good deeds, bought a stuffed head and a bearskin rug for the house, and the next thing I know, I have slayed every monster possible and put their heads up on the wall! It's all nonsense, but people like to tell a tale, sing a song, and believe in the fantasy of it all. They want to *be* the people they sing about."

"But I haven't actually done all the things those stories say," Kern argued.

"I know that, you know that, and Mad bloody Murgan knew that—but the people don't care! Look in any town and watch the kids fight with wooden sticks, pretending they are Kern Ocarn fighting a giant. Do you honestly think they care if you did or didn't kill the giant? Hell, you could probably *tell* people you didn't, but they wouldn't believe you now."

"What happens when the reputation outgrows the man, ever thought of that? What about when every wannabe hard man wants to have a go and see if they can beat *The Man*—then what?"

"You are missing my point, Kern, but don't worry—you'll get it eventually," Jarrow said, gripping Kern's shoulder and smiling.

"Maybe I don't want to get it."

"Maybe not, but it is already written, friend. The fire is burning and getting more ferocious every day, and you are powerless to stop it," Jarrow said.

"I'm hungry," the dwarf said from the back of the wagon. "When are we stopping?"

"Some things never change," Jarrow laughed. He called back, "In a few hours we will be up near Raith's Wood. I suggest we head there or somewhere close. We are out in the open here."

"The tracks head that way, so maybe they camped there too. Depending on their speed, I think we are a day and a half, maybe two days away from them," Kern said.

"So when we find Ty, if he is with the bandits and Conn is a prisoner too, what then?" Jarrow asked.

"We ask Conn where our rewards are for finding the king's gold!" Galandrik shouted from the back.

"I don't know, really. I haven't thought that far ahead. Let him go, I guess—give him the herbs and hope that is the end of all this."

"I can't see him holding a grudge. The king gets healed, you get Ty, and all is good."

"Not really a fair deal, is it," the dwarf added.

Kern sniggered. "You miss the little shit, really."

"I admit it can get a little boring without him. To be completely honest, I had a dog much the same when I was growing up. He was a bloody nuisance, but when I was off for weeks on end, I missed the little shit—then home for one day and I wanted to kick the little sack of shit up the arse!"

Jarrow and Kern both gave a belly laugh. "I know that feeling with Ty. More than once I could have throttled him—well, actually I *have* throttled him. He seems to do everything in his power to push you to the breaking point."

"He does you, because he knows you will bite every time," the dwarf said.

"Yeah, probably," Kern agreed.

"Not 'probably,' he *does*," Galandrik insisted.

*

The next couple of hours went by uneventfully until the elf spoke up. "Look, there are people coming this way."

"It looks like there are quite a few, too. Be on your guard, everyone," Kern said laying his katanas of vanquishing down next to his feet. Jarrow pulled out a bow from behind him and rested it across his lap. The two guards flanked them, riding in between them and the group advancing towards them.

"It's just townsfolk," one of the guards said.

"Don't be fooled, Brendin. Bandits can be as slimy as a snake, and lower too."

"Aye, boss. I will keep a look out."

As the group got closer, they could see it was indeed townsfolk—men, women, and children heading past them towards the Double Dikes. Their wagons were completely full with bags, furniture—everything they owned.

"Greetings!" Jarrow shouted as they passed the townsfolk. Most people ignored him and carried on walking, heads down and blankets wrapped around their shoulders, but one man who sat driving a wagon answered, "Greetings, stranger."

"Where are you heading?"

"Eastern Bodisha. We have travelled for miles, from the northern tip of the Eastern Mountains."

"The cold finally get the better of you?" Kern joked.

"I wish, my good friend! It wasn't the cold—the cold we didn't mind."

"What made you leave, then?" Jarrow said, frowning at Kern.

"Orcs."

Galandrik sat up quickly, straightening his helmet. "Orcs you say, lad? Where?"

"Everywhere. They were as far down as Dryad's Mirror. You'll see, they will flood all over Bodisha before the leaves go green," the man called over his shoulder as his wagon rolled on southwards.

"That is bad news; they must have breached the defences of the north," Galandrik said, shaking his head.

"They will never get this far down. The majority of their armies is situated on the western side of the mountains. The king will pull forces from everywhere to protect Morcas and the lands around," Kern said, referring to the town around King Moriak's castle. The king had renamed it when he ascended the throne, combining the first sounds of his own name and the word castle.

"Can you imagine if they got as far as Morcas and through to Raith?" Jarrow pondered.

"Never happen," the ranger said. "I doubt if there even are any orcs. It's probably just scare mongering."

"Well, let's hope so. Look there is Raith's Wood."

After another hour they reached the wood, just before they lost the light. Kern followed the tracks, which did indeed head into the woods—but only a little way in, to a clearing.

"What the hell," Kern said, entering the clearing. The bodies of the bandits still lay where Gorgon had slain them, and their equipment was scattered everywhere.

"Looks like a massacre," Jarrow said, drawing his sword and standing next to Kern.

Galandrik also stepped up. "I hope none of that is Ty's blood," he said, looking at the big dried pool of Conn's blood in the centre of the clearing.

"Me too. I'll have a look about, see what I can make of it all," the ranger said, examining the ground.

"They bloody stink," Jarrow noted, holding a hand over his nose.

"Indeed. I think we may need to bury them. I can't sleep and eat ten feet from five stinking corpses," Kern said.

"I'll get the others to help load them on the wagon and take them away. No way am I digging here; the tree roots will have sucked this ground dry. You'd still be digging this time tomorrow," the elf said, making space on the wagon.

"I take it you have shovels?" Galandrik asked.

"Oh, didn't think of that," Jarrow admitted.

"Look, take them out of here and burn them, that is by far the best way," Kern said, examining the red dirt. "I think someone was decapitated here. They lost a lot of blood."

They burnt the bodies while Kern cleared the debris and scattered dirt about, covering the signs of bloodshed. Before long, a fire was roaring and a pot of chicken stew boiled above it. Kern sat on a log contemplating, as Jarrow and Galandrik entered the clearing.

"What happened here, then, lad?"

"Well, as far as I can make out, the bandits camped here and removed the cage from the wagon; I found Ty's prints so I know he was let out. Then it's a massive brawl. I can't really tell how many people attacked them, to be honest. At least two, it stands to reason—the trouble is, the tracks are all too close together," the ranger explained. "I think Conn may have also helped, somehow."

"Conn? I thought he was locked up with Ty," the dwarf said.

"Yes, I think he was, but look at the electrical burn marks on that tree. They are recent, and you don't get many magic-using bandits."

"So the bandits let them out and they attacked, and Conn somehow got hold of his staff and fried them?" Jarrow questioned.

"Well, no. I couldn't see any burn marks on the dead—just sword wounds. So it's all a bit confusing, unless Ty did all the damage... but that doesn't seem plausible."

"What about if another party attacked, and rescued Conn and Ty?" Galandrik asked.

"That would make more sense, definitely," Kern agreed.

"Let's eat and carry on," Jarrow suggested.

"Good idea," Kern said, then asked, "Where are the others?"

"Patrolling. They eat as we travel. These parts are rife with bandits and thieves, best not to take any chances," Jarrow said as he filled his bowl.

"Even your driver?" Kern asked.

"Even the driver. Remember what I said: *Reputation*. If I let the driver get too close to me, he becomes a friend, and you tend to treat friends differently. He will probably tell someone back in Breeze that I killed those five bandits."

"You and your reputation issues," Kern smiled.

"I am telling you, Kern, being scared of someone's reputation loses people half their fights. If you were to fight two identical men, one dressed in white and one dressed in red, and someone told you the man in red was a gladiatorial legend and never lost a fight, killed hill trolls for a hobby, you would play out a completely different fight. I am not saying it would change the outcome, but he would have more chances than normal because you would be wary and on the back foot—all because of his reputation," Jarrow explained.

"All right, I get it," Kern said, filling his bowl again.

*

Queen Cherian walked into the war room, the place where every major decision in the kingdom was hashed out. It was a square room with a large window at the end opposite the door, which opened onto a large balcony overlooking King's Square. Every king and queen for as long as could be remembered had stood on this balcony and greeted their people. The walls were lined with images of all the previous royalty that ruled over Bodisha—well, some of Bodisha. The country was split into four sections, and each had their own royal family. Even though all races mixed, there had been a constant battle for soil for as long as anyone could remember. The humans and dwarfs hadn't been at war with the elves for many years, and the humans had never been at war with the dwarfs, mainly because they were so distant from one another. But in recent years it had been Guldir, the elven ruler, who had been making the most trouble. Moriak ruled over southwest Bodisha; the elves had the northwest, and the dwarfs ruled the southeast. The orcs ruled the lands in the northeast, which they called Cragor, and that was where all the trouble lay.

At the war table sat Brithuim, the king's chief in command. He controlled all the armies, and was the mouthpiece between Moriak and the men. He was a hardened veteran of war who always wore his shiny chain mail and was always immaculate, from the red plume on his shiny silver helmet to the sheen on his shiny silver boots.

On either side of him were two generals of the king's armies, Blane and Fiktus. Blane was a fat, red-faced general who was always angry. He felt he had no time for these trivial meetings, and hated everybody and everything apart from his beloved dogs, twelve Bodihain Bullnecks, which he kept at his home, northwest of Phebon. They were a ferocious breed of dog that were used in troll hunts.

Fiktus was his opposite in appearance, a tall skinny man whose knowledge of battle strategies was second to none. He had masterminded most of the tactical placement and defences of King Moriak's armies.

There were also Reddoc, who sat in on the meeting as representative of the Mage Circle in Conn's absence; Devon, who had been promoted to Captain of the Guard after Svorn's death; and three members of the Seer Council, Odol, Piduim, and Granot. These three were really the quill-pushers who controlled the taxation, food supplies, metal exports, and everything else that generated revenue. They had a say in everything, because everything revolved around money. If there were to be a war, they would need more steel for swords and weapons, and more steel could mean higher taxes. They never missed a chance to make a gold piece, and the king trusted them with everything.

"All rise for Queen Cherian," the guard on the door said as she entered, and everyone around the table stood and greeted her. She took her seat at the head of the table, in King Moriak's usual spot.

"Greetings all, and welcome to the King's Council. We need to discuss the war."

"Indeed, Queen Cherian, but please tell us some good news—how is the king?"

"He is stable, and Conn is returning with the herbs as we speak. We have had word that he will be back within three days. Murtal has assured me that the king will hold on until Conn's return," she said. There was mumbling around the table as they all thanked the gods for the king's safe return to health.

"Now, let's talk orc. What are the whispers we are hearing about them breaking our defences?"

"It's not a breach of our defences," Brithuim explained. "All the passes and possible ways through the Craic Mountains are protected and we stand strong, but we think they may be tunnelling through or maybe under."

"Tunnelling through the mountains? Is that possible? Those mountains are a mile wide!" Blane spat.

"The news our scouts have given us is that the orcs have captured gnome engineers and are tunnelling with a massive drilling machine."

"Damn those gnomes," Blane hissed.

"We can't blame them. If they are prisoners, they will do as the orcs demand," the queen said. "So what does this mean?"

"Well," Brithuim continued, "we control the mountain passes and all possible entry points to us through the Craic Mountains. But if they tunnelled through anywhere between these points, it *could* be disastrous."

"Explain," Cherian said.

Fiktus leaned forward. "My queen, if they broke through, and had a tunnel wide enough to move on Bodisha in numbers, we would have only one option. They would be in behind our defences and would have a completely free run straight to here—all our armies would be on the northern side between them and here. They know we would have to pull our armies back from the mountain passes to hold them back from getting here."

"And that would mean we would have no men defending along the mountain passes," Brithium added.

"So they will have a free route here, flooding through the tunnels, and if we pull back to defend this attack they can flood through the mountain passes. Is that what you are saying?" Cherian asked.

"Yes, my queen, that is about the size of it. We can hold the passes with limited men because they are narrow. Once they breach that, it'll be all-out war, and as you know, we are too spread out to go to war on that scale. We cannot lose our foothold in the Craic mountain defences," Brithuim stated.

"So what's the answer?" she said, leaning back in her chair. There was silence. "Please, someone tell me we have a contingency plan for this."

"Ask Guldir for support?" Odol suggested.

"Damn those elves! They would rather join the orcs," Blane said, thumping the table.

"We will arrange a meeting once the king is fit," Cherian answered. "What other choices do we have?"

"What about getting support from Moriak's cousin Threliun?" Fiktus said.

"We have sent a message overseas, but even if they can spare the men it'll take a month for them to get here. Have we got that long?" Cherian asked.

"That we don't know, my Queen," Brithium said.

"What *do* you know, exactly, apart from at any moment we could be flooded with orcs?"

Fiktus spoke up. "We have pulled one hundred men back for the defences and they are patrolling all along the mountain. We know troops of orcs are getting through somewhere, but we don't know where exactly. If they had tunnelled all the way through, there would be hundreds, so we are at a loss."

"They have a tunnel small enough to get through singly, so they must be close," Granot stated.

"Yes, we believe they are. Also, the attacks on the mountain passes are fewer now, and our spotters don't count half as many orcs," Fiktus said.

"So they are gathering to attack through the tunnel—is that what we are saying?" Cherian asked, shaking her head.

"We don't know—"

"I am sick of hearing 'We don't know!' You are chief in command, Brithium! The king appointed you to protect us!"

"Queen Cherian, we will send scouts into their land and find more information," he answered, face reddening.

"If they have fewer men attacking the passes, why don't we also pull men back?" Piduim asked.

"We have considered this, but they might *want* us to think that. As soon as we weaken, they could strike. We really are in a predicament."

Queen Cherian got up from her chair and paced towards the window and back. "What else can we do? We have contacted Threliun and the elves, and we can't pull troops back from anywhere else… What about the dwarfs?" she said, thinking out loud.

"We could send a message, but again, it would take them a few weeks to group and get here," Fiktus said, "not that they would."

"Sod the dwarfs, they can't fight anyway. They are probably digging the tunnel for the orcs!" Blane said, angrily as always.

"That isn't helping, Blane," Fiktus snapped.

"Oh, well you *would* say that, after—"

"Enough!" Brithium interrupted. "If you have no positive input, be quiet!"

"Well said," Queen Cherian said, sitting back down. "So it looks like we are in a pickle. If no one gives us support, we could be heading for a full-out war with the orcs on open ground."

"How many numbers do the orcs have?" Odol asked.

"They outnumber us four to one. If we gathered all our troops back from around Bodisha, maybe two to one," Fiktus answered.

"Damn. This isn't good," the queen said, glancing at Reddoc. "What about the mages, have they got any bright ideas?"

He starred at her, then slowly leaned forward and placed his elbows on the table. "Light up the three Orbs of Protection," he said calmly.

The queen stared at the mage with a confused look on her face. "Light up the three Orbs of Protection? Stop speaking in riddles, mage!"

"You don't believe all that nonsense! This is war, lad, and fairy stories and myths will not help us now," Blane hissed.

"Will someone please explain?" Cherian said leaning back and folding her arms.

Reddoc stood up and retrieved a map from a small table in the corner.

"This is wasting our time," Blane said, standing up.

"Sit down! I will tell you when you can stand up!" Queen Cherian ordered.

"The sooner Moriak is back, the better," he grumbled, sitting back down. "He wouldn't put up with this rubbish."

Reddoc spread the map across the table, placing a goblet on each corner to stop it rolling back up.

"Right, hear me out, my queen. Long before you or your grandfather or your grandfather's grandfather graced Bodisha with their presence, humans went to war with the orcs. They had all the north, long before elves lived in the forests, and humans had the south. Our records show that roughly where we stand right now was where the battle field was. It ran from coast to coast. Thousands of men and orcs died, but eventually we pushed them to the northeast, where they are now."

"This is nonsense. Why are we listening to this bullshit?" Blane spat.

"Guards!" Queen Cherian shouted. "Take General Blane and escort him to the cells."

"What?! I have never been treated like this in my life! Wait until Moriak hears of this," he bellowed as four guards marched him out of the room.

"What a vile man. Please continue," Queen Cherian said as Brithium gently shook his head.

"Thank you, my queen. After the orcs were pushed back and their king was killed—"

"Who was?" Cherian interrupted.

"King Drikdorok."

"He sounds delightful."

"By all accounts, he was as chaotic as it gets. After his death, Aryinel, the most powerful of all the human mages, created three orbs. The scribes state that inside the orbs were Drikdorok's eyes, heart, and tongue."

"And *Drikdorok* was the chaotic one?" Granot said quietly.

"He cast a spell on the orbs," Reddoc continued, "then created three indestructible pillars to sit them on, each standing thirty feet high. One is in the elven forest; one is on the coast, just north of the Voltic Isle; and the other is in the heart of the orc lands."

"How long is this story? Has it actually got an ending?" Cherian said, rolling her eyes.

"Sorry, my queen. Once these orbs were in place, they protected the human lands from the orcs."

"So, light them up! Start them up again, do whatever it takes," she said.

"This is the hard part, my queen. Aryinel used his staff, the most powerful of staffs ever made, to create the magic he cast on the orbs."

"Did this staff have a name?" Piduim asked.

"The only written name we have found is 'the Staff of Aryinel.'"

"How original," Fiktus said, smiling.

"So, use the staff to re-ignite the orbs or whatever it is you do," Queen Cherian said, waving her hands.

"I was getting to that, my queen. Over one hundred years later, the staff was stolen and broken into two pieces, which broke the spell. No one really cared, because the orcs had been suppressed and had not been seen for so long."

"Who stole it?" the queen asked.

"We have a few different writings that contradict each other. One says it was a great thief of the day, who sold it back to the orcs for a lump of gold as big as a barrel. Another says it was Drikdorok's great-great-grandson, who was bred as a half-orc specifically for this task. The last legend is that the power of the staff made Aryinel crazy, and he smashed it."

"So," Cherian looked at Reddoc and shrugged her shoulders, then said sarcastically, "hmm, mend it?"

"Not that easy, I am afraid," he began, as Cherian turned and looked at Brithium.

"How did I know that was coming," she said.

"The pieces were both hidden, and have been so for over five hundred years."

"So why are you telling me all this? I should have listened to Blane; he made more sense than you do. What a complete waste of time," she said angrily, and Reddoc waited patiently until she finished.

"We know where the pieces are," he announced.

Queen Cherian's head jerked around and she locked eyes with Reddoc, now looking more interested.

"How do you know? If they were buried five hundred years ago, why wait until now to tell us?" Brithium said, taking the words out of everyone's mouths.

"We have only just found out. Mages have been working to decipher the ancient writings since the staff was stolen. Two weeks ago we finally made a breakthrough."

"So where are they hidden?" Cherian asked.

"One is hidden in a tomb under Dryad's Mirror and the other…"

"Well, spit it out, man!" Cherian said.

"It's in Cragor, I'm afraid," Reddoc said, sitting down.

"Cragor! You are telling me the second part of the staff is in the hands of the orcs?"

"Yes, in an orc temple called Bagdor."

"Well, that's just brilliant! How are we supposed to get it, just walk in and knock on the door?"

"Queen Cherian, I can't answer that. But if you got the two parts, we could eliminate enough of the orcs to have peace again."

"That's only if this myth is true," Fiktus said.

"Agreed, but it is a possibility," Reddoc said, rolling up his map.

"I will speak to Conn on his return. I have an idea. Now, is there anything else anyone can suggest or add to solve this problem of ours?" she asked. They all shook their heads, and she called an end to the meeting, adding, "Brithium, write a detailed report on troop movement and I will give it to the king when he wakes. Have it to me by morning." He nodded and everyone left. The room was empty and Queen Cherian stared out the window.

"The Staff of Aryinel," she whispered to herself.

Chapter Thirty-Seven
Broken Bones

Gorgon rode Conn's horse and Bok rode in the wagon as they moved north towards Raith. It was mid-morning and the sky was clear blue, without a cloud to be seen.

"You see in the distance? That's Raith. Do you know where Morcas is?"

"It's just north of Raith, isn't it? Why, what are you doing?"

"I'm heading west to the bandit camp to retrieve the herbs. The king relies on me."

"What about me? What if I get attacked?"

"Well, you'll die; *he* will die—" Gorgon indicated the cage— "which will save the hangman a job; I will get the herbs; the king will live, and everybody is happy."

"What should I say when I get there?" Bok asked.

"Don't say anything about what's happened. Just say you were split up from the others and I found you at Double Dikes. I will explain to the queen about Conn and how Ty killed him."

"But what about Ty?" Bok said, nodding at the cage.

"What about him?"

"He will surely talk and blurt everything out."

Gorgon thought for a second. "Cut his tongue out."

"What?" Bok said, frowning.

"Did I stutter? Cut his fucking tongue out, so he cannot talk!" Gorgon growled.

"He would bleed out, surely?"

"No, he won't, trust me. The saliva in the mouth is a good healer."

"Well, if you are sure…"

"I have cut out more tongues than you can imagine. Just knock him out with the hilt of your sword and cut it out; easy! Even you couldn't mess that up."

"It's not something I do regularly, but on this occasion I'll give it a go," Bok smiled.

"Just don't do it here. Head into that clump of trees. They tend to scream when they wake, so cover his mouth, too."

"The Rat won't be so gobby after this!"

"See you at Morcas."

Gorgon rode off towards the bandit camp, and Bok headed towards the trees. Once there, he had a quick glance around and entered using an old wagon path. Travelers only came through here for shelter from the weather; circular groups of trees had been cut down in areas large enough to get the wagon in and to allow other wagons to move along the central path; the remains of old campfires were dotted about in each one. Some even had pots and pans, still hanging on nails stuck into trees. Bok chose an area that was a little deeper off the track, and pulled his horses to a stop as quietly as possible. He waited a few minutes, then peered under the sheet that covered the cage.

He saw Ty laying on his side, and listened to his deep breathing and the odd snore. *Perfect,* he thought to himself. He pulled the two swords of shadows out and laid them on the wagon bed, being careful not to wake the sleeping thief. He looked around the clearing until he spotted exactly what he wanted. Tiptoeing over, he picked up the lump of wood, about a foot long and a bit wider than a spear. Bok swung the wood down a couple of times, visualizing knocking out the thief. *Yes, perfect,* he thought, stepping carefully back to the wagon, making sure not to step on any twigs. He untied the rope restraints that held the sheet in place, and squatted under. Ty was lying, balled up, in the dead centre of the cage. As quietly as possible, Bok reached in through the bars, holding the club above Ty's head. "*One…two…three,*" he mouthed silently and lifted the wood up as high as he could—but to his surprise Ty reached up and seized his wrist.

Spinning around, Ty placed both feet against the bars where Bok's arm came through. Bracing his back against the opposite side, he pulled with all his might.

"Arrrrgh!" Bok screamed.

"Cut my tongue out?" Ty said through gritted teeth.

"It was Gorgon's idea!" Bok said, his face planted against the bars. He felt in his scabbard for his sword, but it was on the wagon over his shoulder beside him.

"I can't believe you would do it!" Ty shouted, still pulling on Bok's arm.

"You're going to pull it out of the socket! Let go," Bok begged.

"Best idea you have had!" Ty said, and began rocking from side to side.

"Stop, please! What are you doing? I will let you go, I swear!"

"Swear at *this*!" Ty yelled. He pushed Bok's arm the wrong way with all his strength, until the arm snapped at the elbow.

"Arrrrgh!" Bok shrieked as the pain raced up his arm. Ty lay all his weight on top of Bok's broken arm as he screamed in agony, then he grabbed the small dagger he had stolen from the bandit camp and help it up, facing Bok.

"No! Please!" Bok screamed, in a mixture of the pain from his broken arm and the anticipated pain of what was soon to come.

"This is from Conn!" Ty shouted, and brought the dagger down towards Bok's neck.

Bok moved just enough for the dagger to miss his throat, and it wedged just above his collar bone. Ty held the dagger and pushed down, trying to inflict as much damage as possible, his face only inches from Bok's as he screamed, "Die, you piece of shit!" But in doing so, he released the weight on the broken arm.

Bok managed to pull free, standing in front of the cage with his broken arm hung limp; his other hand gripped the dagger protruding from his shoulder. Ty grabbed the bars, shaking the cage with uncontrollable rage and screaming, "Come on! Come cut my tongue out!"

Bok's eyes widened as the pain shot through his body; he could feel the warmth of the blood seeping down under his leather armour. He glanced down at the dagger and began to feel faint. He looked up at the sheet-covered cage and saw it rocking, and heard shouting from underneath.

Ty placed his feet between the bars on the floor of the wagon and barged the side of the cage, moving it a few inches towards the edge of the wagon. Again and again he tried, until the cage had slid to the wagon's edge, then twice more he barged it until the cage fell off into the dirt, rolling the thief inside. The door fell open and Ty jumped out into the clearing, fully expecting to see an attack coming from Bok. Spinning around, he looked and waited, holding his fists up.

But Bok was gone.

"Arrrrgh!" He screamed into the air and clenched his fists. He shook his head trying to release his anger at letting Bok get away.

He examined the wagon and found his swords, then opened a backpack and tipped it out. There was nothing of use in it, apart from three lumps of dried beef rolled up in cloth and a canteen of water. He put two of the pieces of beef back in the backpack, and started chewing on the other. He loaded the backpack with some items: flint and tinder, rope, a couple of torches. Another sack sat next to Conn's body; he dragged it to him and took out Conn's spell book, placing it into the backpack. Conn's staff lay on the other side of the corpse.

Keeping an eye out for Bok, Ty started to unleash the horses from the cart, then stopped. *I can't leave him here like this, but if I go back to Morcas they will surely kill me. Damn, what to do? If I get there before Gorgon, I could tell them the truth—no, it'll never work. They won't believe a thief over Gorgon. What about getting the herbs? Yes, grab the herbs, then I have a bartering tool. I could even get some gold out of this and move away, down south, and start again. All right, that's the plan: Get the herbs and start again.*

Ty grabbed the old grey cloak lying on the wagon, wrapped it around his shoulders, and pulled the hood up. Then he sat in the front of the wagon and guided the horses out of the forest and back towards the Double Dikes.

*

Jarrow's wagon rolled on north towards Raith. Galandrik sat up front and Kern snoozed in the back, Brendin and Joff riding ahead.

"Do you think they will let Ty go?" Galandrik asked Jarrow.

"I can't see how they have any other choice but to. You have the herbs."

"True, but it's going to be risky, getting the herbs to them and getting Ty out without getting caught."

"We will work something out. If the king's life is at stake, they will honour their word. Once he is better—well, that's a completely different story."

"That's if Ty is there and… I hate to say it, but he could have been killed by now."

"Come on, Galandrik, that's not like you. Be positive! I didn't get to speak all that much to Mr Ty, but what I *did* gather was that he's a hardened little bastard."

"Oh, he is definitely a survivor. That is for sure, lad."

"You see! You're thinking differently already. I bet you'll be swigging beer with him in no time."

"I hope you are right, Jarrow. I honestly do."

"I am always right. Kern wouldn't be doing this if he thought any differently."

"Yes, I know. He is always positive—he'll probably walk out of this being called 'Kern the King Saver'!"

"You can be sure of that. He is already writing history with song, and this will be another chapter in the book they write about him one day." Galandrik smiled.

They rode on, Kern fast asleep in the back of the wagon.

A few hours had passed when Joff spoke up. "We have oncoming traffic, Jarrow," he said, and the two guards drifted slightly apart. In the distance, a wagon was heading towards them.

Jarrow held his hand up and squinted in the sunlight. "Doesn't look much, just a lone traveller."

*

Ty noticed the wagon heading towards him accompanied by two riders in front. He pulled his hood down to hide his face, leaving just enough room to see. As they drew closer, he could see that the front riders were heavily armed, and three men rode on the wagon. Ty steered his wagon off the main track to make way for them; he didn't want any conflict here. As the riders drew level with him, he peered up at them and did a double take.

Galandrik!

Never one to miss an elaborate entrance, he called, "Hello, good friends," in the most gravelly voice he could muster.

"Hello, friend," Jarrow answered.

"I wonder if you could help me," Ty continued, nearly bursting inside with glee at seeing his old friend.

"Well, that depends on what it is you want, kind sir."

"I'm looking for a dwarf," Ty said, trying not to laugh.

Galandrik's head turned at the word 'dwarf.' "Why, what for?" he asked, arching his neck in an attempt to see the face behind the hood.

"For cleaning my shithouse. Have you seen one?" Ty said, nearly flipping his hood, only just holding in the laughter.

Galandrik stood up on the wagon, "Listen, lad, if you—"

"He is a fat ginger dwarf," Ty interrupted, ready to burst, "and goes by the name of Galandrik. Apparently he is the best shithouse cleaner in Bodisha!"

"Right, let me kill him," Galandrik said, scrambling over Jarrow to get down.

Ty flipped his hood back, revealing the red topknot of his hair. "Kill your old friend," Ty said in his normal voice.

"Well, I'll be an elf's ear!" the dwarf said, jumping down, as Ty did the same.

"Oi, leave the ears alone," Jarrow laughed, but it went unnoticed.

Ty and Galandrik gripped forearms and held each other's shoulders.

"Good to see you, halfling!"

"It's good to see you, too, dwarf!"

"You remember Jarrow?"

Ty stared at the elf, and finally recognised him. "Where the hell did you come from?" Ty said as Jarrow jumped down to join them.

Jarrow offered his own arm for greeting. "Good to see you too, Ty."

"How the hell did you hook up with him again?" he asked, nodding at the dwarf.

"Well, I was trading in the Midas Hills and stumbled across Galandrik… and Lan'esra."

"It's a small world," the thief said. Then his shoulders sagged a little, and he said, "I heard about Kern. I was devastated."

Galandrik turned back to look at the wagon, and spotted Kern peeping, shaking his head. Galandrik realised immediately what he was doing, as did Jarrow.

"Yes, damn shame," Galandrik said sombrely. "He was a good guy."

"Yes, one of the best. A true gent," Ty said, nodding.

"He deserved the nickname Giant Slayer, I always thought," Jarrow said with a sly wink at the dwarf.

"Oh, hell yeah. If it weren't for him, we would never have taken it on. He did the majority of the damage," Ty said.

"I think Lan'esra liked him too. Probably because of his looks, I guess," Galandrik teased.

"Yes, he was quite a good-looking guy," Ty said, kicking a stone.

"If you could have said one thing to him before he died, what would it have been?" Jarrow said, teeing the thief up.

"Hmm. Just that he was more than a friend—he was my brother," Ty said, looking up.

"Well, come give big brother a hug then, boy!" Kern shouted as Galandrik and Jarrow burst out laughing.

Ty's mouth hung open and his solemn demeanour turned to anger. "You bunch of sneaky dogs!"

"Oh come on! *'He's my brother'* and *'He's good-looking'*!" Kern jumped down, laughing.

"I didn't mean any of that old shit!" Ty shouted.

"Oh, yes you did!"

"No! I only said it because I thought you were dead," Ty moaned as Kern stepped in front of him and looked down at the halfling.

"It's good to see you, old friend," Kern said, holding his arm out.

Ty slowly produced a smile and gripped Kern's arm. "Good to see you too… brother!"

"What the hell happened?" Kern asked.

"I will tell you on the way. We need to go south and grab the herbs," Ty said, grabbing hold of the handle to pull himself up and onto the wagon seat.

"No need, lad. We found them."

"Really? What, in the tree?" Ty asked.

"Yes, really. We followed your wagon tracks and saw them hanging—we couldn't believe it. How did they end up there?" Kern asked.

"The bandits had them. I said they were poisonous to stop them cooking them, and they just threw them," Ty said remembering the moment. Then he thought of Conn. "Oh yes, look under that sheet," he said, pointing. Kern stepped past the thief and lifted it.

"It's a headless corpse," Kern said, frowning.

"What?" Ty said, looking at the back of the wagon. "Shit!"

"What's up?" Kern asked.

"I forgot his head," Ty said, searching under the sheet. "I must have left it there."

"Whose head? Left it where?" Galandrik said, just confused as the others.

"That's Conn's body. I left his head in the clearing. Damn!"

"You cut his head off?" Jarrow asked.

"No, I didn't; Gorgon did."

"Gorgon? Where did *he* appear form? Hang on a second, let's rewind here. Start from the beginning," Kern said.

"Well, while you lot were fighting Gorgon, I released the dragons and got knocked out by Conn. The next thing I know, I'm in a cage on the back of the wagon, then whilst travelling through the Dikes pass, we were ambushed by bandits."

"You mean Conn and Bok were?" Kern asked.

"What? Yes, yes, they were. Well, Bok had it on his toes, and the bandits tied me and Conn up together. That's when the herbs got thrown into the tree."

"You mean at that camp to the south?" Jarrow asked.

"Yes, where you found them in the tree. We moved on and the next time we stopped we heard a—"

"'We'—you mean you and Conn?" Kern interrupted.

"Yes, Conn and I—we heard this commotion of swords clattering and shouting. Then it went all quiet, and when the sheet was taken off the cage, Gorgon was standing there! Then Bok appeared."

"And the bandits were all dead?" the dwarf asked.

"Every one of them, dead as a dormouse. Gorgon then proceeded to drag Conn from the cage and, well, slap him about. Gorgon threw him all over the place because Conn left him fighting you and should have helped. While Gorgon was savaging him, he was telling him how he killed his friend Belton. He is one nasty piece of shit."

"Tell me about it. He stuck me to a tree," Kern said, rolling his aching shoulder.

"So he just beat him to a pulp, then cut his head off?" Jarrow asked, intrigued.

"No, I managed to grab Conn's staff and throw it to him, and he blasted Gorgon with a magical electrical display. This massive electrical fist grabbed him and pinned him to a tree. Gorgon was trapped, but that bloody no-good, two-timing son of a pig Bok ran into the clearing and backstabbed the wizard."

"So *Bok* cut his head off?" Galandrik asked.

"No, Bok did not! Let me finish! Bok ran in and backstabbed the wizard twice. This made Conn drop the staff, which released Gorgon from the spell. Conn turned to face Bok, but by the time he had, Gorgon had got up and just calmly walked up behind him and *whack!* His head was spinning through the air!"

"I see. So how did you end up with the corpse?" Jarrow asked.

"Gorgon couldn't find the herbs, so obviously he was angry. I wouldn't tell him where they were, so he dragged me from the cage—"

"And slapped you about?" Kern said.

"No, we had a fight. I gave as good as I got, but he had Bok. Two versus one was hard work and it eventually paid off for them."

"And then?" Kern said, rolling his eyes at Ty's tale.

"Well, I told him the herbs were at the bandits' camp."

Galandrik shook his head. "What bandit camp?"

"The camp the bandits were taking Conn and me to, before Gorgon smashed them all up. It was called Frolin's camp. I told Gorgon that they knew about the king, and that they'd taken the herbs to get money from him, so we stopped half a day's ride north, and Gorgon went west to the camp to get the herbs."

"So how did you escape from Bok? I take it he was still there?" Jarrow asked.

"Yes, well, Bok was worried that when we reached Morcas, I would tell the queen that he had killed Conn and whatever else I might say, so Gorgon told him to cut my tongue out."

"Cut your tongue out?" Galandrik said.

"Yes, cut my bloody tongue out!" Ty said, sticking it out.

"He would have needed a two-handed broad sword," the dwarf said with a laugh.

"Whatever. Well, I overheard this and pretended to be asleep. When Bok reached through the cage bars, I grabbed his arm and bent it the wrong way, snapped it at the elbow."

Jarrow winced at the thought. "How lovely."

"It gets better—when I was fighting with Gorgon, I'd managed to pick up a dagger and conceal it."

"Why didn't you use it, then, if you were fighting?" Kern asked, smiling.

"Er... It was only a small one, and at the time they were getting the better of me. So after I snapped Bok's arm, I thrust the dagger into his collarbone and twisted it as hard as I could," Ty said, exaggerating.

"And did you kill him?" Galandrik asked.

"When Gorgon put me in the cage, he had rolled it over so the door was facing downwards, so I put my feet between the bottom bars and shouldered the side until eventually it fell off the wagon. When I got up and out, he had run off, with his broken arm and a dagger sticking out of his shoulder."

"Then you came here, without Conn's head?" Kern asked.

Ty didn't answer, just nodded and shrugged his shoulder, then winced with pain. "Oh, and I dislocated the old shoulder again. It's giving me so much grief!" he said, stepping past them to his horses.

"You got to love him," Jarrow said.

"His life should be written about, not mine. Look at him," Kern said, pointing. "It's like water off a duck's back. Look, not a care in the world! It's as if it never happened, or it's a normal day in the life of Ty 'the Rat' Quickpick."

"I'm afraid it *is* a normal day, lad," Galandrik said, getting back up onto Jarrow's wagon.

"Who are the others?" Ty called back to them.

"Don't worry about them; they are paid helpers. They will keep us safe, though I think maybe I should have brought a few more," Jarrow laughed.

"I'll ride with you,"Kern smiled, getting up on Ty's wagon.

"I didn't mean any of that. You know that, don't you?" Ty said, as Kern settled in next to him.

"Yes, you did."

"I didn't."

"Whatever, *brother*." Kern sniggered.

"And *I* did more damage on the giant."

"Right, what's the plan now, then?" Jarrow asked, as Ty turned his wagon round.

"Raith, Orc's Armpit—let's have a pint," Ty said, with a grin from ear to ear.

"Sounds like a plan. I could murder a nice pint and a roast hog!"

"We are heading to Morcas to heal the king," Kern said.

"We are doing what?" Ty huffed.

"What I said. We are going to take the herbs to the king."

"He wants us dead! Are you mad?" Ty moaned.

"He's dying! This will clear our names and we can move on. We haven't done anything wrong."

"Hmmm… let me think," Ty said, rubbing his chin. "Killed loads of his men, stole his dragons, killed his wyverns, got his wizard killed… shall I continue?"

"I will go by myself, then. All those who don't want to go can leave on this wagon. The rest can come with me and do the right thing." There was a silence. "Jarrow, what are you going to do?"

"I'm coming with you. This is far more interesting than selling gold in Raith."

"Ty, are you heading to Raith?"

The thief stared at Galandrik, and knew the dwarf wouldn't leave the ranger. "*Fine*, I'll come, but only because you need me. I'd have been better off going with Gorgon," he moaned.

"I knew you'd come around, *brother*," Kern teased.

"That's it—once more and I'm off," Ty said, cracking the horses' reins.

Kern sat back and smiled. *It's good to have him back*, he thought.

Chapter Thirty-Eight
Promises, Promises

The party made the gates of Morcas around eleven the next morning, and they sat in the queue of traders waiting to enter the town. They had divided Jarrow's wares between the two wagons to look more convincing—and to cover Conn's corpse. They had visited the clearing to retrieve Conn's head, but Kern deduced that animals had carried it away: All that was left in the cage was the empty sack that had held his head.

"Right, remember the plan: You are with me and things should be fine," Jarrow said. They all agreed, and before long they were at the gates.

The guard recognised Jarrow straight away. "Hello, back so soon?"

"It's been a good month! Two wagons this time. Bloody bandits everywhere, though, so I had to double the guard," Jarrow said, tutting.

"Must be frustrating for you. Anyway, two wagons is one gold, sorry."

"No problem," Jarrow said, "and here's one for you. Treat your wife… or someone else's!" Jarrow said, moving his wagon through the gates.

"Why, thanks, Mr Jarrow, sir! I will indeed treat someone."

"You do that."

The wagons rode into Morcas; much the same as most towns, it had a market place and all the usual shops and inns. At the opposite end to the town's main gates was the castle, King Moriak's castle, and that had his garrisons on either side. These could hold two thousand soldiers easily, and the king loved the security.

"How can we get a message to the queen about the herbs?" Galandrik asked Jarrow.

"Let me worry about that." Jarrow turned to Kern and Ty and said, "Follow me. We will lose the wagons and discuss things."

"Discuss in the inn, I hope," the dwarf said, to no one but himself.

"Over there, the Welcome Inn. You three go eat and drink—" Jarrow looked at the dwarf and added, "but not too much," with a smile. "I'll get rid of my wagons and be back in twenty minutes. Try keeping it on the low, you don't want any attention."

"I don't think anybody would believe us stupid enough to walk into this place," Ty laughed.

"Maybe so—still, just keep your heads down," Jarrow said.

"What about…" Kern nodded at the sheet concealing the corpse.

"I will store it, don't worry. I know people here. Now go eat," the elf said as he led the wagon away.

"Jarrow!" Kern called.

The elf pulled up on the reins. "What?"

"You couldn't, ah, spare us a couple of gold?"

Jarrow shook his head, reached into his tunic, and threw a little coin pouch to Kern, who said, "Thanks, you know we are good for it."

*

The trio sat in the Welcome Inn, eating bowls of beef soup with thick chunks of freshly-made bread, and waited until Jarrow returned. The inn was empty, apart from a few humans sitting at the bar. Jarrow entered and sat at their table.

"How did it go?" Galandrik asked.

"Fine. Gondal is taking care of my goods, with Brendin and Joff's help."

"You trust them with your gold?" Ty said, raising an eyebrow.

Jarrow smiled. "No, Ty, I don't. I have taken care of that personally and banked my money; they just sell the jumble I have brought."

"So what are you thinking, friend?" Kern asked the elf.

"I think you should ask Queen Cherian for a pardon."

"A pardon? What is a pardon?" the halfling asked, pushing his empty bowl into the middle of the table.

"'*The king's right of pardon is the power to remit any punishment imposed by any court, king, or queen,*'" Jarrow recited from memory.

"But we haven't actually been given any punishment," Kern said.

"Yes, but obviously the king wants you three dead. So if you ask for a pardon—or to be granted your freedom with no one else trying to kill you—in return for the herbs, I can't see how they can refuse."

"But surely they can just go back on their word," Ty said.

"Theoretically, the king cannot go back on his word—unless the pardoned person or persons do something else. Say, for example, *steal the king's gold*. That would obviously cancel it."

"I see. Well, it's worth a shot. What about the herbs? We can't just walk into the palace carrying them; they will take them and pardon us straight into the dungeon," the ranger said.

"That's where these come in," Jarrow said, pulling two red sacks out of his backpack. "These are bags of sending."

"What are they?" Galandrik asked, picking one up.

"They a pair of sending bags. Whatever you place in one will appear in the other after thirty seconds."

"You have lost me. How do they help us?"

"Well, adventurers use these in dungeons when they are farming. When they have gathered enough of whatever it is they are farming, they place it into the bag. Then it will be sent to the *other* bag, which is safely tucked away in their house. This is to stop thieves stealing it from them before they get home."

"Sorry, but I'm even more confused now, lad," the dwarf said.

"It's simple. These bags only have two charges left. I was going to sell them, but if we give the herbs and one bag to Brendin, then we can go to the palace. If all goes well, he can simply send the herbs to us."

"How will he know if it 'all goes well'?" Ty asked.

"We will send something to him first, as a sign for him to send."

"Genius! So we need to get a message to the Queen, then. That will not be easy; we can hardly just ask the guards on the gate to pop in and get her," Kern said, finishing his ale.

"No, but if we go in with Conn's corpse on the wagon, I think they may listen."

"That would definitely get their attention," Galandrik agreed.

"Shall we leave then? No time like the present," Jarrow said, standing up.

"Pity we never found his head," Kern said.

"Oh, so it's my fault?" Ty grunted.

"Did I say that?" Kern replied.

"I know exactly what you meant. Always my fault."

"I didn't mean that, but a headless corpse is hardly solid evidence that it's the wizard!"

"Well, next time I'm fighting in a cage trying to keep from getting my tongue cut out, I will make sure I put the head in my backpack—*that I didn't have*," the thief replied, rolling his eyes.

"Now is not the time," Jarrow said, hitting the table. "Right, shall we *head* to the castle?" he added with a smile.

"Yes, let's go and *face* the queen," Galandrik laughed.

"Ha ha. You lot are so funny," Ty said, getting up.

"I agree," Kern said. "We should leave while we still have a *head* start on Gorgon."

"I'm not going to bite. You lot are pathetic," the thief said, walking towards the door. The others laughed and followed behind him.

*

They collected the wagon with Conn's corpse and staff, and gave the herbs along with the bag of sending to Brendin, explaining what the plan was. Then they headed to the castle gates. The castle appeared in the distance in all its glory. Long square buildings sat either side of them; hundreds and hundreds of huts in perfectly lines of five, guards mingled about and others marched in platoons. Two massive double iron gates stood in front of the path that led to the castle's main portcullis. On either side of the gate stood a twenty-foot-high gold-painted statue of a lion, each sitting and looking at the other, shining in the morning sun light. Four guards stood watch as they approached.

"Let me do the talking," Jarrow whispered. "Morning!" he said cheerily.

"Yeah, we know," the tallest guard said, stepping forward. "Don't come any closer."

"We have come with news for Queen Cherian," Jarrow answered, halting the wagon.

"Of course you have. I suppose you are her long-lost cousin?" the guard said as the three behind him chuckled.

"No, my good sir, we are not related. Could you pass her a message?"

"She is busy. Just be gone and stop wasting our time," he said, turning around.

"Please—it is of utmost importance."

"Look, be gone or we will move you!" the guard said, placing his hand on the hilt of his sword.

"Very well, have it your way. Where can I leave the corpse of Conn the king's wizard? Then we will leave."

The guard drew his sword and spun on his heel. "You had better explain your words, elf!" he hissed.

"On the back of this wagon is the corpse of Conn. We wanted to explain to Queen Cherian what has happened, but as you have—"

"Enough!" He nodded to another guard, who instantly rang a bell that was affixed to the post of the gate. The other two guards drew their weapons. The gates began to open inwards and fifteen more heavily armed guards rushed out and surrounded them, some with heavy crossbows drawn and others with swords.

"If they try anything, kill them," the tall guard said, walking around to the back of the wagon. He poked his sword under the sheet and lifted, and flies flew out in all directions as he peered under. His face changed and he grimaced at what he saw, holding a hand over his mouth at the smell.

"Disarm them and take them inside," he ordered, dropping the sheet.

*

They were marched in through the main gates. Plush green grass lay on either side of the gravel path and beautifully arranged flower beds sat in large square patches. They were marched across a moat bridge, the water beneath filled will brightly coloured fish that darted about and hid under lily pads at the noise of the guards' boots pounding against the wood.

At last they stood in front of the massive iron portcullis. They could hear the cranking as it slowly lifted. Again they were marched through a courtyard where horse-drawn carts filled with barrels and boxes were being loaded—or unloaded, it was impossible to tell. In front of them was an archway, and behind that they could make out the front of King Moriak's castle. They were turned to the right and led through another door, along a corridor, and into a cell.

"Make yourselves comfortable, won't you," the tall guard said.

"Thanks. One more thing," Jarrow said. "Make sure you mention you have Kern the Giant Slayer and the herbs in a cell."

The guard peered through the bars at the quartet and smiled. "Giant slayer, eh? It looks from here like you four couldn't slay a halfling whore!"

"Open the door and I'll show you a halfling whore!" Ty shouted.

"Of course you will," he replied. Then he turned to the other guards and said, "You two stay here and keep an eye on them. And be careful, *they slay giants!*" He walked up the corridor and away, laughing.

Chapter Thirty-Nine
The Queen and the Thieves

Queen Cherian sat in the king's study signing paperwork with Odol. "Do we really need another church in Morcas?" the queen asked.

"They are requesting permission to build in the eastern sector, my queen."

"Why can't they all use the one in the west?"

"Overcrowding, I'm afraid."

"I take it the church is paying for this?"

"Oh yes, every penny."

There was a knock on the door and Cherian nodded to the guard, who opened it. "It's Raffa from the front gate. He says he has important news, my queen."

"Send him in. Excuse me, Odol," she said, putting the quill down and sitting back in her chair.

The tall guard marched in and stood in front of her desk. He nodded and said, "Queen Cherian."

"This better be important," she replied.

"We had a cart approach the main gate, accompanied by a dwarf, an elf, a halfling, and a human. They had a corpse on the back of the wagon, and said it was the body of Conn. We have them imprisoned, my queen."

"Well, was it Conn?" she asked impatiently.

"We don't know. Murtal is having a look now."

"Are you telling me you can't look at a corpse and tell if it's Conn the wizard? Why come to me with this nonsense?"

"Sorry, my queen, but the body has no head."

"It could be anybody! You actually believe this is Conn's corpse? You should have—" She was interrupted by another knock on the door. "Oh my lord! Who is it now?" The guard opened the door to admit Murtal, who came to stand next to Raffa.

"My queen," he said, bowing.

"Tell me and this *idiot* that these jokers downstairs are conmen. They are probably trying to get gold out of us," the queen said angrily.

"I'm sorry, Queen Cherian, but it is indeed the body of Conn. Here is his staff," Murtal said, leaning it against the wall. Cherian rose and picked up the staff.

"These captives—who are they? Did they give their names?"

Raffa answered, "No, my queen… Well, only one name—he said 'Kern' and something about having herbs."

"YOU FOOL!" she screamed, "Why didn't you say this?! Bring them here NOW!"

The soldier nodded and quickly turned on his heel. "My queen."

"What is happening, Murtal, and where is Gorgon?"

"I have no idea. I'm sure Kern will have the answers."

"Odol, you may go. We can complete this later," she said, waving a dismissive hand.

"I think I should stay, my queen, I can help with—"

"Odol, *that will be all*," she interrupted.

"Yes, Queen Cherian, of course," he answered and left the study.

"He has some guts coming into the palace, this… Kern."

"His reputation precedes him. He is becoming quite a name."

"His name grows and our name diminishes! It makes us look like a laughingstock."

There was a knock and the guard opened the door. Kern, Jarrow, Galandrik, and Ty were led into the room, their hands tied behind their backs. Raffa stood in front of them. "The prisoners, my queen," he said with a nod.

"Thank you, Raffa. I am sure the king will be very happy with your work. Now go back to the gate. It isn't going to watch itself."

"I have four good men—"

"That will be *all*, Raffa," she interrupted sternly. With a nod, he spun around.

"That's a good boy, Raffa," Ty said—quietly, but loud enough for everyone to hear. Kern closed his eyes and gently shook his head.

"Don't. Just go," Cherian said as Raffa stopped and turned to the thief. The guard left the room.

"So, where are my herbs?" she asked, standing in front of the four. The two guards on the door moved forward and stood to either side of her, hands on their hilts. Kern looked at Jarrow, who just smiled.

"They are in the town, safe and sound, Queen Cherian," Kern explained.

"Don't play games with me, and don't think defeating a stupid hill giant will make you special here, either. Now which one of you is going to fetch them?"

"None of us is," Kern said coldly.

"You don't understand, *Kern Ocarn*—the king is not but three rooms away, and he is dying. I may be only a woman but I will have all your teeth pulled out one by one until you tell me where the damn herbs are!" she said, fuming.

"We can get those herbs here within a minute. I just want you to pardon us first," he explained.

"A pardon! A pardon for what?" she asked, placing her hands on her hips.

"I want a guarantee that no harm will come to any of us, and that we are free men in Bodisha, who can walk freely without looking over our shoulders for Moriak's men."

"You kill our men, kill our wyverns, steal our dragons, kill the king's wizard, and then want forgiveness?"

"Queen Cherian, the wyverns attacked us, we but defended ourselves, as with any men who tried to harm us. The dragons belonged with their mother, and Conn was killed by Gorgon."

"Conn was killed by Gorgon? Don't be so pathetic!" She laughed, rolling her eyes at Murtal.

"He did! I was there," Ty said.

"And you must be…?"

"Ty, Ty 'the Rat' Quickpick!" he said proudly.

"Ah, Ty the Rat… Yes, Conn mentioned something about you not being all that you seem."

"I know. I was with him when he sent the paperfinch. He said to give us a pardon," Ty added.

"Yes, now that I think about it, that's exactly what he said," she replied.

"I helped him against Gorgon, but that slimy toad Bok snuck up behind him and backstabbed him!"

"But you said Gorgon killed him."

"He did! After Bok attacked, Conn turned round, which gave Gorgon the time and chance to slice his head off!" Queen Cherian frowned. "Sorry, I didn't mean to—"

She raised her hand. "This is so confusing," she said, looking at Murtal as she sat down.

"When Gorgon was attacking Conn, he mentioned something about throwing Belton off a mountain and how his eyes popped out," Ty said, and Kern elbowed him in the ribs for the gruesomeness of his explanations.

The queen looked up from her desk. "What did you say about Belton?"

"Um, Gorgon said he threw him off a mountain. He was beating on Conn and telling him about killing his friend." She stared at Murtal, who raised an eyebrow.

"Go fetch Odol," she said to one of the guards, "and tell him to bring parchment for a pardon. Murtal, please go tell Devon to put twenty of the king's personal guard on the town's gate to take Gorgon prisoner when he arrives." She looked over at Kern and added, "I take it Gorgon *is* still alive?"

"He should be here within three days," Ty said. "I sent him on a wild goose chase to a bandit village. He thinks the herbs are there, but really they were in a tree, and Kern found them just before—"

"Enough! We can discuss trees, herbs, and goose-chasers later," she said, holding up a hand to stop Ty's story. "Go, Murtal, and come back for the herbs."

"Yes, my queen," he said, leaving the room.

Cherian looked the four up and down. "I can't believe you have caused us so much trouble."

"Please don't take this the wrong way, Queen Cherian, but we were tricked into finding 'the king's gold,' for which we were also promised a gold reward. That was all lies. Then we were tricked into finding those herbs—I thought my father was being held captive. The only thing we have done against the king was to return the dragons to their mother. Being yourself a mother, you must see we did right," Kern explained.

She stared at the ranger. "What about Solomon?"

"Bok killed him," he calmly replied.

"Bok would have a lot to answer for if I were to believe your stories."

"Bok killed Solomon on his way back here with the dragon eggs. Bok was chasing us at the time, and thought it was Ty."

"Because they look so alike, don't they," she said disbelievingly.

"Solomon had my cloak on. He rendered me unconscious, stole my cloak, and left," Ty said.

"How convenient—or in Solomon's case, inconvenient."

"This is what happened. We wouldn't have come here if this was all a lie," Galandrik said.

"I do believe you about Belton. Conn didn't think he slipped from the mountain, either. But why would Gorgon want to kill Conn?"

"When your men found us in the Midas Hills, we had a battle. Conn was at the back, where I was fighting Bok, and saw Gorgon in trouble. Instead of helping him, Conn left—with Bok and me unconscious in a cage."

"Are you ever conscious?"

"Conn helped Bok and they threw me in a cage. They got lucky."

"Solomon was lucky, too?" She smiled, then asked, "So Gorgon obviously escaped and caught you up, then?"

"As we were traveling through the Double Dikes pass, we were ambushed by bandits. Bok got away and Conn ended up in the cage with me. That's how I know he sent the paperfinch."

"I see. It's slightly clearer now."

"The next thing we know is that Gorgon and Bok killed the bandits, then they killed Conn."

"So Bok found Gorgon, but why would he help kill Conn?"

"Bok hated him because of what Conn did to his face! Plus he wouldn't dare cross Gorgon."

"I see. So Bok killed Solomon and Conn—with Gorgon's help—and Gorgon killed Belton. We need to have words with those two," she said, shaking her head.

"They are bad men," Ty agreed.

Cherian thought about the stories they told and tried to piece them all together. Strangely enough, it made sense, she thought; *why would they walk in here if they're not telling the truth? Either they are very brave and very stupid, or they are telling the truth.*

It didn't matter which was right—she needed to pardon them to heal the king.

She could always rip it up after.

"Bad men, indeed—ah, here is Odol," she said, hearing the footsteps outside. The guard opened the door, and Murtal and Odol entered the room.

"My queen, this is most irregular. The king really needs to be the one to sign this," Odol said, laying the paperwork out on the table. She wanted to say 'I don't care, we just need the king healed!' But she couldn't.

"The king is dying and this paperwork will save him," she said, picking up a quill and dipping it in the ink pot. "Now, quickly—where do I sign?"

"It is not that simple, my queen. We need their names and then the three signatures: the king's, mine, and the pardoned party's, on two copies."

"Get writing, then," she ordered.

Odol filled in the spaces on the parchment as quickly as he could, while Kern explained that Jarrow was just a friend, and wasn't in any way part of the deal. Then Odol signed the first paper, and passed it to Queen Cherian for her to do the same. When she finished, she held the quill up to Kern, saying, "Sign for your freedom, ranger."

"I would," he answered, "but…" He twisted round, showing his tied hands.

"Bolfor, untie them," she ordered.

When all three had signed the parchments, she handed one copy of each to Kern and said, "You are free, but trust me, Kern Ocarn, if this is all a pack of lies, you will hang. Now give me my herbs!"

Kern nodded at Jarrow, who dropped a gold coin into the bag of sending along with the parchments and pulled the drawstrings tight. Thirty seconds later the bag filled, and he stepped over and placed it on the table.

"Your herbs, my queen," the elf said.

Murtal opened the bag and smiled. Then, with a nod to the queen, he left the room, followed by Odol.

"I want to thank you for retrieving the herbs."

"You can," Ty said, "with gold," and received another nudge in the arm from Kern, but Cherian just smiled at Ty's forwardness.

"Well, I didn't think you would be standing in front of me. This was a turn-up for the books."

"Neither did we, my queen," Kern said, nodding. "We would like to simply earn some money and get on with our lives."

"What are you going to do now?" she asked.

All four looked blankly at each other before Kern answered. "Go kill another giant, I suppose," he smiled.

"Well, as it happens I need a party to do a very important deed. Do you want a quest?"

"Don't think me ungrateful, Queen Cherian, but last time I was offered a quest by the house of Moriak—well, you know what happened," Kern answered.

"This time I will guarantee you fame and fortune—and this is from me, not some wizard," she replied. "And our human lands might just depend upon it."

"How much gold are we talking?" Ty asked abruptly.

"Enough gold for you to stop stealing and retire," she said with a smile.

They all exchanged glances before Kern finally said, "What's the quest?"

"Ever heard of *The Staff of Aryinel*?"

THE END

AUTHOR'S ACKNOWLEDGMENTS

Thank you to everyone who read Book One – *The King's Gold* – and to those who sent me all the lovely comments. I was truly overwhelmed that so many people enjoyed it.

The King's Gold was dedicated to Wendy Wilson, the late mother of my good friends Tryston (Kern) and Gav (Jarrow) Wilson. We often role-played at their family home, where Wendy looked after us all. She was the sweetest and most wonderful woman but, sadly, was taken from us far too young. Without her kindness, none of these stories would ever have been possible. I should also mention Wendy's husband and my very good friend, Michael Wilson; like my own father, he kindly let us play but secretly longed for peace and quiet after a long day's work.

I have dedicated *The King's Promise* to Brian Connell, Jason (Nuran) Connell's father, who likewise allowed us to play *Dungeons & Dragons* at their home in Beresford Road. Brian was a great man who was also taken much too soon. Brian once even helped Jason win the league with QPR on a Commodore 64 football management game, which I am still reminded of to this day! (Aunty) Eileen, Brian's wonderful wife, kept all us kids well-watered whilst Shaun Saunders (the Dungeon Master) took us into a world of fantasy, mayhem, and madness.

Without all these wonderful people, the adventures in these books would never have happened.

Marina and Jason at http://polgarusstudio.com and Ashley at http://www.redbird-designs.net for their amazing assistance and patience again!

Olie Boldador at rboldador@gmail.com for another superb cover design.

Elayne Morgan at http://www.serenityeditingservices.com/ for the editing plus her invaluable assistance and advice. Without it, Book One would still be a dream.

Kim Shue (brit.chick3@gmail.com) for her excellent proofreading.

Jenny Jackson my poetic friend for her superb poetry and advice, and for completing the final read—such a massive help from start to finish.

Lastly, to all my family and friends who have spurred me on to complete *The King's Promise*.
Thank you all.

Printed in Great Britain
by Amazon